GUARDIANS OF THE GROVE TRILOGY

Fury Burns

BOOK THREE

CHLOE HODGE

Fury Burns
Copyright © 2021 by Chloe Szentpeteri

First edition: July 2021

All rights reserved. No part of this book may be reproduced in any form or by an electronic or mechanical means including information storage and retrieval systems, without permission in writing from the author. The only exception is a reviewer, who may quote short excerpts in a review.
This is a work of fiction. Names, characters, businesses, places, events and incidents are either the product of the author's imagination or used in a fictitious manner. Any resemblance to actual persons, living or dead, or actual events is purely coincidental.

Find me at: chloehodge.com
Instagram: @chloeschapters
Facebook: Chloe Hodge Author

Printed in Australia.

Paperback ISBN: 978-0-6485997-8-4
Hardcover ISBN: 978-0-6485997-6-0
E-book ISBN: 978-0-6485997-7-7

Special thanks and acknowledgement to:
Editor; Aidan Curtis,
Paperback cover artist; Erica Timmons at ETC Designs,
Hardcover artist; Niru Sky,
Interior illustrator; Emily Johns,
Formatter; Julia Scott at Evenstar Books.

This book is written in British English.

For everyone battling a little darkness of their own.
You are a warrior. Let your light shine.

ONYX OCEAN
WINDARION
RENLOCK
AQUAFARIAN
PROVINCE
PILYAR
LILLION
DENTON
GATES
MAYNESGATE
BAY OF
TEARS
FENTIR
HOME
SERANON
PURPLE PLAINS
WOODRANDIA
HILLFAIR
MOONGLA
MEADOWS

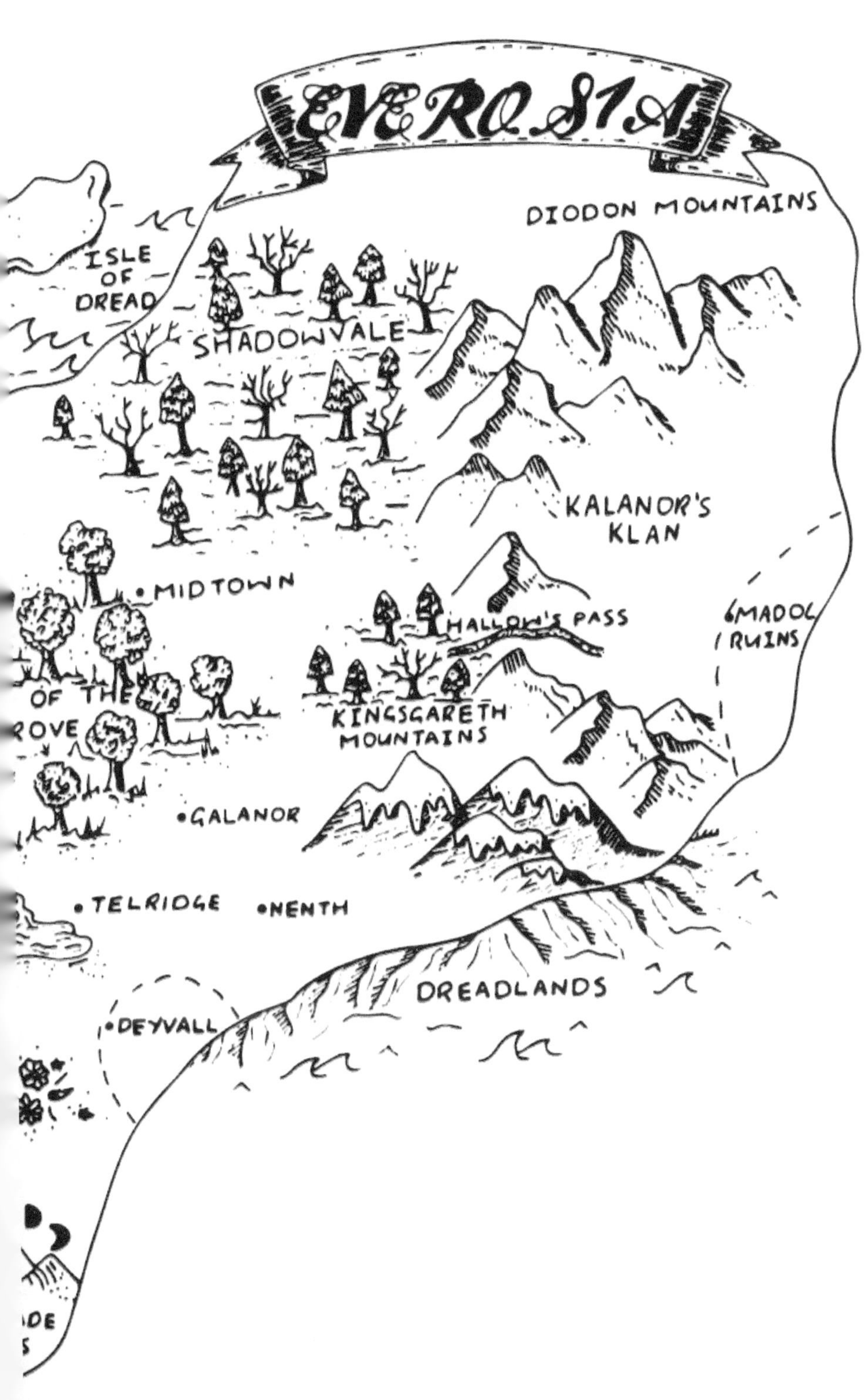
EVEROSIA
DIODON MOUNTAINS
ISLE OF DREAD
SHADOWVALE
KALANOR'S KLAN
MIDTOWN
HALLOW'S PASS
MADOL RUINS
OF THE GROVE
KINGSGARETH MOUNTAINS
GALANOR
TELRIDGE
NENTH
DREADLANDS
DEYVALL

Ashalea Kindaris

Ash-ah-lee-uh Kin-dah-riss

She was the deliverer of vengeance.
The sword of justice.
And her fury doth burn.

A Sobering Thought

YAVAAR

THE WHISKY BURNED as it trickled down King Yavaar Grayden's throat. It was one of the finest he'd tasted, likely having been hoarded in one of the numerous barrels that lined the cellars below Maynesgate castle. He lifted his chalice and marvelled at the amber liquid; so smooth, so textured. Such a fine friend to waste away the hours of the darkest night with.

Whisky didn't command or condemn, it didn't argue or seek to spill his secrets, nor did it vie for better standing or to find itself in good grace. Rather, it freed the king from these burdens, soothing his worries and quieting his mind.

Yavaar sighed before draining his glass to the dregs, revelling in that burn, the feeling of wildfire in his blood.

He yearned for these nights. His routine never failed. It was the same every damned day: breakfast at an ungodly hour, followed

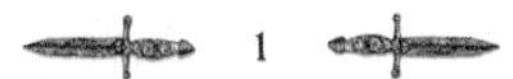

by light training—his opponents conveniently submitting all too easily—then his studies; history, literature, language, warfare and so on. From noon onwards, he would either be holed up in the council room listening to his viziers prattle on, or he would be in the great hall receiving petty complaints from the peasants.

So his days passed, and he would spend every waking hour waiting for that reprieve when the castle quieted, when his servants would excuse themselves, when there was nothing but him and the drink. His silent companion, his escape from the mundane.

He eyed the decanter set on the stone wall of the balcony. The honeyed liquid only stared back, teasing him, daring him to pour himself another. So he did, pulling the glass stopper from the elegant crystal bottle, its shapely curves feeling just right as he clasped its slender neck in one hand and poured.

He breathed in the sharp tang before taking a sip. Some nights he drank himself to oblivion, others just enough to see the little lights of the city become a blur, his bronze eyes forced to squint to see the gated walls that encircled his people.

And it wasn't that he didn't love his city or his kingdom—he was proud to lead this stronghold, this treasure trove of culture and trade. For it was not just the human populace down there in houses both fine and fickle, but elves and dwarves and peoples from lands across the seas.

No, he envied them. For even walls so well made as his, even furnishings so grand and clothes so lovely, the finest foods and the lure of power—even all these things combined—were not enough to allow him to forget that these walls, they were a cage.

The crown upon his head was a pretty jewel for him to wear. Its responsibility was a weight, a reminder that better men had once worn it—once respected its power. But its gilded curves were nothing

but a burden to King Yavaar Grayden—puppet to politics and the greed of other men.

He was trapped in his court, and no amount of wishing or wanting would ever carry him elsewhere. He would never know freedom from his grand keep, but would instead perch on his nest, doomed to roost in his castle, forever cursed to look out across the city and beyond to the glittering seas, to the mountains in the east, to the forests and pastures and brooks that lay beyond his human eyes.

And so he drank, numbing his hopes and dreams until everything blurred together, and he could escape this reality and pretend the nights away. He would think to himself, every now and then, *Tomorrow will be the day I forge a new rule. A day I say no to their demands and deliver my own... I could be a king my people might love; a leader they would follow.*

But they were just words; always just words that he could never bring himself to say—would never have the courage to muster.

A bitter laugh escaped his lips, and he ran a hand through his unruly brown hair. His father, King Dilini, would be turning in his grave if he knew what a weak heir he had sired, what a pathetic king his son would be.

Yavaar pressed his lips into a thin line, the cruel twist of irony suddenly curdling the liquid in his gut. King Dilini, who had thought himself so grand a ruler, so precious a commodity for this kingdom. Yavaar snorted. His father had been lazy, lax in his reign, *greedy*, and through his failings, the city now belonged to the men who had once grovelled at his feet.

Not anymore. Those advisors now held their chins high, their pockets lined with glittering gold, their games more cunning and tones more demanding.

A breeze curled around his shoulders, pushing him towards the balcony, and he swayed on his feet, stumbling towards the drop, the glass escaping his clutch as it plummeted to the courtyard far below. His palms ground into the cold, hard stone, and giddiness clawed at his stomach as he leaned over the wall.

A smash sounded in the stillness, and instantly guards were investigating the source, their torch flames illuminating the crystal shards splayed in a deadly arc from its point of impact. Yavaar could just make out the guards' faces as their heads angled upwards. One quick look at the king and they were back to their posts. A servant was cleaning up the mess moments later, sweeping the shards away, probably cursing their king for breaking yet another glass worth more than what they'd earn in months, maybe a year.

He knew what they were thinking. *Just a normal night for their alcoholic sovereign, drinking himself into stupor.* And for a wild moment, Yavaar considered climbing onto that wall and just ... jumping. He wondered then, what his body would look like splayed over the courtyard. If he'd be swept away just as quickly, just as quietly. Their fragile, broken king, just a pawn to be used, just some strings to be wielded by another's hand.

The thought had the liquor roiling in his stomach, and he felt bile rise in his throat, burning far less pleasantly than when it went down. Suddenly it beckoned to be free, and he bent over double, retching the whisky onto the ground by his feet.

He paused there for a time, gasping, saliva drooling from his lips, eyes stinging and vision blurring. When he had finally recovered enough to stand, he was seeing double as he gazed across the city. A myriad of lights glowed in the dark, sparking to life one after another like embers in the wind.

Yavaar pawed at his eyes, hands rubbing the inner corners

to clear away the haze, but when he looked again at the distant thatched rooves and leaning hovels that made up homes in the lower quarter, the lights began to cluster, forming not stars upon a sea of night, but fire.

Flames. They were flames. And ... there, dashing across the rooftops, barely perceptible against the smoke rising, were shadows. Leaping, running, clambering across his city, their forms not quite solid, their shapes nothing he had seen before. Fire danced along the spines of these shadow beasts, like a phantom come to life.

He squeezed his eyes shut, hoping he was drunker than he thought, that the aroma of rising smoke was a figment of his inebriated state, that these shadows were just nightmares from a fitful sleep.

The bells that began tolling told him otherwise, and as he opened his eyes to a city on fire, the screams of his people carried on the breeze. The doors of his suite burst open behind him with the bellowed cries of, "Attack! We're under attack!"

He whirled to find the faces of his advisors staring back. Eyes wide, faces stricken, they said nothing as they waited, staring at him for confirmation—for direction.

"And who dares breach our city?" Yavaar said with deadly quiet, the tone sounding unfamiliar to his ears. By the widening eyes of his advisors, he wasn't the only one to think so.

Their throats bobbed as the nobles glanced nervously at each other before one offered, "Shadow beasts, Majesty. In the form of Diodonians ... But they can't be. We haven't seen a Diodonian for years. Not since ..."

He needn't have finished his sentence. Yavaar knew of the old campaigns—what dark deeds were once carried out in the bowels of this city. Men who once captured the proud beasts to torture them

and peel away their skulls like eggshells, only to discard the brains when their poking and prodding proved useless.

But those poor souls were long gone, and the Diodonians had long since hidden away in the great desert of the east. It had been an age since they had last been sighted, and though he knew little of the creatures, Yavaar knew that—whatever was in his city—they were not Diodonians. Not in the truest sense anyway. No, these things were not of this world. Which meant ...

"The wizard was right," Yavaar said. "The darkness has come."

The wizard who had sought an audience not so many months ago, who had tried to warn them, to beseech the king to send aid to Everosia—to the many small villages that dotted the land. Wezlan Shadowbreaker—that was his name. Oh, yes, Yavaar had cursed himself a fool for bowing to his puppeteers, for turning that wise man away.

And since then ... his villages had burned, his people had died, and King Yavaar Grayden had done naught to avenge them. To protect them.

"What do we do, Majesty?" It was barely more than a whisper. The question laced with fear, an answer needing direction from a king. *Their king.*

Yavaar truly felt something then—an awakening of fear; a dread that pooled in his heart and filled him with a prompt call for action. To lead, to help his people. He turned, his gaze once again finding the fires that lit up the dark, the people down below screaming, pleading, begging for someone to save them.

The conviction in his voice was true as he said, "We defend our own."

His eyes glowed with the fires' reflections, their warmth spreading—more demanding than the liquor that swam through his

blood, more devastating than the wildfire in his stomach. His stare hardened at the decanter resting atop the balcony and with one swift motion he sent it tumbling over the edge.

He had never sobered up quicker.

Alone

TIME IS IRRESPECTIVE OF ONE'S FEELINGS. The clocks continue to tick, the blossoms bloom and fade, and the passage of nature continues as it always does. For the Guardians of the Grove, time was pressing. For Ashalea, it was obsolete.

As she perched atop a crumbled pillar, lost in the turmoil of her emotions, she felt as broken inside as the ruins surrounding her. The mighty Moonglade Meadows, once a city of wonder, now a fragment of what it once was. Sprawled around her, the ruination was evident in every fallen stone—every crack a cruel caress from the darkness.

So many years had passed since Crinos destroyed this city. She had never seen its true glory, had never walked its halls, but not a day went by where the ruination—the terrible deeds done in this city—didn't impact Ashalea still. Like ripples on the water, his

actions that day carried far into the future, and their paths had converged in a twist of fate.

For Ashalea, that had meant the murder of her family, the battle at Renlock Academy, and the loss of her home. But she had crawled out of the ashes, reborn as a deliverer of vengeance and a saviour of the people. *Her people*. For she was a queen-in-waiting, the hope for a wronged race.

A bitter smile crossed Ashalea's face. Hope was for fools and dreamers. Misery walked in her footsteps, death drank in her sorrow, and everywhere she went, the people she loved died.

Wezlan had died.

It was a stone in her stomach that pulled her down into an abyss. And rather than face this realisation, she instead crawled into the deepest, darkest hollow of herself, curled into a ball, and ignored the passing of days.

Where it was quiet. Where the world ceased to exist, and the cooling calm of nothingness collected her and claimed her for its own. Here, she could drown in silent sorrow. Here, she could—

"Ashalea? Did you hear me?"

A voice brought her careening back to the present and she realised Denavar had been speaking to her. She recognised the same glint to his eyes, in the lines of his face, in the softness of his voice. Concern etched into every crevice, worry alight in those rippling blues.

It was a conscious effort not to drown out his words, to shift her eyes towards his own. "Hmm?"

His lips shifted in a small frown. "I said you weren't present for dinner, so I brought you some food." He settled down beside her on a fallen pillar, propping a bowl on the stone, nudging it towards her ever so subtly.

Her eyes felt so heavy as she glanced at its contents. Steam curled up from the bowl, the aroma permeating the air. And it was that smell that twanged on her heartstrings, her ruptured soul. Soup. Vegetable soup.

Like the one she used to make for Wezlan back in their precious tree, with the stairs of books in precarious towers, the hearth in the centre, the two chairs set by its warmth. One of which would never seat Wezlan Shadowbreaker ever again.

Her eyes burned and bile rose in her throat. It took every effort to offer Denavar a weak smile. "I'm not hungry."

He took a breath. "Ashalea—"

"I said I'm not hungry." The bite to her tone surprised her. She should apologise, should thank him for the offer, but her body felt so heavy, and she was so tired. So, so tired. How much time had passed since Wezlan had left her? Weeks? Months?

She hadn't been sleeping. Every time she closed her eyes, she would see his face. Always the same—Wezlan's smiling weathered face, the crinkle to his lips, the mirth in his booming laughter. But then the dream would shift, and his eyes would turn accusing, angry. "*You did this to me,*" he would say. "*You left me to die.*"

Ashalea trembled, the nightmare so vivid in her mind's eye, haunting her even in her waking hours.

"Perhaps you could spend some time with your mother?" he pressed. "She's been desperate to catch up with you."

Ashalea didn't answer. She had no words ... didn't have the heart and couldn't muster the strength. She felt herself lapsing again, already exhausted from this tiresome subject. Where her mother was concerned, she was not interested. At least, that's what she told herself.

Truth was, she was angry at this woman. Bone deep, blood-boiling angry.

Her mother, who had abandoned her own baby.

Her mother, who Ashalea had thought dead her entire life.

Her mother, who was not her mother at all. She was not the loving, caring, smiling face she pictured, nor the woman who had raised her; the one Ashalea still grieved for, who was slaughtered in bed, lying next to her father on the morning of Ashalea's sixteenth birthday.

No, this woman had failed Ashalea her entire life. The shining star of the Moonglade Meadows, Queen Celiana Anaris Hevenor, had failed her. She didn't sense a looming change on the horizon.

With a sigh, she glanced beside her at the now empty space where the bowl sat, where Denavar had been just moments before. Maybe minutes. Maybe hours.

She didn't process the passing of time anymore, nor did she take pleasure in company, or find peace in sleep. All Ashalea knew was that she was alone, and that her mother hadn't bothered to see her over the many years that had passed. She wasn't about to now.

A Heavy Weight

DENAVAR

S HE WAS WASTING AWAY. Little more than a wraith. A memory of someone who had forgotten their purpose; whose every step was haunted.

Denavar stared at Ashalea from his perch beside the bonfire—one of many that scattered the Moonglade city—and barely registered the conversation. Her ribs were caving in, her face gaunt and hollow, the muscles that once filled that spectacular body now withered and weak.

But it was none of those things that broke him every morning and night; it was her eyes. Those beautiful emerald eyes, now devoid of any spark, lifeless ... cold. They barely recognised him, and when they looked at Denavar, they did not see—did not see the elf who so dearly loved her, who would do anything to make her feel alive again.

She never strayed from her vigil atop that fallen pillar except to sleep and sometimes pick at the food he would bring, drinking the bare minimum to survive. But she was not living. Not really.

Denavar's heart shattered a thousand times over when he gazed upon her. The Guardians—Gods, the world—had all suffered a loss. But none so greatly as Ashalea. Wezlan's death weighed heavily on her—she who had lost so much already. He was her mentor and the closest thing to a father since the darkness ripped away both males who had once filled that role in her life.

First, her biological father, whom she had never laid eyes on. Then her adoptive father, ripped into ribbons by the darkness on her sixteenth birthday. They had all thought the queen of the Moonglade Meadows dead. Finding her alive was the only pleasant surprise from the night Wezlan had died. Just over a month ago now.

Since their surprise encounter with the queen that night, Ashalea had made no effort to bond with her mother. Denavar mused what this meant for them—the elves and all peoples of the land. Would the queen pass her crown to Ashalea? Would she face her son? He didn't expect the latter was likely. Despite all the horrible things the darkness had done, a mother found forgiveness and empathy when the world would not.

He cupped his palms to his cheeks, buried his face in his hands. He knew how badly the queen wanted to connect with her daughter. He knew how scared she was, too. And maybe for good reason. Amends were nowhere in sight. That she had been alive all these years and not gone to aid her daughter ... his fingers twitched with annoyance. Perhaps she deserved the silent treatment for a good while longer.

He felt rather than saw someone slide onto the marble bench

next to him, the soft scent of wildflowers and fresh grass lingering on her skin, her feet bare as she tucked them beneath her. Shara. Even when relaxed she was shadow and smoke. A deadly assassin.

"Still on silent vigil?" she said by way of hello, jerking her chin to his silver-haired elf. Not cruelly, but more a blunt observation. They had often debated what they could do about Ashalea, how they might bring her back to them in all the ways that mattered.

Neither had an answer.

He sighed. "She rarely eats and doesn't sleep. She can barely lift her head to look at me, let alone speak."

Shara was silent for a beat. "She needs time, Denavar."

"We don't have the luxury of time," Denavar snapped. "We have no idea where the darkness is or what he's up to. Wezlan may have slowed him down, but for how long?"

Shara raised one perfect brow, shooting him a glare that could have levelled cities.

He ran a hand through his wavy hair—it was long and dishevelled, as was the stubble on his face—neglected while he spent all his time worrying about the world ... about a certain someone. He was in dire need of some maintenance. He caught Shara's narrowed eyes—following the movement—her small frown suggesting she agreed with him.

"You've seen the reports," he said gently. "More monsters are appearing every day across the southern villages. The elves will wear themselves thin before the war has even begun."

She snorted, pointing at the vegetable soup and assortment of soft cheeses and fruits. "Based on what you eat around here, it's not so hard to see why. You need protein—meat—to stay strong for battle."

He rolled his eyes, but a ghost of a smile crept over his face.

"We're elves, we don't need meat to sustain us like you fragile creatures do."

Her gaze simmered and she puffed out her chest indignantly. "This fragile creature could snap your neck without a second thought, what with it being so scrawny from lack of *meat* and all."

Denavar opened his mouth, a string of curses and not-so-nice names on his lips when someone said, "Whose neck is about to be snapped?"

They both looked up to find the cheery face of Telilah pop into view, her hips swishing as she sauntered up to them. "It's far too fine an evening to spend murdering uncouth elves, not when there's much better things to be done with them." She winked at him for good measure.

He couldn't help but chuckle. The woman was so shamelessly flirtatious he expected half the village would be pining for her now. Not that anyone would dare cross that line if they wished to survive the night. Shara and Telilah ... well, he didn't know what they were, but he was quietly confident that there would be a world of pain for anyone who made a move on the curvy minstrel.

Shara didn't share her things. It didn't matter that they weren't hers to begin with.

But Denavar saw Telilah's bright smile dim as she spied the woman across the square, hunched over, staring at the stars—perhaps beyond, into other worlds—one where her mentor had sacrificed himself so that she may live. So he could live.

Denavar would never forget that moment, when Wezlan gave his life so they could escape. When his eyes—those stormy grey eyes—conveyed the one order that Denavar would always obey: to protect her, to shield her, to be there for her when the wizard could not. And he would do anything for Ashalea for the rest of his long life,

or what remained to be seen of it from the oncoming war.

Telilah crouched in front of him, her brown eyes boring into his own. She tentatively took his hands in hers. "You listen to me now, Denavar Andaro, and you listen well. There will come a time when she remembers this. The heartache, the pain, the anger ... it will fade as raw hurts always do. But she will never forget that you stood by her side through all the anguish, loving her when she had nothing left to give. You are her constant. And constants never quit."

He let her words sink in, breathing deep from her wisdom as he looked once more at his love. His spark for her would never die, just as he knew her love for him would never dim. But that's the thing about love—about life. It's the hard days that make the good ones all the brighter.

A kernel of fierce resolve spread within his belly and, setting his lips in a determined smile, he said, "I know what I have to do."

Shara grinned wolfishly. "Go get your girl back, brother."

Rising, he set his eyes on the prize, preparing himself for a conversation that could go any which way. But before he marched to his destination, he clasped a gentle hand on Telilah's shoulder, allowing a grateful smile to grace his face. "Thank you."

She nodded dutifully before taking Shara's hand and silently departing. He watched them go, curiosity rising as he watched that strange woman. She was a mystery, but fierce of heart and full of fight—perhaps not built for battle, but an old soul through and through that could lead with the power of words and wit.

Denavar turned, striding purposefully. He approached Ashalea and marched right on by; past the ruined columns and architectural wonder of a forgotten city, up the winding path that led towards the palace and, finally, through the open archways of the exterior

throne room, finding his feet planted firmly before the queen of Moonglade Meadows. She was sitting in one of the thrones on the dais, the spare caved in, like the very sky had smote it to ruin.

He didn't need to wonder who had done it, or who had once sat in it. He did wonder why no one had ever replaced it—or removed it. But he supposed it served as a reminder. Of what the queen had lost ... what everyone had lost.

She raised her head, wariness clouding those hazel eyes; her otherwise fine features slightly pinched with the echo of worry, her narrow shoulders rigid in defence. She could sense it then, his anger.

"You wonder why I haven't approached my daughter," she said simply. It wasn't a question.

His jaw clenched at the casual words. "Weeks have passed and still you haven't even tried to bridge the gap with her. She wastes away as we speak, and you can't find the time for a gentle word or to lend a shoulder to cry on?"

She rose in one fluid motion, the folds of a gossamer gown the colour of dawn shrouding her slender form, a clasp with a celestial star holding it in place over her shoulders. It never ceased to amaze him, how like her mother Ashalea was. The curve of their mouths, the wealth of secrets hidden in their eyes. And the hair. Silver waves of starlight. A gift of the bloodline ... or a curse.

Queen Celiana turned, padding gracefully towards the precipice, the open archways and columns of the structure allowing a panoramic view of the city below. He stalked silently to her side, gazing out at the place he'd once called home.

She sighed. "Beautiful, isn't it?"

That's something he could agree on. The Moonglade Meadows was most picturesque at night, when the moon and the stars shone

down upon buildings of smooth white stone, pearly and glistening, giving the city an almost ethereal glow. Soft lines in the old language were carved into archways standing guard at the city's perimeter; Magicka of an old design glowing a white-blue at their centres.

A small brook curled through the city, babbling away happily, children playing at its edge, fireflies hovering above like flying fireballs. This was an old city. Mystical, full of Magicka and the old ways, and there was a wildness to it that could not be tamed. Bountiful green surrounded the structures, growing in every nook and cranny, harmoniously sharing the living space.

Balance. The way life should be. The way of the elves.

"Keeping this city going ... it hasn't been easy," the queen continued. "After the king passed, after what"—she swallowed—"after what Crinos did, nothing has quite been the same. It took time to regain the people's confidence, to regather our forces and to return to some semblance of normal life."

She turned to Denavar now, her eyes imploring, her lovely features twisted with desperation. "After my return from the Grove, after everything I went through—"

"Everything you went through?" Denavar scoffed, anger flushing out all sensibility. "We all lost something that day. Mothers and fathers lost sons and daughters, marriages were broken, friends buried friends. How dare you stand before me and expect pity when you fled the people you were born to rule."

Her face contorted for the briefest of moments in an ugly sneer before she smoothed her features, but Denavar didn't miss the resemblance. The temper he had seen in another face. The disdain he had seen from Crinos.

"Do not forget that I am still your queen," she seethed.

Denavar's stare burned into her own, his furious gaze slicing shards of ice right to her soul—to the truth she so desperately tried to hide. "You have sat on a broken throne watching the years pass in solitude, hiding behind your misty walls, letting the world carry on in turmoil while you wallow in dreams of a paradise long lost. You are no more a queen than I am a king. *You*," he spat, "are a coward."

She opened her mouth, but he wasn't done yet. Not by a long shot.

"You see that woman down there?" He jabbed one pointed finger at the ghost of a girl who looked without seeing, who was alive but not living. The queen's eyes slowly trailed his finger to land on Ashalea. Celiana's face betrayed nothing as she gazed upon her daughter.

"That woman has done more in her twenty years than you have done in the many human lives you've lived. She fights for this world. She bleeds for it, and I would take every cut if it meant she'd be safe. But there are some burdens I cannot bear. There are some roles I cannot play. She needs you now. She needs a mother."

She stared at him then, hazel eyes all but dead as she gazed upon him like an ant to be squished beneath her boot. And for a terrible moment he wondered if maybe he'd overstepped. Celiana was deadly calm, still as a predator before taking the kill. But that was his love down there, and etiquette and punishment be damned. Exasperated, he raked a hand through his hair, gritting his teeth.

"Prianara help me, if you don't say something Celiana, I'll—"

"You're right," she whispered.

His forehead crinkled in confusion, anger quieting to a gentle hum in his veins. He leaned against the column to his right, crossing his arms as he waited, one sceptical brow crooked.

She frowned softly, her nose crinkling just as Ashalea's did when lost in thought. No freckles spattered the queen's face though.

He had to suppress a snort. That would involve leaving this place, and from the queen's creamy complexion, he gathered no sneaky trips had been taken for some time.

"You're right," she repeated, voice louder this time, firmer. "When my husband died and I was at death's door, the only solution was to let Ashalea go. To give her a chance at a better life—a safe life." Her face turned ashen. "I never expected Crinos would discover her, that he would try to finish what he started. I should have gone to her then ... on her sixteenth birthday. I should have brought her home. Maybe if I'd done so, Wezlan would still be here and none of this would have happened."

Denavar sighed. "None of that matters now. We can't change the past." He shoved off the wall, stalking forward to put his hands on the queen's shoulders, forcing her to look at him. "Wezlan knew what he was doing. He gave his life because he believed in something bigger than all of us. He believed in her."

He jerked his chin towards Ashalea, her silver hair, though lank and dull, still a beacon in the distance. "She's a Guardian now. Shara, Razakh, myself? We've got work to do, and the longer we wait here while time trickles through the hourglass ... it is to our detriment. Your son is coming, Celiana. Crinos is coming."

At the mention of his name Celiana winced, and Denavar saw true fear glimmer in her eyes. His anger subsided, replaced by a pang of sorrow for this woman. He couldn't imagine it ... the pain she must be feeling. To have the blessing of creation, to love something more than anything in the world, only to have that child grow into the bringer of death and destruction—to destroy everything she held dear.

Her shoulders sagged under the weight of that burden, and Denavar dropped his hands to his sides. The queen turned, eyes glazing as she lost herself in memories and ghosts.

Uneasiness shifted inside his belly like worms on rotten fruit. He had never discussed it with Ashalea, but Denavar had always wanted children. Their purity, their joy, the light they brought to the world; he fancied he would be a good father, a doting one—the envy of all the other kids. But with war brewing, it was hard to fancy much at all when his own life wasn't assured for keeps.

He looked at the elf beside him. For all her faults, for her lack of courage, he couldn't blame Celiana entirely. She had rallied the people, erected the wards and kept them safe. She might have feigned ignorance to the rest of Everosia, but in her heart of hearts she meant well. And as he watched Celiana staring at her daughter, mouth downturned in sadness, a longing in her eyes, Denavar felt his heart soften.

"I love her, you know," she said.

He uttered a long sigh. "I know."

"You'll protect her, won't you? Until the end?"

Something in her tone made him halt at that. As if she knew what the finale would be. As if she were saying goodbye, giving up before the war truly started. But he offered a grim smile as his fingers drifted to the hilt of the dagger at his belt. "Aye," he agreed. "Until the end and ever after."

She nodded, her body visibly deflating, as if that answer solved all the problems in the world. "Well then, there's only one thing left." Eyes glued to her daughter, she took a deep breath, and slowly, so slowly, she adjusted her gown, smoothed down her hair, and thrust her chin skyward. "How do I look?"

Denavar gave her a mischievous wink. "Like a queen."

The look she returned could have killed lesser males, but she took a deep breath, making her way towards the path leading out

from the throne room. Denavar chuckled softly, turning to take a stroll on the adjacent hills. He was barely one boot onto the grass when he heard her murmur.

"What on Everosia—" she began, but the sentence trailed off to end in a gasp.

He was by her side instantly on high alert, all senses primed for trouble, eyes scanning the city below, the meadows surrounding them. A soft breeze curled around them, the scent of fresh flowers and grass wafting up his nose. But something else tickled his nostrils, a fell stench of decay, of shadow and smoke.

And then true shadows loomed across the grasses, blackening the flowers, shrivelling petals to crisp and ash. Great beasts that looked like ... looked like ...

Horns sounded, breaking through his thoughts, the alarm triggering the city into a flurry below. Elves sprinted to the armouries, children bolted indoors, and a sea of faces turned eyes up the hill to fall upon their queen. Seeking answer. Seeking command.

Denavar glanced at her, but the queen was mute, staring in shock, her shoulders locked, her face dumbfounded. "Celiana," Denavar prompted. "My Queen!" He shook her roughly, but he found no answer in her terrified eyes.

"Hells," he muttered. "If you want something done ..."

Smoke and Shadows

RAZAKH

THE TASTE OF DEATH FILLED HIS MOUTH, a smoky film lining his tongue as he ripped into flesh that was not flesh, blood that was not blood but something other. Something *wrong*. They were an abomination, these non-Diodonians. A perversion of everything his proud and noble race were. He tore ruthlessly at the creature to remind it of that, stared right back into its burning yellow eyes as its life bled out like tar. In a puff of smoke, it was gone.

He spat the gore from his mouth, ruffling his coat in disgust, the red glint to his golden fur rippling as wildly as the flames upon his back. He had met these creatures not so long ago with Shara and Telilah, despising having to do so again.

Horns were blaring, the calls long and deep, the frequency growing frantic.

"Razakh," someone called over the commotion and, turning, he spied Denavar hurtling down the hill, dragging the wide-eyed queen by the wrist. Denavar skidded to a halt, eyes like a stormy sea, game-face on as he surveyed the chaos. Razakh knew who he was searching for, but the silver-haired princess was nowhere to be seen. Shara, on the other hand, was putting on quite the show.

Fighting alongside a small group of soldiers, she pirouetted and slashed with the ease of a dancer, her movements as fluid and graceful as the elves around her. Her golden skin was aglow under the moonlit sky, raven hair curling around her face as she fought with deadly precision. And, of course, the assassin was grinning from ear to ear, as eager as a bloodhound on the hunt, almost maniacal in her delight.

Razakh almost rolled his eyes until he spied Telilah cornered by two of the shadow creatures, her hands shaking on the hilt of a rapier, arms slashing in a panic. With a roar he bounded towards her, the call to arms rallying his comrades. Narrowly evading having her head decapitated, Shara leapt, sliding on her feet, back defying gravity as she slid under the mighty legs of the shadow beast and tore its innards asunder.

And then they were running; Shara and Denavar flanking Razakh as they hurled themselves at the non-Diodonians just as one leaped towards Telilah's throat. With uncanny speed Denavar used Razakh's back as a stepping-stone, sailing into the air before bringing his sword down in a mighty arc, slicing the head off the beast and causing smoke to puff out.

Razakh growled at the elf, who only winked back with that stupid smile humans and elves seemed to melt over. He bared his teeth but Denavar only grinned wider as they circled the other creature. It glanced between the three of them, black coat rippling,

fangs glinting with deadly promise. It lasted all of five more seconds before Denavar lifted a palm and conjured a fire arrow that skewered the beast's heart ... or the place it should have been at least. Its leering face faded into nothing as it became ash on the wind.

"Took the cavalry long enough," Telilah huffed with a smile. "Though," she amended, pointing past the group, "I think you've got bigger problems."

Razakh followed her line of vision, spotting the queen surrounded by a consort of elves fighting valiantly. But the creatures were too many and the city was in chaos. The soldiers were divided—some ushered citizens to safety, others fought in pockets throughout the ruins or amongst the fields of flowers.

"They're everywhere," Shara breathed.

Denavar's shoulders set as he decided on a course of action. Razakh could almost see the cogs turning in his head; the soldier in him taking precedence over emotion, knowing that his beloved city—his people—were once again in peril.

The elf looked to Shara and Telilah. "Take the queen to safety. There's a catacomb underground—you'll find the entrance hidden at the mouth of the brook down the way. The passage will open for the queen. Stay there until someone comes for you. Protect her."

Shara's face crumpled with indignance. "I'm not a babysitter, I—"

Denavar grunted in exasperation, his expression darkening. "Just do it, Shara," he snapped.

The assassin fluffed her hair before grabbing Telilah's hand and running into the fray. Razakh could hear her snapping at the elves to get out of the way, and anything else in her path had little time to talk back before she cut them down.

Denavar turned to Razakh and placed a calloused palm on his

shoulder blade. "I need you to find her," he said. "She could be hurt, she could be ..." The elf's face was stricken as his mind no doubt ran through countless horrid possibilities.

"I'll find her," Razakh promised, already turning on his paws.

Razakh surveyed the city, searching for Ashalea, finding only death and destruction. Flames were spreading throughout the sprawling wildflowers, the air now perfumed with burning foliage and flesh. Elves rallied, their attacks swift and precise. But while they were perfectly in sync, efficient with sword and bow and their footwork pristine, the creatures were savage in ways even elves could not predict. For all their knowledge and grace, brutality was not amongst lessons learnt by these people.

Without leadership they were falling, their numbers dwindling, their circles breaking. Most were unarmoured; long limbs exposed, feet bare, nothing but the steel in their hands or the wood between their fingers as they let fly white feathered arrows. Denavar started bellowing orders, screaming at them to "hold the line" and "regroup". Razakh set off, leaving the elves to fend for themselves, his silver eyes scanning.

The city was in turmoil and everywhere he looked—upon the ramparts of the white stone walls, upon archways and statues and columns and the delicately carved roofs of the homesteads, the shadow beasts lingered.

The river glittered as it snaked through the city, its midnight blue waters sparkling with the reflection of the moon and the fires surrounding it. And still Razakh searched, side-stepping one creature, pouncing on another's jugular, swerving and swaying as he sprinted through the carnage.

Elves felled by the beasts scattered the mossy grounds, some struggling to breathe, others clutching their wounds—their lifeblood slowly returning to the earth as they bled out. Others yet lay still, wide eyes open and glassy, their gift of long life ended in one swift gnash of teeth.

But Razakh couldn't aid them. Not until he found her; the future of this people, the hope for a future for all in this world. A united army. An alliance of races. With a frustrated snarl, he put all his weight into his paw pads and launched onto the parapet a few metres off the ground. He turned towards the watchtower. Its walls glittered pearlescent, elvish runes of warding carved across its smooth stone, and before its open door stood two shadow creatures.

With a throaty roar he descended upon them, gripping one by the scruff and hurling it from the wall, pouncing on the other and raking his claws down its body in one fluid motion, penetrating deep beneath its rippling coat. It was dust before it could blink.

Razakh scrabbled up the tower's stairs, making short work of the climb up several stories as he burst onto the landing above. From there, he had a three-hundred-and-sixty-degree view of the city. Elves rallied below. Archers now lined the walls, sending death from above, and foot soldiers formed rank in squads of twelve. Those better skilled to Magicka advanced in small groups, some hurling electric balls of blue and white, others concerned only with extinguishing the fires.

Some elves linked hands, their lips moving feverishly as they called on water not from the air, but from the river itself—and rise the river did, fingers of water reaching out gently and cradling the fires, diminishing them with tender hands.

The tides had turned. Denavar had marshalled the elves and the forces of the Moonglade Meadows were rising. Their queen would be safely hidden away, protected by the fiercest of soldiers. So, where was the princess? The silver lady? Their broken leader?

His eyes roved over the crowd, their depths swirling furiously as he focused his attention wholly on finding her. But ... there! Was that a flash of silver hair? And another. She was climbing the city castle; not inside taking the stairs but scaling the damn thing like a spider clings to a web.

He watched her grapple over its smooth edges, the building luminescent, blindingly bright as it reflected light like a mirror. Moonstone, it was. A shimmering, radiant, glorious thing of white and blue and purple and pink, shifting like sand as the moon beamed down upon it.

It was not a looming, boastful beast that stretched endlessly on—it didn't teem with servants and cooks and advisers and nobles from across the land. It wore a different kind of nobility. Graceful—ethereal, almost. And of all the places she could be, Ashalea Kindaris was climbing up that damned smooth stone and about to get herself killed.

Razakh's breath caught in his throat as one hand slipped, and she swung precariously for one violent heartbeat until her boots found purchase again and she was once more gliding up the surface. A low rumble shivered through him. *Elves.* No one else could be so confident, yet no other race was so nimble either. He watched on helplessly, too far away to be of help, worlds away from reaching her. All he could do was wait ... and watch. She flew up the domed roof of the castle and beyond to the pinnacle of the tower set in its centre, until at last, she would be but a pinprick to those battling below.

Razakh, with his keen Diodonian eyes, saw the look on her face. A wild determination, a familiar fury he had not seen ignited for some time. It was terrifying and terrific all at once. That this ghost of a woman had returned, burning brightly, if even for the briefest of moments.

She lifted her hands into the air, eyes screwed shut in concentration, jaw set grimly, hair billowing in the wind. The sky rumbled and the night seemed to darken, as if ... as if she were sucking the light from the very moon itself.

As one, the elves and shadow creatures lifted their heads from the battleground below, halting their killing song, eyes shifting uncertainly until all found their mark. Until all found *her*. She was rising now, feet lifting off the ground, like some beautiful goddess, like some terrible wraith.

Razakh looked down to the masses below, spotting Denavar, covered in blood and ash, blue eyes wide and uncertain. And amongst the incredulity that echoed in his eyes and the set of his mouth, Razakh saw fear. Utter fear for this display of power. This ability to transcend gravity itself and float, not unlike someone else they had all come to know. And it wasn't fear of Ashalea herself, but rather for her. For what this rage might cause to rise within her soul.

Razakh's stomach coiled, whether in awe or fear of a different making, he did not know. Ashalea rose, arms trembling with unseen power, face contorted with effort, muscles bunching, and then ... light. Light so profoundly white, so blindingly beautiful that even Razakh had to squeeze his pupil-less quicksilver eyes shut.

The world seemed to fold in on itself, like the very breath stole from his lungs. He had the sick feeling of weightlessness for a moment, and then, like a tidal wave, the light seemed to cascade in a blast, almost throwing him from his own tower. His claws gouged into the ground as he clung on for dear life, still unable to open his eyes for the sheer force of this Magicka.

The air stilled, the dust settled, and finally, when the burn behind his eyes dissipated and gravity returned to normal, he cracked them open. Stillness echoed across the Meadows, an eerie silence replacing the cries of the wounded and the bellows of war. Razakh gazed upon the shocked faces of the elves below, confusion clouding their features, even as their weapons, still half raised, found no opponent to cleave. No enemy to fell.

Every shadow creature, all the abominations, the perversions of Razakh's kind were ... gone. Not one remained, the only evidence of their intrusion left in blood amongst the green and upon the still bodies of once proud elves.

A slight breeze curled through the city, carrying with it the remnants of ash and smoke, purifying the air, cleansing the battleground. She had done this; Ashalea had destroyed them all. Hundreds of shadow creatures vanquished with the power of moonlight. With *her* power.

Eyes wide, Razakh looked to the wraith still hovering in the air, her face now a picture of tranquillity. Somehow, she looked even more fragile in this moment, as if the power itself had eaten away even more of her—the already wasted creature now entirely hollow.

Razakh felt guilt claw at his heart, regret shuddering through his body. How could he have compared her to the darkness? She had only ever used her power for good. What she just did ... it could have killed her. But she would have paid that price willingly to save the ones she loved, to do what was right. Perhaps the risk came too easily, in fact.

Maybe she would welcome death after having felt its presence shadow her for so long. Now that thought—that was more alarming than the rest. He gazed at her, this ghost of a female, and he vowed he would not allow her to take the easy path and give up on herself. Whether she wanted to or not, she would re-join the living. Starting now.

As if in response to his inner monologue, Ashalea's eyes fluttered, she gasped in one heaving breath, and then she plummeted to the tower like a ragdoll, limbs limp and head lolling. A broken girl, inside and out.

5

A Motley Gang

ASHALEA

ASHALEA THOUGHT SHE'D KNOWN PAIN. She was wrong.

Her body ached with a sharp throbbing, like a thousand needles had been jammed into her skin. Her limbs felt barely attached, held together with the tiniest sliver of skin. Every time she moved her body screamed in agony, her vision blurred, and stars would fire behind her eyes. Her bones felt brittle, and to breathe was to feel like her lungs might burst with every inhalation.

And yet pain burrowed deeper, nestled in her heart—to despair, emptiness, sorrow. Bones mended, wounds repaired, and her elven blood meant she would heal quicker, recover her fitness faster, but the people that once burned so brightly could never be replaced, never be forgotten.

She sighed, feeling disoriented as she looked around the room, eyes slowly adjusting to the ray of golden sunshine creeping through the window. It was warm and cosy, elegance etched into every item of furniture, rustic wood gracefully carved into a four-poster bed. Delicate emerald curtains draped the windows and subtle hints of green popped throughout the cream throw rugs and cushions. The ceiling was etched in a carefully constructed replica of the night sky, constellations carved with runic symbols so they might light up in the evening.

It felt like home and decidedly not. For what was a house without the loved ones that made it a home? What were riches and luxuries without a family to share them with?

But he was there. Denavar. Silent, seated in a wingback chair by her bedside, arms folded around his midriff, one leg sprawled along the wooden floor, chin tucked into his chest as he slept.

Ashalea observed the sweep of his lashes, quivering slightly as his eyes moved beneath the lids. His fingers twitched ever so gently. His lips quirked. Dreaming. She looked at the vastness of her bed—the empty space at her side, heart breaking just a little as she realised how wide the rift was growing between them. She had done this. Pushed him away—all of them—so she could mourn in selfish silence. So she could play the petulant child, stamp her feet, cry in vain and beg for things to be better.

She sighed. Nothing would get better. The wheels would not turn towards triumph until she picked up her broken pieces, put a bandage on them and carried on. He would want that for her. Wezlan would want her to keep going. No, not just want ... he would expect it. He would say something witty and wise and smile with that mischievous grin that only Wezlan could give.

He would hate that she'd distanced herself from the others— would tell her to draw strength from them, to confide in them. "A strong man will bear the burden alone, a wise one will share it with his friends," he had once said.

And he was right, she supposed. But Ashalea was not strong and had instead played the part of a fool, her self-inflicted misery the crux of the joke. She closed her eyes, easing herself as gently as possible back into the soft bed. How the mighty had fallen. How the righteous had wronged the innocent.

She felt a calloused palm encircle her hand, gentle and tentative in its touch. Ashalea opened her eyes to see him staring at her, azure peering out in bright contrast to an exhausted face, tired purple shadowing the orbs. But it was those eyes, bright and curious as always, that captured her attention.

It never ceased to amaze, how they changed according to his mood, what he was wearing—even the weather. His lips curled in a soft smile, a little uncertainly, much to her sorrow. She had done that too: dulled his shine, tempered his nature and perhaps that of the others.

"Denavar," she began, little more than a croak. "I ..."

His hand tightened on hers and he shook his head, gaze sad but determined. "You don't need to apologise, Ashalea," he said quietly.

She only squeezed his hand harder. "Yes. I do. I pushed you away. I didn't want to face the truth; I couldn't bear the idea of being in a world without him, so I retreated into my own dark cave like a snake returning to its pit."

"We all die, Ashalea. It is the natural course of life, and Wezlan had a long one. Longer than most who dwell on Everosia, except the elves."

"There is nothing natural about the way he died," Ashalea spat.

The room was silent for a spell, her words lingering on stagnant air. She regretted the poison in them immediately. But then, surprisingly, he said, "Lenith et du idre, adu etua mena sif jaene."

"Live in love, and eternal memory shall be granted," Ashalea whispered. Tears burned her eyes as she understood its meaning. "To be loved is to live on in the hearts of elves, and no matter how long our lives, their memory will never be forgotten."

"He loved you more than anything." Denavar loosed a shaky breath. "His life was dedicated to the people, to the mages, to you. He inspired all with his good deeds, with his courage and kindness. His power was something to be awed, but it wasn't the might of it. It's what he did with it."

A tear trickled down her cheek as she weighed Denavar's words. True. All true. And that made her even sadder, but there was a new hope in this message. An understanding.

Denavar continued, "We will always honour his memory, but to do this, we need to carry on with the quest. Let us continue his work and bring a lasting peace to our lands. It's what he would want, what I want, so that I might live my life in love too ... if you'll have me."

He said the latter with such uncertainty that Ashalea burst into tears, kicked off the covers and threw herself at him, causing both Denavar and the chair to fall to the ground with a forceful *whump*.

Every bone in her body screeched in protest but she didn't care. This male was everything to her. *Everything.* And to have him question that was a thought she could not abide. She squeezed him with all her strength, which apparently wasn't much because he swept her off the floor and into his arms before setting her gently back in the bed in one swift motion.

He sat next to her, brushing a hand across her cheek, tucking limp hair behind one pointed ear. Ashalea took his hand, kissed each knuckle softly, then his wrist, then up his arm until she met the soft flesh of his neck. She nestled her head in the crook of his collar bone, the familiar smell of peppermint climbing her nose.

He held her tight. "I assume that's a yes, then?"

Ashalea leaned back, looked him straight in the eyes—which danced with joy now—and she feasted on this moment, greedily drinking in his full lips, the curve of his jaw, the wayward mop of his thick, dark brown locks, the stubble on his canvas.

"Oh, Denavar. Don't you know? It will always be you. Even locked away in a fortress of my own making, it will always be you."

His lips curled into a genuine smile before his eyes turned serious again. "Just promise me. No more walls. No locked towers, no sealed doors. If you don't let me in, I can't help you, and you can't help yourself. And absolutely NO heroic acts of almost killing yourself to save the populace."

Ashalea cringed. "That bad, huh?"

"You've been out for almost a week. The energy required to perform Magicka of that magnitude ... between being malnourished and not sleeping properly, Ashalea, it's nothing short of a miracle you're alive." He swallowed. "When you—when you dropped from the tower, I almost died three times over."

She leaned back against her pillows in shock, letting the gravity of her foolishness sink in. But, reflecting on it, she would have done it again. She would always risk herself to save the others.

Denavar frowned, his brow creasing like a teacher scolding a child. "I know what you're thinking, and while it's terribly noble of you, it was also stupid."

She looked up at him in surprise, opening her mouth to retort but quickly clamping it shut upon his withering glare. "We need you, as one of the Guardians, to keep on fighting to the very end.

Without you, Goddess knows what would happen. If we could still seal the Gate or not. It's not a risk worth taking." His voice softened and his hand swallowed hers as he moved it over her heart. "But Everosia be damned if it didn't have you in it. I couldn't bear it if..."—he gazed at her imploringly—"just stop putting the rest of us to shame, will you?"

She managed a croaky laugh, but she nodded all the same. She would make no promises, but he was right. Everosia was at risk and becoming a martyr would do nothing for the living. Without the Guardians, without the Gate being sealed once more, the war could last for years. The darkness's army would continue to trickle through his portals until the day Crinos would have enough strength to obliterate the only thing stopping his armies from spreading. He would decimate the Grove—the very core of this land—and all would fall into ruin.

The thought of her brother filled her with rage, tempered only by the fragility of her body and the pain coursing through her veins. Ashalea took a deep breath, wincing as her ribs protested the movement. With a groan she swung her feet off the bed and padded to the dresser. She gazed at her mirror image and had to stifle a gasp at what stared back at her.

A face hollow and pale, with dull green eyes and limp hair that was the grey of old age, not the silver of the stars. She lifted her shift, noting the loss of muscle to her arms and legs. She could count a good number of her ribs, and her stomach was a depressed pit.

No wonder she felt like shattered glass. There was nothing sustaining her body, no nutrients to help her heal. Ashalea had no doubt that she would be dead from that Magicka, had she not been an elf. As it was, it would be an art to put her back together. Her stomach grumbled as if in agreement.

She turned back to Denavar. "I don't suppose—"

He grinned wolfishly. "Already on it." He whistled and their friends came bounding in, falling over each other in their excitement. Shara almost bowled Ashalea over in her haste to hug her, and Razakh joined in, planting a wet, sloppy Diodonian kiss on her cheek.

Ashalea laughed, allowing their warmth to seep into her bones, their love for her a balm against the pain, filling the emptiness in her stomach. Shara squeezed tighter and Ashalea tapped her on the shoulder, her vision dotting from the pain. "Can't ... breathe," she wheezed.

"Oh, right, bag of bones and all. Let's get some meat back on there," Shara said with a wink.

Telilah walked in right on cue, a broad smile on her heart-shaped face as she wheeled in a cart overflowing with food. Sweet fruits and oats, freshly baked breads, mature cheeses, vegetables dripping in fragrant sauces, eggs covered in rich spice, small cakes and pastries dripping with honey.

Ashalea's mouth began watering at the delectable feast, stomach groaning. The normal reactions to food had her heart soaring. She was hungry, and that was ... it was progress. To not only be able to stomach the sight and smell of food but to want to taste it, indulge in it.

Denavar began heaping piles on a gilded plate before gesturing to Ashalea and then the bed. "Eat. Not too quickly and not too much, or you'll be sick. Your body isn't used to it."

"All right, mother hen." She raised a brow but didn't argue, taking the plate daintily before throwing caution to the wind and wolfing down the feast. Shara plonked on the bed beside her, almost upsetting the contents of Ashalea's plate, where she, too, scoffed the meal as if the world might end tomorrow.

When a stillness settled over the room and Ashalea could hear naught but the loud chews of Shara—and perhaps her own—she looked up. Everyone but Shara was staring at her in mild amusement, or in Denavar's case, profound delight at her eating.

Ashalea frowned. "Such poor manners you all have. It's rude to stare in refined society," she tsked.

Telilah looked pointedly at everyone present. "And who here fits that description?"

Shara snorted and, with her mouth still full of food, said, "Speak for yourself. *I* am the daughter of a chieftain."

Razakh's throat rumbled. "*To people who deal death like one might deal cards.*"

"Huh! The dog has a sense of humour."

"He's also got the higher card in this game, dear," Telilah said with a wink.

Shara swallowed loudly and glared at her companion. "And how do you figure that?"

"Well, you're the daughter of a chieftain. Razakh *was* one."

Razakh tipped his head back and howled, to which Denavar and Ashalea raucously joined in. A serving lady who was walking past the room poked her head in with wide eyes, turning her slender nose up before shaking her head and moving on.

The room fell silent momentarily before everyone burst into a fit of laughter. Even Razakh rumbled with that curious sound of utter amusement. Ashalea shuddered over her plate, lifting her arms in defeat, pain racking her ribs as she tried to stop laughing.

But she didn't want to—not really. This moment carried freedom from her pain, from the haunting memories she stored within a locked box deep inside her. The pure joy in being with her friends—her family—was a breath of new hope. A sweeping gale to not create wreckage but instead remove it from her heart.

Denavar, still grinning, took a seat by Ashalea, stealing a chunk of her bread before sinking his teeth into the soft crust. "Welcome back," he whispered in her ear.

Ashalea nestled into his shoulder, looking at her family, and smiled. A broad, unhindered, loving smile. They all caught her eye and soon quieted, even Shara, perhaps sensing her friend had something important to say. She cleared her throat.

"We've all had a hard time of it lately. We've lost loved ones, left our lives behind, abandoned other duties, and—look, I'm not going to lie, I've wanted to give up. I never asked to be a Guardian—none of us did—and yet here we are, for better or worse, together. Just another day in the life, huh."

They all smiled softly at that, most with eyes glazed as they reflected on the paths that led them here. Shara, after her rescue from the darkness and upon standing down from her potential future as the Onyxonite chieftain. Razakh, who had forfeited his position as the Diodonian leader and left his near-extinct brethren. Telilah, after the passing of her grandmother, with barely a coin to her name and nowhere to go. And Denavar: darling Denavar, whose home away from home—Renlock Academy—had recently lost its wise leader and had been stripped of many mages and friends, of Farah ...

But they had all lost Wezlan. Razakh and Telilah might not have had the time to forge a bond so strong as the rest of them, but he had made an impact, nonetheless. As he always did, for better or worse, with everyone.

"You have all stood by me, always been there for me, and it's time I thanked you for that. So, thanks, Guardians—friends—for sticking by me no matter what. I love this motley gang of thieves, killers, pariahs, performers ..."—Telilah brightened at the latter—"I love you all."

Shara rolled her eyes, even as she tried to hide a sniff. "As if it needed to be said."

Ashalea smirked. "Is that a hint of emotion I detect?"

Denavar squinted at Shara, studying her face. "A little ... teardrop, perhaps?"

"Oh shut up or I'll break your balls," Shara snapped.

Telilah sniggered as she stacked everyone's plates back on the cart, and Shara and Denavar rose. Razakh jumped onto the bed, snuffing the flames on his back and curling up, ready to take a nap. The fact he was near the size of a bed himself did not go unnoticed, but she welcomed his warmth and size, like a weighted blanket.

Ashalea yawned. "Couldn't agree more." She burrowed under the covers and snuggled in, trying to get comfortable beside the giant Diodonian. She let one hand sprawl over Razakh's golden fur, soft and snug under her fingertips.

Shara glared at him disapprovingly. "Don't you have work to do?"

He opened one eye lazily. *"Let the elves tend to elvish matters. When Ashalea is well, we shall seek counsel."*

She grumbled at the dismissal, but before she stalked from the room, she tucked Ashalea's cover in around her and whispered, "Love you too, but—by the Gods' balls—don't ever scare me like that again."

"No promises," Ashalea grumbled, eyes closed, already drifting off. "Now get out and let me sleep." She flapped her hand with a vague shooing gesture and heard them exit one by one, the sound of laughter drifting down the hallway.

Denavar pressed a peppermint kiss to her forehead before leaving, and then the world was quiet, nothing but a warm belly and the soft snores of a Diodonian to send her to sleep.

<hr>

She woke to find her mother seated in the chair beside the bed, her fingertips steepled as if in prayer to the Moon Goddess Prianara, her nose scrunched in quiet contemplation.

Ashalea may as well have been looking at her mirror image, her mother bore such likeness to her. The same straight nose and set of the mouth, the wavy hair, the small mannerisms such as the crinkled face when something stirs the mind. Two sides of the same coin. They could be sisters if one didn't know better. Such was the grace of the elves.

But the differences lay in their livelihoods. Time had made its subtle marks on the queen. Age and despair had settled around her mother's mouth, in the sweep of her eyes, the hands clasped before her. But there was a grace to the queen that Ashalea did not possess. Regal stature radiated from this she-elf—the set of her shoulders, the high chin, the elegance in every movement.

The queen had known pain, yes, but she had long since lived in solitude. In peace and prosperity and ignorant bliss while the world fell into ruin beyond her misted gates. Her kin were at risk—Everosia was at risk, and still she had ignored the blight that spread across the land. Still she had ignored the evil, the destruction that her son was sowing, right up until it found her doorstep and stepped through the threshold.

Elves were dead because of her. The blood of innocents washed the streets because she had not prepared for the possibility of war—

had not predetermined that her son would come. Perhaps she couldn't bear the weight of that burden. Perhaps she never would.

Ashalea felt her stomach twist with loathing as she considered the cowardice of this elf. But there was pity too. Pity for a queen so broken by the past she could not open her eyes to the future. Pity that she had lost so much but learned so little. She would not become this broken monarch. Not today, not tomorrow. The darkness wouldn't have that satisfaction.

Celiana looked up to find Ashalea staring at her, and a small but wary smile crossed her face. She reached a tentative hand out—as if to comfort her—but perhaps she saw the coldness in Ashalea's eyes, for she withdrew it, clearing her throat awkwardly.

"You're looking better," she said with a bright, pasted-on smile.

"My friends brought me refreshments earlier," Ashalea replied bluntly, emphasising the word 'friends'."

Her mother cringed, taking a deep breath, as if that would help her navigate treacherous waters. "Ashalea, I know I haven't been there for you in the past but—"

"There for me?" Ashalea interrupted. "You gave me away when I was just a babe! And sure, I can understand that you did that for my protection but what about the years after? What about when my parents were murdered by your *son*?"

Celiana flinched but her resolve hardened. "It was too risky to leave The Meadows. The darkness has spies everywhere. If just one of them reported that I was alive and well ... if they had followed me and led him to you it could have been disastrous."

"For whom? I almost died on my sixteenth birthday; did you know that? If it wasn't for Wezlan, my body might be rotting in a ditch. Where were you?" she spat venomously. "Where were you when I was bleeding out, when their throats were cut—your best friend and most loyal servant—where were you when Wezlan died?"

"I am not to blame for their deaths. What he did was vile, but I will not be a scapegoat to bear the brunt of your pain. I know you're hurting. I know there is much to be repaired between us. I am not asking for your love, your forgiveness or your pity. I wish only for a chance to get to know you."

The room fell still as Ashalea considered her words for a long minute. "Know this," she said with deadly quiet. "I will not scorn you or turn you away, I will not let our past stain the course of the future, and I will give you a chance to redeem yourself. But if your actions put my family—my real family— in harm's way, I will see that you pay an equal price."

Slowly, with predatory intent, Ashalea rose from the bed so she stared down upon the queen. "We are at war. This world is at war. Rise to the occasion or build your own pyre because this isolation is at an end. The blood spilled thus far is on you. See that you avenge them."

The queen's face was pale as the moon, eyes wide—fearful, even. But she merely nodded, her movements stiff, her shoulders turning inwards.

Ashalea stalked towards the door, but before she left the room, she turned on the spot, chin high, eyes alight with purpose. "You will send missives to the dignitaries of the Everosian races. Request a council meeting at Renlock Academy in one week's time. Tell them that to miss this meeting is to declare their allegiance as hostile. Tell them war is coming."

With that, she turned on her heel and prowled from the room, leaving the queen to sit silently in baffled wonder.

Bodies of Work

DENAVAR

A LIGHT BREEZE CARESSED HIS CHEEKS, the smell of wildflowers tickling his nose as he observed the city from the balcony's edge, the air still laced with the slightest scent of decay. Much of the surrounding meadows had been burned from the shadow beasts, the green slopes marred by blackened earth.

His fingers tightened where they clutched the white stone, curling with anger. His skin heated as he gazed upon the homesteads down the valley, upon the elves who worked tirelessly to restore what they could of the buildings, the crops, their livelihoods. Yet another reminder of the darkness's corruption. How quickly it spread, how easily it devoured.

Denavar turned, stalking back to the library within; a place he had always sought for solace and time to think. Floor-to-ceiling shelves lined the walls of the three-tiered building, and a giant chandelier twinkled from above, giving the room a warm glow to read by. Dotted between shelves were cosy couches in emeralds and sapphires, accompanied by roaring hearths that crackled merrily. They were all lit today, fighting off the bite of crisp weather.

But it was the dome at the library's peak that he loved most. Atop a curling staircase, encased in glass and nestled into a pedestal upon the rooftop lay a glittering moonstone gem the size of a large bird egg. It shimmered like a beacon, and its smooth surface could be seen rippling under the starlight.

The city library had been his favourite haunt as a child—a quiet haven of knowledge and wonder, adventure and promise. He'd spent many afternoons within the nooks and crannies, the cosy corners and the rafters amid the high ceilings. It had been the source of a game of hide-and-seek he would play with his parents. Somehow, he'd always manage to find a new place to hide, until his mother or father would pretend to give up and he'd come racing out, laughing as they scooped him into their arms.

He was making his way towards the dome, trailing a hand fondly across the leatherbound books and dusty spines of the tomes amongst the shelves when he sensed her. The softest of footfalls announced her presence as she curled an arm around his waist and warm, soft lips caressed his neck and jawline.

He growled low in his throat, turning on the spot to pin her against the shelves. Beneath a dove-grey cloak, she was wearing a lavender gown that was cinched deliciously tight at the waist, the material nearly sheer over her legs. Her emerald eyes sparkled brighter than he'd seen them in weeks, her cheeks and lips full of colour.

A few days of rest had done her well—that, and she'd been eating more, even dragging him out of bed at the crack of dawn for some slow runs to ease her back into training.

Denavar laid his hands on her hips, hoisting her towards him so her breath huffed, and her neck arched. "You, my dear," he said as he trailed kisses up her throat, "are looking positively divine." He clutched at the folds of her dress, surprised to find the thin chiffon gliding open at the thigh. He raised a brow. "And, might I say, scandalously dressed for a library."

She smirked, arching into his touch. "I had to lure you away from these musty rows somehow."

His hand crept higher, thumb trailing small circles over her skin, curling towards her inner thigh. "Why not stay awhile?" he said in a low voice. "I could think of other ways to pass the time. Other bodies of work I would very much like to read."

A soft shudder escaped Ashalea, and she wriggled beneath his touch, his hand drawing higher, her legs feeling warmer. Denavar kissed her gently, tentatively, and she groaned beneath his lips.

His blood heated as she sank her nails into his arms, before searching the lines of his back. Her tongue crashed into his, relentless, dominating. He gave into that bliss, allowing her to fully claim him.

Fingers curling up her thigh to the wet warmth that awaited, he was about to lean down when—

Laughter rippled through the library as two she-elves swept into the hall, their animated chatter growing louder as they approached the aisle. Denavar straightened quickly, smirking at the flush creeping across Ashalea's cheeks. He cupped a hand to her face, sending her a smouldering gaze that promised they would continue this later.

Ashalea grinned, but the joy in it faltered, her eyes glazing as she drifted away somewhere he couldn't follow.

"Hey, stay with me," he said, and her glance came snapping back.

"I was so alone, Denavar," she said softly. "So trapped in my despair, unwilling to make room for anyone else. I don't want to shut everyone out. I—I don't want to be alone anymore."

Pulling her close, he wrapped her in his arms, standing there for minutes until their breathing eased, their bodies cooling. He leaned back and stared at her, deeper than her eyes, deeper than her soul. "You won't be," he said finally. "We're in this for the long haul, you and me. Come, there's some people I'd like you to meet."

She stared at him, bewildered. "Who?"

A wolfish grin followed. "My parents."

"Introducing her eminence, Princess Ashalea Kindaris of the Moonglade Meadows, Guardian of the Grove, lucky partner of one Denavar Andaro."

Ashalea shot Denavar a glare before shifting her attention to his parents, who bowed so gracefully he had to stifle a laugh.

"Just Ashalea will do," she said. "No need for etiquette."

His father straightened with a beaming smile. "Well, in that case, Ilius Andaro, and my wife, Rhelia."

His mother rose gracefully from her curtsy before rushing to embrace Ashalea. "Thank goodness you're not another stiff," she whispered. "We prefer to dispense with formalities in our household."

"We get enough of that with the royal council," Ilius said with a wink. "Please, come, sit."

Ashalea smiled, and it was free and unrestrained. He almost

wilted with relief. She had not been amused having had the announcement of meeting his parents dropped on her earlier. And after changing that delicious, flimsy thing she'd been wearing, they were now in his old home.

Denavar glanced around the house as they were led into the dining room. It was still the same as he remembered; white walls dressed in gold trimmings and patterned ceilings, warm floorboards and furnishings of cream and tan, with sapphires and navies adding a pop of colour to the rooms. Elegant yet homely, with odd trinkets and paintings giving the house a sense of identity, uniqueness.

He had loved this home as a child. A place full of happiness and love, learning and growing. But the faces opposite him as he took his place at the table—those he had missed the most.

His mother's face was most like his own. High cheekbones and a smile that promised mischief, eyes like true sapphires, bronzed, golden skin. His father was slightly fairer, with salt and pepper hair, hazel eyes and a slight, yet tall, build.

Scholars and ambassadors—and both stubborn to boot—they were well suited to their roles as council members in The Meadows. What they lacked in swordsmanship or Magicka skills, they more than made up for in diplomacy.

"I've been wondering when we'd get to meet you," Rhelia said as she swirled a wine goblet idly. "Besides your duties as Guardians, Denavar speaks of nothing else these days. Not that I'm blessed with the pleasure of his company often," she remarked with a glare in his direction. "His poor mother, left to rot while he cavorts around the country."

Denavar snorted. "Grease the pan some more why don't you. You're hardly rotting, what with this bountiful spread and the copious wine before us."

Rhelia sniffed. "A spread I prepared myself I'll have you know."

Ilius leaned towards Ashalea, a hand over his mouth. "Avoid the pumpkin stew at *all* costs."

Ashalea laughed as Rhelia slapped him on the wrist. "I'm sure it's all very lovely, and I haven't had a meal like this for some time." Her gaze wandered. "I haven't had many meals at all lately, truth be told."

Denavar took her hand, squeezing it gently. "You're here now, and that's the most important thing."

Ilius smiled softly. "We can go without food for some time, but the soul, when starved, is a tricky thing to mend. You've taken the first step, the next will come easier."

Ashalea's stomach grumbled in answer, and Rhelia laughed. "Well I'm pleased to hear you've an appetite after all. Dig in, and don't listen to my husband. He thinks himself a food critic despite having a palette measurable to a dwarf. He will eat anything."

"A trait that runs in the family then," Ashalea grinned as she glanced slyly at Denavar.

"What can I say? I know my way around a meal," he said with a wink.

⊰•◦•⊱

"You're off to Renlock tomorrow then," Ilius remarked once they had finished dinner and were reclining on the sofas huddled together on the terrace. The night was dark, giving way to the starry sea far above, and Denavar marvelled at their beauty, and the freedom of the night.

He glanced at his father, lips twisting into a frown. "The races meet to discuss the war. The future that awaits us all. Not a task I look forward to."

Ilius rested one leg over the other's knee as he carved a wooden token—a hobby of sorts, usually one he took to when the mind was full, and his thoughts were heavy. "Don't bend before them. Stand strong as the roots of a tree. Do not give them an edge they can work against you."

Denavar shook his head, his gaze drifting to Ashalea and Rhelia, the pair chattering as they took a stroll through the gardens. His heart softened to see them together, and he burned the memory into his mind, fearful he might not see such an image again.

His gaze snapped back to his father, the wood he whittled so easily, like peeling skin from an apple. "You're worried," he stated.

Ilius barked a laugh. "I'd be foolish not to be. But my concerns ... they lay close to home. The city falls further into ruin. The people lose faith in their leaders. We are a forgotten race. Our pride buried beneath the rock and ruin of this once-flourishing city."

Denavar leaned forward, clasping his father's knee with one hand. "So remind them who they are. Who they can be. Convince the council to open our borders, to join the living once again instead of walking among ghosts and memories of an old life. We are warriors. They only need reminding of it."

His father's eyes darkened. "I hope you're right, son. For our sake ... and for yours."

7

The Everosian Accords

SHARA

NOBILITY OF ALL EVEROSIAN RACES ARRIVED AT THE MEETING— even the dwarves, who had proved on more than one occasion most difficult to negotiate with. Thankfully, none had opposed gathering at Renlock. It was a haven for all races as both a Magickal hotspot of energy and an educational facility for those gifted with Magickal prowess.

Not all had come, though, given the recent attack that had swept through the land like a plague. The darkness had hit all the larger western fronts: Maynesgate, Woodrandia, Windarion and the Moonglade Meadows. An attack had also hit Shadowvale, though Kalanor's Klan—given their secret whereabouts—and the dwarves of Kingsgareth—with its city hidden beneath the harsh peaks of the mountains—remained unscathed.

Maynesgate had been hit the hardest. As the thoroughfare for merchants of all races, and the largest Everosian port for sea-trade, the shadow beasts had burned their way through the city, destroying much of the lower capital and rendering a high number of civilians without homes and means of survival. The city was in turmoil, the streets rife with protests and crime as the starving took matters into their own hands. The farmland surrounding the city had also been largely burnt.

Shara gazed at the faces surrounding her; young and old, handsome and not. It was an odd sight, truth be told, to see elven, dwarven, Diodonian, and human nobility and their retinues surrounding her. Present were the Guardians, King Tiderion of the Aquafarian Province, Lady Nirandia of the Woodrandian Realm, King Yavaar of Maynesgate, Chieftain Linar of the Diodonian Klan, and—of course—her brother, Flynn, representing the Onyxonites.

Which left the dwarf king: Kano Rivken, of the Kingsgareth Mountains—the city beneath the snow. He was surprisingly tall for a dwarf, with long blond hair bound in intricate braids that tied back from his face. In the flickering candlelight, his hair appeared as white as the snow-capped lands he hailed from, as did his icy eyes. Shara glanced at his lips, in such a thin line she suspected he seldom smiled.

Amusingly, King Tiderion sat beside him, looking just as irritated to be there, powerfully corded arms tucked in.

Ashalea had been delighted to see her friend, Erania of the Woodrandian realm, within Lady Nirandia's entourage. From what Shara understood, the two had become fast friends when Ashalea had first set out with Wezlan, not long before Shara met them in Maynesgate. It seemed an age ago now. Back when her marks were her only concern, and death was her duty; her kills were clean and quiet, unlike now.

Shara glanced at Ashalea again, standing beside Erania. The duo chatted animatedly, albeit in hushed tones, in the corner of the room. A genuine and free smile flickered over her friend's face, and she was glad of it.

"It does my heart good to see her happy," Denavar whispered to her, noting her observation.

Shara chewed her lip. "Remember what I said, though. She's trying, she's putting on a brave front, but only time will heal deep hurts. You know this as well as I." He ran a hand through his hair, a long sigh escaping his lips. She nudged him in the ribs. "On the plus side, you shaved, bathed, and had a haircut. Bravo. Much more respectable, at least in circles such as this," she smirked.

He rolled his eyes. "We're meant to be Guardians. The least we can do is look the part."

"We *are* Guardians," she replied with a snort. "And I always—"

"Yeah, yeah, you're naturally gifted, beautiful as the Goddesses above. Give it a rest or your head will explode from that big ego of yours."

She held in a cackle as Queen Celiana entered the room at last, and all fell quiet while she took her seat, as did those who were standing around the chamber. The party looked expectantly at the queen, whose face was as rigid as the chairs beneath Shara's ass. Hard. Unyielding. A little painful to put up with.

It's not that Shara had any personal vendettas against her, unless she counted the fact Celiana had hidden behind her foggy fortress and left Everosia to rot. Or that she was a pathetic excuse for a mother and, by now declaring herself alive and ready to play parent, she had likely caused deep trauma and damage to Ashalea's psyche.

Scowling, Shara found her hand reaching for the blade

sheathed at her leg, until Denavar discreetly stomped on her foot. She rolled her eyes but fell silent, waiting for the first hammer to strike. The room was still even as an undercurrent of tension rolled through the council chamber, like clouds gathering before a storm.

It was strange to be here again so soon. Renlock, the famous Academy of old, which had been a killing ground not so long ago. The green hills and bountiful gardens that surrounded the grand building were now a barren landscape after the slaughter.

The people knew bloodshed that day. Many had died, and the energies residing beneath Renlock had failed to regenerate the fields surrounding the Academy.

Shara surveyed the room. The council chamber was the same as ever. Cream walls, polished oak floorboards, a round wooden table, and chairs of black steel. No décor dotted the room, keeping its purpose simple and practical. Comfort was not a priority here.

The chamber itself was on the fifth and final floor; the highest level before the stairs that led up to the rooftop itself. To the place where the darkness had ended her life, and miraculously, where Ashalea had cast all her Magicka, all her hope, and Shara had been born again. Her hand drifted to her throat of its own accord and she swallowed hard.

Denavar's eyes flashed to hers, concern etched into eyes of stormy blue. He didn't miss a thing, and in so many ways, he reminded Shara of Wezlan. Even more now that he had the wizard's power. Every last drop had been transferred to him, according to Ashalea. She wondered how that might change a man, let alone an elf. Having more power than one knew what to do with. For all she knew, he could be as powerful as the darkness.

Someone cleared their throat pointedly, and all eyes shifted to the dwarf king. "You called us here for a purpose," his loud voice boomed. "Let us be on with it, then."

No grand introduction, eloquent speech or bowing and scraping. Just straight to the point. Shara liked his grumpy ass already.

Celiana dipped her head slightly and began. "My lords and ladies, thank you for attending. You were called here today to revisit the accords of our races. To discuss our alliance and our standing as a united people."

"Oh, aye," Kano scoffed. "You speak of unity while you hide behind your walls. You ask us to review our alliance, but what have you to offer? You, who have ignored the reaping of our land, the calls of your brothers and sisters." His mouth curved into a thin sneer, pure mockery lacing his words.

"Careful Kano," Nirandia said with unnerving cool, voice a deadly sleet of ice. "You yourself have not been so amenable in recent discussions. Wouldn't want you to play the hypocritical fool."

"Pah! We have patrolled the lands to the east, kept our city safe,"—he looked to Yavaar, who it seemed he held no qualms with—"kept the surrounding human villages safe too."

Yavaar nodded his thanks, but kept quiet, his brown eyes keenly intelligent, though sorrowful. This was not his fight, Shara realised. It was smart to stay silent until the elves and dwarves ended their quarrel. Smart to intervene when the moment was opportune ... or maybe he was just too damned tired for any of it.

She studied the king carefully. His face was lined with exhaustion, which was understandable; his was a large burden to bear. His city had been half decimated, his people cut down in the night, his resources dwindling. Even so, his eyes were clear and attuned to everything, it seemed.

Shara frowned. From what Wezlan had said of the man, he was

little better than a schoolboy following orders, taking direction from a gaggle of advisors—men and women of high stature and position. He was rumoured to be fond of the drink, lazy and un-intuitive. But this was no boy king: this was a man who had come into his own. Not a warrior, judging by the thin frame, unmarked dark skin and smooth hands, but a man of intelligence.

Discord crackled through the room on whips of cutting tongues. The elves and the dwarf king kept at their squabbling, and Shara thought it a little unfair he was outnumbered, however sharp his tongue may be. And as entertaining as it would be to watch them shred each other to ribbons, Shara knew their reason for being here far outweighed this pettiness.

She was about to intervene when a quiet but firm voice said, "Stop."

Somehow, Ashalea commanded the attention of the room in a second. The Lady Nirandia's features softened when she looked at her, but Tiderion and Kano only narrowed their eyes. Shara could tell Yavaar's interest was piqued and, as for Linar, he might have been napping at the table by the look of his drooping eyes. Not surprising. Her brother merely caught her eye and grinned with wolfish delight.

"And who are you to speak at this table?" Kano asked Ashalea warily.

"Oh, for Goddess's sake, Kano, use your damn eyes," Tiderion snapped. "You're addressing the next queen-in-waiting of the Moonglade Meadows."

"Gentlemen, please," Ashalea said, and though her face was schooled into neutrality, Shara saw her right hand fisted in her midnight blue skirts. They were scattered with crystals, so they sparkled like stars in the candlelight. She was the very picture of nobility, even with the still hollow face and jutting ribs, but her eyes burned bright and clear. "You're here today because I called this meeting, not my mother."

The queen bristled ever so slightly at the casual address but said nothing. Ashalea's eyes hardened as she surveyed the room. "We are at war. The recent attacks were not the first our country has faced, but merely coordinated simultaneously, rendering efforts of aid impossible for all races. This is what the darkness wants—to have us isolated from each other, to keep our eyes only on our immediate surroundings, not that of the bigger picture." She shook her head. "It is not enough."

"What would you have us do?" Yavaar asked, propping an elbow on the table to lean on his fist.

"I would have you fight, as I would have all able warriors of Everosia fight. If we combine our armies—if we are a united front—we might stand a chance at beating the darkness."

"Easy for you to say, *Guardian*. You will not be the one bleeding on the battlefield," Tiderion said coldly, upper lip curling.

He had never liked Ashalea and herself. As soon as he had heard of Ashalea's encounter with the water dragon back in the Aquafarian Province, jealousy and anger had overcome him. It must drive him mad, to know the dragon had chosen to speak with her and not the king. Tiderion was spiteful, egotistical, and Shara hated that he thought himself better than her—better than humans altogether.

The sheer arrogance in his tone set Shara's teeth on edge and it took every effort not to have him kiss the end of her blade. But the ire on Ashalea's face was as great as any counter.

"How dare you sit there, crowned in self-righteousness, mocking my duty to this war. I will fight, as I have since the day I learned of my task. I will bleed as I have already bled for our people. I will walk to my death if it means I can seal the Gate—if I can protect the ones that I love."

She walked around the table to stand before Tiderion and leaned over so she was inches from his face. Her fury burned like the stars above, and she said in a dangerously quiet voice, "By undermining me, you mock him—a better man than you, and one more deserving of this world. So, speak to me like that again and you will understand just how well I fight. Understood?"

The king blinked, his face contorting into ruddy rage before it ebbed to a simmer. He nodded like a petulant child, sulking after being thrown off his high horse. At least he was smart enough to stay silent.

Shara could have broken out in applause; Ashalea was back. Her vengeful she-elf, her fierce friend whose loyalty to her family would ignite wrath of epic proportions. Shara snuck a peek at Denavar, and the elf was positively beaming with pride. And so he should, for she was right. They would fight, and anyone who thought otherwise could be damned to Fari's Dungeon. Let the beast from the Isle of Dread square off with Tiderion. Now that would be a sight.

Seemingly satisfied, Ashalea nodded and returned to her chair, where she serenely clasped her hands together, looking every bit a queen as she held her chin high. "I know I ask much, but the truth is a simple as this: without an alliance, we will be decimated one by one by the darkness's armies. The Grove will burn, the Gate will be ripped open, and there will be no stopping what walks into this world. All the misty mazes, the highest walls, the tallest peaks, will not save you. For he is coming, and he is death."

Kano tapped his fingers on the table absentmindedly. "What makes you think he will assemble one army to attack? Why not continue raiding our cities as he has done? Pick us apart little by little?"

Ashalea shook her head. "Crinos has been biding his time, growing stronger, amassing his armies beyond this dimension. I have seen with my own eyes how vast his army spreads. Like black clouds on the horizon, endless, ominous. It is not his style to pick us off one by one. He is impatient, cocky, and he takes pleasure in seeing our pain first-hand. He has already taken our greatest ally."

"The wizard? Wezlan has passed on?" Linar asked, finally breaking his silence. Those not accustomed to his telepathy winced as his voice infiltrated their minds. The nobles had wasted no time starting this meeting, so she supposed Razakh hadn't had time to confer with his chieftain.

Shara couldn't help but notice Linar flash his teeth at Yavaar. Shara knew the wounds of the Diodonians' past still cut deep. Razakh had told her his story, the story of his ancestors—of Kalanor's Klan—and how his own mother had been butchered to satisfy the curious and careless minds of men.

To ally with humans ... Shara knew it would not be easy for the Diodonians. Not when merely looking at them would be a reminder of their dead kin—of those wronged beasts that were stolen away, experimented on, mutilated—all in the hopes that their executioners might find the secret of their Magicka. Even Razakh, sitting stoically, proudly, could not hide the rigidness to his powerful shoulders, the silver eyes that swirled just a little quicker than usual.

"He passed in another realm," Denavar said quietly. "Facing off against the darkness and,"—he glanced carefully at Ashalea—"allowing our return to Everosia."

The mood shifted, an eerie silence shrouding them like a heavy fog. The high tempers and petty squabbles all but forgotten as the rulers of these great races considered this news. Many heads bowed in reverence to the wizard. For whether all knew him personally or not, his name would forever mark the tomes of history—right alongside battles of old and deeds most wondrous.

"He was a great man, Shadowbreaker." Kano shook his head solemnly. "A great man."

"You knew him personally?" Ashalea asked.

The dwarf nodded. "There was a time when the dragons of old were the greatest threat to our lands. They had an understanding with the elves—a kinship of sorts—but men and dwarves were not so lucky. The dragons thought us greedy, hateful, taking from the land, destroying her. Most would pick off the wildlife, cut us off from resources, even cause rockslides from the great peaks above. Others, the ones that played with us for sport, they would freeze us on sight—for they come in many forms, those wicked drakes.

"Fire, water, ice, for the most part. Gods only know what other kinds may dwell in different dimensions." Kano sighed, a muscle twitching in his jaw as he recounted his story. "They terrorised my people. Had we not dwelled under the mountain there might be far less of us to tell this tale. It just so happens, though, that your great wizard was passing through on whatever business wizards be doing, and after hearing of our plight, he climbed to the highest peak of our great mountains, summoned the biggest beast of them all and struck an accord."

Shara smiled to herself. Wezlan would have known about the dragons frequenting the mountains, would have had his reasons to meet with he who ruled the roost. Small ripples have great reach.

Denavar merely smirked. "Of course it had to be the highest peak. Good ol' Wez-man. If you're going to face the most powerful of beings, why not do it in style."

Kano raised one thick brow and Shara smirked. "Don't mind him, a family joke is all. Carry on."

"Ahem," the dwarf cleared his throat. "Well, Wezlan offered the dragons passage to another land beyond our own. In another dimension. He offered them a peaceful world—one untouched by man, elf or dwarf. One wild and wholly free. They accepted, though it is said some may have stayed, to honour their alliance with the elves or some such rubbish." Kano snorted, a great rumble that had the mouths of elven nobles lifting in distaste.

Shara looked sidelong at King Tiderion, who kept his mouth firmly shut. Ashalea and Denavar stayed silent too, sharing a quick glance with each other. The water dragon was not common knowledge then. A card to be played when the time was right.

"The wizard came to warn me of the darkness," Yavaar said suddenly, eyes focused on a long channel through the wooden table. "He asked me to send aid. I refused him. My ignorance has cost many lives."

One of Yavaar's advisors—an especially thin and pasty man with a stern nose—approached him. "My King," he began, grovelling as he pawed at Yavaar's fine tunic, and Shara eyed him in distaste. Wezlan had been right about the company the king kept, of that she had no doubt. But the king merely raised a hand in irritation, and the advisor smacked his lips together, retreating instantly with a flicker of annoyance on his face.

"All the more reason to fight together now," Ashalea said firmly, ignoring the interruption. She looked around the room, staring down every noble, daring them to say otherwise. "Long has the darkness spread, casting his shadow across our lands. His army grows, his resolve strengthens. If you do not fight you choose bondage or death. You choose blood."

"Blood will spill no matter the outcome," Tiderion retorted.

Ashalea turned a flat stare on him, coldness rippling from her in waves. "Aye. Blood is a price that must be paid. But would you send warriors—trained soldiers—to stem the tide, or would you cower in your crystal palace while the screams of the innocents beat as war drums in your city?"

Tiderion's beautiful features turned ugly. His golden face purpled into mottled rage, and in a heartbeat his sword was drawn, the tip angled up the column of Ashalea's neck. "Don't patronise me, girl. You speak of war as though you have lived it." He lifted his face, lips curving into a cruel sneer. "You don't know the first thing about it."

The room exploded.

"Treason," Yavaar's nobles blustered angrily and all at once.

Shara aimed two shurikens at the elf, Denavar with a ball of electricity crackling in his fingers. Even Razakh had leaped onto the table, great maw bared viciously. The elves at Tiderion's back spun their double-bladed spears in a blur, the sharp ends pointed at the Guardians.

"Try it and you'll have a fancy new accessory right between your eyeballs," Shara hissed.

Razakh growled to Tiderion, *"Unless I remove your head entirely first."*

The nobles backed away, all except Kano, who watched the encounter with a toothy grin, eyes alight with amusement. Flynn, Nirandia and Celiana also sat calmly, the latter pair tittering quietly together, and if Shara didn't know better, *gossiping* at the unfolding events.

"Does this happen at every meeting?" Celiana whispered incredulously to Nirandia.

Nirandia snorted softly. "You'd think Tiderion would have mastered his temper in all his long years, but no. Still as cranky as ever."

Ashalea stared Tiderion down, her teeth bared, her eyes daring him to move a muscle, her own twitching as if itching for conflict.

"She has lost more loved ones in her youth than you might in a lifetime," Flynn said quietly, flatly, though his words were sharp as knives. "I have been a pawn of the darkness; I have seen what he's capable of. I was a prisoner in my own skin, unable to control my movements, trapped. I have done things you couldn't dream of. I tortured my sister at his behest. I killed innocents. So don't pretend you know what pain and suffering is. Because these Guardians ... they have lived and breathed it."

Shara smiled faintly, pride coursing through her veins. This ... this was the future of the Onyxonites. No longer a boy, but a man taking ownership for his actions—for his wrongdoings. And despite all he had been through, her brother seemed stronger for it.

Good, Shara thought. A man who can look at his flaws and be at peace is someone lesser men will follow. A man who will give rise to banners and have a sea of black at his back. She nodded her approval.

"Enough!" Celiana rose from her seat, movements fluid and graceful, though her tone was sharp. "You all have much to think over. For now, I suggest we take a break, lest this council soon be torn to shreds. Talk with your parties, discuss your options, but when we reconvene at this table, I expect civility from all of you."

Tiderion let his sword drop uselessly, and Ashalea glared at him before turning on her heel. Celiana's icy stare left no room for argument, save a few grumbles from Kano and a dismissive swish of a cloak from Tiderion. Everyone began to trickle out the room, leaving just the Guardians and Telilah.

Shara leaned back in her chair, propping her boots on the table, a smirk on her face. "I think that went swimmingly, don't you?"

King of Men

Denavar

ASHALEA RAN HER HANDS THROUGH HER HAIR IN EXASPERATION, a low snarl ripping from her throat. "How can Tiderion be so blind? If we don't band together, the darkness will squash us all like bugs underfoot."

Denavar felt her rage like a blast furnace. The very room was rife with it, simmering as she prowled in circles, wearing the rug thin. He strode to the window, cracking the doors open to provide some relief, relishing the cool breeze upon his face.

"Tiderion is no fool. He knows Crinos must be stopped no matter the cost. If he pulls his soldiers back from Renlock, if he cuts ties altogether, he risks much. Tiderion is a proud elf, but he will do what's right for his people."

"His arrogance will get us all killed," Ashalea countered, huffing her irritation. "We need his army, Denavar. His lands are larger than that of Woodrandia or The Meadows. He has the numbers and a respectful unit of Magickally talented elves."

"Tiderion respects strength and cunning more than anything," Denavar deadpanned, turning on the spot. "He respected Wezlan not just on merit alone, but because Wezlan's power was unrivalled among Everosia. As a wizard, he was powerful, his stature almost unattainable ... and Tiderion knew it."

Ashalea cocked her head with predatory intent. "I know that look. What are you getting at?"

"The Aquafarian king has no respect for the Guardians because he does not understand them—us. He thinks us weak because our primary focus is the Gate and not the battle itself." Denavar grinned, the beginning of a plan forming. "Well, I'm going to show him just what strength is. I will sit the Academy's test and I will become a wizard. The only wizard alive in Everosia."

Ashalea blinked. "But how? The Divine Six were the only ones capable of performing the examination and they're all dead."

"A severe oversight on their behalf to form such a limited council," Denavar frowned. "But there are some who can oversee the test. Those who have lived long enough to know the old ways."

"The elves," Ashalea breathed.

Denavar grinned; a wicked, feline thing. "The very people we are trying to convince. And won't we put on a show."

Ashalea's answering grin was nothing short of devious.

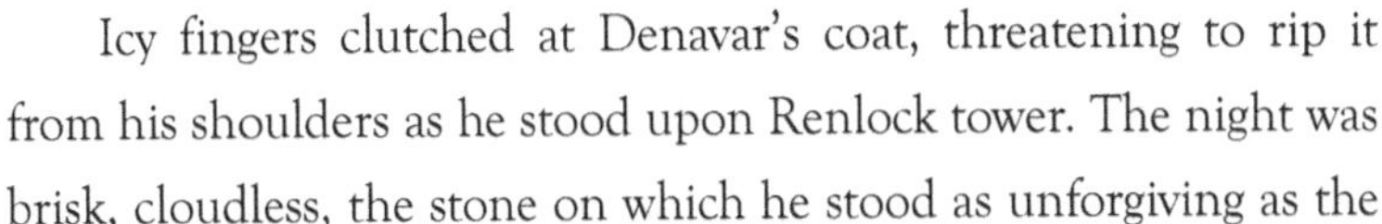

Icy fingers clutched at Denavar's coat, threatening to rip it from his shoulders as he stood upon Renlock tower. The night was brisk, cloudless, the stone on which he stood as unforgiving as the

memories he recalled here.

His stomach twisted as he gazed upon the tower floor, eyes roving over the place that Shara had died, however momentarily. He remembered the crunch of her neck snapping, like the first bite of an apple—one leaking poison and pain.

Ashalea had summoned enough power to bring her back—something unheard of in Magickal history. Even Wezlan had not had the strength to perform such a feat, though he hadn't been surprised that Ashalea did. Nothing had unnerved that man, always ready to weather the oncoming storm. And it had remained so in the face of death, too.

Denavar sighed, raising his eyes skyward. The glory of autumn was over, and the first snows would soon be approaching. He could smell it in the air, taste it in the skies above—a newfound awareness that exceeded even his elven senses. Power gifted to him by Wezlan. A life force given before it was taken away.

It frightened him, to a degree. The Gods and Goddesses had deigned to gift him a natural affinity with Magicka—understanding it, wielding it, harnessing the natural energies of the world. Magicka was not equal among all who shared its power. But now? Now his strength was twofold; far more than anyone could fathom. His veins sang with it; a chord so beautiful, so infinite in its sweetness, known only to him.

But the power was dangerous, addictive. Its calling was like the whispered words of a lullaby, gentle and seductive—a bottomless pit that hungered to swallow the world. Denavar would not succumb to its lure unless the price meant the darkness would fall. If it meant protecting the ones he loved, then he might fall into its embrace.

He strode to the tower's edge, feeling the wind lash at his face as he eyed the drop to the landing far below. The Aquafarian lake sparkled in the distance—serene, yet somehow solemn, as if it too felt a shifting of the tides and the winds.

Denavar sensed the slap of footsteps on stone before he heard it. Someone approached from the stairwell, their steps heavy, sluggish. Not so elegant as an elf, not so heavy as a dwarf. King Yavaar appeared, eyes hooded, rimmed with exhaustion. If he was surprised to see Denavar he did not show it. "Only he whose mind is brimming seeks solace in sleeping hours." Yavaar gestured gracefully to the landing. "May I?"

He offered a small bow before nodding, but the king merely waved a hand. "No need for formalities. Save that for councils and placating angry elves."

Denavar laughed softly. "I'm afraid not even the most courteous of kings could soften Tiderion's temper."

The king withdrew a small leather pouch and pipe from his tunic, packing it with tobacco before stuffing it in his mouth. A frown replaced his smile as he patted his pockets in search of a light. "Perhaps not. Your lady certainly enflamed it. Speaking of," he said with a mischievous glint to his eye, "I don't suppose you could ..."

Denavar clicked his fingers and a flame sparked to life in the pipe. Yavaar took a puff, eyes crinkling before he blew out a plume of smoke, stark against the cold, blustery night. They leaned over the wall together in companionable silence for a time. A moment of peace between neither friend nor foe.

The elf cast a sidelong glance at the king. Besides his obvious distress at the massacre at Maynesgate, there was a certain boyish hope still alight in the man's eyes. As if he'd found purpose— meaning within the mysteries of life. But a burden still lingered in the depths of his haunted eyes. Of the countless murdered souls of his city, yes, but something—or perhaps *someone* else entirely. A

puzzle. One Denavar hoped to piece together.

"I don't suppose I need to ask what drives you from sleep?" he said quietly, arms bundled against the cold.

"Ghosts," Yavaar replied. "Of my people, of kings past, of my father."

At the last, his voice hitched ever so slightly. A sore point then. And from the stories Denavar had heard of Yavaar's father, he could understand why. He had been hated amongst the human populace for his greed and ignorance of the people's plights. "King Dilini's reign achieved little, true," Denavar said begrudgingly, "but perhaps his greatest achievement was in bearing a better son."

Yavaar smiled but it did not reach his eyes. "You elves spin sweet words, but my father had no hand in raising me, unless it was to my face and that of my mother. He was cruel, greedy, weak. He ruled with a closed fist; always taking, taking, taking, never giving back to those who needed it. Never improving, expanding or building the empire but letting it lie fat and stagnant."

Denavar turned to face his companion. "So be what he could not, change what he would not, and give your people a true king. Show them that you're willing to fight for them, that you'd bleed for them. Forge the alliance and join us against the darkness. You reap what you sow, King, and we shall all bear the brunt of this war one way or another. It's time to decide what's worth fighting for."

"You are a warrior," Yavaar said, straightening his back defensively. "A leader. It is easy to speak of fighting when those instincts—the skills—are in your very blood."

"I may know how to fight, but you are a king with countless resources to call on. Provisions that are sorely needed in a war. But more than that, you are the face of your people. Someone to rally your forces and the many cities of men across Everosia. You may stand and have all bow before you, or you may ask them to rise—rise and band together as one. What do you think will happen to the villages when the darkness comes? They will be destroyed one by one, great pyres that will burn in your honour if you abandon them."

Yavaar stared at Denavar for a long time before he uttered an incredulous laugh, bitterness etched in its thrum. "Well when you put it like that, what choice do I have?"

Denavar offered a grim smile. "We all have a choice, king of men. That's what makes us free. You may be a slave to the crown on your head, but with that pretty piece of jewellery comes the choice to save the lives of innocents. Think of this in your bed tonight: whatever choice you come to bear, it will be written in the pages of history."

"Aye," Yavaar said unhappily, "or written in blood on a battlefield."

Denavar grinned, clamping a hand on the king's shoulder. "Aye, but then you'd be dead and who the hell cares after that?"

He made to descend the stairwell when a change in the atmosphere made him look up. The stars blinked above, glittering in celestial wonder in oceans of black, and slowly, softly, white flakes began to fall, caressing the world around him. He outstretched a palm, and a perfect snowflake kissed his calloused skin.

The new season was upon them …

And war was coming.

A Dangerous Game

RAZAKH

IT MIGHT HAVE BEEN THE HAPPIEST DAY OF RAZAKH'S LIFE. Snow fell in droves around him, soft pillows of white powder shaken down from the skies. He loved the feel of it on his coat, loved the playful bite, the crunch of it—so different from the red sands he hailed from.

Had there not been an audience he might have bounded amongst its ivory sheets and rolled within its embrace as he walked through the Academy grounds earlier, but as it were, acting like a juvenile would do naught for his status. Not to mention a certain wretched assassin would have had a few things to say about it if she saw.

He was with the Guardians now—Telilah and Flynn too—all gathered in Denavar and Ashalea's shared bed chamber. It was lavishly decorated, with dark wooden floors and walls, and a huge bed covered in rich red quilts trimmed with gold. Chairs surrounded the fireplace, which had a shaggy white rug before it and shelves built into walls full of thick, leatherbound tomes. A small dining room sat adjacent, for the busy wizard who might take meals in his or her room.

It was fit for a king, or a queen-to-be in Ashalea's case, though it remained cosy rather than overbearingly formal. And, he had to admit, the bed on which he sprawled was rather comfortable.

Still, a growl rumbled from deep within his stomach as he gazed out the window of Ashalea's suite. His delight at the change of weather had been brief, and he had been stuck indoors for the better part of a day whilst various dignitaries prowled the halls and tittered together in groups, some at his expense.

The mages were less irritating but remained intrigued by his presence. Razakh supposed he should preen at their attentions, but he was bored more than anything and loathe to remain indoors. The wild was calling ... as was fresh prey. The creatures in the small forests and the expansive plains lacked the intelligence of the desert beasts, too used to their freedom, used to the scents of wolves and pack animals. But not his kind. If he could just—

"Hello?" Shara waved a hand in front of his snout and he snapped at it playfully. She rolled her eyes and draped herself on a nearby chaise, pulling a blade out and twirling it lazily. "Stop drooling over your next bunny and pay attention."

"*I was not—*" he huffed. Okay, maybe he was. "*Bunnies are not a sustainable meal for a creature of my stature,*" he retorted instead.

Shara picked her teeth with the blade. "A-huh, tell that to the cooks who had to clean up the bloody mess you left yesterday morning. A massacre of cute and cuddly creatures, you big scary beast," she teased.

Razakh eyed her off. *"Says the woman who just devoured a roast chicken, gravy still stuck to your fingers."* He sniffed. *"And you call me an animal."*

She shrugged, lounging on the chaise like a feral cat just learning what luxuries lay in life.

Denavar snickered from his perch on the arm of a chair by the fireplace, one arm casually—almost protectively—looped over Ashalea's shoulders as she sat with her knees up against her chest. She was far away from the conversation in this room, that haunted look gracing her gaunt face, emerald eyes unfocused.

As if sensing his attention her eyes snapped to his and she shook herself, physically shaking away her daydream. Razakh cocked a head, and she nodded, confirming she was okay. His eyes darted to her plate on the table, still heaped with food she had not wanted or could not finish. But it was a start. Eating at all … it was a start.

Telilah cleared her throat, clever eyes noticing everything. "So to recap, Denavar is performing the examination tonight of which Nirandia, Celiana and Tiderion will be judging. Are you sure about this?" She chewed her lip. "What if Tiderion finds a way to stop your ascension?"

What if indeed, Razakh thought. Broaching the subject of the test had gone down with the elves about as well as an Uulakh carcass—tough, chewy, and hard to swallow. Tiderion had objected, as Denavar knew he would, but ultimately with no wizards left to oversee the exam, the elves were in no position to refuse him. And Denavar, at least, had some sway with the Aquafarian king, given his previous work as both spymaster and Magicka user for him.

If anything, it was that Denavar had abandoned the king for other endeavours which might have infuriated him. That, and the she-elf on Denavar's arm these days. Razakh couldn't fathom

Tiderion's distaste for Ashalea, but perhaps their stubbornness was the root of that. Their pride and impulsiveness and, on Tiderion's behalf, jealousy.

Razakh had always had a knack for sensing emotional behaviour and responses—it seemed even more heightened with other species who tended to act on their hearts rather than by logic alone. And Tiderion, he was dripping with jealousy. A primal rage that Ashalea possessed something he did not. That she was chosen for something beyond ruling. Perhaps this was the very obstacle stopping Tiderion from seeing sense.

But Denavar shook his head. "Not even Tiderion would dare intervene with this test. It is sacred, and a right for all mages to undertake it. I wish others would step up and brave the exam, but I fear Renlock's education and training have dwindled of late. The battle, the deaths, it's too much to expect these students to step up to such a mantle when no one showed them how to wear it. And after Avari Ventiri—"

At the mention of his name Ashalea hissed, and Flynn looked up from cleaning his blade, eyes narrowed. The air rippled with sudden rage, leaving him curious to know more. He cocked his head, tail swishing with intrigue.

Ashalea took a breath. "Avari is—was—a former councillor of the Academy. It was his duty, among others here, to maintain order and oversee the education of students."

"But he betrayed us," Denavar spat. "Sold us out to the darkness in exchange for riches and fortune. There's a backdoor in this place, you see. Tunnels that would give the mages, their families and anyone unfit to protect themselves safe passage if they needed to escape." Denavar's voice grew thick and Ashalea laid a hand on his arm in comfort.

"Under Avari's advisement, the darkness sent his minions through the tunnels," she continued for him. "They ... they killed everyone on the lower floor. Healers and—and children. It was a bloodbath."

Flynn uttered a string of curses. "He got what was coming to him in the end."

"Good," Telilah said, shoulders squared. "The bad guys always die in the end. You think they'd learn." Everyone stared at her in disbelief. "What? All the old tales end in damsels being saved, monsters being slain, or wars being won. The hero reaps the rewards, not the villain."

"Maybe in children's bedtime stories," Shara scoffed, but Razakh noted the way her eyes lingered on Telilah, the soft smile at the other woman's optimism and cheerful demeanour.

"*It's true,*" Razakh agreed. "*We have heroes amongst our kind, too. Berian the Brave, Vanador the Vicious, Siviki the—*"

"Scandalous?" Ashalea offered.

"Solemn?" Flynn grinned.

"Stupid?" Telilah said, immediately withering at Razakh's growl.

Razakh stared at them blankly. "*You're all idiots.*"

The group cackled in earnest, and even Ashalea snickered at their banter. The rest of them had enough good sense not to stare.

"Point is," Denavar said, "the test cannot be interfered with. I'll ace it, put Tiderion in his place and we'll have an alliance before dessert. We get Tiderion, we get the rest."

"I didn't know you were a gambler" Ashalea teased.

"Only when the odds are stacked against me."

"You play a dangerous game, Denavar Andaro."

He grinned cockily. "The only one worth playing."

A Master of Magicka

DENAVAR

THE ROOM CRACKLED WITH POWER, as though a bubble of Magicka surrounded him, encasing him in its aura. For whatever reason, the testing hall had always contained the most energy, had always been the most sacred. To stand here was to harness the lifeforce of the land, to pull and be pulled by the energies of the world.

This test was a gift, one that demanded balance before unboxing. For only the worthy could attain the rewards, only the pure of heart and mind. Denavar wasn't sure he was either. He had always wondered at that—how anyone could be perfectly aligned— for no one was naturally good or evil, and he had always thought dreadful creatures slept in all who walked the earth.

He didn't know if the good took up more space than the bad, or if one should set up the scales that he might be evenly weighted.

But he did know Wezlan always had a reason for his actions, and it wasn't Ashalea that he poured his lifeforce into. It was Denavar, so he could damn well go mad searching for that reason, or he could be grateful for that gift and prove how much he deserved it. Let a greater power decide his fate.

Five tests awaited: mastery of the elements, psychic ability, healing, portal travel, and the ability to mould darkness and light. The last would be the ultimate test, balancing good and evil in one's very soul. If Denavar could not pass that, he would never again have the chance to become a wizard.

In truth, Denavar didn't fully understand what went on in this room. No one knew except the Divine Six and wizards long before their time—when Everosia was a new and lovely thing, unchanged by any. The Academy decided what tasks to bestow upon its students, and not even those judging could know what would happen. But all knew it was dangerous to attempt.

Denavar took a breath before striding to the centre of the hall. It was plain—nothing but stone floors and walls, and ceilings that seemed to disappear high above into blackness. Clearing his mind of doubt and everything except the task ahead, he sat down, closed his eyes, and waited. A shroud of silence enveloped him until he sensed the aura shift, Magicka crackling in eagerness, energies ebbing and flowing around him.

His eyes snapped open as a light flared beyond his eyes. Before him hovered a brilliant white spear, glittering with a deadly tip—and it was flying straight toward him.

<hr>

With a yelp he dove to the side as the ice shard swept past his body, narrowly missing his heart as it shattered upon impact with the far wall. More spears formed mid-air, winking to life one by one, and Denavar was on his feet in a heartbeat.

Sprinting, he muttered an incantation, forming a golden shroud around his form just as two shards pierced the shield and skittered over the floor. Without thinking, he forged a path towards the exit, diving into a forward roll as he sensed another spear hurtling towards his head from behind.

The door was just a few feet away—safety, warmth, and his friends waiting just on the other side. But he skidded to a halt. This was part of the test. If he took one step out of this room before it was done, he was finished. His chance at becoming a wizard, forfeit.

Think, think, think. He shrugged one shoulder to the side, a spear sailing harmlessly past. They were growing in intensity now, glowing like fireflies as they swarmed, a barrage of deadly frost. They began spearing towards him, ice shattering in a wild dance before his eyes. His shields would only last so long against their onslaught. His time was running out. It was death or the door ...

Panic began to overtake him, hot flushes racking his skin as beads of sweat formed on his brow. His lungs constricted, heart pumping with fear.

No. He could do this. Wezlan had believed in him, trusted him, and he would not break that faith. So he reached deeper inside himself, hauling on that line of power until it was stretched taut and shivering with anticipation.

He gave himself fully to his power—all of it. The Magicka came flooding out of his core, filling his being with pure energy ... and darkness. A myriad of both surged through his veins, chaotic, hungry, fighting each other. He stumbled with giddiness, the war within making his heart pump with adrenaline, his mind feeling out of sync with his body, like a delay had set in. His back arched with the onslaught, mouth in a silent scream as it raged.

Use me, his Magicka seemed to whisper. *I am yours now.* Denavar burrowed down, down, down into the deep recesses of his mind and soul, to the depths he had been too afraid to uncover, too fearful to let loose. But he realised now that power was not a wild, dangerous thing. It glimmered with promise, with purity, with ... love. As if the power itself held friendship within its core.

And so Denavar dove into that raw, pure, raging Magicka sparking through his veins, and he whispered to it, soothing it, quelling its rage. *I am your master now*, he told it with a soft caress, *I am yours, as you are mine.* There was silence for a moment and a release, as if the power sighed, sated, until his consciousness came shooting back to the surface in a blast of ecstatic energy. His muscles drank in the vigour greedily, his veins sang, his eyes burned. And he knew what to do.

He needed no incantation. Not a flick of the hand, not a fist to direct his intent. He simply willed it and watched in awe. *Fire.* Embers sparked to life, curling into great flames that stretched up the walls high above, whirling about him in a storm, eating the ice, so furious and so intense that the building itself could have crumbled down upon him.

It burned so brightly that his skin should have stripped away, the meat of his body shredded, not even ash left to linger. But the blaze tore around the room oblivious to his form, and finally the ice spears stopped coming, not a drop of moisture left in the air to take shape from.

Once sure that it was safe, Denavar extinguished the flames, and in a blink, they were gone. The floor simmered in their wake, and somehow, the room was still intact, as if the energies of this strange place willed it so.

And then a storm of a different kind began. The hall rumbled in discontent, thunder clapping in great booms that shook the very foundations of the Academy. Lightning gathered above, white flashes threatening to erupt from behind clouds of black turmoil.

"Oh hells," Denavar muttered. "A change of temperatures, and you throw this at me."

He ran to a corner and crouched down, running through his options. Fire, water, earth, ice, lightning? All useless against this foe. Perhaps he could use wind to blow the storm away? It was a poor plan, but the only one he had.

Curling his fingertips he lashed out before him, creating a vortex and hurtling it through the room, whipping the clouds like cream for a cake. They rumbled in answer, the room blackening with every second until great booms rocked the ground beneath him. Denavar winced, his elvish ears protesting the intrusion. The pain was replaced by fear when he saw the forks of lightning skitter in the blackness above.

With renewed urgency, he grunted as he sent the whirlwind above him. Picking up dust from the floor, the gale spiralled towards the dark and angry clouds, dissipating them before the lightning within could form pathways through the air. With half a thought, Denavar opened a portal and sent the vortex through, closing it with a small zap that left the room in eerie silence once again.

A single flame sparked to life in the room's centre. It floated, flickering almost playfully, beckoning Denavar to approach. *Daring him.*

So he stretched his arms above his head, squared his shoulders, and, gritting his teeth, he strode towards the next task.

Not My Queen

ASHALEA

ASHALEA PUSHED HER FOOD AROUND THE PLATE, eyes glassy as she stared at the mush that recently resembled a vegetable pie; the rich gravy and flavourful vegetables now something of a gloopy paste. They were seated in the dining room joined to her bedchamber, but food was the furthest thing from her mind.

Hours had passed since Denavar had begun his examination and her stomach was churning from the wait. Was it meant to take this long? She knew the power he possessed was well up to the task. She also knew he could back out at any time, but he wouldn't do that, of course. She frowned, nose puckering in irritation. Denavar was not one to shy from a challenge, especially when everyone was relying on him.

From her perch across the table, Shara sniffed, narrowing her amber eyes at the meal. "Are you going to eat that or not?"

Startled, Ashalea scowled at her friend. "How can you even think about food at a time like this?"

The assassin rolled her eyes. "For starters, I'm always thinking of food. And secondly, Denavar is more than capable of passing this test." She shrugged. "What are a few tricks to someone with his power?"

"Tricks," Ashalea echoed softly. Wezlan had said something similar once, when they were fresh on the road and spending the night at an inn. *"What's a wizard without his tricks?"* he had said. Indeed, they had scared the poor innkeeper witless, pretending to be tax collectors for the king. Their convincing performance had scored them a free meal and had sent the nosy owner scurrying, to which Ashalea had felt bad for after ... just a little. Still, a small smile tugged at her lips from the memory.

Things had been easier back then. *She* had been easier. Consumed with ideas of vengeance, of heroism, adventure and a chance to wet her sword, her bow and arrow, against more than wooden targets or the staff of her mentor.

Her smile vanished. That was before death had stolen her friends away on blackened wings. Before Kinna and Ondori had died, before children had been ripped from this world, before ... before ...

She couldn't say his name right now. Couldn't think it. There was loss and then there was utter emptiness. Yet, she would try. She would try so hard not to fall back into that quiet corner of her mind—for her friends. For this world. For Denavar. And ... for *him.*

She didn't miss the quick glance between Shara and Telilah. They must think her so breakable right now. Unpredictable. She swallowed her rising anger. They were just looking out for her—as friends are supposed to, but she couldn't help feeling like every movement was noted, every action tracked—as if monitoring her growth, calculating her healing. Would every smile or laugh be a milestone? Would every horrid thought be a case to analyse and lay bare?

Ashalea sighed, the happiness from that fleeting memory now marred by irritation. She handed her dinner to Shara with a small frown. "Here, seconds for the bottomless pit," she uttered with a small bite.

Shara ignored the tone, barely nodding her appreciation before wolfing down the food.

"For a species that uses utensils out of courtesy, you make animals look like model citizens," Razakh drawled from his vantage point on Ashalea's bed in the adjacent room. It seemed no matter where they travelled, her bed would presumably be co-shared with him from now on. She couldn't decide if it was for her protection, or simply because the Diodonian had taken kindly to the luxurious silks and velvets beneath his rump.

She suspected it was more of the latter.

Ashalea's mood softened. "Indeed. So says the common house cat lounging on his bed," she said with a raised brow.

The Diodonian huffed before jumping off the mattress with feline grace, his fiery mane flaring to life just once in reply. He then took to slumping before the table, looking ever so awkward next to the arranged chairs.

Ashalea bit back her laugh, but she dared not remark further. His pride could only allow so much indignity. A sly glance at Shara confirmed the assassin was too busy shovelling grub into her mouth to notice.

Telilah snorted from her seat by Shara's side, noticing Ashalea's amusement—and slight disgust at the splattering food. "She's a

species all of her own, this one. There's no taming her."

Shara swallowed a giant mouthful. "Don't pretend you don't love my wildness. You didn't complain when my hands were—"

"Nope," Ashalea said with a laugh. "A lady never shares her intimate secrets; you can keep those to yourself."

"*Hardly a lady*," Razakh interrupted, to which Shara ignored him.

Ashalea folded her arms. "There are more pressing matters we should discuss."

Shara groaned, swallowing her last mouthful before lounging back in her chair. She uttered a contented sigh, patting her stomach. Beside her, Telilah daintily blotted her mouth with a napkin, her manners equal to those of an empress.

"Are you done eating the mages out of house and home?" Ashalea smirked at Shara.

She offered a crooked grin. "Quite."

Telilah rolled her eyes before she glanced between Ashalea and Razakh, her face quickly sobering. "I know you're worried, Ashalea, but I have faith that Denavar will pass the test. He's strong and he's smart."

"*And he's stubborn,*" Razakh added. "*He won't give up without a fight.*"

"That's what I'm afraid of," Ashalea said. "And even if he passes the test, what then? If we convince Tiderion to take the stick out his ass and the others follow suit to form an alliance, where does that leave us?"

Razakh's tail swished gently. "*The final Guardian awaits us in the dwarf kingdom. Perhaps we can journey with Kano, prove our mettle and strengthen our alliance. If he warms to us, we'll have better luck finding who we seek.*"

With Denavar's new Magicka, we won't need to, Ashalea thought. He was now the most powerful elf—maybe even the most powerful of all races—to dwell on Everosia. Except the darkness. She suspected it could be an even match, but what that meant for the immediate future, she didn't know. She didn't want to go down that path, for if there was to be a final battle—as there always was in the old stories—the most powerful of warriors would face each other.

And maybe that didn't mean her. Ashalea was strong, gifted with the power of her people, but her Magicka was weaker than Denavar's. She had noticed the shift in strength—where her fire had burned bright as the sun it now paled next to Denavar's. And she didn't mind, not really. Her mentor had given her something far more precious than power alone.

Time.

All the years spent protecting her, teaching her, loving her like a daughter. It was worth every drop of Magicka on this world and all others. She wouldn't begrudge Denavar his new gifts. Not when he deserved every kernel. She had seen no one work as hard for their people as he did. Not her mother, not the Woodrandian elves, not the king of Maynesgate.

His passion for this place—for all the mages that dwelled in Renlock—was as undeniable as the bond she shared with him. And that connection deep within told her she was needed. No, Denavar wouldn't stand against the darkness alone—all-powerful being or not. For she'd be right there with him, two sparks, who, when put together, were fire incarnate: burning for vengeance, for redemption, for a better world.

A world that she might one day be proud to rule a quiet corner of. And it struck her, suddenly, what that might mean for her and Denavar. Would he take his place as the leading council member of

Renlock—as wizard of the esteemed Academy? Or would he perhaps sit by her side, co-ruler of their birthplace.

Would he be her king? Is that something he would want?

Ashalea shook her head. Lingering on hopes and dreams did little for the present and she needed to choose the roads that would lead her to her future. Firstly, the alliance. Secondly, the dwarves. Third? War. Bloody, brutal, damnable war.

She cleared her throat, slicing through the silence. "Kano," Ashalea said. "What do we make of him?"

Shara yawned, stretching her muscles out like a cat. "He's not to be trifled with, that one. Gruff as an old goat but fiercely loyal. He would do anything for his people. They are his pride and joy." She smirked as she slipped a shuriken from her belt. "You can also bet he knows how to wield the heck out of his weapon. Did you see his broadsword?" She whistled. "A dwarf his size could lop your head off with one sweep. Thing is as sharp as a teenage princeling's prick."

"Aye," Ashalea agreed. "Mighty is the sword ... if he can reach his enemy's head."

Even Telilah chuckled at that, much to Shara's delight. The assassin was positively beaming at the woman beside her, and Ashalea detected how her amber eyes lingered a little too long, something like longing within their depths.

Good, Ashalea thought. *I hope something comes of it.* Shara had told Ashalea about their little night spent together at the inn back at Galanor. It was meant to be harmless fun, the Onyxonite had explained. A means of stress relief. But then the girl's grandma also happened to be Wezlan's mysterious contact—the woman who had boarded their horses while the party trekked into the Diodon Mountains.

Fate sure had some clever cards to play. As far as Ashalea was aware, the duo had not yet shared any more intimate moments, though not for lack of trying on Telilah's part. The girl was utterly shameless—a complete flirt. If Ashalea didn't know better, she might have been a courtesan in another life. But for whatever reasons, whenever the girl got too close, Shara pushed her away, always holding her at arm's length despite the want she so clearly carried for the girl.

Ashalea understood. Shara had known pain, sorrow, loneliness all her life. She wielded them as weapons, used the negative energy behind those feelings to enflame her affinity to inflict pain on others. Never mentally, always physically, but Ashalea supposed it was an outlet, nonetheless. It was a mask of sorts, to hide what lingered beneath the surface.

That's why she kept her walls up; always joking, always challenging, her passion as fickle as her pride. It's what made her so fierce, so protective of what small comforts she had in life. And those comforts now included Ashalea, the Guardians, and Telilah. And maybe a knife under her pillow, but who was she to judge?

Tearing her eyes away from the tension so clearly simmering between those two, she eyed off Razakh with amusement, who was still seated like a perfect gentleman at the table, simmering in his own way.

He caught her looking and merely huffed. *"Procreation is not a joke. We Diodonians take it very seriously, given how close we came to extinction."*

Shara winked at him. "Oh, I bet you do, boyo. Gotta sire the next big bad and all."

Ashalea and Telilah roared with laughter as the Diodonian snapped at Shara's face, his grumpy expression setting them off even further.

Shara pouted, her eyes twinkling as she said, "Poor puppy."

His warning growl was nothing short of deadly. *"Perhaps we can focus on our plans again?"* His throat rumbled for good measure, much like an old man clearing his throat.

Telilah leaned forward and gave him a consoling scratch behind the ears, to which the beast seemed to calm immediately, silver eyes shuttering with pleasure.

"Denavar becomes a wizard, Tiderion backs down, we make merry with the dwarves and find ourselves a Guardian." Shara shrugged. "Simple."

Ashalea noted Telilah's fingers picking at invisible lint on the ruby table runner, its fabric adorned with silver swirls—a decidedly good make, not a thread out of place. Her gaze travelled to the woman's face, her teeth worrying her lips.

"Telilah?" Ashalea asked softly. "Something wrong?"

The girl looked nervously between the Guardians present. "It's just ... where do I fit in?"

She's worried, Ashalea realised with a jolt. Fearful that she has no part in this scenario, no place within the Guardians. And why wouldn't she? Telilah had no Magickal skill, she was untrained for battle and would likely be a distraction for all of them if she fought. She was a creative—wildly passionate about art and music and the pleasantries of the world. Telilah was an entertainer, a curious and clever wanderer. Yet none of these things held merit when a war was looming.

She peered at Telilah's brown eyes, intense as they stared right back into Ashalea's. She knew. The woman knew, and ever so subtly, she nodded once, just once—an understanding, and permission.

"What are you talking about?" Shara scoffed. "You're coming

with us of course."

Ashalea sighed. "No," she said softly but firmly. "She isn't."

Razakh shifted in his seat beside her, not saying a word, but she could sense the approval. He, too, had thought it through. Telilah would better serve the cause in the safety of the Academy. She might not know how to fight or how to harness the energies of Everosia, but she had intuition. She had cleverness, and she could lead these people by helping to prepare the Academy and the allied races for the oncoming war.

Shara's eyes snapped to Ashalea, narrowed with confusion. "What do you mean, no?" she demanded, her voice low and cold.

Ashalea took a breath, but it was Razakh who replied. "*Telilah has many gifts, she is a joy to be around,*"—Telilah nodded at his kindness—"*but she cannot fight or defend herself and we cannot afford the distraction of protecting her. It would be unfair and selfish to the many soldiers who will one day soon fight by our sides.*"

"Selfish?" Shara said incredulously. "How dare you?" Her eyes darted furiously between Ashalea and Razakh. "How can you sit there like royals and demand what a person can or cannot do with their freedom?"

Telilah rested a hand gently on Shara's arm, the simple movement enough to quell Shara's no doubt colourful speech had she continued. The minstrel smiled prettily, softly, even as sadness lined her eyes. "They are right. I am unfit for battle; I have no position, no standing or aid I can offer. All I would do is get in the way or get someone hurt. I couldn't stand that. I won't."

Shara sputtered, "But ... you're a part of our team now. You're one of us, Guardian or no."

Ashalea set her palms atop the table. "And she always will be, Shara, but Telilah can do so much more to help us here. Safe, with the protection of the mages and all our allies.”

Shara glared at her, such rage radiating from her pores, and it was all directed at *her*. “You don’t make the rules, Ashalea. You are not the leader of this group; you aren’t and never will be Wezlan.”

A slap in the face would have been better. Ashalea felt the sting of those words sink deep into her soul, latching on to every fear, every shred of sorrow. The room fell deathly silent as she bit back her tears and swallowed her pride, feeling like a child as she tried to hold her head high.

“Let’s make something clear,” Shara said, her hands splayed on the table as she leaned towards Ashalea. “You do not order me around. You do not order Telilah around. I am not your subject and you,” she jabbed her finger menacingly, “you are not my queen.”

With that, she grabbed her cloak and was out the door before Ashalea could open her mouth.

***

“She didn’t mean it,” Telilah said softly. “And—and I understand. I agree it is the right thing to do.”

Ashalea gave her a small smile even as her insides warred against rage and nausea that her friend was so, so angry. *At her.* They had quarrelled before, but it had never been personal. And the things she had said—what she had implied ... Ashalea swallowed the rising nerves. Shara had a temper and no leash on her emotions but not once had she been harsh. Not like this.

To mention Wezlan’s name with such carelessness and to imply Ashalea would ever ... No. It was too much. She was already on edge with Denavar being gone so long. She stood abruptly, feeling suddenly too warm, too caged within this room. “I’m going for a walk," she declared to no one in particular.

Telilah clicked her tongue. "Are you sure that's—"

"I'll be fine," Ashalea said sweetly, cutting her off. She knew precisely what Telilah would say. A carefully worded question suggesting it wasn't in Ashalea's best interest to be alone right now. She had every reason to. There was also the risk of crossing paths with the warhorse that was Shara, though perhaps talking it out would be a good thing.

But the time for waiting was over, and she could no more sit around and stuff her face than she could keep up pleasantries. Not while Denavar was being tested. Not while his life could be at stake. She riffled through the armoire for a cloak, settling on a simple black one and throwing it around her shoulders in one swift motion. With her back still turned, she patted down her legs, checking for the reassuring weight of her knives.

She could feel Telilah's eyes glued to her back, but as she turned, the minstrel merely smiled. Telilah's eyes roved over Ashalea's attire, narrowing at both the cloak and, no doubt, its colour, but the woman kept her full lips shut.

"I'll see you soon," Ashalea said with a nod, careful to remain indifferent, setting the lines of her face to show mild distress— nothing concerning to note, just an elf worried about her man and stressed from fighting with a friend.

"*I'm coming with you,*" Razakh said, already at the door, his fiery tail swishing back and forth eagerly. His silver eyes blazed into her own, and she once again marvelled at the almost otherworldly intelligence within.

She raised her brows but nodded once, and she quickly cast a genuine smile at Telilah. At her friend. "We all care for you very much, you know," she said quietly. It was the best she could offer, and maybe it wasn't enough but ... she opened the door and shut it behind them, leaving Telilah on her own.

I'm such a horrible person, she thought miserably.

"*No you're not,*" Razakh said simply. She briefly wondered how often he combed through her mind. He went on, either oblivious or wisely choosing to ignore her afterthought. "*Sometimes leaders are forced to make tough decisions. Not everyone will agree, not everyone will be happy about it, but that's the price one must pay. And you are a leader, Ashalea. Born to it or not, it's in your marrow.*"

She didn't answer. Later. She would deal with Shara later.

The corridor was silent, the hour growing late. Any mages not within their dorms would no doubt be curled up in the library with a good book, lost in worlds of different makings. Perhaps even sharing tall tales around the fireplace in the common room.

The ruling elves—King Tiderion, Queen Celiana, and Lady Nirandia—would all be somewhere near the testing room. They weren't allowed to interfere with the examination, nor were they allowed in the room with Denavar, but they had to be judging it somehow. Perhaps through a—

"*Through a scrying pool, no doubt,*" Razakh interrupted.

She frowned at him, but after tonight's events she hadn't the heart to berate his eavesdropping in her head.

She set her eyes on the wooden door that crowned the upper floor—the examination room. It loomed at the end of the hall, its wooden frame limned with light from the sconces either side, the reflection of the flames glinting on the brass handle.

"*You've the look of a hunter tonight,*" Razakh noted, following her line of sight. "*We're not just going for a walk, are we?*"

Her eyes shifted to Razakh and she grinned mischievously. "Not just," she admitted, "and hunters always need their hound."

His answering grin was all droopy skin and fangs.

Tried and Failed

DENAVAR

"I T'S TRYING TO KILL ME," Denavar panted as he conjured portal after portal, his sense of direction now utterly lost. If not for his keen elvish senses, he might already have been skewered by the sharp spikes lining the pits around him.

He had passed the elemental tests before being tested in his healing ability. Now he had seemingly moved on to portal travel, for unless he sprouted wings there was no other way to avoid the sudden pitfalls that formed throughout the chamber, lined with crude wooden spikes no less.

For every pit there formed a pillar, interchanging in a steady rhythm, too quick to vault onto, but not so fast he couldn't portal to safety. It was madness—everything solid and safe was suddenly a moving maze, and one wrong step, one wrong turn ... but Denavar was good with puzzles, having studied many ancient texts and deciphering riddles and codes for both the elves and Renlock. He had just finished a mental mapping of the room when the frequency changed, and he stumbled through his next portal—with no pillar to step on.

Cursing, he propelled himself out of certain death's embrace with a gust of wind, sending him toppling onto the ground, his head slamming into the wall with a loud crack. Wincing at the sharp pain atop his crown, his fingers found blood when he pulled them away. With stars threatening his vision, he leaned his back against the wall and breathed in deeply, calming his heart, ignoring the dull throbbing in his head.

Fine, he thought, gritting his teeth. He would shed blood for this task, but Gods let this blasted test be over. As if in answer to his silent prayer, the testing room began to reform its original shape, and Denavar sighed in relief, not even caring how this place defied the natural laws of the world.

Sweat slathered his skin, a river running down the curve of his back. He had but a moment's reprieve before the Magicka would send something wicked his way. Denavar rolled his neck, groaning from the headache already forming—and no doubt an egg-sized bruise to accompany it.

"Do your worst," he dared the Magickal energy.

It did just that.

"Denavar?" a voice called, and his head snapped up at the familiar tone. He squinted, peering into the gloom that now settled over the floor. A flash of red peeked through the mist and his stomach filled with dread.

"Farah?" he whispered back, leaning towards that voice, slowly, carefully, rising to his feet.

The figure stepped out of the gloom, and there she was. A

mane of untamed fire, round glasses, blue eyes of the clearest sky. A skinny girl with the face of an old friend, and the heart of a would-be lover.

"It's me, Denavar," she said, reaching for him.

He let his hands hang loosely at his sides, ready to defend himself at any second. But a part of him hoped, a part of him dared that perhaps ... perhaps she was not gone after all. Perhaps he had not failed his friend in this, at least. Perhaps Finnicus—his once best friend who had died in the filthy streets of Maynesgate—perhaps he wasn't turning in his grave, cursing Denavar for letting his sister die. For sending her to battle knowing the risk, knowing the cost.

But she had died on the bloody fields of Renlock not long ago ... hadn't she? He remembered her hair fanning out, her crushed body, her eyes open, sky blue staring at blue sky.

His mind was fuzzy, the world tilting. Perhaps he'd hit his head harder than he'd thought. Or perhaps—

He jolted when her hands, cold and clammy and feeling very real, clasped his arms, and her fingertips slid up to wrap around his neck. "It should have always been me," she said, voice hollow and cold.

"What?" He held her back, cocking his head to ascertain her meaning, studying her eyes. The blue burned feverishly, and something within their depths struck a haunting chord within him.

"You were meant to be with me," she hissed, fingernails suddenly biting into his golden skin. "I loved you, but you chose her. That silver-haired wretch. That plague upon the earth. She brings death. She brings darkness."

Denavar withdrew, a shiver spider-walking up his back. "I'm sorry, Farah. I love you like a sister, but it could never be more than that," he said softly, tucking a strand of glimmering red behind her ear. "Ashalea and I are together now," he said more firmly. "You will not disrespect her in my presence."

Her answering smile was wicked—cruel almost—and he took a step back in uncertainty. "This isn't right," he said to himself, shaking his head. "You're not real, this isn't real."

"Who are you trying to convince, Brother?" chimed in another voice, the speaker directly behind him, a puff of icy air tickling the nape of his neck.

Denavar swivelled, fists raised, only to drop them in awe. "Finnicus," he breathed.

"In the flesh," his friend answered. He was exactly as he remembered. Red hair with a mind of its own, a lopsided grin, a strong jaw and nose. But ... 'remembered' was the key word, Denavar reminded himself, because Finnicus was dead. And that, he knew, was a fact.

Denavar looked between the twins, gaping at seeing them side-by-side, their eerie smiles broad but emotionless. "You're dead. You died in an alleyway in Maynesgate. I held your head in my lap, I tried to heal your wound."

Finnicus stared at him, face pallid. "Yes," he said. "Tried and failed." His chin sunk to his chest as he stared, eyes slowly—ever so slowly—drifting down. Farah grinned beside him, unblinking, her white teeth luminous in the dark.

Denavar followed Finn's eyes, landing on the man's chest. Blood blossomed from a wound, branching out like roots seeking water, and Denavar, transfixed, looked on in horror, nausea climbing his throat just as blood filled his friend's.

Crimson petals fell from Finnicus's lips until the liquid began bubbling, spluttering out in a cruel re-enactment of his death.

"Stop," Denavar said, but the blood kept spilling. They both kept smiling and Farah began to laugh. A once sweet sound now twisted and wrong. His stomach dropped and he tasted a metallic tang on the air, shoving its way down his throat.

Finnicus was still bleeding, still smiling, and Denavar—having absolutely no idea what to do—strode up to his friend, took him by the shoulders and shook violently. "Dammit man, stop this. You can't be here. This can't be happening." Eyes wild, he looked pleadingly at the room. "What must I do?"

Farah's laugh grew louder, her cackle bouncing off the walls, and the blood kept flowing, kept spreading in an endless wave until the floor was drowned in it. Denavar backed up against the wall, sliding down it in despair. He squeezed his eyes shut, burying his face in his hands, trying to block them out—trying to find reason in this task.

But even with his eyes closed they haunted him, and Farah's laugh grew louder as she and her brother sat down beside him. "You let us die," Finnicus murmured finally. "You let us die, die, die."

A sob escaped Denavar, and even as he clenched a fist in protest, the first tear fell. For perhaps the first time in his life, Denavar had no tricks, no plans, no idea what to do. He rocked on the balls of his feet and let the madness consume him.

<hr>

He didn't know if minutes had passed or hours, but fear like he'd never known clawed at his chest, suffocating him. Denavar lifted his hands to his face—they were coated in blood. His friend's blood, who should be dead. *Was* dead. No matter how much he wiped them on his tunic, they remained stained. A reminder of his failures.

Yet the weight beside him, real or not, was too solid to ignore, as was the petite frame of Farah on his other side. This couldn't be happening. Only Magicka of the darkest forces could reanimate the dead or conjure wraiths to walk the earth. This was an abomination of the highest order; a perversion of Magicka, and it held no place in this sacred space.

He bolted to his feet, forcing deep breaths in and out, closing his eyes to gather his wits about him. Not real. They weren't real, the blood wasn't real. Whatever phantoms haunted him today, they had not sought to harm him ... yet.

The presence of Farah and Finnicus shifted at his sides and he suppressed the shiver seeking to wrack through his body. Wrong, it was all wrong. Their presence here, this twisted game, whatever darkness had leeched into the energies that formed the foundation of this place.

Could Crinos have tainted the pure energies here? Or perhaps the bloodshed that stained these hallowed grounds? His mouth set in a hard line, muscles bunching in anger. Yes. The Magicka may have decided it had been abused enough already. For Crinos had slaughtered countless lives in this place. At the recent battle for Renlock, and long ago when he *became* the darkness. When he was denied that which Denavar was currently being tested for.

Divinity. Wizardry. The highest respect and the most revered seat of power in both Renlock and, at least in terms of Magickal prowess, across Everosia.

He swore under his breath. He should have known. And this— this was the result. He didn't know of any incantation or spell that would send his dead friends back to whatever plane of existence they came from, nor how to free their souls from this abhorrent abuse of nature.

Had they been elves, he would have expected their energies—their souls—to return to the earth. But as humans, it was widely believed their souls travelled elsewhere, to a better place, far from this land. But maybe this was a punishment for him. For all the mages. Maybe being this close to the energies meant seeing his worst fears.

Grimacing, he did a mental list of the powers available to him and came up empty. For all the gifts Wezlan had given him, he could think of nothing that would banish the evil in the room. Farah cackled beside him, as if sensing his frustration and ineptitude.

"Oh do shut up," he snapped, and Gods have mercy, she, it, snapped its mouth shut.

Massaging his temples, Denavar did the only thing he could think of. Reaching into the deepest recesses of his mind he pulled on his nerve endings, searching for his memory bank, combing through his Magicka until he established a link—a direct channel to her mind.

"Ashalea ..."

Scars and All

SHARA

S HARA LOOKED UP AT THE GLITTERING SNOW floating down upon the tower, settling into slick pools within the stone cracks before her. In her anger, she'd stormed around the top floor of the Academy, almost wearing tracks into the carpet runner and causing any passers-by to turn the other way, before finding herself on the roof.

The roof, she realised with a start. Perhaps the very last place she'd want to revisit in this Gods awful place. She hated the Academy; hated the four walls around her, the stares and titters of the mages, the ghosts that walked the halls—her mind—but most of all she hated how she didn't fit in, how useless her skills were in this place.

Magicka surrounded her, yet she felt none of the energy from the wellspring on which the tower was built; felt nothing but pain and sorrow. Renlock was like a cage, which she supposed was why she'd sought the fresh air. Despite what had happened here—despite the memories that came flooding back, colder and crueller than winter could ever be.

But right now she needed that flood to quench the heat radiating through her bones, the anger eddying in the depths of her stomach. After she had given so much, she was about to lose something that made her happy—or rather, someone. A woman who made her *feel* again, made her smiles genuine, her laughter true.

And maybe she'd been pushing that someone away for fear of what it all meant, but it was better than that shell she'd settled into. Better than the emptiness and the memories. Around Telilah she didn't feel like she needed a brave face or a mask, she could just be herself, whoever that was these days. Shara gulped down the frigid air, savouring its embrace as it stung her throat. She placed her palms onto the rampart and hissed as the cold stone bit at her fingers.

Gentle, warm hands curled around her own, and Shara looked up to find big brown eyes, softened in their gaze as they stared at her.

"You'll catch a cold without extra layers on," Telilah said disapprovingly, letting go to drape a spare cloak around Shara's shoulders.

Shara wished she hadn't let go. Wished she could cling to that warmth and the creamy, uncalloused skin. Always so thoughtful, thinking of others even as Shara could see a sadness pinching the lines of Telilah's face, the angle of her brows drawn. Her soft, doe eyes almost glassy.

"How did you know I'd be up here?" Shara said softly.

Telilah raised a brow, a playful smirk forming. "With that

temper of yours, it wasn't hard to guess."

Right. Shara opened her mouth but Telilah continued, "It's for the best you know," she said quietly. "Ashalea and Razakh are right, and I don't blame them for that choice. There are things I can do here, to help the mages, to prepare for the war. I've never truly felt all that useful. My talents aren't exactly essential to hard times like these but ... but maybe I can bring some cheer back to this place. Fill the halls with music again, and beyond that, maybe I could be a diplomat of sorts for the alliance."

Shara turned to her, taking one of Telilah's soft hands in her own, offering a small smile. "You'd be perfect for that. I can think of no one better to shed light in our darkest hours." She meant every word.

Telilah blushed, the rosy pink already gracing her cheeks from the cold deepening into a warm rouge, like mulled wine on a winter's day.

Shara brushed a thumb down Telilah's finger. "There is one thing you're wrong about though. You are essential ... to me."

The woman ducked her head, shyly looking up from behind fluttering lashes, her mouth opening and closing as if she were contemplating what to say. "Shara, I—"

Shara stared at Telilah's lips, and every part of her being wanted to claim them, to taste her, to hold her close and never let go. Telilah bit her lip and it sent delicious want coursing through her veins. Shara leaned in ... but merely tucked a strand of Telilah's long brown hair behind an ear, turning to watch the snow shimmer across the fields. It was falling heavily now, dusting the world in white; the long stretches of green that had housed bodies and blood not so long ago were now coated in the promise of something new. A change for all.

The trees of Shadowvale—too far to see even from the tower—would be standing proudly, the village she loved well protected behind their spindly arms. The Onyxonites would have lit bonfires, celebrating the first snow as they danced and feasted and embraced each other in carnal delight. Winter brought them to life—their bones singing with the cold, with the instinct to survive and prosper.

They would embrace their impulses, drown themselves in wine. She remembered what it meant, this first day of snow. Winter had always been a challenge her people rose to wholeheartedly, for it was the one thing that was truly a danger. Shadowvale had its few small luxuries, but it was no city of jewels or decadence or comforts. Her people lived day to day, fending for themselves. They survived through strength. They survived together.

The Onyxonites looked winter in the face and told death in not so many nice words to bow down before them. The weak grew stronger for it, the untested grew hard, and even so, there would always be warmth if they stuck together.

Shara sighed. She wasn't really a part of that tribe anymore. Not in her heart. Her destiny had forged a new path, and perhaps, if she survived the war, it might never be a home to her again. Her brother, her father—as much as she loved them, maybe they weren't the family she needed right now. Maybe a small part of her was okay with that, but still her heart stretched thin, and she turned her sights to another direction.

The Aquafarian lake shimmered in the distance; its gentle waters would soon freeze over, protecting the creatures that dwelled within its depths for the season. She considered what that might mean for Gruvar—the most delightful animal she had ever met. Its form something like a colossal bird crossed with a turtle, its temperament perhaps akin to a dog.

There was something even bigger that dwelled in that lake, too. Something ancient. The water dragon. What he thought about the oncoming storm that was the darkness, Shara could only guess. She frowned, considering how many pawns on the board might be played, and how many might fall should they all fail. Should her princess fall—and Ashalea was just that, despite what Shara had said.

She had regretted the words before they had finished leaving her mouth; words fuelled by such fierce rage that she sometimes forgot lingered within. Always burning, no matter how she tried to ignore it. Ashalea had been cut deep and Wezlan ... Shara had not dishonoured his name in such a way before and her stomach roiled at the thought of insulting his memory like that.

He had been Ashalea's mentor, her closest friend when there was no one else. He had been Shara's too, but there was no time for mourning. Only anger.

It had always been a tool for Shara, when she'd been a lone wolf in her work. It had helped her survive, helped her block out emotion—fear, empathy, regret. These things did not exist when she was an assassin. It was a crutch she leaned on heavily.

But as a Guardian, as a friend ... She was quickly realising there were more weapons in her arsenal, and sometimes—sometimes her anger backfired. She had been angry at Ashalea because she'd been the only one brave enough to speak the truth, when really, Shara should have been angry at herself. For denying that she, too, agreed it was in everyone's interest for Telilah to stay behind.

She let out a huff of irritation, the air pluming white before her, and she turned around to lean against the wall. Slowly, her eyes travelled over every crack, every stone, to a mark on the floor. To where she had almost—

"I died up here," she blurted, the sound suddenly abrasive and wrong in the quiet of night. Beside her, Telilah's back stiffened, her eyes widening as she too, turned towards the tower's centre.

Shara pointed with a shaking finger, "Right over there. It was the night of the battle, I'd come racing up here, too angry and upset to think straight, and he"—she swallowed—"he grabbed me, and he was so strong, so strong that under his grip I was nothing more than a toy for a dog to shake around, to tear into."

Telilah's hands reached for her own. She barely noticed their warmth, lost in the memory, eyes glazed as they replayed the moment in her head. "I was nothing but a puppet on strings, broken and afraid. After he tortured me—after Flynn tortured me under his spell back at his base I just ... froze. I couldn't do it again. Couldn't think with his hands around my neck and so I—I shut down. I gave up. I let the others down."

"I didn't know," Telilah whispered, stroking her arms gently. "I didn't know you'd been through so much pain."

Shara barked a bitter laugh. "I didn't tell you because I couldn't stand to see the pity in your eyes. The same sorrow I see now." She looked up, a grim smile on her lips. "Dying wasn't so bad, one *snap* from his hands around my neck"—she emphasised the word and Telilah flinched—"and I was gone before I hit the ground."

Telilah's face did indeed twist into horror, followed by remorse. There was silence for a few beats, then, "How?"

"She brought me back. Ashalea, somehow—Gods bless that elven saint—she broke the damper on her Magicka, called on the power gifted to her by the Moon Goddess herself and, well, here I am." Shara shook her head. "The greatest gift someone could offer, and she wasted it on me."

Telilah's hands travelled up her arms to squeeze her shoulders tight. "Not a waste. Never that." She leaned in, so close Shara thought their lips would touch. Her body shivered, blood pumping loudly in her ears; the hairs on her skin standing up with anticipation. But the woman placed a gentle kiss on her cheek instead, leaving the skin tingling from her touch.

When she pulled away, Shara could only stare at her in awe, but she could wait. She would do it right, for this woman, as slow and steady as needed. And whatever happened, if Shara survived this war, she would court this woman like she'd never done before—never wanting or needing to until now.

As if reading her thoughts, Telilah lifted her chin, big brown eyes staring into Shara's soul like sunlight in dark corners. "I will have you one day, Shara Silvaren, scars and all—even the ones we can't see. And once this war is done, we'll heal them one by one, together."

Shara smiled, extending a hand. "I would like that very much."

14

Dark Magicka

ASHALEA

ASHALEA REACHED FOR THE BRASS HANDLE, her reflection in its polished edge a mask of determination, yet her hand halted halfway.

"*What's wrong?*" Razakh asked, tilting his golden head inquisitively.

She bit her lip. "I don't know what the rules are for these tests, but if we go in there, we might jeopardise Denavar's examination. Interrupting him might not be the best idea."

"*So we think of something else,*" the Diodonian suggested, baring his teeth in what might have resembled mischief. "*Perhaps pay a little visit to the judges instead.*"

Her mouth opened to reply when Razakh stiffened preternaturally beside her, his hackles raised, teeth bared in defence, a warning growl rumbling deep within his chest. The fire rippling

calmly down his mane in soft, blue hues suddenly morphed into angry red and orange, the heat near singeing to the hand placed on his back, the other still midway to the handle.

She almost shivered at the pure animalistic aggression in his frame. Had a mage happened to see him, she was convinced they might have relieved themselves on the spot. "What's wrong?" she repeated his earlier question, this time with deadly quiet, her own senses on alert.

"Whatever is inside that room," he hissed, *"defies the natural order of the world. A perversion of Magicka. You were right, Denavar needs us."*

"Ashalea," a voice echoed in her head. Not the melodic ringing of Razakh, but the timbre of another, deeper chord, full of urgency and ... fear.

"Denavar," she breathed, her resolve hardening at his tone, at the thought of him frightened or hurt. "Test be damned."

Ashalea didn't bother with the handle. With one swift kick and a slam from Razakh's shoulder, they busted the door down, the old wood groaning before splintering under the force of her assault, Razakh wild beside her as she sprinted inside. What she saw made her skid to a halt.

Farah, along with another red-headed man, stood beside Denavar, their twisted features leering, broad smiles not touching their feverish eyes. Their cold, lifeless eyes and flat expressions chilled her to the bone, the nape of her neck tingling with fear. "Get away from him," she growled as their eyes swivelled at the commotion.

Razakh leaped in front of her, embers from his mane threatening to catch on their withered bodies, his great maw snapping as he steered them away from Denavar. Ashalea gasped as she spied his face, pale and drawn, not just from expending Magicka for hours on end but being trapped in here with these things. With a dead girl whom he'd loved like a sister. And from the uncanny resemblance, a man who she could only guess was Denavar's old friend and Farah's brother, Finnicus.

Also deceased. Also wrong in every sense of the word as his awful face twisted into a sneer, his teeth slick with red, as was the shirt he wore. As was the entire floor of the room, Ashalea realised. In her hurry to get to Denavar she hadn't even noticed.

But the metallic tang she'd smelled outside the door—that's what it was. The iron scent of blood as it drowned out fresh air, so strong it climbed her nose and coated the tip of her tongue. Bile slithered in her stomach at the awfulness of it all, but she swallowed, forcing all thoughts away as she brushed her knuckles gently against Denavar's cheek, Razakh guarding their backs against the wraiths.

His face was stark, mouth set in a hard line as he slowly turned his eyes to her face. Recognition filled it, and his features softened. "The darkness," he said by way of greeting, gesturing around the room. "He must have tainted the energies at the battle of Renlock." He ground his teeth, brushing past her to stalk around the room. "Whilst I believe the mages are still safe, and our individual energies remain clean, this is the result of his being here again. A sick joke—a mockery of anyone who would dare take the examination."

She nodded grimly. "It's a good thing then, that no one else has entered here since. But these ghosts, if you would call them that, what do you suppose...?"

Denavar surveyed his old friends with disgust and sorrow. "I expect the dark Magicka manipulates the test, shows he or she who is undertaking it their fears or their regrets."

Ashalea glanced between Farah and Finnicus, saying nothing. Later. They would discuss this another time, when they weren't standing in blood, or what made for a convincing illusion at least. She wasn't even sure what was real in here, besides Denavar and Razakh.

"*What do we do now?*" Razakh asked, not moving an inch as he kept the siblings cornered, his tail flicking in warning. Their eyes followed its movement, teeth pulled back in hideous grins, their faces contorted in death.

Neither Denavar nor Ashalea had time to answer as Tiderion and Celiana stormed through the door, their sharp eyes quickly assessing the room before falling on Ashalea. Her mother's face paled upon seeing Farah and Finnicus, whereas Tiderion's eyes only hardened.

Nirandia rushed in behind them, her lavender dress swishing to a stop, the bloodied floor seeping into the scalloped edges of her gown. She looked at it wordlessly, mouth pursed, before studying the wraiths and then Ashalea and Denavar.

"This examination is over," Nirandia instructed, ever the queen commanding her subjects. "Denavar, you will assist Tiderion and myself to cleanse this chamber." She glanced at Celiana, who looked ready to swoon as she held a dainty hand to her throat, and Nirandia's lips deepened to a frown.

Dismissal, Ashalea noticed, and disappointment—as if Nirandia had hoped her mother would rise to the occasion. Ashalea almost snorted, and her own appraisal of Celiana deepened, the anger within her stomach coiling like a pit viper ready to strike.

She shook her head, striding to her mother and taking her not so gently by the arms, steering her to the exit. "Come, Celiana," Ashalea said, suppressing a long-suffering sigh. "Let's give them space while we get a warming pot of tea."

Ashalea jerked her head at Razakh, who followed in her

footsteps, but not before she glanced at Denavar, who gave her a tired smile. Nirandia nodded her thanks just once before turning to the task at hand.

Once her mother was back in her rooms without a word exchanged between them, Ashalea headed to her own, Razakh padding by her side. She collapsed on the bed, feeling the mattress sink as the Diodonian curled into a ball beside her, his flames extinguished. She ran a hand along his spine, the golden fur soft as silk under her fingers, and she stared up at the ceiling, waiting, wondering.

Denavar didn't return that night.

A New Order

ASHALEA

H ER BOW WAS A COMFORTING WEIGHT IN HER HANDS, the smooth white oak firm under her calloused grip. She tested the string, frowning at its disobedience before thumbing the feathered tips of the quiver nocked against it. Her muscles had declined, and despite her rigorous training, her body—still nimble as an elf—lacked the agility and strength she had once worked so hard to achieve.

"It's because there's no meat on your bones," Razakh drawled beside her.

He had been eager to expend some energy after the previous night's bizarre events, and Ashalea hadn't said no when he'd asked her to join him. She scrubbed a hand over bleary eyes, cursing at the lack of sleep. After finally nodding off in the early morning hours, she'd been visited by the wraiths in her dreams, waking drenched in sweat and fitfully thrashing, much to Razakh's alarm.

Ashalea hadn't got a wink after that, her body still feverish from the nightmare, her mind sprinting through what had happened—and why, for that matter. But she already knew that. Crinos. All the awful things in her life were a result of him. Her brother. She wanted to spit just thinking of him.

Emerald eyes turned to the skies, observing the morning light; rose, ochre and periwinkle blue painting a pretty canvas as the sun bid good morning on its arc overhead. She marvelled at the snow glittering in its wake, fresh white powder shining like one big diamond beneath her feet.

It was the perfect morning for a hunt, and though she would not eat any game they found today, there were others within the keep who would benefit. And Razakh was right, she thought miserably, there was no meat on her bones. No muscle either. She felt the curve of her ribs, one idle hand able to count each one until she reached the plane of her stomach—more filled in now, but still not the toned, feminine curves she once had.

Yes, she had lost far too much weight. She would need to eat more, train more, or she'd soon be wraithlike herself. Ashalea turned to Razakh, who was regarding her with those eyes of moving metal. His fur glinted in the rising sun, strands of ruby shimmering amongst the golden hue. Beautiful. As if reading her thoughts, he hummed low in his throat, what she supposed passed for amusement.

"Oh, stop reading my thoughts, you big brute, and go fetch us some deer," she snapped.

Razakh pulled his mouth back to display his canines. "*Touchy, touchy,*" he purred, then bounded off into the thicket. The woeful death knell of an animal greeted her not moments later, and she cringed, feeling shameful even with her good intentions.

She sighed as she rolled her shoulders and readied her bow, leaving the elf behind and becoming the primal predator that dwelled within.

<hr>

They returned to the Academy several hours later laden with a menagerie of animals, tied onto a makeshift wooden rack and draped over Ashalea's shoulders. Razakh carried his kills on his back, some even hanging limply in his mouth.

The head cook—a plump woman with bow lips and chubby cheeks—clapped her hands in glee and barked at her assistants to begin skinning the carcasses. She nodded approvingly at Ashalea and even went so far as to reach for the birds tucked between Razakh's clamped jaws, soon thinking better of it after a warning growl.

Ashalea smiled sweetly. "Just mine and the ones on his back. He plays for keeps," she grinned. Razakh just spat his meal out on the floor and began tearing it to shreds, blood and feathers making a right mess on the clean stones.

She winced before raising her hands apologetically. The cook's eyes merely widened before she quickly stepped away, trying vainly to ignore the Diodonian whose teeth and claws would make short work of all present.

"I'll see you upstairs," Ashalea muttered, which the Diodonian ignored while he chewed, bones and all, some audibly snapping as he swallowed. The mages on duty flinched at each crack, the youngest among them gaping in awe as the boy stared with pure wonder in his eyes.

Trudging back up the stairs to her room, she groaned from the morning's work. Her back and neck ached with the strain of carrying the animals, her bow arm stiff from the tension on the string. She was frozen to the core, shuddering underneath a cloak wet from sweat and snow.

When she finally made it to the top floor and had shut the door behind her, she yelped in surprise at a very naked, very amused Denavar spread out in full display on the bed.

She clamped her mouth shut, pretending to ignore him as she removed her bow and quiver, and wriggled out of the heavy overcoat, tossing it on the floor. The movement caused her to groan in protest, and Denavar was there in an instant.

His sturdy fingers made short work of the lacing binding the cloak underneath and soon she was standing in her shirt and tights; he even went so far as to gently remove her boots. He glanced at her from his perch on the floor, blue eyes dancing, and slowly, his hands trailed the length of her legs, up and up until his fingertips circled tauntingly at the waistline of her pants.

Ashalea shivered at his fingers on her bare skin, the heat of his body warming her frozen waist until it travelled down, until the tickle of his fingertips had her shivering for a different reason. He rose, gently peeling back her pants, shucking them off as she stepped one foot out and then the other.

She brushed a finger along his jaw, halting his movement, gently pulling his chin up and towards her until their foreheads met and she stared at him lovingly. This beautiful elf, this fierce lover. Their lips met and she savoured the taste of him, his lips a cushion of warmth and softness against hers, his tongue exploring her mouth in a gentle caress.

When they pulled back, she whispered, "I was worried about

you."

He kissed her neck in answer, pecking at the space beneath her ear, sending a tremor through her body. "I know," he said, continuing to kiss her neck, her jaw, her cheek. "But I'm okay, we're all okay. The ghosts are gone. The Academy is safe."

Hearing those words, she deflated, neck releasing that tension—that weight she'd held since the moment she heard his voice in her mind, frightened and unsure. Something she'd never heard before despite everything they'd been through.

He seemed to understand that too, as he wrapped his arms around her, inviting her to nestle into the hollow of his neck, to the space above his heart. Denavar stroked loving, understanding lines down her spine, and she sighed in relief. "When I heard you in my mind, when I saw you, I—I didn't think. I just acted. Hearing you so worried, feeling that desperation ..." She looked at him then, imploringly, lovingly. "If anything happened to you, I don't know what I'd do."

Ashalea's lips wobbled, and he brushed a hand over her silver strands, coiling them around a finger, a knowing smile on his face. "What happened to you after—" he paused, searching for the words, though she knew he meant Wezlan's death. He tried again, "You will never have to feel that way with me. I swear to you, I am with you, to *our* end, not yours or mine alone. Not until nature takes us, as is the way."

She believed him, though deep down she knew he couldn't promise such things. Not with war approaching or while her brother still breathed. But those words comforted her all the same, preventing that abyss from yawning open and swallowing her again.

Nestling in, breathing in that peppermint scent, she wondered how they'd managed it; how they had restored the natural balance of this place. But Denavar seemed to know that too, for he merely smiled at her, his lips widening to reveal white teeth, his eyes blooming with newfound joy.

Cocking a head, Ashalea studied him, wondering what in the Goddesses' name might cause—

"You did it," she breathed. "You son of a—you really did it. Amongst all the chaos and the corruption of last night." Her eyes widened and her heart did a merry dance, hope coursing through her as she searched his eyes.

"I passed the test, Ashalea," he confirmed, crooked grin widening even further. "Together—Tiderion, Nirandia and I—we found the source of the corruption and we burned that bastard's power until naught but scorched earth remained. It was buried beneath the earth through a hidden pathway that led to the wellspring. The energies there, they judged us, weighed our intentions, and allowed us passage through."

She couldn't imagine it—seeing something so ancient, so magnificent. Until now she hadn't realised the wellspring, as the mages liked to call it, was an actual place one could touch or see with their own two eyes. She had merely thought this place had been blessed, pre-ordained as the birthplace of Magicka or something. Shaking her head, a small, disbelieving laugh shook through her. "How?"

His eyes creased, laughter booming from his own chest, hands lifting incredulously. "I don't know. It's hard to explain but it felt like the Magicka called to me—implored me to cleanse it, make it right. I followed its call through the hidden tunnel that leads from the foyer, down and down into the earth. Far, far below where no one would find it without guidance. And it was unlike anything I've ever seen, Ashalea. Not a well, not anything solid or explicable, but a vast being that was nothing and everything at once. Its power was ... astounding. And it chose me," he laughed again, kissing her joyfully on the lips. "It accepted me, judged me as pure and balanced."

"Balanced?" But her own grin grew as she voiced that aloud. "The final test to become a wizard," she recited to herself, looking at Denavar with respect and admiration. The only thing that had stood a chance at preventing him from becoming a wizard. The one test that weighed an individual's character and asked them to walk a fine line between good, evil, right or wrong.

He merely nodded, giving her time to work through her thoughts. "The balance of darkness and light. The final test that, should one pass all others, will make one a wizard."

Ashalea grinned, her heart alight with genuine joy—perhaps the first powerful emotion she'd felt since waking up after the attack on the Moonglade Meadows. It stirred something in her, coaxed a piece of her heart back together—a shred of her soul settling back into place.

She looked at him then, really looked at the elf before her, now the only one of his kind. A wizard. Denavar was a wizard. The last Divine being. No longer one of the Divine Six, but the first of a new order.

Smirking, she flicked his nose and winked. "So what shall we call you now, oh Divine and graceful one?"

His answering grin was predatory as he conjured a blast of wind that sent her drifting to the bed. She flopped onto the downy quilt in surprise, a sharp retort on her lips, but as she saw his ravenous expression, she bit back her reply. Something flared hot and heavy inside her at the way his eyes devoured the bare skin of her legs, her shirt now cinched halfway up her waist.

"Less talk, more play," he growled before striding across the room towards her.

And pounced.

An Allied Army

RAZAKH

THERE WAS AN AURA ABOUT HIM NOW. Razakh could sense the Magicka settling over Denavar like a golden cloak, cradling his shoulders with pure affection and unwavering loyalty. The elf was a wizard; the only wizard to walk Everosia, and he wore the mantle well. To be picked by the land itself? Well, there was something to be admired about that.

Razakh didn't fully understand what had occurred these last few days. How the Magicka itself had chosen Denavar as a vessel, as a bearer of its divine energies. He didn't care to know why, only that it was well-deserved, and as part of a larger picture, worked favourably for the Guardians.

Indeed, as Denavar sat at the council table, back straight and chin high, the elves looked to him with a newfound respect—perhaps begrudgingly on Tiderion's behalf. Yavaar dipped his head, and Kano, the dwarf king, had merely clapped Denavar on the back with a hearty laugh before they had all taken their seats.

As Denavar was now a wizard, his mantle carried new weight—responsibilities that accompanied his title. Renlock Academy, for all intents and purposes, was his charge now. His burden to bear, his vassal to protect, as were all the mages within it.

Razakh knew Denavar had much work ahead of him. A leader's job was never finished, and his friend would have some hard decisions to face soon—some that carried the fates of his people and whether many would live or die.

Indeed, not a day went by where Razakh didn't question his last orders as Klan chieftain of the Diodonians. That mantle had passed to Linar now, but not before Razakh had commanded the warriors of his tribe to partake in the war to come and align themselves with the other races once again. The elves and dwarves weren't the issue, but the humans ... Razakh's tail swished with agitation. He prayed the Diodonians kept their anger—their hostility—in check. An alliance was one thing on paper, but the soldiers who would fight under the treaties? That was another matter.

Razakh huffed, sending his worries scattering. Now was not the time to debate such matters. Today, they must focus on securing the favours of all races, which is exactly why Denavar's new position would hold great sway over the leaders.

His eyes landed on the wizard and the elven lady at his side. Ashalea was resplendent in blue so dark it was almost black, her gown shimmering like starlight, her silver hair coiled into a coronet atop her head. Where she was a moonlit queen, Denavar was the sun; his skin glowing, his white tunic, though simple, was well fitted and embroidered with golden trim. Together, they personified night and day, sun and stars. They were each other's equal, neither lesser nor higher than the other. Balanced.

It had been Telilah's idea, to present them as such. A careful calculation on her part, and one which had certainly made an impression on their audience. Dignitaries of all the royals present had tittered and nods of approval had circulated. Even Ashalea's mother, Celiana, after quite the scare of seeing the wraiths, looked on with pride, her fierce eyes clear and burning.

Denavar cleared his throat, and the low hum of conversation immediately stilled, all eyes swivelling to him in earnest. "Thank you for meeting tonight," he said, bowing his head slightly. "The last few days have been trying for us all, presenting unexpected challenges that we, as allies, have conquered together."

Razakh noted the squeeze of Denavar's hand resting casually upon Ashalea's arm, and she smiled at Denavar before turning and looking every royal in the eye. "What the darkness did to this sacred place is inexcusable, and we thank you for your aid. Renlock is one of the few wellsprings of natural Magicka that reside in Everosia. To see it corrupted, abused, is to see the very fabric of our world become unstitched." She breathed deeply, and Razakh knew she was steeling herself, finding the words.

"You have all seen what the darkness is capable of," she continued. "Besides Renlock, his monsters have raided your lands, murdered your people, poisoned your way of life. How long can we let this stand before he grows too powerful? His numbers too endless? Until his darkness eats away at us and there is no light left to live by? We need to act now. Before it is too late. The Guardians have our mission. Will you rise up to yours?"

Kano stroked his beard. His eyes, usually chips of ice, softened. "What would you have us do?"

Ashalea glanced at Razakh, and he dipped his head. "*The Grove is the key to all of this. Should the portal lie unprotected, the darkness will have unlimited access to this land, as will all his armies. He will be able to come and go as he pleases, meaning all is lost should he gain control of it. That is why we need you"*–he looked at Kano, Tiderion, Nirandia, Celiana, and Yavaar in turn–*"to fight. To give the Guardians every opportunity to ensure the portal remains closed ... forever."*

Nirandia nodded as she looked at Kano. "Only Razgeir, the Diodonian Guardian, and Shirilea, the elven priestess, are left to stand their vigil. Both are not long for this world, so it is only a matter of time until only the Keepers stand in the darkness's way. If we are to have any chance at winning this war, the Gate must be protected at all costs." Nirandia looked to her second—her brother Caelor—waiting for confirmation. Approval, perhaps. He nodded just once, and she turned to look at each of the Guardians.

"The Woodrandian elves will fight," she said, a steely glint to her eyes Razakh had not yet seen from the forest queen. "Our armies are at your disposal."

Ashalea said nothing, but she stood and bowed deeply, the movement so graceful one might have thought she'd been doing it for years. Razakh felt hope surge in his heart. Of the elven realms, Woodrandia had been the most likely to join them. Nirandia had ties with Ashalea and had been of great assistance to the Guardians of late; her title and neutral position with the dwarves would also hold sway over the others.

Razakh turned his head subtly to spy on Celiana and, as if feeling the weight of his gaze, her hazel eyes shifted—her daughter's eyes in all but colour—to him. Without fully knowing why, he sent a tendril of thought into her head, his telepathic powers burrowing into her mind, his gold-flecked essence searching every nook until every thought was laid bare.

She was afraid—terrified, even—of what the oncoming war would mean. Not for her people, for the bloodshed or pain that would ensue, not even for her daughter. No, she feared only for herself. A once proud and noble queen who burned so bright with purpose and love ... reduced to nothing but ash on the wind. A husk of what she was and what she could be.

Razakh rifled through her mind with disgust, feeling no guilt at this violation of privacy. Her mind was a confused array of regret, sorrow, and despair. Cowardice, however, reigned at the top of that list, and Razakh saw the path it led to. She would say no to this alliance. Despite everything, she would reject the treaty, the Guardians and, most importantly, her daughter.

Razakh's snarl echoed through her head, only hers, and she flinched, eyes widening. Like the rabbit he ate for breakfast, she backed into a corner, scrabbling at the walls of her mind, her own powers trying vainly to shove him out.

He only dug his claws in harder, letting their wicked curves trail down the sensitive tissues of her head. *"I will say this only once,"* he whispered, and she had the decency to shiver at the icy tone. *"Should you abandon us all in this war, your future promises only death and misery. Your queendom will fall, your people will despise you, and your daughter will* never *forgive you. And if she doesn't end your pathetic existence, I might rip your head off myself."* He bared his teeth in emphasis, tilting his head so the candlelight glittered off his canines. *"You have the power to change the course of history. So think carefully about your choice. Make it the right one."*

Razakh tightened his grip on her mind, choking it at the source, letting her stew until he withdrew, and the queen gasped for air as he released her, the mental onslaught as torturous as if he'd throttled her throat. "My Queen?" her steward approached;

concern etched into his sharp features.

Celiana waved him off. "It's nothing," she snapped. Ashalea straightened, studying her mother with interest before her eyes darted to Razakh, a slight frown creasing her lips. He merely rolled the muscles in his shoulders and yawned, casual as could be.

Kano folded his arms, boredom carved into the set of his mouth, cold blue eyes raised at the interruption. He cleared his throat loudly. "As I was saying," he said pointedly, and Razakh realised he'd tuned out the council entirely while in Celiana's mind.

"The darkness has power beyond all present here, except perhaps our newest wizard. His army is vast, the numbers limitless. What chance do we stand against him?"

Shara scoffed. "We've fought him before and won. It was just a taste of the horror to come, but if we stand together, we can win. With the mages and the elves using Magicka, with the might of the Diodonians and the Onyxonites at our back, we can dispense our forces tactfully."

No one appeared convinced.

"It will not be enough," Tiderion said coolly, a reproachful gleam in his eyes as he took in each of the Guardians, his mocking stare lingering on Ashalea and Shara most of all. "Even with our forces combined, it will never be enough to take on the darkness. Best we look after our own."

Shara glowered at him. "Careful, Tiderion, we don't all have pretty jewelled walls to hide behind or ships to sail away in. One might think you a coward."

"At least we have walls to guard us, unlike those shoddy spikes that encircle that cesspit you call Shadowvale."

"Tiderion." Nirandia's voice was low with warning.

The elven lord only sneered, sharpening the wicked, beautiful lines of his face. His next words dripped poison from a honeyed tongue. "I suppose I should be thankful, should the darkness take a few dishonourable thieves and assassins down. Less vermin to clutter the streets."

Silence ticked over for what felt like an eternity, and then chaos.

Shara and Flynn had their swords drawn, the latter leaping up and sliding across the table in a blink of an eye, but Tiderion was quicker. His Magicka uncoiled, lashing out at the twins and sending them sprawling into the adjacent wall. Tiderion's delegates stepped forward in one motion, one hand on their spears, shielding their king.

Enough was enough. Razakh pounced on the table and then dove clear over the heads of Tiderion's guards and right onto the king's chest. Tiderion crashed to the floor, arms pinned by Razakh's two giant paws. When the elf was helpless and Denavar had swept the surrounding guards aside like debris—a mere wave of his hand sending their weapons hurtling across the room—Razakh roared. He roared with the full might of a Diodonian, the cry so bloodcurdling, so primal, it travelled down every floor of the Academy and had Tiderion turning white as the snow falling outside.

"*Enough,*" he demanded, and a graveyard silence fell over the room. "*You can hide behind your walls and watch the world burn, or you can be the change that ushers in a new day. But we will fight, and should you flee then more will fall. At least have the dignity to meet your foe on the battlefield. And if we are to die, then do so with a sword in your hand and fury in your heart.*"

Razakh backed off, and Tiderion shook his tunic out with heated cheeks. The Diodonian turned and sat on his haunches. "*I stand with the Guardians. My tribe will stand with all of you. As we speak, the Klan makes its way through the mountain pass. We wield no weapons but that of tooth and claw and mind."* He gazed at Yavaar then. *"The past will never be forgotten, but perhaps we can learn to forgive the deeds of humans. We will stand by you. With you."*

It would be a long road for the Diodonians, but Razakh believed—genuinely believed—that there could be an accord once again between the two races. Humans would always be fickle creatures, but there were some—he looked at Shara, at Flynn, at Telilah—there would always be some that proved honesty, friendship and loyalty existed.

Yavaar was a fresh king, but something told Razakh he could be a great one. He was a man of few words thus far, seeking to listen and learn rather than demand he be heard. There was a quiet strength to him, a trueness, as though he had faced troubles of his own and come out a better man for it.

Razakh's words must have struck home, for even in the stillness that befell the council, Yavaar moved with grace, his every stride purposeful. He was clad in dove grey, the smooth, silky fabric cut to fit his slim figure, a velvet cape trimmed in black fur clasped at his neck with thin chains of black. The cape fluttered as the king halted before Razakh, and the royal kneeled before him, head bowed.

Gasps echoed around the room as his retinue gaped; his viziers clearly at a loss for what to say or do. Eventually, they echoed the king's actions and Razakh looked in awe as every human bar the Onyxonites knelt before him.

"What happened to you and yours is a crime that has stood the test of time. To see such an honourable, proud race be hunted and exterminated for being different—vastly superior in many ways—is a sorrow I will always carry. But I, Yavaar Grayden, King of Maynesgate, ruler of the human populace, vow to you that it shall not happen again. Should this happen under my rule, I swear to you, I will relinquish my throne under the eyes of our God and all Gods above."

"Majesty," one of the advisors cried out. His balding head shone like oils on a canvas, his pointed chin as harsh as his grating voice. "You can't—"

One look from Yavaar silenced the man immediately, and he continued, "I will stand with the Guardians, and with all Everosians to see this threat overcome. My people have suffered enough, it is time we rise."

Razakh peered at the man, his flames burning bright as the sun, his confidence restored. *"So stand, King Grayden, and rise with us against the darkness."* Razakh dipped his head in respect before he lifted his quicksilver eyes. *"Let us rise together ... and watch them burn."*

A boom rattled the room, and Razakh quickly realised it was Kano. *Laughing.* The dwarf slapped his meaty hands to his chest, the shock of white-blond that crowned his head and fell in forked braids down his chest jiggling as he shook his head in glee. "I'll be damned. Humans and Diodonians working together, and what next? Dwarves and elves, no less."

Razakh cocked a head, the gesture asking what he did not voice. Kano nodded, his body still shuddering with amusement. "Oh, aye, young Diodonian. The dwarves wouldn't miss a chance to show our mettle. We shall bring the mountains down with our war song, and our hammers and shields shall clash as thunder in the heavens. This shall be one for the pages."

Oh yes. Razakh liked this one. He wondered how deep that courage ran or if his words were pure swagger. But, by the steely glint to his eye, Razakh was inclined to agree the dwarves would prove most useful in battle. Which left the Onyxonites, Tiderion, and Celiana.

Naturally, Flynn stepped forward, his crooked grin the twin to Shara's smirk, and fisted a hand over his heart as he looked at the Guardians in turn. "Shadowvale shall answer your call." He winked at Ashalea for good measure, and she grinned wolfishly right back.

Tiderion, still disgruntled from being knocked on his ass by Razakh, straightened his tunic and rolled his shoulders. "Windarion shall honour the alliance," he growled, albeit begrudgingly. As if that signalled the end of the meeting, he stalked out the door, his retinue of elves clambering after him.

Shara winked at Razakh knowingly. A proud elf such as he would not allow his ego to be bruised, and Razakh realised she'd been baiting him all along. It seemed that small slice earlier was really deep enough to sever, to wound. "*You knew he would bite,*" Razakh whispered, his words directed only to her.

She picked at her nails, a blank expression on her face. "*I'm an assassin, Razakh,*" she thought, knowing he'd pick up on the comeback. "*I always go for the kill.*"

He shook his head in wonder. "*Incorrigible snake.*"

Her response was full of mirth. "*Oh saintly mutt of mutts.*"

Razakh snorted, startling a few of the nearby diplomats. They edged subtly away, and he swished his enflamed tail teasingly, much to their alarm. But, still connected to Shara's mind, he quickly realised her body language was tense, her mind sharp.

His eyes darted to hers, only to find them fixed on Ashalea. The silver-haired elf was staring at her mother. Celiana was the last one, he realised. The last one to accept an alliance and declare her forces on the offensive against the darkness. Against her son.

He hoped his performance earlier had been enough. Razakh bared his teeth as he saw the strain in Ashalea's expression—the worried line of her mouth, the nose scrunched ever so slightly,

Denavar's hands atop her own the only thing halting her fidgeting.

"Well?" she blurted out, the question clearly directed at Celiana, whose shoulders were curved inward, her posture small and helpless as a mouse. Nirandia and Kano observed, both wisely staying quiet—the dwarf's eyes cold and calculating, arms once again folded against his chest, as if daring her to say no.

"I—" Celiana looked nervously around the room, and Razakh noted the white-knuckled fingers clenching, opening and closing around the folds of her dress. "I can't," she declared hurriedly, and bolted from the room, leaving everyone stunned in her wake.

Razakh would never forget the look on Ashalea's face, for he remembered what it was to feel that way. Abandoned. Helpless. Alone. Only, when his mother died, he had not blamed her, of course. She had been taken against her will, killed for reasons he had not fully understood as a pup. But his father ... Razgeir had left for a greater purpose. To protect the tribe, to ensure Razakh's survival via a different means—a noble goal. He had learned that over time and throughout maturity.

But Celiana? She had no greater calling. Nothing holding her back but fear. Razakh noted how Ashalea's hands clutched at Denavar, her chest heaving with quickening breaths. But it was the expression on her bloodless, crestfallen face that cracked Razakh's iron heart.

For this hurt would not be mended, and her broken soul would fracture just a little more.

Bitter Disappointment

ASHALEA

S HE BURST INTO HER ROOM, keeping it together only until she stepped through that door, slamming the wood closed behind her. That's when the tears came. They burned as they fell hotly upon her clammy skin, cleaving paths of salt-ridden despair down her cheeks.

Celiana had abandoned her again. Her mother, lost for so long, had deserted her in their greatest hour of need. As every other realm, every other race had pledged their allegiance, it was her mother that had failed her. Failed all of them.

Ashalea stalked in circles, too furious to pass out in bed, too exhausted to do more than rage and cry. What a cruel joke, to find that which was lost, only to learn they were not worth finding at all. She had thought her mother dead, and upon realising that she was yet flesh and blood, a piece of her heart had sung, however briefly.

Her sorrow at losing Wezlan had taken up too much space to fully embrace the revelation that someone who was meant to love her, someone who was a part of her in blood and family name, lived. But now ... now it seemed a mockery. A disgrace that her adoptive parents—who had been so much more to Ashalea than this woman ever would—lay dead and gone. That they had been killed for playing house just because they dared to love her; dared to love the person who was sister to a foul, evil, hideous perversion of an elf.

Hands balling into fists, body shaking, her Magicka threatened to spill out of her pores and level the furniture. Sobbing, she collapsed, knees thudding to the polished floorboards, nails biting so deep into her palms that angry red welts formed in half-moons, raw as her bleeding heart.

Ashalea didn't hear the soft click of the door as it opened and shut, didn't hear the soft steps padding towards her or feel the sturdy hands as they gently directed her to the bed. Silently, he peeled away her shirt to reveal Ashalea's naked torso, bare as her soul.

Denavar rubbed his hands together until they glowed with blue light, directing its energy over her spine. Down through the muscles and tendons, his Magicka easing the stiffness and cooling her anger. Eventually, the pain muted to a dull throbbing, and her tears ceased their endless torrent.

He kissed the back of her neck before gently replacing her shirt and wrapping his arms around her, cradling her from the world. He held her for a long time before asking, "Do you need to talk about it?"

"I thought it would mean something, to have her in my life again," she said quietly. "I thought seeing me alive—seeing me fight—would give her a reason to rally. Mostly, I thought maybe I'd be able to rely on her, have her at my side as we faced the darkness."

Denavar shifted so he could look her in the eyes. He was silent for a moment, contemplative. "Grief affects us all in different ways. Your mother, she chose to shut out all the good, shield herself from the bad, and in doing so built walls around her that ensured she gave up on life altogether. She hides behind those walls as if they might guard her from reality. I think"—he sighed, running a hand through his hair—"she retreated so far into herself that she's forgotten how to live. What's worth fighting for. Until she learns to look in the mirror and accept what she sees there I'm not sure she will really see anyone else. Even you."

Ashalea's eyes welled at the wisdom in his words, even as they stung, and it still felt like her mother had utterly given up. "She doesn't love me," she said.

Denavar brushed the curling strands of silver from her face. "She does. Deep down I know she does, but that love leaves her vulnerable and open to pain. She will shield herself from it, but I think, given time, she will understand what that vulnerability means and embrace it."

Ashalea let out a bitter snort. "If we don't all die first."

He smiled gently. "Aye, that would be a good start."

She puffed out a shaky breath, crossing her legs and planting her face between her hands. "So everyone is on board but The Meadows. Honestly, I'm surprised we even made it to this point."

"The other rulers know the price of this war, but they would pay a higher cost if they sought to stand against the darkness alone. It's in their best interests to band together—some might even profit from it in some ways."

Ashalea raised a brow. "You're referring to Yavaar."

Denavar nodded solemnly. "His city took a huge blow.

Commerce will be difficult to maintain until the surrounding farmlands bring new seed in the spring, and the dockyards have been rebuilt. As the centre of trade, it is a hit to all our races, but none so much as the humans. The king will need provisions, perhaps even to relocate much of the populace if they're going to survive the winter."

She pursed her lips. "The Meadows has ample room to house them this season. I shall speak to my mother about it. Hopefully, she will bend to this, at least."

Soft, soothing strokes resumed up her spine, quenching that anger before it began boiling in her blood. He leaned in close before nipping at her ear. "One step at a time, my love. One step at a time."

18

A Bond Restored

SHARA

ER BLADE SANG AS IT MET FLYNN'S SWORD, the block sending reverberations shaking up her arm. She clenched her teeth, thrusting forward as they met again and again. Her brother's annoying grin—the twin to one she so often wore herself—only incensed her further, and she struck venomously.

"Your emotions are getting the best of you," he taunted as he shifted, his boots a flurry of movement as he danced to the rhythm of war.

"Then my sword shall laugh with me when I defeat you," she gritted out with a grin.

Sweat poured down their faces, the Academy's training room slippery with their perspiration. They had been sparring for over an hour, releasing some pent-up energy gathered from tedious talks with the other races.

Flynn gazed at her, his face the picture of calm, his body betraying nothing ... at least not to a stranger. But Shara knew his tells as only a twin could. His fingers twitched on his free hand, and she pounced, grinning madly.

She swiped his legs out from beneath him with one boot, and he toppled to the ground, somehow still graceful as a bird as he landed on his back and vaulted to his feet with the momentum.

"Don't cheat a cheater," he purred, and she almost yelped as three shurikens came tearing through the air towards her face, the last of them slicing off the smallest lock of hair as she vaulted sideways.

She stood there, panting, eyes narrowed as she spied the raven hair on the floor. When she glanced at Flynn, he was backing away, like cornered prey. "You do not mess with the hair," she spat.

She sent an arc of her own shurikens before she was upon him, sword swinging. Her blade scraped along the sharp metal of Flynn's sword, and she grunted as he twisted his rapier, the hilt catching the tip of her blade. It flew from her grip and he thwacked her on the ass with the flat of the sword.

"That's for being so careless," he grinned triumphantly.

Shara's nostrils flared as she somersaulted, twisting so her boot hit him square on the nose. He flew to the ground, his body shifting into a plank as he landed, as he prepared to rise. Her dagger was upon his throat in an instant.

"Not so fast," she whispered, tapping the flat of it against the exposed skin.

He laughed, raising one hand in defeat. "I submit. In honour of your vanity."

She smirked as she offered him a hand, pulling him up with a grunt. "How noble of you."

He draped an arm around her shoulder and tousled her hair, and the action was so casual, so *normal*, that after a moment she realised that she hadn't recoiled. Hadn't cringed from his touch or spiralled into memories of a monster of a man who had tortured and abused her at another's bidding.

Flynn seemed to realise where her thoughts had gone, for he gently lifted his arm, backing away a step. "I can't apologise enough for causing this ... this rift between us. What was done in the past, what he made me do—"

"Stop. Just stop," she said, stepping forward to place a hand on his shoulder. "I don't think I ever said it before, and it's well past overdue but I don't blame you for what happened. You were a pawn, a body bent to another's will. I can't fault you for that. I won't."

Flynn swallowed; his eyes soft as a deer's as he glanced at her. "I should have tried harder."

She shook her head, tears in her eyes as she looked at her twin. Her other half. "Don't tread down that road, Flynn. It's time to let go. We both need to let go."

He nodded, exhaling a shuddering breath. "In shadows we dwell, in darkness we die," he whispered, reciting the Onyxonite oath.

Shara smiled sadly. "How true that turned out to be. But I am one with the shadows no more, Flynn. I want to live in light, I want to find joy and love. I want to want things for myself. Just for me ... as a free woman."

"Then I hope you find every happiness beyond Shadowvale. You deserve the world."

"I'll settle for a fraction of it."

His answering smile was beaming, and he jerked his head

behind her. She turned, swivelling to find Telilah waiting quietly at the room's entrance, looking like a lost puppy as she shifted between two feet.

"Don't keep your fraction waiting too long," he said with a wink, and then he was striding away.

Shara smiled to herself, feeling a weight lift from her shoulders, her heart feeling freer than it had for some time. It had been horrible, to feel so untethered to her brother, to feel like he was worlds away even when right beside her. And this talk ... she had needed it.

But there was one thing left to say. "Flynn," she called.

He ran a hand through his brown hair as he glanced back at her, eyes questioning.

"I forgive you."

A tear tracked down Flynn's face as he smiled, and he walked out of the room with shoulders held high. A weight lifted ... and a bond restored.

Shara's heart soared, her soul singing with happiness at the progress she'd made with Flynn. It finally felt like she was on the path to really fixing things with her brother, to restoring balance to their relationship. He was her twin, after all, and she loved him dearly ... even if her family had an odd way of showing such emotion.

Giddy, and still elevated with adrenaline, she slowly turned to face the woman waiting across the hall.

"Hey," Telilah said coyly, making her way across the floor.

"Hey yourself," Shara said with a smile. "What brings you to these sacred halls?"

Telilah laughed. "Only you would refer to the training room as such."

Shara stretched her arms above her head, relishing the groan of her muscles, still feeling pumped from both the fight and her conversation with Flynn. "Call me a worshipper of weapons, if you will," she smirked.

Telilah shrugged. "I pray only to the living."

"Not the gods?" Shara raised a brow.

Telilah shook her head, a devious smile upon her lips, skirts gliding across the floor as she stepped into Shara's space. "I'd rather give thanks to more physical forms. Mortal ones I can touch, smell, taste," she crooned.

Shara's skin shivered as the minstrel reached a hand up her arm, across her collarbone, between her breasts. The implication set her flesh prickling, the awareness that they were all too alone in this room firing through her.

"And how might one pray to said mortals?" Shara breathed.

"A reverent touch," Telilah whispered, palming Shara's groin, so near her core that heat instantly pooled there. "A soft embrace," she continued, her hand splaying over one breast before the other. "A simple kiss," she said finally.

Their lips collided before Shara could blink. Telilah's jasmine and sandalwood scent was heady in her nose as she breathed all of her in, greedily claiming her lips, her tongue, her everything.

They kissed and kissed, forgetting the world, falling harder into each other's spell. Shara's hands clutched at Telilah's waist, slipping over sinful curves, before winding around her neck.

She didn't know how long they'd been there when they finally broke apart. It took all her willpower not to go beyond that kiss. A kiss that was anything but simple. Shara wanted so badly to take her somewhere dark and disappear for a while.

But what they had ... it meant more to her than sex. More than stolen kisses or secret meetings. She thought of what Flynn had

said about not keeping her fraction waiting. And maybe she was too chicken, maybe she wanted to wait to develop this further, but she didn't do all the wild things she imagined.

She simply held Telilah in her arms for a while.

And it was enough. For now it was enough.

Honest Work

Denavar

T HEY DIDN'T STOP TALKING. For two days they had awoken, met in the council chamber and discussed all that was to come, planning for the days ahead. And as necessary as it was, Denavar couldn't help but eyeball the clocks and the hourglasses, sand sprinkling lazily through the tube, as if every second didn't lead them closer to the war.

Renlock was a hive of activity and, aside from the council meetings, he had been all but locked away in his study, writing inventories, assessing stocks, and attending to his duties as the apparent new ruler of the Academy. He wondered what Wezlan would think, to know Denavar was now running the place.

Sighing, he took a swig of cocoa from his mug, feeling the warmth spread in his stomach, enjoying a quiet moment, just for a minute.

His study door banged open, and he cursed under his breath, nearly spilling the cocoa over his lap.

"If I have to deal with Tiderion for another moment there's going to be blood on these walls," Shara barked, planting her hands on his desk with a huff.

He raised a brow, noting the red cheeks, steam practically fuming from her flared nostrils. She swiped a mound of papers from the wooden surface, the sheets fluttering to the floorboards.

"Feel better?"

She breathed deep before stalking to the settee and plonking down. "Yes. I do," she sighed.

He leaned back in amusement, propping his boots on the free space. "Good," he said. "I'd had enough of paperwork anyway."

Shara glanced at the discarded papers before throwing an apologetic smile his way. "I'm sorry, I know you have bigger things to worry about than my troubles. I just need to get out of here, do something worthwhile. This place"—she swallowed, fingers fidgeting in her lap—"I don't enjoy being here again. It brings back bad memories."

He understood. Renlock had been stained by battle—quite literally on the lower levels—and the evidence of those deaths showed in the halls just a little quieter than before, in the families reduced by ones and twos. Especially those who had lost children.

But Shara had died at the hands of Crinos himself. She would still be dead if not for Ashalea. It had been a miracle what she had done, bringing Shara back to life. He still didn't know how it was possible—whether it was the will of the Gods, the Magicka that lay beneath the Academy, or simply a power awoken by sheer stubbornness.

"It's a good thing then, that you'll be leaving these halls

tomorrow."

Her head snapped up in surprise, amber eyes narrowing. "You're serious? To find the final Guardian? About time," she grumbled.

"I know," he replied. "Time is running out, but the dwarves are headed home tomorrow. You, Ashalea, and Razakh shall accompany Kano as his guests, and while you're there, you will look for the Guardian."

She pouted. "You're not coming with us?"

He wanted to. Gods did he want to. But ...

"I can't," he said begrudgingly. "With the other embassies still here and the mages needing direction, I must stay. We will need to continue meeting, get the wheels turning and soldiers on the front."

Shara winced. "You're got your work cut out for you. But I would trust no one else. You're a good card to have, Denavar. A jack of all trades. Better you than I when it comes to politics."

He cocked his head, sharing a crooked grin with his friend. "I think I'd rather fight with a sword in hand. At least it's honest work."

The Dwarven Stronghold

SHARA

SHE HAD NOT EXPECTED THE MAELSTROM that was the Kingsgareth Mountains. Or, what raged around its steep slopes at least. The snow whipped and whirled around them as they teleported to the gated walls at the base of the great dwarven city. The namesake of the range loomed above, its great jagged edges and monstrous peak invisible against the whitewashed sky.

Her amber eyes squinted against the ground, burning as she peered around her, cheeks stinging with the threat of frostbite should they linger. Grumbling, she shifted her rucksack higher over a shoulder, bundling her fur-lined cloak tighter against her chest. The fingerless leather gloves that clad her hands did little to staunch the icy wind as it shrieked, ripping at her clothing.

In spring, she had been informed earlier by an unusually cheery

Kano, the peaks were a sight most beautiful. Roiling green teeth that split the sky, tears of water trickling down their faces and mists that formed rainbows in every which way. In certain spots where the sun hit just right, wildflowers would blossom, finding root in cracks and fissures, rosy pinks and whites and blood-red petals sprouting, totally oblivious to the world.

She supposed that did sound rather nice, but as her nose silently screeched in protest at the biting wind, the images swept away, and she huffed in irritation. Even Ashalea's teeth clattered, the she-elf having begrudgingly taken a fur cloak from the dwarven entourage earlier given that she owned nothing suitable for the wild weather here.

Denavar pulled her closer, and even the wizard looked ruffled by the endless snow. His eyes travelled the ascending path that would lead them to the giant doors guarding the city nestled within the mountain itself. His handsome face was strained, jaw clenched, the usual sparkling blue of his eyes now a sombre grey. Shara suspected that had less to do with the cold and more that he would not be staying, leaving his better half to the mercy of the other Guardians.

Indeed, out of the four of them, Razakh was the only one with bright eyes, his golden coat rippling as he bounded through the snow. *Gleefully*, Shara realised with a smirk. Like a puppy he sprang about, tongue lolling as he inhaled the cool air, the fire on his back dancing with elation.

The dwarves watched him with bemused expressions, knowing that this great, floundering beast could tear their heads off in seconds. But here he was, rolling in the snow like a great, big idiot, fangs bared with pure joy.

She shook her head. "Do try to rein in that happiness, Razakh," she huffed. "You're ruining my bad mood." His answering grin was a mess of skin, teeth and tongue, and she chuckled under her breath.

Kano, the last to come through Denavar's portal, strolled up beside her, a huge grin on his usually gruff face. His hair, white as the winter world around him, tinkled slightly as the beads that clamped his numerous braids clanged together in the wind. But his eyes were upon that mountain before them, and he gestured with one sweeping, meaty arm. "Home."

Not just the city underground, but the roaring landscape, the ruggedness, the freedom of it all. Untouched beauty ravaged only by the harshness of the seasons—the bite of wind and water, and the animals that roamed its peaks and troughs. And as he stood there, eyes glacial, smile proud, he looked every inch a dwarven king of old. A wrothful god, who would bow to nothing and no one but the people he protected and the great mountains he ruled under.

He clapped a hand on Shara's back as she looked at Kingsgareth with a new appreciation, seeing as if through his eyes, and he winked at her knowingly. Her heart thawed just a little, like the first signs of spring on a frozen lake.

She squared her shoulders, not just against the bitter cold, but against what lay ahead. The tasks to come and all they would face. Kano, stout as his legs were—however proportionate to his short stature—ploughed through the snow in thick socks and metal-toed boots with jagged bottoms to make trekking through the thick powder easier.

His retinue followed their king; axes, broadswords, hatchets and hunting knives all clacking in their sheaths or against the rounded metal shields strapped to their backs. Shara grinned. Certainly not weapons she'd opt for normally—and certainly not worth hauling to an allied meeting—but she had to respect their enthusiasm. It was always better to be prepared, even if a few of them could be seen shuffling awkwardly in the snow under all that weight.

Denavar and Ashalea came to stand before her, Razakh slinking towards their semi-circle. "This is where I leave you," the wizard said, a grim smile on his face.

Ashalea pouted. "You're not going to stay just one night?"

"I am needed back at Renlock. There is much to do and apparently I've been lumbered with the responsibility of seeing it done." He frowned, as if the idea of roosting at that nest was appalling.

"Poor wizard," Shara crooned. "All powerful but left to clean up the messes. Good luck with that."

He elbowed her in the ribs. "Try not to make any new ones while I'm not around?"

She threw up her hands. "I'll be on my best behaviour."

Razakh's snort suggested he doubted that very much and Shara sent him a withering stare, though it was more of a half-hearted squint in the white glare.

Denavar merely grinned before pulling his girl in close, sharing an overly intimate kiss with Ashalea before them. Shara glanced at Razakh and rolled her eyes, the Diodonian's tail flicking with agitation.

"*Your scents are disturbing the fresh air,*" he said matter-of-factly.

"Oookaay," Ashalea said, untangling herself from Denavar, but she grinned wolfishly at the elf. "Remind me to send him for a walk when we're alone again?"

Razakh growled, lifting a paw as if to bat them apart. Ashalea clucked her lips, leaning in close to squeeze Denavar one final time. "I'll see you soon," he said, turning as he conjured a portal—a flurry of mages going about their business visible through the crackling window. But he looked back at them all and smiled, his eyes landing on Ashalea once again.

The love conveyed through that gaze was enough to melt the very snow-caps from the mountains. "I love you," he whispered to her.

Then he was gone.

The three of them stood awkwardly. His absence was immediately strange, as if pulling apart left a little hole. Shara was certain she wasn't the only one who felt that way, and she wondered if perhaps it was because of the Guardianship they shared. The duty that somehow bound them, maybe in a more profound and Magickal way than she'd realised.

"It's possible that we Guardians are tied together on a deeper level, through the will of the Magicka or the ancient forest itself," Razakh mused, obviously having tuned into her thoughts. She scowled at his uninvited presence.

"Busybody," she retorted.

He only nuzzled his golden head against her leg—like a common housecat does when expecting dinner. She trailed a hand through his fur absentmindedly, but something inside warmed a little at his words. To think they'd always be connected, like an invisible string tethered them to each other. Her friends. Her *family*.

"Come," Razakh said, taking point at the head of their trio. *"The family is yet to grow by one."*

For one more Guardian lived within that mountain. One more piece to their puzzle. She took Ashalea's slender hand, the she-elf suddenly withdrawn now that Denavar was gone. And, setting her jaw, they took the first steps that would change the course of their future.

◆ ● ◆

Kingsgareth was more wonderful than she ever could have imagined. After being underground in the hidden passage back in the Diodon Mountains—and nearly getting mauled by a giant centipede creature—Shara had expected the worst of the underground city.

She had felt claustrophobic then. Cold, small, helpless. But this ... this was the very opposite of that horrible place. After stepping into the great cavern, warmth immediately hit her. Warmth—and light.

A dome stretched overhead, the very mountain itself smooth like alabaster. A mural depicting the dwarven history sprawling in bright splashes of reds and golds and vibrant hues every colour of those spring rainbows. Gilded chandeliers dotted the great hall; candle-less but somehow Magicked so eternal fire burned bright and inviting.

Balconies encircled the room, jutting out in perfect increments, broken only by a myriad of winding stairwells and dwellings. Even underground, the dwarves were elevated in their homes. Rich velvet drapes in sapphires, emeralds and amethysts adorned both dwarven homes and various winding streets in the marketplace, and Shara breathed in awe.

It was colour and light and richness; bustling streets carved into the rock and nestled amongst columns of unyielding stone. The pillars were gilded with crawling veins of gold and silver, minerals and gems encrusted in the stone.

And the people smiled and laughed and carried on with their day. The dwarves—so often described as gruff and stubborn and hot-headed—all working together in tandem, all a living, breathing tapestry of life. A good life. Children ran through the cavern, and tradesmen of all varieties lumbered about with some of them carrying frames and woods and metals of impossible weight.

The clanging of metal echoed deeper underground; the sounds of miners hard at work unearthing things of great beauty—priceless and yet worth fortunes untold. But her wandering eyes halted as her attention snagged on the smell.

Lamb roasted on spits. Herbs and garlic scented the air, with the juices of other meats wafting towards her. A medley of vegetables curled like a promise up her nose, and spices akin to those used in Shadowvale had her stomach growling and her mouth suddenly salivating.

"It's ... it's—" she sputtered, for once at a loss for words as she devoured the sights and smells and gloriousness of it all. Ashalea nodded mutely by her side, her own emerald eyes wide. Even Razakh's snout was upturned in the direction of food, his muzzle flaring at the barrage of scents.

"It's home," Kano said again, his grin broad and face relaxed. She wondered if she had imagined him ever appearing otherwise. Indeed, the stern, somewhat grumpy dwarf was like a different person upon stepping into this hidden wonder. His delegates had ambled into the cavern without a word, no doubt eager to find loved ones or return to their various duties.

But as soon as they had departed, a group of servants appeared, taking Shara and Ashalea's possessions wordlessly, their beards cropped short, their hands nimble and practiced. She raised a brow at Kano, who boomed a laugh. "You'll be reunited with your arsenal later, but for now ..."—those stark blue eyes twinkled—"come with me."

Kano began weaving through the masses, his people bowing and smiling or offering warm tidings and welcomes. He politely returned every smile, even knowing many of the dwarves' names and enquiring about their families or their health.

Shara glanced sidelong at Ashalea, but her friend was staring intently at Kano—studying him, watching the ease of which he met with his people. Still set apart as a king, still granted the respect his station commands, but it was obvious they weren't just his subjects—people he lorded over. No, these were a people with whom he had connected, shared stories and built the city.

The strain in her eyes and the set of Ashalea's jaw suggested she was thinking much the same thing and, no doubt, comparing that to the reign of her own mother. And it wasn't that the Moonglade Meadows was in any way inferior to this city. It was vastly different, yes, and perhaps not teeming with light and life, but it was more a division among the people.

Where Kingsgareth City was a bright beacon that offered endless opportunities, The Meadows was a cold, dark thing that slumbered quietly as if waiting to wake up. As if begging its ruler to unite its citizens and let life bloom again. Celiana had withdrawn so far into herself that she had abandoned her people, even while walking among them.

Shara leaned over and squeezed Ashalea's hand, stopping her from falling too far into the murky waters of her mind. A pretty smile—if a little restrained—bounced back, and the pair followed Kano together. Razakh was up ahead, presumably convening with the king.

"I'm sorry for everything I said," Shara whispered quietly while they walked, and Ashalea squeezed her hand back tighter.

"As am I. I wish things could be different," the elf said softly. Shara couldn't help but share the sentiment, even if they both knew it couldn't be.

Shara chewed her lip. "I was wrong for bringing Wezlan into our fight. I know I've a temper, but I went too far. I was angry and wanted to hurt someone, when really that's the last thing I want to do to you. And I lied. I'm not one of your people, nor an elf, but if I had to choose someone to follow, a queen to rule fairly, it would be you."

Ashalea's brows rose, but she smiled gently, and her shoulders seemed to sag with relief. "You will always have a place in my court," she said. "Always."

And that was that. The tension Shara had been holding melted from her bones, and she breathed deeply. Some bonds were too important not to mend, and it was a weight off her own back to now be able to focus only on their mission instead of emotions and hurt feelings.

As they ascended a spiralling staircase Shara could only stare in awe, each new vantage point allowing her a better view of the city. Once high enough, she could see forges burning brightly down the long cavern, their metal jaws opening and closing, hammers on anvils clanging away. If she squinted, she could just make out an armoury adjacent to the forges, lined with all manner of glittering jewels. Ones she'd much rather wear than those that clasped around necklines or wrists.

Eventually, their seemingly endless trek up winding stairwells and through curving passageways led them to another hall—this one designed more for comfort than the decadent cavern that sprawled below. But the stately chamber was still elegant and refined—a place for welcomed guests to retire like any humble being of the earth, able to shed their royal skins and heavy mantles of responsibility.

Kano shrugged off his fur cloak, throwing it unceremoniously on an adjacent chaise of crimson and gold brocade, its golden clawed feet peeking out beneath. The room was full of creature comforts; a fireplace crackled front and centre, embers spitting merrily on the dry wood, and art in gold and bronze frames speckled the walls, dwarven faces—bearded all—peering out from within. Dark cherry wood gleamed from every surface. Throws and carpets and silk lampshades of reds, maroons, golds and soft beiges dotted the floor.

The dwarf king slumped on the chaise; his arms once more folded against his chest as he surveyed his three guests. A servant strolled into the room right on cue, long flaxen hair tied in a complicated braid from the crown of her head right down to her waist. She curtsied, wearing a simple white gown and corset, eyes of grey seas drinking them in.

Shara was shocked to see how slender the female dwarf was. Perhaps not the finest of features and certainly packing some muscle, but pretty, nonetheless.

Kano smirked, gesturing at the lady. "Surprised? Our females are not bearded beasts as those damnable elves might suggest." He looked to Ashalea at that, but she merely raised a brow in amusement. The female only blushed, her gaze landing anywhere but the king. Satisfied, he continued, "This is Ehren, she's charged with the staff and upkeep of the royal wing. A walking planner for myself too, she would say."

"It is an honour," Ehren said, and Shara wondered how much she knew about them and the purpose of their visit. But the dwarf only continued, "I will show you to your rooms and you may freshen up. Dinner will be served at sundown. In the meantime, I hope you are comfortable. Please call for me if you need anything."

With that, she turned on a heel and strode down the adjacent corridor. Shara turned back to Kano, shuffling awkwardly. "My ... err ... My King," she said, bowing.

He grunted, waving his hand errantly. "Kano is fine and one butchered bow is enough, girl."

Razakh hummed in delight, tail swishing in amusement, and Ashalea bit back on her laugh, fighting to stay poised. Shara might have strangled them both, but she merely nodded and stalked stiffly after Ehren. The king's laughter followed her steps.

Ehren was waiting outside two doors of mahogany, their handles sculpted to appear as snarling wolves. She expected the dwarves would indeed be equally fearsome should they be crossed or threatened. Ehren gestured with a slender, calloused hand and Shara spied new blisters, raw and peeling.

Jerking her chin, she said, "You train with the warriors?"

The serving girl cocked a head, considering. "All dwarves have the right to bear arms in Kingsgareth, even servants and lesser merchants. Those who wish to may train as lads and lasses and are classed by skill until reaching an age where they may be picked for the king's army. A select few are occasionally picked by the arms master himself for tutelage. Rare, but over the years there has been a few dwarves to merit their mark in the history of our people—of battles waged and wars won."

"I'm impressed," Shara said. "How many dwarves take up this training on average?"

Ehren's answering grin was devious. "All of them."

Razakh's eyes swirled with interest. "*Your masters must be quite the teachers if they train countless students.*"

"Their skills are unparalleled," Ehren said, chin high, "and losing is a rare thing indeed. We call them the king's wolf pack and there is one among them who has never lost in the ring."

Ashalea snorted—actually snorted—and Ehren looked to the she-elf with raised brows. "Oh, you think you can beat our master dwarves?"

Shara grinned. "Screw washing up. When do we start?"

A Lesson in Humility

ASHALEA

T HE THREE OF THEM STOOD BEFORE THE YAWNING JAWS of Kingsgareth Mountain, facing out towards the surrounding peaks. The surrounding mountains were smaller, almost as if bowing down before their king. The landing was covered in a white blanket, though somewhat protected by the curving roof of the mountain's natural hollow. Beyond, the wind howled, shredding all in its path, and snow dumped down from the heavens, the Gods showing little regard for their denizens below.

It was blistering cold, and bundled as they were, Ashalea felt the harsh bite of winter as it dug sharp claws into her skin. The dwarves, on the other hand, looked unbothered by the fact, utterly used to the savagery of the season in their homeland. Some even seemed to revel in its harshness as they trained.

For this pocket of the mountain was their arena. A place to test both strength and endurance of the body and mind. Indeed, the ringing of metal tolled around her as dwarves clashed with swords and axes and heavy shields beyond the slight reprieve of the cave mouth and out in the wild weather. She swallowed at the sheer drop down the mountain; there were no fences, gates, Magickal wards or anything of the like preventing them from death by error or foe.

On her left, Ashalea saw row upon row of wooden dummies of varying sizes—some stout, others tall and slender. Children thwacked equally wooden blades on those, angling their swords, thrusting again and again under the watchful eye and barked orders of a squat dwarf. Beneath the snow-crusted beard his hair was ember red, styled like a mohawk, and he reminded Ashalea of a rooster with ruffled feathers. A master, if she wasn't mistaken, given the cunning eyes and sharp tongue of a teacher who wasted no time.

To her right, a group of young adults trained in hand-to-hand combat, and Ashalea noted the pairings were divided equally between boys and girls, with some of the smaller fighters versing opponents of brute strength and bunched muscles. Not exactly a fair fight but ...

Her thoughts must have been clear enough because Ehren leaned in close and whispered, "Keep watching."

Ashalea's eyes snagged on one pair in particular; a short boy—short even for a dwarf—mousey and timid and yet to grow into muscle, paired with a hulking beast with meaty fists and arms so large it was almost obscene for his age. But she watched, eyes narrowed and locked on.

Meathead swung wide while Mousey ducked under his blow, landing a punch in the sensitive skin under the arm. But the bigger boy didn't even flinch, instead whirling to uppercut the little one's jaw.

The boy went flying and Ashalea cringed at the blow, eggplant purple already spreading along his cheek as he landed in a pillow of snow. She was surprised to see him jump up almost instantly, his only reaction to the hit being to spit blood out and shake his head, as if he knew he could do better. He resumed circling his opponent. The little one was fast, maybe just fast enough. He dashed under Meathead's wide swings; the bigger boy slower as he put all his weight into his punches. But everywhere his fist flew, the Mouse ducked and twisted, dancing just out of range, jabbing with sharp punches, wearing his foe down.

His punches were careful, precise, and in three more hits he had the match. A palm to the ear, a jab to the throat, and the arm of the brute pinned up and behind his back at a threatening angle. Spluttering, a vein bulging on his red face, the big boy slapped the snow three times, signalling his defeat.

Ashalea saw pride flicker for the most fleeting of moments, and her heart sang for the little guy, but not two seconds later the boy fell to his knees, agony written on his face as the backs of his legs were beaten by a sharp stick of black metal.

Its bearer frowned down at the boy, pale as the snow, as stern as a winter's day. Lips, blue from the cold sneered in a thin line, and eyes of shocking blue as piercing as any blade narrowed. His head was almost bald, the blond hair almost white, as if the man were stripped of life.

"A walking corpse would have more vigour than that guy," Shara joked.

"*Aye, like his very bones have been picked clean of joy,*" Razakh agreed.

Ashalea said nothing as the dwarf's eyes lifted, meeting hers. "Pride inflates ego and breeds indulgent brats," he said to the boy, even as his eyes drove into Ashalea's. "Pride leads to carelessness, which leaves one vulnerable to?"

The boy bowed his head. "To death, Master."

The master nodded once before jerking his head to the other boy standing silently, eyes downcast and hands clasped behind his back. "Continue."

"What a piece of work, eh?" Shara nudged Ashalea's ribs.

Ehren's grin was infectious. "You have no idea," she whispered, but her smile straightened as the master glided towards them, practically floating on graceful feet. Ehren cleared her throat, stood a little taller as the male stopped before them and peered up the length of his nose at Ashalea and Shara. Somehow, the effect made Ashalea feel small, despite his stature.

Whatever that icy glare searched for apparently found them lacking, for he sneered before turning towards Razakh. To the Diodonian he bowed his head, the only sign of respect he had or apparently would show.

"Master Erik, may I present Princess Ashalea Kindaris of the Moonglade Meadows, Shara Silvaren of Shadowvale, and Razakh of the Diodonian Klan, all Guardians of the Grove. They come in search of the next member of their order."

Erik stroked his chin, clean shaven unlike most of the other dwarves who wore their beards braided and forked. It somehow made him more threatening, highlighting the sharp planes of his face, the hardness to his body—wiry yet rippling with muscle. Based on his earlier demonstration of education, the male's heart was just as hard too.

If Erik was surprised at their purpose here, he didn't show it. Nor did he deign to recognise Ashalea's title, which she thought tasted a little sour given the situation with her mother. Instead he said, "You are here to fight the Masters."

Not quite a question, but Ashalea eyed him off boldly, mustering her best effort at haughtiness. "Aye. That's right. We challenge you, all of your pack, to a contest."

Erik sneered. "Little more than a peacock preening feathers. How I will delight in plucking them out."

Her nostrils flared as she took in his measure, feeling Shara bristling at one side, seeing Razakh's hackles rise on the other. Oh how she would enjoy knocking him down a peg. She smiled, no joy in the telling, and retorted, "'Tis only a male can be called as such, but I assure you, our claws go deep before we close the kill."

His eyes glinted, lips curving like a scimitar before the sweep. "We shall see."

⬥•●•⬥

The main ring was cleared not five minutes later, all other training either paused or moved to another location. Apparently whispers of this challenge had spread faster than diseases in a brothel, and an audience was already gathering on the outskirts.

The matches would be simple: victory to he or she who drew first blood, or if one opponent yielded. Magicka was against the rules, and it seemed the dwarves were loath to raise a blade against a Diodonian—apparently, the dwarves thought them as close to Gods as any mortal being on Everosia—so Razakh was forced to sit out, despite his grumblings and growls.

So close combat it would be with weapons of any choosing, and Ashalea was up first. She flexed her arms, rolling her neck until it popped and swaggering towards the weapons rack, knowing her confidence would irk Master Erik. *Let him watch, let the condescending bastard see me ace this challenge*, she thought.

Ashalea ran a finger over the handles of the various blades. The craftsmanship was exquisite, she'd give them that. The steel gleamed; polished to perfection, rounded edges, sharp points and spikes all sharpened to deadly precision. Runes were etched down blades and along the wicked curves of axes, an ancient language unknown to Ashalea. No doubt they depicted various dwarven Gods and odes to war and strength, as such values were highly praised among this race.

Two short swords glinted at her, their hilts wrapped in black leather, their make exceptional—as were the twin dragons etched down their side. She tested their weight in her hands. Near perfect, the only imbalance not in the blades but herself. Ashalea sighed, silently cursing herself for losing so much muscle mass and weight. She couldn't afford to lose her fitness or strength. Not with all at stake.

She snuck a peek over her shoulder at the awaiting master. He was stocky, with jet black hair dusted with pepper and chocolate brown eyes. And despite the muscle clearly bulking up his form, she was sure some of that considerable girth had softened on the insides—like a gooey caramel beneath a hard shell. But, most amusing of all, he was equipped with an axe, to which she almost rolled her eyes.

Predictable.

Yes, the short swords would do nicely, even if it had been some time since she'd practised with two blades. With a small nod, she turned, stalking towards the ring. Bets were being exchanged between the onlookers, and with no small amount of dismay she realised the majority were betting against her; the Everosian crown flashed on golden coins as they were flicked through the frigid air.

Pride bristled, her own hackles rising at the insult, but she would show them. Master or not, he was going down. With a wink at Shara and Razakh, she then bared her teeth at the dwarves, some of whom had the right idea to shuffle out of her way as she approached her opponent.

He squared off; beady eyes somewhat hawkish as he assessed her from head to toe. His eyes widened slightly at her choice of weapons and she grinned as he hefted his axe before him, gloved fingers tightening on the handle. "Master Helvhan, I am told?"

The master said nothing to her, the only appraisal that of the glance he gave her pointed ears. Oh yes, she was an elf and damn proud of it. Let her heritage be the last thing he sees before she flips him on his ass.

They bowed, as was respectful, and then Helvhan was off, a broad arc cleaving through the air. A strong start, nearly taking her head off had she not arched her back and slid along the snow. She swiped at his groin, letting him know she wasn't playing, but he deflected with ease. Ashalea had barely righted herself when his axe was singing through the air, whistling towards her midriff. He was strong—his strength superior to her own—but what she lacked in muscle, she made up for in speed.

She parried with blades crossed, slashing in a flurry of motion, teeth clenched as steel met steel and the dwarf grunted as he blocked all blows. But she feigned the last strike to his stomach, and he lowered his weapon to guard right as she jammed her elbow in his nose, an audible crunch sounding the horn of victory as she held the point of her blade to his throat.

A drop of crimson splattered onto the white canvas at their feet, and his eyes swivelled upward in astonishment, blinking as he realised—

"Your loss, *Master*," Ashalea said, the title hissing out her teeth in mockery. She bowed with dramatic flair, tilting her head to ensure he got a good look at her ears. She made sure to glance at Erik as she did so, graceful as a bird as she rose to her full height.

His narrowed eyes burned holes in her skin, and she could taste his disdain on the air. Ashalea almost felt sorry for Master Helvhan, for she suspected he—and the rest of the wolf pack—would be met with his wrath later. Once she and Shara swept the floor with them all.

The following battles passed at much the same speed. Shara had disarmed her first opponent in less than five seconds, to which it appeared the master might die of embarrassment. But the games went on; Ashalea's next fight as laughable as the first. Dwarves swore with reckless abandon as most lost large sums of money—oh so sure of their famed wolf pack who had thus far been as savage as a pack of pups. Those that kept on winning beamed, their eyes round as saucers as they gathered purses of gold.

It wasn't until Ashalea and Shara had won their first two matches wearing only a few small bruises and scratches post-fight that they stood before the final master. The wolf pack leader, the alpha of them all. Erik. His thin mouth puckered like he was sucking on sour lemons, his aloof stance making him appear large and threatening.

"Since our numbers are at odds, I will face you both in the final match," he drawled, words as icy as his demeanour.

She exchanged a glance with Shara, whose only tell of astonishment at this announcement being a slow blink. Hushed voices muttered around them, low and gravelly as the dwarves debated the odds.

Ashalea nudged Shara before she could mumble a rude retort.

There was no point arguing with him. This was his den, and they were his dinner. But wolves hunted in groups, and they had already culled the weak. Perhaps they could be cunning instead.

Where dwarves had been howling and booing and cheering from their positions encircling the ring, they were now still and silent as the dead. Ashalea stood side-by-side with her friend, staring down this master warrior. She glanced at Razakh, a beacon of red that refused to be swallowed by the snowfall and drowned by winds shrieking like banshees.

The Diodonian nodded just once to them both, his metallic eyes full of dark secrets and primal challenge. His paws twitched, almost shivering with anticipation, as if he too wanted to jump into the fight. And Ashalea knew he would have in a heartbeat, that the animal within that intelligent mind wanted to roar and rage and be released.

But not today. Erik's lips curled into a faint smile as she looked back at him, taunting her, daring her to let loose her own wicked claws and raging beast. And as he bent his head in a show of respect, he said for Ashalea alone, "Pride."

She could have sworn the boy he reprimanded earlier flinched at the word.

Ashalea launched, driving power into her right sword as she swung viciously, but to her shock he flicked aside her blow as if swatting a fly, launching a barrage of his own. He was fast, nimble for a dwarf and deadly with the broadsword he wielded—a severe oversight on her behalf.

Cursing, she rolled to the side, curling her body in tightly to avoid having her head smashed in by his gigantic blade. She had speed on her side—could dance all day if she had to—but Erik had a rhythm of his own. Despite the hindrance one would normally expect from his large weapon, it seemed more an extension of his arms, granting him range that Ashalea didn't have. His footwork was impeccable, his every move calculated.

She vaulted back onto her feet and Shara took her place, pressing the advantage with a sweeping staff, frost-licked at the ends. It whistled with blinding speed as the assassin twirled it around, her hands a flurry of movement as the baton moved as though on invisible wings.

Shara got a couple jabs in, the last smacking the dwarf soundly in the stomach, winding him and giving Ashalea her chance to jump back in. But Erik's eyes were furious, burning like the forges beneath the mountain—not filled with molten gold but blue fire. Apparently, taking a hit was an insult he couldn't bear.

With a grunt he struck his sword point first into the snow and, fast as an asp, caught the end of Shara's baton between his palms. She struggled, amber eyes wide as she fought to pull her weapon back, but he only tugged her closer and, realising her mistake too late, he hefted his mighty fist at her face. She crumpled to the ground, out cold and nose bloody.

Ashalea gaped at her friend, but Erik was wasting no time. He advanced like a battering ram—broadsword somehow already back in his hand—and she knew her barriers would fall. Her elven blood could only go so far. Her body was failing, her breaths little more than ragged gasps as the bitter cold burned her throat. Despite the sweat slicking her back and coating her hands, her fingers were numb, her hair so frozen it would snap off if pulled.

But still she gritted her teeth and lunged, avoiding the arcs of his broadsword, jumping over a wicked sweep that would have sliced clean through her legs. She struck hard and fast, her blades singing, but he parried every move until his riposte had her arms shaking as she crossed her blades above her heart, knees buckling under the savagery of his blow. Her body howled in protest, energy dwindling as their blades shivered and his broadsword began to push until it threatened to carve her like a roast pig with her own swords.

His face was calm, almost serene, and Ashalea knew then he was always going to win. Not because he was stronger or faster—stronger, yes—but because he was the better swordsman. A master who had earned his title through years of honing his technique, assessing his opponents, knowing the art of the sword and understanding it far more than Ashalea would likely ever know.

Her arms wobbled as the last of her strength gave out, but she refused to back down—to yield. He might be the victor, but he was still a condescending bastard. And just as the first of her blades tasted flesh, cutting through her layers and slashing a thin red stripe down her chest, he swiped her blades away and stood back.

They clattered on the snow, a small drop of blood trickling onto the white, and at last, Ashalea sank to her knees, her energy spent, muscles dancing a jig as they spasmed from the exertion.

Exhausted, she glanced at the still form of Shara a few feet away, crumpled and helpless, her raven hair swept over her face. At least one of the dwarves had thought to drape a cloak over her shoulders.

But she could ignore Erik's shadow no longer. It towered over her, and she realised how pathetic she must look. What a mockery of a warrior—of an elf for that matter. For all their speed and strength she had made a pitiful example of her race. As she lifted her head and glared into the stark face of Master Erik, she decided she could not care less. Not as he offered her a hand, clasping her own in one meaty grip and pulling her up.

Ashalea stared at him—not a trace of mockery or smugness on

his face. And that was the lesson. *Ego.* She had wanted to beat him, had scoffed at the skills of this race. Suddenly she felt ashamed, that perhaps the rivalry between elves and dwarves ran deeper than she realised, and perhaps she thought she could beat him because she was entitled to. How young and foolish and *wrong* she had been.

It reminded Ashalea of her brother. Because he was powerful, he thought all others inferior; that they should bend their knees and that he could conquer worlds simply because he wished it. His ego, once wounded when he had been denied the honour of becoming a wizard, had since inflated beyond reason. Like a chided boy, he had rampaged and wrought havoc in his tantrum—killed and maimed and done cruel and terrible things, so that he might carve out a throne of entitlement for himself.

She would not walk that path. She would not become that person. And so, even as her limbs screamed in pain at the movement, she bent the knee to Master Erik, bowed her head, and whispered, "Thank you."

And as she at last raised her emerald eyes to his of uncut ice, his answering smile was genuine. A lesson shared not among elf and dwarf, but among teacher and student.

Equals.

Hunting for Guardians

SHARA

"I MUST ADMIT, *it gave me some small satisfaction to see that serpent's smile wiped off your face,*" Razakh drawled from his perch by the fireplace, the Diodonian lounging like a prince lording over his subjects.

After their spectacular failure against the master, Shara and Ashalea had practically crawled to the bathing chamber to wallow in both misery—at least on her part—and within the heated waters. They were now all three sprawled around the fire, enjoying a lazy hour or two before they had to prepare for dinner.

Ashalea was surprisingly chipper after the fight despite her loss. Shara had hounded her about what happened, but nothing the elf had recounted should have given cause for happiness. The elf had only tapped her nose, as if it was some guarded secret.

Shara groaned, "Could you not tease a little later? My head is pounding and your barking in my head is making it worse."

Razakh merely swished his tail—flameless for now—in her face. She scrunched her nose as the fur tickled her cheeks and she immediately winced from the bruised flesh. She waved his tail away in annoyance. Ashalea watched them, eyes dancing with amusement even as tiredness filled her bones. The elf had certainly lost her edge in the arena, and Shara frowned as she surveyed her friend.

"Do I have to wring it out of you?" Ashalea asked with a smirk.

"I was just thinking, after our pitiful performance today, that we should double our training. You're a skinny slip of a thing, your strength is lacking, and your fitness is average. You should thank your stars you're an elf and have Goddess bloody gifts to fall back on."

"Tell her what you really think," Razakh snorted.

Ashalea shrugged. "She's not wrong. We might have beaten the other masters today, but I need to be better. I can't rely on my elven blood to keep me alive. We need to be better, individually and as a unit."

Shara pinned her with an indignant stare. "Excuse me, but I—"

"Your guard was down, and you were cocky. If we were in battle, you would be dead."

"It's true," Razakh added, trying to be helpful. *"Your technique was off, and you were slow."*

Before Shara could respond with a cutting remark, Ashalea said, "We should use this time to train with the masters. We might learn some useful skills, and training in a different climate would be an added benefit. I don't know about you, but snow is new ground for me. I've always known the woods and wide-open plains. We didn't get snowfall like this on the western coast, and I certainly never had cause to fight in it."

Shara crossed her arms, head tilted in thought. "Fine. I am used to harsh winters, but never for war. We should take every opportunity to hone our skills, and you"—she glanced at Razakh—"need to stop treating winter as a play pit and learn to use it. You also stick out like a sore thumb. Not great for stealth."

Razakh bared his teeth at her. *"I am a hunter. Stealth is what I do, but I would like to train amongst other species, get a feel for fighting alongside allies. It might help to observe the way you move and how you fight."*

"We're going to be fighting monsters, Razakh, not humans, elves or dwarves," Ashalea said.

"Monsters come in all shapes and sizes, my friend. You must be truly naive if you think men will not fight for the darkness."

Shara had considered that. The darkness would need men—beings whose intelligence outweighed primal hunger and a thirst for blood—if he hoped to expand his army and build structures and weapons and gather resources for the war.

A shiver crept down her spine as she recalled his other reasons for keeping men at his disposal. She had lived with a handful of horrible humans in the darkness's cells, back when she was imprisoned by Crinos and tortured by her brother. The darkness had experimented on those men, hoping to create a new kind of monster.

She could still recall their screaming ... would never forget the sounds of their terror morphing into something else altogether unhuman, their cries turning into guttural grunts and moans. Those sounds haunted her in her sleep, nightmares often placing her back in the darkness's prison, her body being carved by her brother, her days folding into one endless stream of agony and despair.

Sometimes her dreams were sound and smell and thought

instead of visions, and those guttural screams would echo and echo, the stench of metallic blood, urine and excrement permeating the air. Upon waking she would occasionally taste the blood on her tongue or reach for a phantom wound. Sometimes the horror would send her hurtling for the chamber pot to vomit her fear away or urge her to find a mirror so she might spy her scars, white and rippling in stark contrast to the olive skin of her back.

She hated those scars. Hated and admired them, for they were signs that she was alive; that she had survived and would keep on fighting.

And though Shara had never seen the result of those experiments—only knowing that bad people went in and worse things came out—the thought of those monsters terrified her. That horridness and evil in its most base form could be twisted into something worse. Creatures not born but made, and whatever they were, she knew deep down in her bones this war would be their playground. And, if they weren't stopped, could be the end of all things.

Shara breathed a shuddering sigh, that horrible thought jolting her out of the past and careening into the present. "What about the experiments?" she said quietly.

Her friends didn't answer immediately. Ashalea hugged her knees to her chest and Razakh growled. *"Abominations. We know nothing about them, and even the Diodonian scouts searching the sands of my homeland have found no evidence of them. We destroyed the darkness's base, but he could have set up elsewhere. Most of the Klan are on their way to Renlock as we speak, but a few Diodonians were left to guard the females, pups, and the weakest among us."*

Shara had forgotten about the bonds Diodonians shared—a kind of invisible thread linking the Diodonians' minds. Once connected, they remained tethered, allowing the beasts to communicate across great distances. A trait that would be most handy indeed for the oncoming war. Razakh had informed her the process was similar for that of other races too. Once a Diodonian linked to another's mind, it would leave a lingering imprint. Only the Magicka blurred here, making it impossible to speak across great distances unless a ritual had been performed.

A 'ceremony of power' Razakh had called it. A weaving of hearts and mind not to be taken lightly, for he had said it was personal for both subjects. But what better way to stay informed, to effectively be in two places at once? If the Guardians had that power, they could keep each other safe, provide instantaneous reports. Eagerness warred with uncertainty. Still ...

"I want to do the ceremony of power with you," she blurted.

Razakh blinked, and the flames on his tail almost guttered out. *"You would form that bond with me? I am honoured but ... why now?"*

Shara had rarely seen him so flustered, but the Diodonian looked uncertain as he chewed on her words. She shouldn't have cared but a small sliver of hurt fired through her. They were not lifelong friends, sure, but they were that. *Friends.* Something she'd never dreamed of having what felt like a lifetime ago. And yet, she had shared things with Razakh that the others had not heard—even Ashalea. There was a kinship between them, an understanding of pain and sorrow, a character flaw that they both shared.

He must have been listening, or perhaps her hesitation was written on her face, for he said in her mind only, *"It is not that I shy from the connection, but I do wonder if you might one day regret it. The bond is ... complicated. It allows us to speak wherever we are in our world, yes, but it can also translate thoughts—flashes of emotion or colour. As I said, it is not to be performed lightly. I worry you would one day regret the intrusion."*

"Excuse me," Ashalea interrupted, looking back and forth between them. "Am I missing something? Ceremony of power? What are you talking about?"

Razakh explained while Shara stretched out by the fire, groaning as the warmth leeched into her skin, melting the tension from her muscles. She propped an arm up, leaning on it lazily as she watched Ashalea's face flit between awe and intrigue.

"Incredible," Ashalea breathed when Razakh had finished. "To have a power like that would prove most useful. Granted, those with the gift have the ability to use telepathy too, but ... unless the receiving subject has Magickal affinity, it's a one-way conversation." She shook her head, clearly impressed by this ancient Diodonian rite.

Razakh bared his teeth in a clumsy grin. *"It is beneficial, to be able to speak with others. I suppose Diodonians are beasts in our most base form, but whether it was the Gods' will or the very essence of our land, our intelligence surpasses that of common animals."* As if to gloat on that fact he began grooming himself with a long pink tongue.

"Telepathy has always been one of my weakest skills," Ashalea admitted. "Though, I haven't tested it much. Only on my horse."

Shara laughed. "You've had conversations with Kaylin?"

Ashalea frowned. "I'll have you know he's quite the gentleman." Shara snorted, to which the elf added with a grin, "He speaks to me in the elvish tongue, given he's a Woodrandian steed."

"Oh, the common tongue is beneath even your horses now?" Shara began howling, her laughter seeming to stir even the fire in the hearth, and Razakh began humming too, his quiet melodic equivalent of joy.

"I hope he's okay," Ashalea said softly.

Shara chuckled. Her friend had always been a gentle soul where animals were concerned. "I'm sure he's happily munching on Moonglade Meadows grass, destroying your fields."

It felt good to be at ease amongst friends. To forget, however temporary, the worries of the world and the last few months. Laughter was still new to Shara, still foreign on her tongue like a language she had yet to master. She hadn't had the luxury of happiness before. It had always been about the next job, the next mark on a seemingly endless list. And there would always be people who deserved death or things far worse, but it was nice not to be the one to dole out their punishment.

She had once thought she enjoyed the kill—the adrenaline was addictive, the feeling of power much like a drug. She had tried potions before, feeling them addle her mind and sway her grip on reality. It wasn't for her. But she had seen others take drugs in various forms too, and she had also seen the shells of the people it left behind. No, she would much rather live in the now, even if the world was a bloody mess, even if her dreams and memories plagued her.

But there was something to be said for friendship, for love. It was altogether risky in a different way than she was used to, and that realisation made her feel more alive than ever. More determined to clutch at the still-healing tendons of her heart and stitch them back together, making her less likely to sink back into that unfeeling, tactful creature that she used to be. The crutch that was being an assassin.

How things had changed. How Shara had grown, from a careless killer to someone who had a reason to fight. People to fight for. If only her father knew just how much more she could be—how much that mould she had been squeezed into as a child no longer fit like it used to. Because she was not Onyxonite anymore. She was a Guardian. She was a friend, maybe a lover, maybe one day not a villain but a hero.

Ironic, really, given her previous line of work.

She looked up at the faces of her friends; Ashalea, so fierce and brave and giving. So beautiful inside and out, despite the horrors that had slowly torn pieces of her apart. She was a rare creature—powerful—whose wrath had been ignited, whose fury burned.

And then Razakh; wise, strong of heart and mind, courageous. He had become a fast friend despite their rocky start, and Shara knew that was only because of their similarities. But like calls to like, and they were both wanderers of heart and soul. Both eager to see the change on the horizon and live to see better days ahead.

She hoped with every fibre of her being that they would. He looked at her then, as if to say he would think on her offer, and she nodded silently, lapsing into her own contemplation. Shara sighed, rubbing her temples as her head increased its dull thrumming to a steady pound.

Ashalea snorted. "I suggest you take a tonic. We've got work to do tonight and I need your wits sharp." She studied first Shara, then Razakh. Straightening suddenly, her gaze turned thoughtful as she asked, "Has anyone felt different since arriving? Like a powerful Magicka lingers within the mountain?"

Razakh stretched his powerful legs before the fire. "*I have sensed something strange since we entered the city. Not exactly Magicka but an energy, a kinship.*"

"The Guardian?" Shara asked. In truth she'd felt a little off since arriving, like an itch that could not be scratched. Given that she didn't have a scrap of Magicka running through her veins she'd dismissed it entirely, but could it be that there was a very real thread binding them?

"*It would make sense,*" Razakh said, interpreting her thoughts. "*As the current Guardians of the Grove fade and their strength wanes, the balance of power shifts to us. I have felt it these last weeks. Their time is short. I have ... feared for a while now, that their vigil is close to an end.*"

Ashalea began, "But your father—"

"*Is dying,*" Razakh snapped, and the elf winced at the tone. Shara studied her friend, the only sign of his frustration the tail swishing madly behind him.

"Why didn't you say anything," Shara said quietly. Ashalea threw her a warning look to drop it, but she ignored her.

A low rumble stirred from the beast and there was silence for several long moments until, slowly, he bit out, "*He chose his path long ago, and I have learned to accept it. We have our own ends to meet, our own journey. I do not have the luxury of time to go see him.*"

His words were laced with misery, regret dripping from every syllable. But Shara understood why he would not leave. If his father, Razgeir, and the elf who stood vigil were about to drop dead, then there was no time to waste. A sickening thought jolted through her.

"Razakh, if you can sense the shift of power, what if someone else can too?"

Horror dawned on Ashalea's face. "You mean to suggest the darkness might know the Grove is vulnerable?"

"*I think he knows far more than we give him credit for. The Grove is essential to his plan of conquering Everosia. The moment it is left unguarded, the moment that portal is left for the taking, he will strike. The Keepers will protect it with all they have, as will our armies, but their Magicka is limited. The forest will burn, and they will fall.*"

Shara felt her insides liquify, fear spreading through her like toxin. She swallowed the dryness in her mouth. "Crinos is smart.

He'll have spies watching the Grove from all over the continent. Whatever our move is, we need to make it fast."

Ashalea nodded. "So tonight we dine, then we strike. Lay our demands on the table, have Kano arrange for his armies to march to Renlock."

"And while his armies prepare?" Shara asked.

Her friend smiled grimly. "We find ourselves a Guardian."

23

Feast For All

SHARA

ER GOWN WAS RESPLENDENT, breath-taking, if only because the body it fitted like a glove was all curves and curiosities beneath it. Shara did a slow spin before the mirror, admiring the gemstones that glittered down her crimson dress like droplets of blood. It was backless, a daring plunge that ended at the indents beside her spine before spilling out from the waist. Gossamer cradled her skin with loving fingers, and sheer wisps encircled her arms before dripping over the tight corset, also somewhat daring as it showed off her assets.

She'd had Ehren trim her hair and attend her nails, for even a woman who had little to no beauty routine required indulgence every now and then. And she liked it, this new vision in the mirror. She gleamed and shone from every angle—a perfect lady, if one didn't know better—and anyone who thought otherwise from the daggers strapped to lacy strips around her thighs surely wouldn't know it for long.

Her mind drifted to Telilah, wondering what she'd think of the dress ... Shara wished she could see this version of her. Polished and glamorous.

Shara glanced at Razakh, who was regarding her from the four-poster bed in the corner of the room. If his coat had been shiny before his bath, it was now radiant; like a sunbeam lighting up the night. The gold rippled with the slightest movement; the copper hue shining like the vibrant red of autumn leaves. He had moaned and growled about his bath earlier, but Shara sensed he'd enjoyed some indulgence too, no doubt happy to be rid of whatever filth found its way into his fur.

"What do you think?" she asked, clutching her gown like a true lady of the court, curtseying with as much grace as she could muster.

His rumbling chuckle told her all she needed to know about the gracelessness, but he nodded. "As *far as humans go, you look ... Well, I'm sure you'll have even the dwarves transfixed tonight.*"

"As far as humans go?" She raised a brow, but she supposed that was the best she'd get from the lazy beast. He sprawled out on the bed, nuzzling his head into the silky sheets. She chuckled but couldn't blame him. The room really was extravagant.

Hers was bedecked in plum and gold trimmings. The wooden walls—so dark they were almost black—bordered with golden filigree, and white rugs and throws dotted the room, softening the hard and dark interior. A fireplace crackled away; a desk tucked into the corner so one might work in the comfort of the room. Golden hairbrushes, gilded handheld mirrors, and women's jewellery cut with every gem imaginable were laid out along a vanity. Ehren had certainly done her homework. Shara didn't know how the serving girl knew who her guests were or what they might need, but she suspected the king had his ways. Royals were sneaky like that.

A gentle knock at the door signalled Ashalea's arrival, and when she stepped in the room Shara gasped. The last time she had dressed up was for the council meeting, regal and poised like a ruler of the starlit sky. Beautiful, but deadly.

Today, she was spring eternal. A tight bodice of lily green chiffon was embellished with golden vines, pastel pink roses climbing the fabric. The sleeves were sheer green, and the skirt flowed like soft waterfalls, sparkling under the light. The colour could not have been more perfect, bringing out her emerald eyes and complementing her golden skin.

Her silver hair, curly and glistening, hid her pointed ears as it cascaded down her back, and Shara wondered if it was to her favour that Ehren styled it as such. Not that her angled jawline and high cheekbones, combined with her height and general slim build could be anything but elvish, Shara thought with a scoff.

The lack of muscle was evident in the thin arms visible beneath the translucent fabric, and Shara noticed how painfully small Ashalea's waistline now was. But there was no denying the glow that still highlighted her lovely features. She had been eating frequently and had started running and doing simple exercises in quiet moments. Her friend was healing slowly, but roses needed time to bloom, and Ashalea's thorns were withdrawing.

When the elf needed to talk about Wezlan or her mother or anything else, should she ever want to, Shara would be there. As they all would. Shara just hoped she knew that, despite the small fights that seemed to erupt from their fiery natures.

Ashalea's eyes lit up when she saw Shara, and she shook her head. "You look–"

"Stunning? Radiant? Like a Goddess?" Shara fluffed her hair. "I know."

Razakh rolled his eyes as he jumped down from the bed. "Shameless flirt," he teased. "*Why you creatures feel the need to dress up in frilly, lacy things is beyond me. Your useless skins need warmth in this weather, not paper-thin costumes.*"

Shara sighed. "Razakh, the first thing you need to know about women—females—is that we defy the natural laws of the world. The second is that our frilly, lacy things allow us to wield the second-most important weapon in our arsenal."

"*Dare I ask?*"

She snorted. "Our bodies, of course."

Razakh huffed. "*And the first?*"

"A wit as sharp as a sword and a honeyed tongue," Shara winked.

Ashalea scratched the soft spot behind Razakh's ears, and he purred. "You have a lot to learn, my friend, but probably best you don't sniff too far down that rabbit hole."

His bewildered expression suggested he agreed, and Shara patted him on the head. "There's a good boy."

Before he could bite the hand she quickly withdrew, another knock at the door sounded, this time belonging to Ehren. She beamed at her three masterpieces and nodded, as if satisfied with her work. "It's time, ladies, gentle friend," she said. "This way please."

They filed out the door, their guide taking them along the corridor and into a staircase that filed up from the king's hall and into another passageway of connected rooms. It was incredible how sophisticated this mountain was. A labyrinth with wealth and history etched into every wall, painting and tapestry.

She asked, "How did the dwarves build this city?"

Ehren cocked her head as she walked, her long sheet of hair swaying from the motion. "The mountain goes deep, its roots planted far below the earth for longer than history could recount. When the dwarves first found the mountain, we were a broken people, ravaged from wars amongst other races, and creatures such as the dragons who hunted us like sheep. The king, oldest of his line, despaired, for his villages—once a bountiful, thriving flock built at the very base of this range, were burnt down by the dragons and plundered by monsters from the marshes. He wanted peace, safety, security for the dwarves, and when he came upon the highest peak of Kingsgareth he swore he would burrow deep, far away from firedrakes and sky serpents, and embedded in earth where wet things do not dwell.

"He beseeched the rare, gifted dwarves among them to move the very earth and, upon hearing his plight, mages from across the land joined the cause. And they built. Weeks, months, years ... they built deep into the soil, and then they built wider, higher, until a city was birthed. And tools of mass production were built, allowing the dwarves to carve as they willed without Magicka. Since then, Kingsgareth has been the jewel of our people. A haven for our kind."

It was the kind of tale Shara's mother might have told long ago when she was a little girl. Back before the beatings and the starving and the cruel, calculating ways that fathers trained their daughters and sons, and assassins begot assassins. Back before her mother died of pox and Shara's memories of her became twisted and foggy and forgotten. But she remembered, vaguely, the soft voice that spoke of adventures and mythical beasts and warriors who sought out fair maidens.

But it turns out some of those stories had merit. They were damn well living in one, after all. War would reveal who the victor would be, only this time the fair maidens would wield weapons and Magicka and—hopefully—send that corrupt, woeful cretin into an early grave. The idea of the darkness's smirking lips curled instead in a howl of despair gave her great pleasure.

"Thank you for sharing your tale," she said to Ehren, sweeping aside thoughts of vengeance. "I admit, my knowledge of the dwarves is limited. The Onyxonites, as I'm sure you are aware, are taught many different lessons than history as a child." She grimaced. "We focus more on muscle memory than anything else."

Ehren didn't bat an eye as she led them towards two crimson doors towering above them. "I have heard about your people," she said. "We value strength here and hold similar methods of training, though ours is optional and comes at high risk of death."

"Who would choose to endure such a thing?" Ashalea asked.

Shara's mood darkened momentarily. "Who indeed," she said quietly, thinking back to her childhood, both her body and mind bearing the scars of her own training. But she forced thoughts of her family and her people away. Tonight held a different purpose.

Two guards stood at attention on either side, and they fisted hands over hearts before opening the doors to the feast that lay beyond. The smell was the first thing that hit her. Lamb roast with rosemary and thyme, crispy potatoes and gravy, vegetable medleys arranged in spiralling patterns, colourful dishes she had never seen before, covered with exotic spices, freshly baked bread ... all wafting towards her. But the pride of the table was a giant hog placed in the centre, a bright red apple wedged in its mouth. She was salivating before she took her first step inside the hall.

Shara wondered if the trade routes were still clear—whether

merchants could freely traverse the paths leading to the mountain. With the increased sightings of monsters lately, she suspected not, but it would seem the dwarves would be well stocked for the winter ahead. She perused the spread once again ... perhaps not if these feasts were nightly affairs.

Razakh had a few strands of drool escaping his maw and, with a frown, she kicked him subtly, to which his jaws quickly snapped shut and he ducked his head in embarrassment. Shara had to stifle her giggle as she strutted into the hall, the eyes of every dwarf on the trio as they strolled in.

She smiled with scarlet lips, going as far as to wink at one of the more handsome nobles as she sauntered to the table. She almost tripped as she noticed the view from the windows—windows, for the dwarves had carved a damned balcony into the side of the mountain. Glass several inches thick both insulated the room from the cold and protected those within it.

The room was high up, and through the frosted window she could see the surrounding mountains; their jagged points reaching high into the blackening sky above. Trees embellished their sides—great pines splintering the earth—and a ravine snaked its way between them, its river frozen solid.

Shara turned and took in the room's high ceiling and sweeping banners as their crimson and gold velvet draped from all corners of the room to tie neatly like a bow to the giant chandelier dangling above their heads. It was quite possibly the most exquisite thing she'd ever seen, for not only candles sat within its many arches, but gems ... every gem imaginable gleamed above, casting refractions of all colours throughout the room.

It took every effort to stop her jaw from hanging open as her eyes travelled down to the king at the table's head. Kano's face was impassive as he watched the three of them enter and gawk at his underground palace, but just as suddenly he grinned and threw his arms out wide, "Welcome my friends. Come, take a seat at my table."

Temperamental bastard. Shara loved it.

She swished her way towards a plush velvet chair, plopping into it without ceremony. She caught a few of the dwarves staring at her—some with interest, others with dislike—but she merely grinned and blew a kiss, much to the king's joy.

Ashalea settled by her side with much more grace befitting her station, chin high and eyes bright, and Razakh hopped to the empty space at her other side like a noble himself.

The dwarves looked at him reverently, hearts practically bleeding out their eyes at the Diodonian.

She swivelled to face the king, eyes settling on the two males at honoured positions on either side of him. He caught her gaze, his grin turning wolfish as he gestured, "My sons, Prince Sven and Prince Jyorden. My third-born will not be joining us tonight."

Shara shrugged at the missing son, instead focusing her amber eyes on the two males present. The former was the mirror image of his father, though she sensed the unimpressed line to his mouth was in no way faked as he stared at her. His hair was almost white, eyes of cold grey narrowing as he examined her. He wore a grey, form-fitting tunic to match, the sleeves cut off to reveal stern strokes of ink twisting down rocky arms. The ink portrayed wolves and hammers, mountains and whorls. She wondered at the stories they told.

But her eyes were quickly drifting to Jyorden. Where his brother was cold and unforgiving as cut glass, Jyorden's easy smile and sparkling blue eyes were as fire—inviting, catching, but just a little bit dangerous. His hair rippled down his back like a flame, its wildness contained by leather bindings, his beard styled in a similar fashion. He wore all black, cut like his brother to display bulging biceps.

She sized them up immediately and sensed, despite the bigger build and obvious strength Jyorden bore, his brother was the biggest threat. Shara smiled at them sweetly, to which she received a broad grin from Jyorden. Sven just bared his teeth ever so slightly. A challenge then. Her favourite.

"We are honoured to dine with you tonight," Ashalea said, her sweet disposition slicing the tension like a knife. "I must admit I am yet to try dwarven fare."

"Better than the rabbit food they serve down with your lot," Sven said.

Ashalea's eyes whipped to him, but to Shara's surprise she laughed. "Our fare is not to everyone's taste, but I don't need to eat my weight in said rabbits to find my strength."

Kano's laugh bellowed down the table as he clapped his son on the back. "Don't mince your words with this one, laddie, she'll carve your self-esteem up for breakfast."

Sven scowled as he shrugged off his father, but Jyorden winked at the she-elf before turning to Shara. "I'm told you hail from the Shadowvale tribe. I have always been fascinated with your history."

She shrugged, sipping wine from the goblet before her. "It's a bloody trail that began with a deep-seated grudge and a fascination for jewellery." She fingered the hollow at her throat, suddenly feeling the absence of her Onyxonite talisman. When she had been captured by the darkness, it had been taken from her, along with all other possessions and her damned dignity too.

Ashalea followed the movement, eyes narrowing as Shara

withdrew ever so slightly. "I've met the Onyxonites," she cut in smoothly. "They are a proud and noble people who dispense their own form of justice to criminals across Everosia. Assassins, yes, but there is a code among them, and their skills are exceptional. Aside from your Master Erik, Shara is the best combatant I've seen."

Shara threw her a grateful look, not just for the compliment but the save. She didn't want to talk about her people, with the dwarves or anyone. Flynn was their leader now, and he would serve them well but ... she had never felt so disconnected to her heritage. She was transforming, shedding her skin to wrap herself in something stronger, more meaningful.

A servant leaned in to refill her wine, startling her, not even realising she'd sculled the whole thing. Conversation drifted around her, and she let Ashalea and Razakh take the lead, exchanging pleasantries while she drenched her tastebuds in every dish on the table. She almost groaned at each mouthful. Rich, exotic, fulfilling food that made her feel like she could fight ten battles. She would use this energy tomorrow, to train until she passed out.

When the feast was over, the table cleared and most of the lesser nobles dismissed, Kano leaned forward and eyed the three of them like a hawk. With niceties out of the way, he lost his easy smile and shifted into that gruff, hardened dwarf they had first met at Renlock. The mask of a general. Of a king.

"Now," he said calmly. "You have been wanting to ask me of my armies since the moment you sat down."

Ashalea looked to Shara, offering her the floor and so, taking a breath, she told Kano everything Razakh had mentioned earlier regarding the current Guardians, and their suspicions about the darkness. "... And so we need your armies to move immediately. Ready the dwarves, prepare your city, gather whatever food and supplies you can. To prepare and march your army, it could take over a week, given the weather."

"*What if they teleported instead?*" Razakh suggested. "*The mages at Renlock would be more than capable to carry small groups at a time. It would be taxing on their energy but, given the circumstances, worth it.*"

Ashalea clicked her tongue. "The snow is unseasonably heavy so early this winter; it poses a risk for travelling through the mountain passes." She tapped her nails on the table, mouth pursed as she considered his proposal. "I agree. Denavar's power alone might be enough to—"

She halted, suddenly on high alert as her gaze swivelled to the adjacent window. She shot from her seat, gown swishing as she bolted through the door and outside onto the slick balcony. Bitter wind and drifts of snow cleaved its way into the hall in her wake.

"What's going on?" Kano bellowed, his face incredulous as Shara and Razakh sprinted after their friend. She ignored him as she raced after Ashalea into the dreary night, the snap of cold teeth biting into her skin immediately. Cradling her arms around her body, she shivered as she skidded to a halt on the balcony, scanning the mountainside below.

Her amber eyes saw nothing but white and black and grey space in between clusters of trees and boulders cutting the slopes. "What do you see?"

Ashalea shook her head, mouth pursed as she maintained her search. "It's not what I see, it's what I heard. An alarm, far in the distance. Something is wrong." She stiffened again, deathly still as she turned one pointed ear out.

Razakh leaped up to lean his front paws on the stone edge, cocking an ear. "*I hear it too. Horns.*"

By now Kano and his sons had barrelled out the door to join

them. "What's all the fuss about?" the king grumbled. "What—" but he stopped cold as this time a chorus of horns sounded, clear as bells and loud enough for human and dwarven ears alike.

"Who dares?" he breathed, fury in his eyes. The king turned to his sons. "Go."

Sven and Jyorden were already halfway out the door before the king looked back down the mountainside. Signal fires began to light up the dark one by one from their staggered perches below, and movement skittered in the shadows. Shara ground her teeth, flexing her fingers as she watched. Whatever they were, they could not be human. Not from the way they darted with alarming speed in the snow.

"What the hell are they?" Ashalea murmured, her spine rigid as her keen eyes saw what Shara's could not.

Shara leaned forward, eyes narrowed to slits as she strained to identify the shapes, moving so fast they were little more than blurred shadows. She hunched further over the balcony, crying out in alarm when a large dark mass careened over the stone wall claws first, using her chest as its landing board.

Pain rattled through her as it raked down the tender skin below her collar bone, blood staining the already crimson gown she wore. The creature arched back with teeth sharp as daggers flashing before her as it lunged for her neck. Her body barked in pain, her skin tearing as she blocked with crossed arms, muscles straining under its weight, grimacing as its foul, rotting breath leeched up her nose and into her mouth.

She almost gagged from its snapping jaws and flailing arms—the fangs dangerously close to her jugular. And then arms were hauling it back, Ashalea's grip unwavering as she grabbed it by the neck and *snapped* it with a sharp twist.

Shara staggered back, half crawling as she retreated against the wall with a moan. Her chest was in ribbons, blood pouring out between folds of skin and she cursed loudly. She dared not look too closely, but Ashalea and Razakh's eyes said enough of the damage.

Kano crouched, hiding the body from view while he inspected it. Despite the frigid air whipping around them, the air seemed corrupted; a wetness belonged to that rotting creature, as if mould clung to it and festered. Kano's face was grim as he said, "A creature from the Dreadlands to the south. They have made their move."

Damn her useless human eyes and pathetic ears! Shara should have sensed it coming, should have had her blade unsheathed from her thigh before she went outside. "Got the drop on me," she said with a half grin, but talking was too hard. Her energy bled out in waves, body rallying its defences as her mind scrabbled to process the pain.

"Let's get you inside," Ashalea said softly, and Kano helped carry her into the hall before jamming the balcony door shut. The elf was instantly on alert, scanning the room. "Bar the doors," she barked at the remaining nobles, their eyes wide but alert as they nodded hastily, and the screeching of furniture echoed as they began dragging bits and pieces towards the door.

Razakh came to Shara's side, nuzzling her hand with his giant head. His eyes bore into hers, and she swore she could read the concern in those orbs of pure silver. Or perhaps it was his mind leeching unguarded thoughts into hers. She smiled weakly, waving him off. "I'll be fine, you big dope," but even as she croaked the words, she could feel the blood rising, leaking into her lungs.

Ashalea looked at her sharply, nostrils flaring as she sniffed before crouching to inspect her wound—scenting the blood on the air, no doubt. And the wounds were as rivers spilling out of her, so much of it that the warmth was almost soothing to her cold body. The pain began to dull, and Shara felt her eyes grow heavy, her brain foggy.

"She needs a healer immediately," Ashalea yelled to anyone who would listen, not turning to see who would obey. But her hands cupped as she reached them to Shara's chest, white light flashing from her palms. There was a faint tickle, somehow soothing, and her head began to droop. "Juss ... little ... sleep," she sighed.

"Don't you dare," Ashalea hissed, and even as Shara's eyes closed the light grew blinding as the elf poured her Magicka into the wound.

"Not too much," Razakh warned. *"You'll need your strength."*

Shara felt drunk as his voice swam through her murky thoughts, but the pain had stopped, the foggy veil was lifting, and she felt renewed vigour flow into her veins. Healing. Ashalea was healing her. She swallowed, throat dry, eyes fluttering open as she gripped her friend's arm tightly. "Stop," she rasped. "Just enough to save my ass from dying."

Ashalea's emerald eyes glowed as ethereal power shone from within, and, with a sidelong glance at Razakh, she sagged. She inspected the wounds, which were still oozing, but no longer fatal. "Fine, but you're to see a healer."

Shara sat up too fast, feeling a rush of dizziness. "I'll be okay. I can fight."

Razakh shook his head. *"No, you're in no state and you'll only slow us down."*

"I'm coming," she stated firmly, feeling her blood heat with frustration.

"Damnit, Shara, no," Ashalea snapped. "Stay here, wait for the healer and for Goddess's sake just listen for once in your life."

The king was already gone and Shara realised he must have slipped away when he discerned Ashalea could heal her. Only a few nobles remained in the room, which Ashalea stalked up to, looking down at them with a steely gaze. "Look after her. If anything happens while I'm gone then so help me my face will be the last thing you see."

She turned on her heel and gave Shara a quick nod. Razakh licked her cheek with a long, scratchy tongue, and then, like smoke and shadows, her friends were gone.

The Mountain Shall Conquer

RAZAKH

HIS NOSE TOLD HIM WHERE TO GO. Down the many accursed stairwells he leaped, legs pumping beneath him and paws splaying with every pounce. Ashalea sprinted down the bannisters with ease, now suitably geared up in a grey material as soft as spider silk and flexible as sponge that hugged her like a second skin and shone like moonlight. Her torso glittered with a steel breastplate and spaulders, leather vambraces providing support and protection for her lower arms.

Razakh noticed her bow and quiver were strapped to her back too, the magnificent white oak almost glowing under the candlelight. He had little time to study its make, for the stairwells grew crowded the closer they came to the main hall. The city knew.

Dwarves flooded the staircases; mothers intent on herding their children to safety, males and females alike running, presumably, to their battle postings. Word spread of the attack in the king's private quarters and Razakh bared his teeth in frustration. Kano was not so thick as to spread undue alarm through his city, which meant one or some of the nobles had let it slip. *Curse them,* Razakh thought. They would never get through at this rate.

"Get out the way," Ashalea hissed, but the common folk were either too scared or too obnoxious to pay heed. Razakh snapped his jaws, a warning growl rumbling in his chest. If they refused to listen, Razakh had other tools at his disposal. One flash of his canines and the crowd parted like the sand above a Wyrmear, those giant beasts of the dunes and roots of the Diodon Mountains.

Calls of *'move aside'* fell like dominoes down the stairs, and Razakh hurtled after them, Ashalea opting to slide down the bannisters instead. When they had reached the cavernous hall, Razakh sniffed the air, the scent of metal and flame beckoning. *"Come,"* he demanded at Ashalea, and they picked their way through the crowds, the hall slowly but surely thinning as all who could not fight fled to their homes. A drill Razakh had no doubt they had practised, but one he surmised had not been necessary for an age.

They bolted past markets still filled with the smells of juicy meats, rich spices and the tangy citrus of various fruits. Past empty stalls decked with rolls of silks, velvets and furs, antiquities and jewellery, shoes and talismans ... all manner of materialistic things that dwarves, humans and elves seemed to delight in hoarding.

Taverns and restaurants lined the smooth granite or marbled streets, with everything one could think of dotting the smooth archways and coiled pillars of carved rock, from tinkerers to woodcarvers to furniture makers. But it was not the rich tapestry of life that Razakh was aiming for as they sprinted through the great city, but the forges of old.

And finally, as they dashed into a new hall filled with metal teeth and wooden contraptions, they saw it: the armoury. Where dwarves gathered in organised chaos to obtain their weaponry and armour, and file out to the wilderness and bloodshed beyond.

That familiar flash of Magicka hummed through him as they approached, and he glanced at Ashalea. *"Do you feel that?"*

She nodded. "The Guardian ... the power linking us calls to me. But it's ... dull. Hidden almost, as if there are too many minds, too many bodies to sniff it out." She shook her head. "The Guardian must wait. We have other matters to resolve."

Razakh skidded to a halt, spying a dwarf who stood out from the rest, his shoulders draped in a burgundy cloak clasped together by a chain of pure gold, emblems of snarling wolves cinched at either side. He was dressed in chainmail and steel so dark it was almost black covering him from head to toe, a plume that looked like a wolf's tail striping down from his helmet.

"Where is the king?" Razakh demanded the dwarf. Whether he was surprised to see a Diodonian and an elf interrogating him, he didn't show it. Not that Razakh could see past the helmet shielding his face anyway; only eyes that glittered like black diamonds peered back.

"He fights," the officer said, jerking his head towards the open archway. "What do you want with him?"

Razakh chewed on the thick accent the dwarf had, having to spell out his words a little slower. Impatient, Ashalea stepped forward. "We fight for the king," she stated simply. "Where do you want us?"

The dwarf stared at her, a little too dismissively for Razakh's liking, but he just jerked his head toward her bow. "How good with that thing are you?"

She raised a brow. "Better than you I'd wager."

He merely snorted and jerked his chin at her, "You, to the upper ramparts linin' the mountain, and you"—he looked at Razakh with a wolfish grin like the beasts emblazoned to his cloak—"come with me."

Ashalea looked loath to leave him, but Razakh dipped his head. He had seen her wield a bow and arrow like she was born to it. Muscles lacking the strength to match the demands of the string, perhaps, but a talented eye and judge of the elements. It might have comforted him to know she'd be safer on the ramparts, allowing her to kill from afar after having expended energy training earlier today and healing Shara.

He wondered how Shara was doing as he padded after the officer. She had taken a nasty blow, and he wasn't sure he'd ever forget the stripped flesh and the waterfall of blood that had gushed from her wounds. He sent a silent prayer of thanks to the Gods above—to the elvish ones especially—for granting Ashalea with such a gift of healing. He knew it was taxing for her, even with how much power she possessed. And, even though a kernel of guilt lodged itself in his stomach for leaving Shara in some pain, she would live. Ashalea would too, having stopped the healing before Shara's wounds could greedily lap up her strength and leave the elf's body weakened.

Ashalea may have lost much of her physical makeup after losing weight and muscle, but she was smart—if her body failed her, she would utilise her surroundings, she would lead. But right now, Razakh had his own mission to think about. Once he stepped into the outside world, he assessed the battleground ahead.

Dwarves were staggered across the mountain at intervals—ranks of soldiers lining the foothills on flatter ground, some fighting in small groups across the mountain, perched precariously on the slopes. Archers gathered in pockets, picking targets off one by one.

To Razakh's left and right, dwarven-made stone was carved upon the rock wall, forming ramparts accessible only from this vantage point on the mountain. Clever, though they left no room for escape if the enemy brought catapults or struck via the sky. Yet Kingsgareth was reasonably well equipped to deal with a land army, given the dwarves had the high vantage points and could send scores of arrows raining down on their foes. In addition was their knowledge of the territory—which parts of the mountain were generally safe to tread across and which led to one's doom if not traversed carefully.

But the Dreadlands fiends were not deterred by the terrain or the climate. Their claws found purchase in the ice, their bodies—secreting an oily residue—slick and slimy and unbothered by the cold. They dwelled in wet, dead places deep within the marshes. A land none but the most detestable of beasts lived within.

Razakh's spine tingled as if clammy hands had stroked a finger down his back. They fought below, these reedy creatures the colour of moss and mildew, claws long as knives jutting from between splayed hands and feet. They were a mess of gills and spines with ridged bones, needle-thin teeth and skin that was dotted with pinprick holes all over.

Normally Razakh would take great pleasure in the hunt, but these things? He could smell them even from his vantage point—rot and wrongness and mucus. He decided he'd rather not sink his teeth into them at all, but it seemed the dwarf had other plans, for their trek took a turn and they veered down the mountain to see—

Wolves. Giant white wolves with eyes of gold to his silver. Intelligent, majestic beasts that yipped and snarled, hackles raised as they scented the air of the corruption below. The alpha uttered a low growl and, as Razakh came before it, all in the pack quietened. Razakh sucked in a breath through his muzzle, approaching them cautiously, prowling slowly towards them. The dwarf, for his part, was content to let them work it out, standing with arms folded across his broad chest, watching, waiting ...

The alpha was huge—almost as big as Razakh, and it was ... female. Her white coat was adorned with faint swirls and whorls of cerulean blue that pulsed softly under the stars. Ice, Razakh realised. Veins of ice that crept over the hides of every wolf, though none so brightly as this one. He had no idea what this magnificent beast was, for it was unlike any wolf he'd ever heard of. Respectfully, he dipped his head, and ever so gently, he let the flame along his spine flare to life, shrouding him in an ember glow of his own.

He tried to connect with her mind, to speak, yet her thoughts were indecipherable. She thought not in words, but pictures and colour. They could not converse then, as he would with other species. The wolf startled, growling slightly, but she sniffed the air as if gauging Razakh's intentions. She stopped and stepped closer, touching her snout ever so gently to his own.

Razakh exploded. Energy pulsed through him at the touch like bells ringing an ancient tune; the sound so sombre, so hauntingly beautiful, it stirred something powerful inside. He thrummed with energy; a new sense of being that forced him into true wakefulness. The wolf touched its forehead to his own and a flash of memory unfolded before his mind's eye.

Light and colour and sound and feeling. The scent of this great beast filled his nose, their souls brushed against each other, and a vortex lit up the sky—red and blue and fire and ice.

Razakh bowed, as he never had in his entire life—as he perhaps

never would again. Submissive only to this mystical, glorious creature. And she copied the sentiment, her pack mirroring her movements behind. Then, as one, they looked down the mountain, and they ran.

Together, Razakh and the alpha took point, the pack fanning out like an arrowhead behind them, cascading snow down the mountain. The first of the creatures cowered before them, and they sprang.

His jaws met the sinewy neck of the first marsh creature, canines sinking into its slimy skin as he snapped the bone with a resounding crunch. He made the mistake of swallowing after and shook his head with disgust. It tasted of death, the mucus sliding down his throat and sticking to the walls of his mouth.

Claws it would be, then. The wolves converged, maws snapping at tendons and bones and the sensitive flesh of the creatures' throats. Then he saw them—more creatures than he could count scaling the mountain. Dwarves began to fall as the spreading shadow grew too heavy, the creatures slicing off limbs, some proceeding to feed on the meaty skin of their prey. For every axe that swung in broad arcs of power, lopping off heads like a scythe reaping wheat, for every dwarf that bellowed with fury, a creature was there, stabbing with razor claws.

Their unearthly moans of victory were the most terrible part. Not the blood or the stench or the litter of limbs, but that horrifying keening as it wailed across the snow. Razakh bit down on the fear that bubbled within, finding his next mark, and the next, and the next.

Leap, rip, rend.

Leap, rip, rend.

The wolves were a shield of teeth and claws around the alpha, working as a unit, as one weapon against their foes. But when they were surrounded by a writhing mass of marsh monsters, the real weapons came out to play. As one, the wolves dug their claws into the earth and howled. Razakh's hackles raised at the eerie call, its echo bouncing off the surrounding mountains. Ice rippled in crackling veins beneath the earth, travelling the ground like a quake. The blue energy found its target and surged into the creatures, freezing them. Other monsters bloated, swelling the murky, corrupt waters inside their bellies and turning the monsters into splintered ice.

It wasn't enough. Even as masses crumbled, falling like dominoes to the ground, more came. Razakh leaped before the alpha as she recovered, whipping his tail of flames at a creature, the oily slime upon its belly igniting on impact. He shredded its chest with his claws, and its throat gargled as it choked on its own blood and bodily fluids.

Razakh gazed up the mountain, his keen eyes spotting Ashalea's silver hair from afar. He sent a thought snaking out toward her mind and she turned, elven eyes narrowing as they focused on him. *"We need assistance. Quickly."*

She steeled herself as she fired an arrow. *"On it,"* she sent back, and the elf disappeared behind the dwarven front lines.

He didn't have to wait long. Where arrows had cleaved through the sky almost unheard and unseen, fire now lit up the dark in a crescendo of flames and rained upon the battlefield. She must have gathered every able dwarf who could wield a bow, for their arrows carved red hot ripples through the night. Creatures dropped in droves, arrows through throats and eyes and hearts.

A horn blared from above—a signal for all to retreat, and on their stout little legs the dwarves began the incline, huffing and puffing from the weight of their gear and the thick snow. The fallen remained, eyes wide and glassy where they had died, others moaning in pain but too far gone to attempt moving. Creatures flocked to those vulnerable dwarves, their moans turning to cries for help that broke the hearts of all who abandoned them to their fate.

Their screams split the world in two, shrill and unnatural for the typically low timbre of these proud males. Razakh could hardly bear it, and instead of turning for the ramparts above he preyed on those creatures, taking extra care to make them feel every moment of their deaths, teeth tearing more than necessary, claws curling as they sank into soft flesh.

He could not kill them all, but perhaps he had saved a few lives that day. Some who, if this fight ended anytime soon, might survive the blistering cold and return to the warm embrace of loved ones.

The alpha snapped at his heels, eyes imploring as she looked up the mountain, then to Razakh, and back again. He understood. It was time to go. He didn't know why these wild animals obeyed the dwarves—whether they were pets, friends, or protectors of this land, but something told him the white wolf knew when to follow orders. The look in those golden orbs promised more blood would be shed. But not here. Higher up the mountain and behind the safety lines.

There was a crackling in his mind, a distorted voice that rang with urgency until it became clearer, fully audible. "Get back," Ashalea screamed. "Get back to the keep NOW."

His eyes found her on the ramparts, bow now slung over her back, palms stretched before her pointing at him—no, at the creatures behind him as they regrouped and began to swarm up the slopes. The skies crackled, an angry rumble echoing above, gathering the growing dark. Forked flashes of purple and white veins split the night, and Razakh realised then, what she planned to do. What she'd need from every gifted dwarf present in order to help her achieve this crazy idea.

So crazy that it just might work. New energy surged through his limbs and he sprinted, legs pummelling, the pads of his paws so hot he swore the snow melted from every step. Dwarves gathered either side of Ashalea in an endless line, mouths set in determined lines as they, too, held their hands skyward. The wolves retreated to the gate by the barracks, the alpha's eyes gleaming as she led her pack to safety. Razakh reached the city gate, flying up the ramparts until he ground to a halt next to his friend.

Ashalea smiled, though it was strained as she tunnelled deep into her reserves of power. "Ready?"

Razakh knew this would take a toll on her—perhaps too much, so he nudged her leg, pressing himself flat against her side. "*Use my energy, Ashalea. I can't do this for you, but I can be your strength.*"

Her eyes flashed as she weighed the odds. At last she nodded; lips set in a stern line as she focused. "I'm glad you've got my back."

Razakh stood tall, readying himself should Ashalea need to draw on his energy. The creatures were gaining and would be upon them soon. They were a plague—decrepit, disgusting things that seemed to leech all the goodness from the earth. Ashalea must have noticed their proximity for she stiffened at last, and he felt the Magicka raging under her skin, the air around him shifting as the energies of this wild place began to change, answering her call.

Razakh roared, his war cry the deliverer of death; primal and ancient. Dwarves beat their axes upon shields and bellowed along with him, their faces hungry for blood, their own veins rushing with the adrenaline of battle.

His call to arms was echoed by the wolf pack standing guard on the landing below. The Magicka users all raised their arms in unison, and Razakh bared his teeth in anticipation. *"Let them burn,"* he said, and he opened his telepathic channels to extend the order to the mind of every dwarf present.

Power erupted from a fan of living flame, the fire from each dwarf converging into one giant beam wielded by Ashalea. It swirled hungrily, the light so blinding, the heat so searing, everything in its path melted in submission. The dwarves below crouched and covered their eyes, their beards and braids whipping about from the force of this reckoning.

Razakh peered into its wrath, perhaps the only one present whose eyes remained unaffected by the bright glimmers. The fires' rays could have matched the sun; they were so unearthly, so beautiful and yet so destructive.

And beyond the flames, the very snow melted as the ground burned. Creatures fell in droves, their skin's toxicity a fuel that the flames gobbled greedily and spat out as nothing but husks. Yet still they kept coming as that fire formed a wall of red and orange, and it swept over the battlefield in a wave.

When the dwarves began to crumple from exhaustion one by one—the last of them holding on for considerable time—the mountain was stripped of ice and snow. Nothing but brown, scorched earth stretching down towards the landscape beyond. But they had been careful, the dwarves, and where the fire had blasted, water remained in condensation and puddles of melted ice.

Ashalea sucked in a breath besides Razakh, her forehead beaded in sweat, her skin clammy from releasing her own fire upon the world. But she was not done yet. With a boom that cracked and had even the hardiest dwarf flinching, lightning threatened to pull apart the seams of the world. One, then two, then three flashes of it lit the sky, and then with a scream she let her energy loose.

Every kernel of Magicka that dwelled within her bones fired from Ashalea's fingertips, and the very heavens came crashing down.

The marsh creatures stood no chance against her vicious plan. Their bodies lit up like blue fireflies in the blackness, the water a conductor. Every creature fell, each one burning, their horrible screams quickly cut short. Ashalea wobbled beside him, a hand dropping from exhaustion as she stumbled slightly. He was there instantly, pushing his body beneath her palm. *"Take it,"* he ordered her. *"Use my strength."*

He almost felt the reluctance as her fingers coiled into his fur, her grip tightening as she sucked on the bond they shared. Her Magicka bounced from her skin into his own and back again, each time taking more and more as it circled between them. The drain was immediately obvious, his muscles groaning, his mind protesting at the intrusion, but he noticed her stand a little taller, her one hand glowing a little brighter.

It was almost done, this murder of a monstrous scale. It gave Razakh no pleasure to watch them die this time. Not as that rotting stench carried with it the scent of charred skin and blackened organs. Not as his friend wilted like a flower losing its petals, curling inwards. She didn't let go until the last creature fell. Until there was utter silence shrouding the mountainside.

The heavens seemed to breathe a sigh of relief as the thunder and lightning diminished above. Then there was cheering and raucous woops of victory. Howls from both dwarves and wolves alike.

Ashalea's knees buckled, and she collapsed, Razakh quickly stepping in to stop her fall. Her body tumbled over his, and he shifted her weight, so she dangled over his back. Around him dwarves congratulated each other and celebrated their win, but a growing dread filled Razakh's belly.

The darkness had known the races would seek to ally; he had predicted the dwarves would join the fight and sent these creatures as a test. But how many more tricks did he have up his sleeve? How many more battles would they need to fight until the true war began?

Thousands of monsters had almost breached the city today. And yet something told Razakh this was just a fraction of the darkness's army—just a taste of one of the many creatures within his hordes.

The warrior in him relished the opportunity to rain hell on those creatures and the traitorous men amongst them, yet logic had him wanting to curl his tail between his legs and retreat.

But there would be no cowering from this fight. No altering the playing field.

Not anymore.

A Deal So Divine

DENAVAR

H E HAD MINIONS NOW. Hundreds of them, running around doing various errands, some even trying to please him because of his newfound status. There was no shortage of work to do—the week without Ashalea had been long and exhausting, filled with preparing for the oncoming war and working alongside the other allies.

Tiderion was swiftly getting on his nerves, arguing at every opportunity or offering a sneer during every silence. For all the time Denavar had once spent working with him in the Aquafarian Province, Tiderion had never been so tiresome. Whether it was because he felt a sense of betrayal from Denavar, was jealous over his position as a wizard or Guardian, or because he seemed to loathe Ashalea, he didn't know.

He sighed, rubbing his temples. At least he wasn't the only one having teething problems with the elven king. Nirandia was at her wit's end, her brother and Denavar perhaps the only ones keeping her sane. And Yavaar, usually cool and collected, had shown some grit too. It was perhaps a blessing that they would all return to their various castles and keeps tomorrow morning to organise their armies. Denavar's scouts had informed him the Diodonians were already waiting at the meeting point—a grassy knoll midway between Telridge and Galanor.

Of course, the beasts did not have the means to begin preparations for the camp, so Denavar and Yavaar had sent a small force of mages and soldiers to work with the nearby towns to assemble lodgings and supplies. Whilst the camp would be open for all armies, each respective contingent would have their own 'block' to sleep and train in, should they wish. All royals had at least agreed on that—better not to push the boundaries of friendships between some of the races. At least for now.

Queen Celiana had left promptly after Ashalea's departure, making her position in this war all too clear. She would not join them. The Moonglade elves would not fight. It had taken all his strength not to throttle Celiana upon hearing of her abandonment. She had been given numerous opportunities to redeem herself, failing every time. But Denavar had swiftly sent correspondence to his parents in The Meadows.

His mother and father, Rhelia and Ilius Andaro, were both members of the council, and he had tasked them with overseeing—much to his own chagrin—every order from the queen. It wouldn't do for any surprises, and Celiana was unpredictable and dangerous—to herself and others. He would not have her doing anything drastic or considering options that might align with the darkness's interests. He didn't believe her to be a traitor, but she was a coward, and cowards held little regard for morals where murderers were considered. Not if it put them at the receiving end of a sword.

Denavar just hoped she would not hurt Ashalea again. He could not bear to see the look on her face—shock, disappointment, heartbreak, right after losing Wezlan. Right after he'd just got her back.

Oh how he longed to be by Ashalea's side again, to hold her in his arms, to kiss her full lips, to keep her safe. He cursed under his breath, hating the darkness even more for the latest attack made on Kingsgareth Mountains. Kano had been thoughtful enough to send a missive detailing the attack, which had been couriered by a dwarven servant with Magickal abilities. The dwarves had managed, thanks to Ashalea and Razakh, but it had certainly caught them off guard.

A knock on the door drew him out of his thoughts, and he sighed, mentally preparing himself for an onslaught of questions from mages or a summons from Tiderion. But it was Yavaar who popped his head in.

"I come bearing gifts," the king said with a wry grin on his face.

Denavar smiled softly upon spying a tray of tea and cakes in the man's hand, wondering what Yavaar's advisors and servants made of the gesture, but he groaned, "Nothing stronger?"

Yavaar grimaced. "I'm afraid liquor and I are having a disagreement." The tray shivered in his hand before he set it on the coffee table and plonked down on a small sofa, its plush white cushions sucking him in.

Denavar had noticed the shakes. They had come quick and sudden, leaving the king looking slightly mad during meetings, or sweating despite the crisp, cool weather. Withdrawals, he had suspected, and now he knew why. It was gossiped that Yavaar was an alcoholic, and with the state of his city, Denavar understood how desperate the need might have been for a drink. He admired Yavaar's refusal to bend to the drink even more.

"No matter," he said cheerfully, pushing out from behind his mahogany desk and joining the king on an opposite sofa. He had taken to hiding in this room in rare moments of quiet. The study had once belonged to Wezlan, bearing all the remnants of the wizard's wayward nature.

Towers of books curled around the room, the dusty tomes ranging from history to Magicka to the study of anthropology. He had even spied fantasy and romance novels amongst the disarray and had smirked softly at the thought of the old man getting his romance kicks through the pages of a book. Cluttered in disorganised heaps were also maps and scrolls bearing complicated spells that Denavar could only guess at.

Creature comforts dotted the room, such as the sofas in their white silks, grey throw rugs, golden antiquities and whirring devices that hummed a soothing rhythm while Denavar worked. A stash of biscuits was kept in one of the desk drawers which had made Denavar smile. He never knew Wezlan had such a sweet tooth.

He hadn't the heart to change anything in the room. As much as his fingers itched to make reason out of Wezlan's system of chaos, as much as he kept losing important documents amongst the trappings of paper and ink, he couldn't bear the thought of sweeping away the wizard's identity. His absence—the loss of his wit, his wisdom, his kindness and infectious joy—was still such a heavy weight.

"You miss your old friend," Yavaar observed, noting the sweep of Denavar's gaze. The man sure did have a keen eye.

Denavar smiled wearily, crossing a leg over the other as he

thought of Wezlan. "He was a wise man, powerful, honourable—all the traits one would expect from heroes and legends of old, and his deeds were worthy of such admiration too. But his true power lay in his kindness. There was a light to him that could not be dimmed. Ashalea loved him like a father and I—I miss him," Denavar admitted.

Yavaar nodded. "The tales of him are true then. The great wizard who defeated the darkness long ago. One of the Divine Six and ally to all races of Everosia." Yavaar mused over his cup of tea, long fingers still trembling as he sipped it slowly. "If all men of power aspired to reign like him, the world would be a better place."

Denavar snorted. "If all men held themselves accountable, there would be no need for great men like Wezlan."

"Ah, truer words have never been spoken. My father might have learned a thing or two from him."

There was a bitterness that laced those words, and Denavar studied the king. He said, a little boldly, "You never held love for your father."

Yavaar's eyes widened, but he sighed. "His greed was boundless. His reign, cruel. The people hated him—for the steep taxes and neglect, for not protecting their villages and cities from bandits and murderers, for letting them rot. While his coffers grew fat with coin from the impoverished, his city became a division of the forgotten and the elite. It will take time, so much time, for me to change things for the better. For me to gain the people's trust. Especially after the darkness's attack. Maynesgate is ..."

The king shook his head, sadness filling those soft brown eyes. Denavar studied him thoughtfully. It was true that Maynesgate had suffered under King Dilini's rule. Its people had suffered, its streets had grown dirty, and the mecca of trade was a shadow of its former self. And this man, he seemed to care about those that lived in destitution and dismay. He had dreams, and perhaps Denavar could see them become reality.

So before he could think twice about the offer, he said, "I will help you."

Yavaar's eyes turned sharp as they narrowed in on Denavar. Distrust lingered in their glistening depths, and why wouldn't there be? He was a king, so young and already so tired of politics and the pawing of people who wanted to take and offer only empty promises in return. Denavar had seen the company the king kept—useless, arrogant fools whose true colours flashed in envious shades of green and self-indulgent hues of angry red as they whispered in the king's ears. Poisonous snakes. They did not think of those who needed, they thought only of those who wanted. Themselves and the elite.

But there was hope there too. A courage that would not be so easily stomped out. And Denavar had no plans for that.

"I will help you," he repeated. "When the war is done, the mages and I will help to rebuild you a new city—one worthy of its people. Trade will prosper, riches will flow, and your people will know happiness and equality. We will navigate the seas and extend trade routes, discover new civilisations. And all will remember what it is to be ruled by a fair and just leader."

Yavaar straightened, eyes glowing fiercely, as if this world flashed before him in fleeting wonder. There was a roguish charm to the king that promised to rebel against what was done and instead chase the idea of what should be. What *could* be a better future.

But the king was clever enough to know nothing comes without a price. "It all sounds wonderful in rehearsal, but you want something in return."

Denavar grinned as he popped a cake into his mouth. A buttery shortbread that oozed strawberry cream as he bit into its gooey centre. Delicious. He took his time, chewing slowly, savouring the flavours as he enjoyed letting the king stew.

Yavaar only raised an amused brow in return, his mouth quirking to the side. "You should try the sugar puffs," he drawled. "They're *divine*, and oh look, there's only one left."

Denavar stifled a choke as the king smirked. There. That backbone, that challenge, was what he had been waiting to see. For what Denavar had planned, the king would surely need it. And, if Denavar was being honest with himself, he liked Yavaar. The man reminded him of Finnicus, and Goddess knows friends would make mightier allies in times such as this.

He swallowed, took a sip of his tea and leaned forward in his seat. "I want to be your emissary—for both the elven allies and for Renlock Academy—which will receive a generous donation for the mages' efforts in due time, I'm sure."

Yavaar's lips curled at his forwardness, and to Denavar's surprise, the king laughed, eyes twinkling as he set his cup down upon the table. It was a hearty sound and no doubt a rare occasion for the human king. Indeed, Yavaar almost spluttered as if he realised it too, yet his expression sobered as he leaned forward in his chair, extending a hand.

To seal the deal—and perhaps to offer more than that. Friendship. The king was in short supply of it, Denavar knew. And truthfully, aside from the Guardians, Denavar had been so focused on his work, so intent on keeping to himself—having set himself apart from the temptation of friends for so long—that he'd forgotten what it was to share in its joys.

So he offered his own hand, clasping the king's firmly, a genuine smile on his face as he accepted that offer—both offers.

"I hope you're prepared," Yavaar said as he regarded Denavar with amusement. "It's going to be a bumpy ride from here."

Denavar snorted. "Your Majesty, I've been the star actor in this show for years. Now"—he waved a hand, gesturing for the king to join him as he stood—"let's talk about those leeches of yours. First order of business, get rid of those pompous pricks before they suck you dry."

Yavaar laughed. "Done. Anything else?"

Denavar's eyes narrowed. "Now that you mention it, there is one thing ..."

A Familiar Face

ASHALEA

"I'M DYING," Ashalea moaned as she sat up in bed, Razakh nestled in like a furnace against her side.

Shara rolled her eyes. "So you borrowed the weather for a night and fried a bunch of slimeballs with lightning. Get over it already, it's been a few days now."

She frowned at the assassin, who was lounging at the end of the bed, playing a game of catch the grape as she threw each one into the air. The girl only blew her a kiss with a mouthful of juice, and Ashalea nudged her playfully with a foot.

"*You're just jealous you weren't there to see it first-hand,*" Razakh mumbled. "*It was spectacular if you could ignore the noise and the smell of burning rot. It'll take me weeks to rid myself of the scent, you know.*"

Ashalea stroked his fur apologetically, letting the pair exchange rebuttals as she pawed the sleep from her eyes. It was too early for arguing, and her muscles were much too stiff to bat them both away. She yawned, stretching her arms above her head before crawling out of bed with a stiffness not akin to corpses in the grips of rigor mortis.

She had slept for a few days after the battle, her energies all but spent on the Magicka used to destroy those foul creatures. Thankfully, this meant she missed cleaning up the mess and the wrath of Kano, whose rage was, according to Shara, 'like being in a horde of hungry Uulakhs'. Ashalea couldn't blame him. Dwarves had died in gruesome ways, feasted on like a veritable banquet set out just for the marsh monsters. He had lost good soldiers because the attack had caught them off-guard—his scouts patrolling the southern border of the mountains had been massacred, not one left alive to spread the news of the incoming army.

Vigilance was key now. Mistakes like that could not be repeated, not as every race in Everosia planned to march, leaving their cities vulnerable to attacks. She just hoped the rulers planned accordingly. The elves would have better luck—Magicka came naturally to the gifted mages, and wards could be erected that would, at the very least, provide due warning of any approaching danger.

Denavar knew this, and she suspected he would be taking extra measures on behalf of the mages to ensure all allies were sufficiently protected—at least from the monsters. If the darkness deigned to fight his own battles, things could take a disastrous turn.

Which was why Ashalea would be scouring the city for the next Guardian today. She had felt something the night of the battle—a calling, a thrum of power humming a low chord no one else seemed to hear except Shara and Razakh, who said they had felt the same thing. It had been strongest before the battle truly began, yet with dwarves milling about, and their focus on the task at hand, Ashalea was unable to discern who it came from.

But perhaps today would be different. He was a soldier, that much was true, for she had only felt it upon entering the fight—after leaving the confines of the city's labyrinth of streets and feeling winter's kiss upon her cheeks. Yet even with vigorous training under the Masters' tutelage over the last few days, she had not felt it flare so brightly again.

So she would scout the arena today, check every home, shopfront and back alley if she had to. Right after her training this morning, which she expected would result in another embarrassing failure at the hands of Master Erik. The male had her respect now, but she still hated him just a little.

The thought of getting pummelled, flipped, prodded and poked again made her want to crawl back into bed but she slunk behind the changing screen and began donning her leathers and fighting gear. She sniffed, her delicate nose scrunching in protest. They reeked of sweat and staleness, but the dwarves hardly had anything to fit her, and by now she was used to the grime from many days spent on roads and in the undergrowth.

She shimmied on her breaches, lacing up the waist as tight as it could go, which was apparently not tight enough. Her elven blood had quickened her recovery, the muscles growing faster than a human's would, her fitness returning. But her hips were still slender, her navel all sharp planes and jutting bones. She sighed. Maybe she *should* try meat. Protein would certainly help with packing on mass and muscle and given the state of the world, she didn't think the elvish deities would begrudge her that.

"*And it tastes very nice,*" Razakh said. "*I don't know what these dwarves do with the meat, but it positively melts off the bone, and that gravy ...*" He licked his lips, lost in a world of free-for-all buffets.

Ashalea pictured gesturing rudely at him in her mind, to which he responded with a throaty snort. Shara threw a grape at his head. "Stop dreaming of food again, you're drooling all over the silks."

He snapped at her before turning to Ashalea, echoing her thoughts about today's tasks. *"The Guardian we seek must be someone of high station here. A commanding officer of the king's army, or perhaps a noble of sorts."*

"A noble? Please," Shara scoffed, fluffing her hair. "Even the dwarven nobility is a bunch of self-indulgent sheep. They've had nothing useful to offer during our meetings"—she glanced at Ashalea—"and before you fret about missing them while you were asleep, you'll be happy to know nothing valuable was gleaned. And if I must spend another moment discussing which female might be most suitable for the king's sons, or if I have to watch them ogle the next buxom wench that waits on us, I'll slit someone's throat."

"They do seem to be rather pre-occupied with the female breast," Razakh said with a frown. *"But I don't understand … I never see any children with the … what did you call them? Wenches."*

Shara whacked a hand over his head. "I'm not even going to touch that one. Honestly though," she grumbled, "I think they're just there for the food."

Ashalea laughed. "They certainly do have an appetite. But I must agree with you, if one of the nobles in the king's good graces was a Guardian, we'd know it by now. An officer—someone the king can trust beyond politics and the power of words—that's who we're looking for. Dwarves favour strength, right? We'll find our mark in someone who has this trait."

Shara winked at Ashalea. "If we don't die first."

⸻ ◆•●•◆ ⸻

Ashalea was wheezing by the time she reached Master Erik's checkpoint, which was much too high up the mountain for her liking. The air was too thin, the cold unforgiving, and she felt like one step might send her tumbling off the cliff. But that was the point, she supposed. Erik never did anything by halves, and this run up the mountainside was conquering *her*, not the other way round. Erik was probably gloating in the arena below.

Doubled over, lungs on fire, muscles screaming with exertion, she suddenly felt sick, stomach roiling with the threat of—

She emptied its contents into the pillowed snow before her feet. She had been running regularly but training on flat terrain was nothing compared to taking on this beast of a mountain. Shara rocked on her heels beside her, patting Ashalea on the back with amusement. It felt less like a comforting gesture than a confirmation of her weakness.

Ashalea sat back, wiping her mouth with the back of her hand. She hadn't eaten yet and cringed from the acrid taste coating her tongue. The vomit was already freezing over, bright yellow and glaring, much to her disgust.

She glanced at Shara. "Not a word."

Her friend only grinned and threw her hands up incredulously. "I wasn't going to say anything. But we should get moving, you know he'll be timing us."

Ashalea groaned as Shara took a hand—the clean one—and hauled her to standing. "Slow and steady, yeah?" the assassin said, her gaze darting to the sheer drop on their left. Indeed, now would not be the time to start sprinting. She glared at the red flag perched in the snow, its banner rippling, unimpressed, in the wind.

But she would not be defeated by the mountain or anything else. Ashalea gazed out at the rugged landscape before them. There was so much beauty in its wildness. Creatures small and large made their livings here—amongst the treetops, burrowed beneath the snow and far below lakes frozen over for the winter. So fascinating, each of them fighting hard for the next day and the next. She supposed, in their own way, the races of Everosia were doing much the same thing. Only, their threat was bigger than the change of seasons, crueller than winter's bite could ever be.

But she would fight. Today, the next day, the next. She would hone her body so it was once again powerful and strong, she would train her mind and Magicka to be a weapon and, brother or not, she would destroy the darkness.

She would have her vengeance even if it destroyed her in the process ... she just had to get through training first.

With a last look at the snowscape around them—a wistful glance at the rosy rays of the rising sun as it tried so hard to pierce through clouds above—they trotted down the path back to the arena. Ashalea reminded herself with every pang of pain that it would make her stronger, that her elven blood and bones would speed up the process of regaining her fitness—her health.

Erik, of course, said nothing when they returned, his thin lips giving little away. He merely waved a dismissive hand. Apparently, training was finished for the day. Shara rolled her eyes before turning to Ashalea. "You search the city for the other Guardian, I'm going to speak with the king—see what help he needs in moving his army or preparing defences for Kingsgareth."

Razakh bounded over, the Diodonian having had a successful hunt given the bloody maw he sported and the lazy grin. Ashalea saw a white wolf waiting for him, and she smiled softly. The alpha of the pack he had run with; the duo had been near inseparable since the battle, her friend slinking off at every spare moment to spend time with her. She wondered if perhaps ...

"*I'll help you look,*" he said to Ashalea, cutting off her thoughts, but she swore he looked just a little guilty. "*You take the smithies and the barracks; I'll search the bowels of the city.*"

"Oh?" she said with a brow raised. "Is that all?" She jerked her chin to the wolf and Razakh's fiery mane flared to life—as close to a blush as one could get from an intelligent beast such as he.

Shara leaned in for the kill, and Ashalea left, a broad smile on her face even as she ignored whatever jibes they exchanged. They were insufferable in the best way, their friendship somehow set apart, unique. But she didn't mind, feeling glad that Shara had someone besides her to rely on. Denavar and Shara were close too, but she suspected Shara had always felt on the outs when it came to their once trio.

There had never been much room for jealousy, but it was comforting to know that there was now another who would keep an eye on Shara. The girl had always been brash, stubborn, fiery, but to have someone to temper that flame couldn't be a bad thing. She just hoped the next Guardian didn't encourage it further.

Ashalea made her way indoors, shrugging off the feather-soft snowflakes and smoothing out her hair. She coiled it into a bun above her head, shoving stubborn tendrils into a leather tie. It would be polite to take a bath—her muscles would sure appreciate it too—but she was eager to begin the hunt, and damned if she cared what everyone thought.

She rubbed her hands together as she stalked down the steps, her fingers scaly and raw from the cold; they felt like an Uulakh's skin—she probably looked like one too.

The city was back to its usual bustling self after the scare of the attack—more so now that orders had been given to prepare for the war. Dwarves hurried about with their own missions, various supplies in hand to pack in wagons to be drawn, assumedly, by the white wolves, given that there were no horses here. The slopes were too precarious, Ashalea assumed, though the height ratio between dwarves and horses could just as well be the issue. She chuckled at the imagery her devious mind concocted.

Children scattered between the adults, laughing, playing with toys and chasing 'marshland monsters' of their wildest imaginations. She smiled at their innocence and joy, so pure, so unaware of the greater threats the coming months would bring. The adults were less impressed as the little terrors darted under bolts of fabrics, nudged cooks whose dishes threatened to topple, or outright hurtled over and through the stalls lining the streets.

The city buzzed with the hum of a people who knew their roles and responsibilities—who would perform and get the job done post-haste. Many of these dwarves would fight, and many would fall. Ashalea studied their faces even as the morbid thought swept through her. She tried and failed not to sear every detail into her brain, as if by remembering each one she might do their memory a service or honour their person.

She had no doubt those children would be hugged tightly come dawn, for she had spoken with Denavar and he had agreed to send mages to begin transporting soldiers and workers to set up camp. Come tomorrow, the camp would host a contingent of all allies, and that's when the fun would truly begin. She hoped—prayed—there would be no mishaps, that the allied armies could play nice. But it would only be so long before fights began to erupt, before soldiers grew irritable from the cold, the rations they would no doubt be fed, and the lack of action ... or not.

There had been no sightings of the darkness, no movement of

creatures around Everosia except for the marshland monsters. In fact, it was decidedly quiet across the land, with no raids or murders or mutilations in sight. Ashalea's brows drew together, her nerves aflutter. This ignited her fears even more. The lack of knowledge for what he was planning and having no contingency plan of her own worried her.

One step at a time, she warned herself, balling her fists together. She wended her way through the crowd, sighing in relief as the streets emptied the closer she got to the forges. If possible, the hammers smashing on anvils and the shouts of blacksmiths barking orders at assistants seemed even more urgent as she approached. Heat puffed in tired breaths, warming her cheeks as she wound towards the barracks.

She felt, in every sense of irony, dwarfed as the towering metal jaws yawned open around her, their tongues red-hot with dripping golds and silvers. Moulds were ingrained into blackened slabs in neat stations—impressions of swords, axes, and various other blades just waiting for molten liquids to be poured in, cooled, and tempered with hammer and anvil.

The blacksmiths' arms rippled with power and strength as they struck again and again. Each wore leather aprons and thick gloves, with most opting for bandannas or caps that tucked away their braids. Many had tattoos that snaked up their necks—a mean looking hammer with intricate workings of text along the axe head. She wondered if, among them, it passed as a sign of respect and pride for their station.

As fascinating as it all was, her heart sagged as she strolled through. The next Guardian was not here, though she shouldn't have been surprised, really. While she respected this art, and there were many legends of dwarven master blacksmiths, it did not speak to a greater calling.

But ... there! The hum of that familiar power; it thrummed ever so softly in her veins, almost invitingly, as if wanting to be found. It felt playful, like a game of cat and mouse—only her prey wanted to be hunted, wanted to be joined with her. United with its kin.

Her boots gobbled up the stone as she quickened her pace, long legs striding with eagerness, and she was headed right for the barracks. It was plain in comparison to the city proper—nothing adorning the stone walls, no rugs or decoration. It was stern, but warm and bright from the many sconces lining the walls. And she supposed it needed no embellishment, for it was a room of war, and war promised no niceties.

The main room was neatly lined with racks of weapons, all separated according to type and size. The walls formed a production queue that progressed towards a gigantic door leading, assumably, to the cliffside beyond. Armour crowded Ashalea first, all in glistening plate mail, shiny greaves, spaulders, pauldrons and vambraces. Heavy armour, to ensure protection from head to toe for foot soldiers, which made up the majority of Kano's army. Dwarves were generally not as proficient in archery, preferring instead to meet their foes eye to eye—or eye to chest, in the dwarves' case—before lopping their heads off.

Strength, Ashalea reminded herself. They valued strength, honour, and the pride that came from taking lives, from their name living on after death through great feats in battle. There was a barbaric undertone to that, for war was not something to be revered. Perhaps respected in a way, but never mounted on a pedestal of glory. But dwarves relished the fight; they were born with the song of war in their blood.

After the armour came the weapons. The craftsmanship was

impeccable, with the swords being well-balanced and light, the axes and maces both vicious and beautiful. She marvelled at their make, even as that Magicka began to pound insistently, her blood alight with adrenaline and power and—

She bumped into something solid as a rock, letting out an undignified squeak as the impact startled her from the distraction of the Magicka. Her emerald eyes travelled down to the top of the bearer's head. White-blond hair ran down the middle of his skull, trailing down in thin ropes to join in one thick braid down his back. One side of his head was tattooed, detailing a snarling wolf that curled from behind his ear as if pouncing.

He turned around slowly—so slowly—shoulders bunching, meaty hands fisting, and for a heartbeat Ashalea wondered if she was about to learn first-hand of dwarven strength and anger. But she almost stumbled into him again, knees weak as the Magicka raged within her, the aura now pulsing, the invisible chord stretching from her to—

The male faced her, confusion taking over the *very* angry set of his mouth and the stern eyes of pale blue that pierced her own. He lifted a hand to his heart, a small shudder racking through his considerably muscly, rigidly tense body.

But his eyes widened, and then they narrowed in accusation. "You," he said, one meaty finger almost poking her eye out, his cheeks ruddy with anger.

Ashalea thrust her hands out in supplication, a weak smile on her lips. "Me?" she said, cringing ever so slightly.

"You," he repeated. "I've met you before. On the road to Maynesgate. You bumped into me then too, and I don't forget a face, hood or no. Bloody elves."

Something about that phrasing sent a spark of familiarity

through her. The haughtiness, that accent ... the memory flashed before her. She was indeed on the road to Maynesgate with Wezlan when she had bumped into a dwarf. She had been so excited to see one—the first she had ever laid eyes upon, though certainly not the nicest. Wezlan had chuckled and said something about dwarven moods, or lack of good ones.

"My Gods," Ashalea mumbled, eyes widening. "You've got to be kidding. You're the next Guardian?"

The dwarf bristled, a corded muscle flexing in his neck as he stared at her incredulously. "Oh, aye, you remember me now, eh? No manners I'll note. And what's this about Guardians?"

Ashalea just stared. The dwarf, for all his bluster, was clearly a male of importance. His armour, golden and glistening, screamed at nobility. And his burgundy cloak was clasped at his throat with a wolf emblem. She could see Kano in his features; in the blue-grey eyes, the hard lines of his face and the white-blond hair. And there was the tattoo on his head, something perhaps any loyal soldier might adorn themselves with but ...

She felt it bubbling in her stomach, surging up and up her throat until she could hold it in no longer. Ashalea laughed, the sound melodic and light even to her ears. His thick brows drew downwards, red cheeks deepening into the burgundy of his cloak. But the scowl was what undid her. She howled, bending over as tears slipped down her cheeks.

"What the blast is the matter with you? You're nuts. Deranged," he said, his expression changing to that of a sane person regarding a madwoman. It quickly morphed into suspicion, his eyes narrowing to chips of ice. "What the bloody heck are you doing in my barracks? And what in two hells have you done to me?"

He clutched his chest again, seemingly feeling the same effects as she. Ashalea's laughter died as the Magicka seemed to let out a final triumphant flare at her recognition before easing into a quiet slumber. She sighed in relief, quickly stamping out any more uncalled for laughter. It really wouldn't do to be thrown in the dungeons before she could explain herself.

"You better start speaking, witch, or I'll have you thrown in a cell and tied up before you can say Guardian."

She almost howled at his odd insult, but Ashalea took a deep breath, standing to her full height as she lifted a chin. "I am Ashalea Kindaris, princess of the Moonglade Meadows, Guardian of the Grove, and sister to the evil threatening this land which you may know as the darkness. And you, Your Highness"—she smiled coldly—"are going to help me kill him."

We Are Lions

Ashalea

HIS NAME WAS TOFIN RIVKEN, general of the dwarven king's army, and Kano's son, third in line for the throne of Kingsgareth Mountains. He was also the next dwarven Guardian, which had been confirmed after a quick appraisal by Razakh and Shara.

Ashalea might have wept with relief. They had finally done it. They had finally gathered all the pieces of the puzzle, all the parts needed to defend the Grove. Only, the next Guardian was proving to be stubborn as an ass, and as venomous as pit vipers; his tongue sharp and grating as he spat all kinds of profanities.

They were seated in the king's dining hall, lunching on the possibilities of war and the burdens of duty. Tofin, it seemed, was less than pleased to take his place as Guardian. It left a lump in Ashalea's throat that had nothing to do with the food. For his part,

Kano seemed just as perplexed whilst his son cornered him with accusations.

"You spring this blasted lunatic elf on me and expect me to abandon our armies and hide within a bloomin' forest?"

Ashalea bristled. "We will be fighting alongside all armies," she interrupted with a glare levelled at Tofin, "and when the timing is right, we will close the portal. Until all allied armies have convened, we will not know the particulars of our plan."

The general scoffed. "Well you can be sure the darkness is not going to let you waltz in to take away his one shot at dominion."

Shara's amber eyes looked at him with boredom, and perhaps a little disdain. "You're forgetting we have a wizard on our side. One whose powers recently received a considerable raise from the *last* of the Divine Six. Denavar's Magicka combined with Ashalea's ... the darkness will have a run for his money."

Tofin glanced at Ashalea. "I have seen your power first-hand. Granted, it is strong, but your thunder and lightning show will not be enough to stop him."

"*Perhaps not,*" Razakh mused from his position on the nearby chaise. "*But she has been granted considerable gifts from the elven Goddess, Prianara. To restore life to a non-beating heart, to harness the power of the very lunar system ... that is no small feat.*"

Tofin's grey eyes widened. "You—you brought someone back from the dead?"

It was the only inkling of interest he had yet shown in their party. Interest and ... fear. She supposed all manner of folktales passed down from kin to kin would have twisted ideas of the raised dead and their unearthly vendettas. But what had occurred with Shara was quite the opposite.

Bringing her friend back to life had brought out the purest

of Magicka; something so holy and divine it had blotted out the dark with its brightness and swept aside stars. Her eyes burned at the memory. It had been a sense of helplessness, with only the strength of hope to ignite the fire within. To stoke the bravery of a girl who dared to believe, who would have given anything to hear that beating heart again.

Shara smiled at her, sadness deep within those amber eyes, but an understanding passed between them that she would have done the same if she could. She would have given everything if she had the power. It was the type of friendship one only dreamed of or heard about in stories—one that Ashalea would fight for, because aside from Wezlan, Shara had been her first and only friend. Now she was privileged to have found not just companions in the Guardians, but a family. One she'd fight for with every kernel of strength in her body.

"*As will I, little one,*" Razakh purred in her mind.

Ashalea flashed him a smirk before she opened her mouth to answer Tofin, but it was Shara who beat her to it. "She brought me back from the dead. And it's a good thing too," she said with a toss of her hair, "this body is a temple that should be worshipped for every second of its prime."

Ashalea winked at her friend. "Your ego knows no bounds. But enough games." She leaned back in her chair, tilting her head to the side as she studied Tofin. "You have two choices. Join the Guardians, help us seal the portal and prevent the darkness from leeching his monsters into our lands ... or don't and watch everything you love turn to ash in your mouth. Your kinsman will fall on the battlefield, your females will be broken, your children will line the bellies of his beasts, and all around you Everosia shall burn. Burn as the darkness destroys this world for spite."

There was silence as her words sank in. And they knew—everyone knew—her words rang with truth. And it was not the meaning behind them that struck fear into their hearts, but the knowledge that all would come to pass should they fail. If, ultimately, the Guardians failed.

"Tofin," Kano said softly as his son paled, "there would be no greater honour than fighting with you on the battlefield, and that we will. A fight that poets will write epics for and bards will sing ballads about. Your name will forever mark the pages of history. But your destiny lies beyond a worthy death or the crash of shield and hammer. You must complete the circle of Guardians. You must prevent the darkness from accessing the portal."

Tofin's hard grey eyes lifted to stare into Ashalea's, empty of all bluster and argument, full only of resignation. "For you, Father, and for my people, I will do my duty."

Kano nodded with approval, clapping a hand on his son's back. "There's a good lad. Now, you'd best get moving. We leave come dawn."

Shara's brows drew up. "Your soldiers are ready?"

"As they'll ever be," the king replied. His mouth set in a grim line. "I would have you return to Renlock and inform Denavar we shall await his mages at first light."

Ashalea nodded. "It shall be done." She looked to Shara and Razakh and raised a brow.

The assassin rolled her eyes before sending daggers at the dwarf. "Fine," she said with a huff. "Razakh and I will join the dwarves at the war camp. Someone has to whip these armies into shape."

Razakh's enchanting eyes swirled violently. *"And so we sheep shall flock to the slaughter."*

Shara snorted. "We are no sheep. We are lions, and we come

to claim our prey."

<hr>

Peppermint tickled her nose as arms of chiselled muscle crushed her against a warm, solid chest. She nestled into Denavar, relishing this haven, nuzzling her head into the hollow of his neck. "I missed you," she breathed.

Her hair mussed as he breathed her in and stroked curling tendrils of silver hair behind her ears. "And I you. Dealing with Tiderion has been taxing to say the least. I forgot how insufferable he can be."

Ashalea snorted. "Are you kidding? He thinks trees should bend before him. It wouldn't surprise me if he shat out gold bars with his face imprinted on them. Then everyone worthy would still be indebted in some regard."

Denavar chuckled. "He's as grumpy as a bear out of hibernation, but he certainly holds influence, and his soldiers are some of the best. But I don't want to talk about him now." He kissed the top of her head, tilting her chin up so he could look upon her face.

His ocean eyes reached depths it would take years only an elf might reach. And she wanted to explore every inch, every shallow wave, every violent delight beneath the crashing layers of turmoil.

They roamed over her face now, studying every freckle, the curve of her lips, the planes of her bone structure as he sat next to her, their knees touching. "You are so beautiful," he said, and the words pulled at her heart. She smiled shyly, which drew his gaze to her lips, his eyes turning ravenous.

She had never cared much for being desired, knowing sexuality could bring out the worst in males and females, and that beauty could be a curse in a world full of the ill-intentioned. But to be wanted—not just skin deep but in every sense of her being—was a gift. A welcome surprise on a journey so wrought with pain and loss. She considered how lucky she was to have him, to have found someone to quicken the rhythm of her beating heart and encourage her to grow.

He drew her closer, began kneading the muscles in her back, and she arched into his touch, letting the last week drain away, ignoring the world momentarily. She was tired, wiped out after training and defending the keep of Kingsgareth, and he knew it. "Do you need anything?" he asked. "Are you hungry?"

"A little," she admitted. Her grin grew razor-sharp. "But not for food right now."

His answering smile was feral, greedy, and he pulled Ashalea onto his lap, her legs straddling his. A small groan escaped her lips as he began trailing featherlight kisses along her jaw, travelling down her neck and up again. Exploring, cherishing, *wanting*. The sound only increased his eagerness, the kisses becoming firmer, a hand that had been massaging her back now possessive as he cupped the nape of her neck and pulled her mouth to his own.

Soft pillows cushioned her lips as she parted them, the seam of his own fitting perfectly. The soft sigh of heady breath rushed as his tongue crashed against her own, igniting the well of heat in her core. His body answered in earnest, and her stomach tensed with need.

She ran fingers through the brown waves of his hair, pulling sharply as she yanked his head back and claimed his neck, grazing her teeth along the soft skin before nipping gently. Her other hand went to work on his pants, unlacing the breaches before sliding a hand under the material to the warmth of him.

Gently, lovingly, she stroked every inch of him, his breath hot and heavy against her chest until she pushed him playfully back, his glorious body stretching out underneath her. He was steel and gilded treasure made flesh, an artform of the body, a masterpiece for her eyes only. And he was hers. Every bone, every ounce of blood in his veins, every sorrow and every smile.

She told him so as she increased her movement, and he shuddered beneath her, the need deepening. With a snarl he tore Ashalea's tunic in two, the tattered remains half covering her breasts as they swelled with desire, peaking at the cool air. He slid warm hands over each, tongue flicking out.

A groan escaped her lips, and he wrapped corded arms around her waist, lifting her from the bed and carrying her to the wall. He set her down gently before claiming her mouth, their passion roiling together, their lips a crashing wave of desire.

Denavar worked his way down her neck, her breasts, the curve of her stomach, until slowly, so slowly, he began peeling away her breaches, thumbs teasing the soft planes beneath her hips all the while. Ashalea rocked her legs back and forth impatiently, and he grinned with lazy, predatory intent.

"So impatient," he crooned, and she growled in frustration, trying to paw at her pants. But he batted her away, his teeth pulling them down until, finally, she was free and bare and ready for—

He swept in with too clever a mouth and she gasped. Heat pooling in her core; her body reacted instantaneously, head thrown back and eyes squeezed shut at the sensation. She wriggled with pleasure, but he snarled as he rose, pinning her hands above her head, claiming her in every sense of the word. She was panting, his movement quickening, her blood rushing and, just as her knees were about to buckle, he scooped her up and slammed into her, unsheathing every wondrous inch.

They sucked in a breath in unison, and she wrapped her legs around his torso as he rocked. His hands firmly planted on her ass, fingers tightening on her skin as he moved in and out. The pictures on the wall threatened to topple as he struck again and again. She plunged her hands into his hair, stifling her cries as their dance quickened, their bodies becoming one as they neared climax.

His tongue snaked up her slick neck before crashing into her mouth, the moan of her name hot as coals as he panted. And the honour it held as he uttered those syllables, the love it bore undid her. She curled her arms around his neck, raked her nails down his back and he arched, pleasure and pain all twined into one.

They finished together, their breaths quick and sharp, the fires quenched as their dance reached its end and the song quieted to a silent embrace. He held her there for a time, head cradled against her neck, with nothing but the feel of each other, the steady rise and fall of their chests, and the comfort of arms wrapped around one another in a protective shield.

After a time he lifted his head to survey her. "I love you," he whispered. "I've loved you from the moment I saw you; moonlit hair and starry eyes as beautiful as the night sky."

Ashalea frowned. "You love me for beauty alone?"

He smirked before placing her lovingly on the chaise and stalking to the far wall, where he filled a small bowl with water, oils. Grabbing a cloth, he padded silently back to her, kneeling like a knight before his queen. The faint smell of sandalwood and jasmine floated before her.

"I loved you," he said as he began to wipe her skin down, the cloth warm and tingling on her flesh, "when I saw your dirt-streaked face in the gardens of Windarion, fighting with the spirit of a thousand Diodonians against Shara. I loved you when I learned of your fiery nature, your sharp tongue, so unafraid of what the world might think." He smirked. "Or what I might think."

She huffed before spreading out luxuriously on the chaise, ensuring every inch of her body stretched out before him. His eyes glinted wickedly as she said, "You were following me around like a lovesick puppy."

He laughed. "Orders were orders."

"Which I'm sure you were all too happy to indulge in."

"It's not every day you get to woo a princess," he said with a wink.

Ashalea nudged him with her elbow. "I'm quite sure Tiderion asked you to spy on me. Not court me ... or bed me for that matter."

Denavar shrugged, his grin lazy. "He didn't explicitly say not to. I would have disobeyed regardless, and it was getting boring in Windarion. Were it not for Kinna and Ondori I would have gone mad long before you showed up."

His smile faded, and Ashalea felt the pang of sorrow too. "I miss them," she sighed. And it was true. She had not known the two Windarion elves long, but they had become fast friends. She recalled their smiling faces, always mischievous, always seeking to break rules. They were beautiful inside and out—unique, right from the top of their turquoise and purple heads down to the last loyal toe. But their friendship was never meant for the ages, and the two elves had fallen on their voyage to the Isle of Dread, lost to the Onyx Ocean's depths—and the mouths of monsters.

Denavar gently took her chin in his hand. "We will remember them—all of them—when the war is done. We will hold feasts in honour of the fallen, and ensure their names live on through the passing of time."

Ashalea smiled softly. "If we survive the war."

His grip tightened—not hard enough to hurt, but to reprimand that way of thinking. To remind her that they were a team, *Guardians*, and they would not give in. "When we survive, we will host a celebration fit for the ages, with so much mead and the biggest spreads that even the dwarves will find their bellies fit to bursting."

Ashalea chuckled. "I wouldn't count on it. I've seen the way they eat, it's almost barbaric how feisty they become when feasting."

"Well, when you become queen, you'll think of something, I'm sure."

She shifted uneasily. "My mother has shown no sign of stepping down or moving any which way for that matter. She is a lost cause, and my heritage perhaps along with her."

Denavar's muscles tensed. "That *queen* will be the death of our people. The Meadows has been left to rot in ruination for far too long. We need a strong ruler, someone who will fight for it with every breath. Someone like you."

Ashalea's eyes narrowed, and she sat up slowly. "You're not suggesting ..."

"An insurrection? Absolutely." His voice was light, but Denavar's features were grave.

She groaned, placing her palms against her temples. "I might be angry with her, and we might have a lot of issues to work through, but I couldn't do that to my mother, Denavar. Not after everything that's happened."

"Why not?" he challenged. "Think of what we could rebuild once the war is done. The Meadows was once a bright beacon of life—a city of wonder and Magicka. Now, it is overgrown with age and disuse, even the Magicka itself is slumbering as if it's too tired to wake. There would be no need for wards or mists or shutting the world out."

And it sounded wonderful, it truly did. But if the cost were shaming her mother, inciting dissent among the people—elves who she would then have to rule over—it didn't seem right, and it certainly didn't seem just. She would have to prove to both Celiana and the Moonglade elves that she was worthy.

"I cannot dishonour my mother's name, nor my own, by seeking to overtake her. Not at a time like this. Not when her son is the very root of all our problems."

"Politics shall be a crown you will wear whenever in positions of power," Denavar argued. "You need to learn to play the game, Ashalea, or no one wins."

"Perhaps I don't want to," she snapped. "Perhaps I don't want to be anything of importance once the darkness is dead. Maybe one more loss, even if it is that dreadful bastard, will be too much weight to handle."

And maybe she hadn't wanted to admit it to herself, but a small part of her was terrified of what she must do. That killing the darkness, however necessary, would tear a piece of her soul from her forever.

"Ashalea," he said slowly, "I know he is your brother, but this must be done. He threatens all of us—our lives and our land. He has killed more people than I can count."

She threw her hands up, eyes burning. "You don't think I know that? After all that we've been through? He's destroyed everything I've ever loved. And I'm tired, Denavar. I'm so damn tired of him haunting my every step. But if we should win this war, if I should succeed in destroying him, then what will I become? I'm afraid ... afraid of the anger in my heart. I'm terrified that once this is over, I will burn until my fury consumes me. Until I am nothing but a memory of a girl you used to love."

Tears swept down her face, hot and angry, and she took a deep breath, the air shuddering out. Denavar was silent as he stared at her. Not piteously or regretfully, but with relief, she realised. An unusual calm that followed her outburst, and suddenly it clicked.

This was perhaps the most emotion she had showed—had allowed herself to feel—since the Moonglade Meadows. The rage coursing through her veins made her feel alive, gave her purpose in this life. But as she looked at Denavar, as she cupped his face and felt the steadiness of him, the reliability, it made her realise ... he would give her purpose in the next one.

A world free from Crinos. Untouched by monsters of his making, of death and despair. One where she might laugh and smile, make memories, make *life* instead of taking it. With him. With Denavar.

She looked at him then, at that knowing smile—a wizard too clever for his own good. He reminded her of Wezlan in that moment; he always knew just how to ignite her temper ... or soothe it.

Denavar rose, shifting onto the chaise to take her by the arms and lift her to his lap, leaning his head forward so their temples met, and their noses touched. "You think your anger stifles you, that it consumes the good, but I say it's your greatest ally. Vengeance sowed the seeds of your quest; retribution shall be what defines it. But not you, my dearest Ashalea. You are more than a Guardian or a queen or a deliverer of evil. You are loved, and you are cherished. And ... if you'll take this rather charming, dashing wizard, you'll be my wife and the mother of my children one day."

Ashalea leaned back slowly, searching those ocean blue depths, sparkling as if the sun itself gilded their calm surface. A small smile crept to her face, an ember of hope igniting in her chest. "Denavar," she said, lips tilting slyly, "that sounded suspiciously like a proposal."

He grinned, wild and wicked and dripping with delight. "Don't be silly. Peasants can't ask for a princess's hand."

She laughed, the heat of her temper quickly fizzling out. The rage of that prior moment already swept aside. "Peasant? I would hardly call the only wizard left in Everosia a peasant."

Denavar rolled his neck before throwing her a cocky grin. "I suppose that does give me some bragging rights, though I think I rather like the idea of you asking me. Makes me feel dignified. Turns the tables on traditionalism."

She scoffed. "Archaic, if you ask me. But I'll think about your proposition. Mull it over a little."

He was apparently pleased with her answer, and they shifted, lying down on the chaise, her settling into his side, him bracing a warm, protective arm over her back. Forever seemed a long way away, but she could dream.

For now, she could dream.

Murderous Heathens

SHARA

HE WOULD NEVER GET USED TO THE WINDOWS. Bright and blue and fizzling with energy. To leave one part of the world and just pop into another was a phenomenon Shara could not wrap her head around. But it wasn't the Magicka that deterred her. It was memory.

For stepping through one of these portals had once set her on a long and torturous path that had ended in her death. She remembered it so clearly—the touch of that clawed hand, the reek of rot, the despair on Ashalea's face as she was ripped from her friends and thrown in a cell beneath the earth.

She shuddered now, breath forming white clouds from her ragged gasps. Razakh must have sensed the change in her, for he stepped to her side, brushing his great head against her leg before looking into her eyes.

He nodded just once, as if he knew the root of her fear, and she knew he would burn her doubts away if he could. But it was enough, the solid weight of him by her side, the warmth of his fur. She clutched a fistful firmly in one hand; not enough to hurt, but so she felt like nothing could separate them.

Razakh waited patiently. It took all her willpower to ignore the trepidation, all her strength to force one foot in front of another and break through. But together, they made it. Like opening a door they simply moved through and there it was: the war camp.

Row upon row of tents in neat, huddled lines that spread as far as the eye could see. Yavaar's camp lay before her, bustling with soldiers set to work, their hands efficient, their steps sure as they each went about various tasks. They barely gave her party a second glance, no doubt used to the arrivals of all the races by now.

Shaking, she stepped into the bleary scene, instantly thankful for the extra layers Ehren had insisted she wear. The weather was miserable, and the wind howled as it sliced through her attire. She gritted her teeth and found even the dwarves seemed to glare at the sky as they poured through one by one.

She glanced sidelong at Razakh, his golden coat already dusted with white, though the beast seemed unbothered by the weather. "*Thanks,*" she thought, and he dipped his head regally.

No sooner had Kano and his sons stepped through the portal when a familiar voice said, "You're late."

Shara smiled. Caelor, the Lady Nirandia's twin and general of the Woodrandian army. The elf looked resplendent in his bronze armour, hazel eyes sparkling as he approached the dwarf king, his blonde hair pristine. Kano's answering gaze could have levelled mountains, tension overflowing into the white expanse.

"Surely we're not going to have a pissing match within the first five minutes," she whispered to Razakh, knowing Caelor could hear. She swore she spied the slightest twitch of his lips as he stared down Kano.

She could hear the mirth in Razakh's reply as he said, "So *uncivilised.*"

To Shara's surprise, the males burst into broad grins, clasping hands and clapping each other on the back.

"We both know the party only starts once dwarves are in the mix," Kano said. He looked around him, a quick study of the camp that lay ahead. "What, no beastly Tiderion to greet me? What have I done to offend his lordship today?"

Caelor chuckled. "His esteemed grace is settling his army in the northern encampment. He didn't want to sully his nose with dwarven filth." He put his hands up as Tofin and the other brothers bristled. "His words, not mine."

Kano merely barked a laugh. "Then we shall wait for the breeze to turn upwind to announce our arrival."

Shara snorted, and Caelor winked. "My lady. Guardians," he nodded in turn. "And I suppose we have a new member now?"

"Aye," Tofin said, looking none too happy about it. "That we do."

If Caelor was surprised, he didn't show it. "Well earned indeed. But let us continue this conversation somewhere warmer ... lest I lose some extremities."

Shara noted several shoulders wilting in relief, her own among them. She was eager to be moving—to assess the camp, to familiarise herself with the layout. She wanted to know where every lord and lady resided, where every armourer, blacksmith and healer tent sat, all the exits, all the vantage points. She was a Guardian, yes, but she was still every inch the Onyxonite. In training at least. In blood.

Caelor led them through the winding tents, neatly assembled in orderly fashion. Shara clutched her furs tight around her shoulders as she stalked through the war camp. It was bitterly cold, and she was thankful for her sturdy boots as she plodded through the sloshy path, muddied and slippery from the footsteps of many.

Her amber eyes studied every tent, every soldier, as she patrolled within their group. Razakh padded by her side, his silver eyes missing nothing. They headed towards an allotted space for the dwarves first. It was a good spot—the grassy knolls inclined ever so slightly, enough for a good vantage point of the plains that bordered the eastern front. Guards would have a clear view of any threats.

Kingsgareth Mountains loomed in the distance, but it was the blackened blight to the north-east that Shara couldn't look away from. The small village of Galanor; the inn that Shara had first met Telilah, her grandmother's home ... gone. Nothing but ash and the bones of the innocent. A stab of regret pierced through her gut, and thoughts of Telilah flashed through her mind. So much pain and suffering. So much needless death.

She shook herself free of the distraction, remembering her duty. Galanor was but a crumb for the darkness to sweep aside, to feed to the rats that worked for him. But she wouldn't let him have Everosia. Not without a fight.

Kano strode before her, his bright eyes searching the land. Apparently satisfied, he nodded and waved to the many dwarves trudging behind him. They set to work immediately, rolling cart after cart pulled through the muddied snow by the giant white wolves, their muscles bunching with the effort. Shara was still pissed she'd missed seeing them in action during the battle. Especially the alpha, whom she'd noticed Razakh had grown rather fond of. She thought he might be smitten.

The wolves came to a stop so the dwarves might set up tents and unload supplies. Efficient as they were, Shara knew that a new kind of wild would overtake these plains come nightfall. A hive of activity, every worker bee assigned to a task.

They left Kano's soldiers to it—an organised chaos taking shape, the beginnings of their life here for the foreseeable future. Until the next move would be made, with the only question being who would make it.

She found herself walking beside Tofin as they explored the rest of the camp. Caelor listed off areas of note; soldiers and workers of all races barely sparing a glance as they went about their various tasks. The north-eastern flank was left open for the Diodonians and to the north resided Tiderion's army, the soldiers gleaming in aqua green or vibrant purples, according to their status as foot soldier or mage.

To the west, Nirandia's soldiers fletched arrows and sharpened blades, all huddled around airborne fires of the Magickal kind. They were slightly more welcoming to the dwarves than Tiderion's host, and Shara had to wonder why anyone bothered with the archaic notions of animosity at all. They were different—one race tall, elegant, prone to knowledge and nature, whereas the other was brutal, proud, strong and, oddly enough, the more inviting of the two.

"They don't break the chains of their ancestors because they are afraid of what is different," Razakh said, and she had to glance around to spot the flash of his flames between dwarves. They were so damned wide she had trouble seeing anything at ground level. Though, she thought with a smirk, she had clear view at head height.

"Always so wise," she smiled to herself, knowing he'd hear her mutter.

"What're you mumbling about?" grumbled Tofin next to her.

She looked down at the wolf tattoo snarling at her from the side of his head and frowned. The cold weather was already souring her mood, and she didn't have the energy to spar with their newest member today. "Nothing to concern your lordship, so take a hike."

His cheeks flushed a murderous red. "Just who the bloody—"

"One of your new colleagues, that's who," she stated with a sweet smile. "Now let's get one thing straight: we've already fulfilled the position of sassy, moody Guardian. So don't be stepping on my toes."

Razakh nudged at her conscience. *"Perhaps a little more tact? He is one of us now. We want him to help us … not have him storm away before we even take a chance."*

If Tofin was irritated before, he looked positively enraged now. "Guardian or no, you're speaking to a prince and a general of my king's army. I could have you whipped like a dog."

She flinched at the mention of whipping, shying from its sting. She knew all too well what it entailed. The darkness had made Flynn do it on occasion, back when he was a puppet without strings, marionetted through mind and soul.

When he wasn't carving her with glittering blades, Crinos would have her whipped with metal tips. The pain was excruciating, of course, but the blow was in its humiliation. The degradation of it—a cruel spin on a common form of Onyxonite punishment.

It had made her hate him even more.

She swallowed her fear, casting the flashing memories aside like a snake discards its skin. Shara huffed. Razakh was right, of course. It wouldn't do to try and close the portal with a dwarf prince set on flouting his duty as Guardian.

She bit back the scathing retorts she longed to unleash and

instead sighed, clearing her mind and forcing her pride to retreat. She breathed deeply, surprised at the words she was about to say. Surprised even more that she wanted to say them, to reveal a small truth and an even bigger burden.

"I'm sorry. I have a habit of lashing out when I'm stressed or feel cornered. A coping mechanism to deal with, well, everything that's going on up here," she gestured to her head. "Working with others is ... difficult for me at times. There is a lot of anger inside, a lot of pain I'm still working through. But we are allies now, and we must work together."

It felt good to be honest, to humble herself before another. And it was overdue. Perhaps this façade of strength and cockiness was a mask that no longer fit. Perhaps she could shed her armour for those worthy of her trust. That was something she could try to do, right?

Tofin looked at her then, pale blue eyes wary but intrigued, the tension easing from his muscles as understanding registered in his eyes. "It's forgiven," he said simply, and Shara wilted with relief. "It takes courage to lay your own truths bare before you, let alone others. We are all our own worst monster."

Shara put a tentative hand on his shoulder. "I will remember that, when the dark is closing in. Thank you, Tofin. I know you don't want this—to be among the Guardians—but the truth is, I didn't at first either. I had other duties, to my father and my people."

She supposed he could relate. He was a prince, after all, and general of the army. Not a position one stepped down from lightly, certainly not a responsibility to pass unto others easily.

The dwarf sighed, stroking his beard with a meaty hand. "Duty is purpose and honour. To have it stripped, to step away from my place at my father's side ... 'tis not easy."

"Your honour remains true," Shara said softly. "To be a Guardian is a position of respect and power. It might not entail glorified halls and gilded thrones, but the blood and sweat you spill in service of the Grove will ensure a future for all of us."

Tofin studied her, the stern lines of his face smoothing. "You're not what I expected."

Her lips curled in amusement. "Why ... because I'm an Onyxonite?"

"Aye. I had you lot pegged for a bunch of murderous heathens."

Shara laughed. "You're not entirely wrong. But we have a code and, believe it or not, we have morals."

He raised one thick, white brow. "Like slitting throats while your targets sleep?"

Shara shook her head slowly. She was used to being judged. There was a prejudice against her tribe. To be Onyxonite was to be alone. So instead she bit her tongue, took the higher road.

"Like making a woman who had been raped and abused all her life feel safe again. Like destroying crime syndicates before they have a chance to destroy a city. Like offering justice to a man whose entire family had been murdered by thugs." She offered him a sad smile. "Our deeds are not heroic, our kills perhaps not honourable, but every death has a purpose. Every act has a flow-on effect that restores the balance."

Tofin's lips puckered beneath his beard. "There may be good in what you do, but I'd be a fool to believe all your kills are justified. Who governs you? What laws hold your own people accountable?"

Shara laughed. "In my town, darling, we are the law. We keep to ourselves because it suits our needs, and the world keeps away because not seeing us makes us easier to ignore."

"Death should be met face-to-face, with sword in hand and a fire in our bellies," Tofin replied with a sniff. "Not met by a phantom, struck in the back with a blade. I would rather meet my foe head on than slip away in my sleep. "

"Then you are a rare male, Tofin Rivken, and I hope your axe swings true, and the sounds of hammer on shield shall be the storm to sing your end."

"But not yet," Tofin said with a grin.

"Aye," Shara said, returning a grim smile of her own. "Not yet."

29

The Threads of Magicka

RAZAKH

THEY WERE ASSEMBLED, all leaders of the races, for a war meeting in what Nirandia politely referred to as the commons—an agreeable space for all party leaders to meet in *civility*. She had stressed that word when he had spoken to her prior. It seemed the elves and dwarves were already having spats despite Kano and his contingent arriving just this morning.

Razakh huffed. Why they couldn't set aside disputes ahead of the oncoming storm, he couldn't fathom. They were all the same inside—what skins they wore made little difference to him. He wished he could speak for all Diodonians, but unfortunately his own Klan had yet to smooth their hackles when around the humans.

Still, the camp had been carefully mapped out by Nirandia and Denavar, with the former arriving not long after the Diodonians to begin preparations. A clever move indeed on Nirandia and Caelor's part to keep Tiderion's elves and the dwarves in separated camps, likewise for the Diodonians and humans.

Despite the Diodonians' wariness, Razakh was relieved to see they had settled in just fine and were, for the most part, left to themselves. They would fare well in the cold weather, with their flames serving to keep each other warm, especially at night when they huddled together. Still, Nirandia had seen fit to erect several pavilions, lined with cushions and blankets, even going so far as to carve out hollows in the ground like those back in their sandy dens for pack members to curl into.

He was grateful for her. That kindness alone would go a long way to gain his soldiers' respect—maybe even tempt them to engage with the other races. It had certainly pleased Linar, the new chieftain. It had been a boon for Razakh to see that familiar, scarred face. The gruff Diodonian may not have agreed entirely with Razakh's wishes to have the Diodonians reintegrate with the world once more, but he had led the army through the old tunnels of the Diodon Mountains and straight to the plains.

Thankfully, no Wyrmears were noted on their trek, though Linar had mentioned his disgust at a monstrous corpse of one that lay rotting in the lower tunnels. Razakh had hummed with glee, launching into his and Shara's tale and everything the Guardians had done until now. He refrained from smiling now, lest he frighten any fainthearted elves. It seemed Kano was quite capable of doing that on his own.

"So that's it then, we just wait until the bastard comes gliding in to slaughter us like lambs?" Kano grumbled, clanking his goblet on the table, causing some of the nobles to jump.

"We don't know where the darkness is hiding," Razakh replied for

all to hear. *"His base, the size of his army, the weapons at his disposal, we're left in the dark."*

"Which is exactly how he wants us," Shara drawled. "When last we saw him"—she glanced at Ashalea and Denavar—"when Ash and Denavar escaped the other dimension, Wezlan wounded him, forced Crinos to unleash his powers. But it's been a couple months now and not a whisper of news has come our way. What game is he playing?"

"He could be waiting us out," Caelor suggested. "It looks to be a hard winter, and if the cold doesn't take us, the lack of food surely will."

"I think not," Yavaar said, shaking his head. "We have mages under our command—access to supplies, the blessing of Magicka to keep us warm. The only thing we risk by waiting is the sanity of our soldiers."

Nirandia nodded along. "Idleness breeds bad temperaments, but that's nothing hard work can't fix. There is much to be prepared. If we're going to stand any chance, we will need more than Magicka to save us."

"I might be able to help with that," Jyorden said with a wild grin, fishing in his pockets for some notes. "I have been working on some blueprints for mechanisms that will increase our reach on the battlefield. If they work, they will wreak havoc on the enemy."

Shara sat up straight, reaching a greedy paw out over the table. "May I?"

He handed over the blueprints, toothy grin broadening as he saw her delight. From what Razakh could see, the structures looked to be catapults of sorts, but their descriptions were scrawled in unintelligible script—for a Diodonian anyway.

A wicked glint filled Shara's eyes as she stared lovingly at the means for more bloodshed. "Oh, Princeling, you shouldn't have," she crooned.

"I aim to please," the dwarf said, and his brother Sven coughed at his side.

"Enough," Tiderion grumbled. "If your toys work then we can utilise them, but for now strategy is key. How to strike and when."

"He's waiting ..." Ashalea said, eyes glassy as she clasped her hands together. "Biding his time until we grow desperate enough to venture to the Grove."

Tiderion leaned forward in his chair, eyes narrowed as he looked at each of the Guardians in turn. "When *are* you going to the Grove? I should think, while the rest of us line up for the slaughter, your priority would be closing the Gate."

He really was detestable. His words were honeyed in that melodic tone, but Razakh could hear the edge, razor sharp and dripping with condescension. *"If we go to the Grove before our armies engage, we will be at a disadvantage. With his power, the Guardians don't stand a chance at taking him alone. There's nothing stopping him from opening a portal right outside the forest, but if we bring the fight to him and he's distracted, tired, wounded even ... that's when we strike."*

Tiderion sneered. "Is your wizard not capable of protecting his flock? After all, that's what your little test was all about. A show of power to convince us all to unite?" Tiderion scoffed, turning to Denavar. "I was born a long time ago, boy, and I see right through your thinly veiled plans."

Denavar's nostrils flared and Ashalea gripped his arm tightly, a balm to cool his rage. Razakh felt his own flames surge with annoyance, and he was just about to argue his point when—

"For all the Gods and Goddesses, would you please shut up, Tiderion?" a voice replied, its bearer waltzing into the room in a tumble of snow.

"Mother?" Ashalea said, her jaw gaping as the Moonglade queen swept in, looking every inch a warrior queen in a sleek navy tunic, furs clasped around her neck, silver hair in a slick braid.

Celiana winked at her daughter, and strode to a vacant seat at the table, ignoring the shock on everyone's faces ... everyone except Denavar and Yavaar. They shared a quick glance, but Razakh didn't miss the exchange. The pair had been inseparable, and Razakh wondered if their alliance went deeper than the others.

"Celiana, you will join us after all?" Nirandia asked as she clasped the other queen's hands in welcome.

It was odd, Razakh thought, that she would show at all given her declaration. He scanned the room, perking his ears to listen beyond the tent walls. He heard only the guards posted around the tent shuffle slightly outside and the muffled voices of soldiers around their nightly campfires. No elven nobility, no guard of her own, no horses.

Celiana had come alone.

Ashalea's shoulders wilted, Denavar's face tightened, and Shara outright rolled her eyes as he conveyed this message to the Guardians. Tofin's face remained impassive as he watched the elf closely, but Razakh was coming to realise the dwarf was a hard study. Grumpiness was fast becoming his sole personality trait.

Flynn crossed his arms, his expression of scorn near identical to his sister's. "And what, my dear lady, can you offer us if not soldiers and supplies?"

She shifted in her seat, the confidence from moments before quickly disintegrating. "I came to support my daughter," she declared, almost proudly, as if it were something she should be congratulated for. "And"—she added with an uneasy glance at

Razakh—"I bring ill tidings."

Everyone perked up, their attentions recaptured, the air itself frozen in time, set to shatter with the slightest knock as everyone held their breath. Razakh felt every hair stand on end, his stomach churning with premonition.

Celiana glanced at everyone present, her lips pulling into a thin line as she took a deep breath. "Shirilea, the elven Guardian, is dead. I don't know what the cause was, only that the Magicka of the Grove hangs by a thread, the power at its heart stretching thin as its Magicka dwindles, linked to one last life.

Silence blanketed the room as all eyes fell on Razakh, and he understood the full weight of Celiana's words. His father was the last remaining Guardian of the first order. His father, Razgeir, was the only one protecting the Grove.

The last one left before age took his body and soul ... or the darkness did.

30

The End of Redemption

ASHALEA

"JUST ONE LEFT," Ashalea whispered, the cold clutch of fear gripping her chest. She glanced at Razakh, trying to decipher the violent swirls of those silver eyes. She shut her eyes momentarily, blocking out all sounds but the frantic beating of his heart.

He was afraid. Of course he was. The last living Guardian—his father. Razakh had to go to him, they all did, before Crinos made his move. Before it was too late. She wanted to rant and rage and scream at its unfairness. How did the elf die? Better yet ... her eyes travelled to her mother, the picture of sorrow as she spoke softly to Razakh. How did her mother know?

"This changes things," Nirandia said gently, though her voice was firm and loud. She looked to her twin, commander of the Woodrandian army. "We need to act now. Caelor, suggestions?"

He masked his emotions well, now wearing the helm of a soldier, motioning his most loyal soldiers to his side. An elf with long honey hair stood at attention, her brown eyes watching Caelor carefully. She was beautiful, even with a ragged red scar encircling her throat.

Ashalea gathered she was Caelor's second, and the other soldier—a male with auburn hair tied in a knot, his body sleek and all sharp lines—was his third.

"I want the guard doubled around the camp's perimeter and soldiers at intervals around the forest's edge. Send runners to warn the nearby villages, and scouts in every direction. I want all nooks and crannies searched. Understood?" He tilted a head at the Aquafarian lord, all business. "Tiderion, I advise you appoint some of your own soldiers to join them."

Thankfully, Tiderion's sour mood had dissipated, the latest announcement filling the room with an urgency and panic. He simply jerked his head at his closest soldier. No nonsense communication. The soldiers had their orders, and soldiers always obeyed.

"*Take a squadron of Diodonians,*" Linar's gruff voice rumbled. "*We are fast, and our noses better than even yours, lordling.*"

Caelor smirked at his mannerism but nodded, and Ashalea guessed the Diodonian chieftain was sending his own orders out, drifting along a pipeline of communication to the pack camped in the north-eastern edge. As it were, she heard no voices in her head, so if anything was said, it was for Diodonian ears alone.

The soldiers received their dismissal, and then they were gone.

Sven sighed, his stern face looking for all the world like everything and everyone inconvenienced him. Without addressing his father, he upped and left the room, supposedly to relay his own orders to the dwarves. With Tofin now assuming his role as a Guardian, the crown prince to the Kingsgareth throne would be stepping in as general. And, despite his unfortunate lack of social skills, Ashalea thought him a good fit. Where others might bend to emotion, Sven, the eldest of Kano's sons, was rock solid. He would lead well.

Ashalea set to work on unravelling a large map of the area, a myriad of tokens scattered across the table that resembled the four armies and the darkness. She plucked one of the pieces, rolling the smooth wood between her fingers. It was carved to the likeness of a Diodonian, and she marvelled at the craftsmanship.

Such a small thing, a simple beauty that became so much more than a piece of wood. She wondered who had carved the piece, had marked the etchings, had given it enough thought to make it feel real. To make it recognisable.

And then she felt an odd lamentation, looking at the little Diodonian. For this one piece was not one at all, but many. An army of Diodonians. And if this piece—the section it claimed on the map—if it burned, if it crumbled to dust, then they all would.

She set it down on the map with steely resolve, letting her mind's eye open to the possibilities, imagining the many-headed-beast that was their army. Where it would snap, where it would claw, and where they might rip the head off another.

This was war. And she had every mind to win.

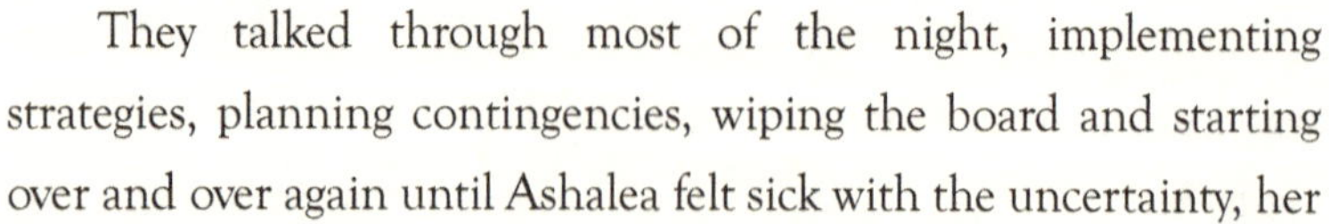

They talked through most of the night, implementing strategies, planning contingencies, wiping the board and starting over and over again until Ashalea felt sick with the uncertainty, her eyes blurry with tiredness. The darkness's armies would bleed the earth black. She knew that. Their snaking tail would go on and on, for he had worlds at his disposal.

For all the time Wezlan had thought him banished to one portal, he had been free to traverse his prison—to find any number of beasts and the cruellest of creatures. And when his strength had grown enough, he plotted, and portal travelled, and promised his minions a world full of life—life from which they would feast until all was grey and ghostly.

She sank onto the furs of her cot with exhaustion, already half asleep when she heard the folds of the tent swishing together. Dagger in hand, she was in a defensive position before her disturber had fully entered.

"Oh!" her mother exclaimed, lifting her hands in fright. "It's just me."

Ashalea sagged, relief filling her veins, but wariness too. "What can I do for you, Celiana?"

The queen frowned, and Ashalea saw herself in her mother's features—in the puckering nose and the upturned lips. It was somehow unsettling, rather than comforting. "You can call me mother, Ashalea. No one is listening now."

"I know," she replied, a hint of steel to her tone. Her mother's face fell, and Ashalea felt a pang of regret. But she didn't trust her yet. Not when she might run off at the very mention of *his* name. The darkness? Crinos? Son? What *did* she call him?

Celiana took a seat on the edge of the cot, and she reached out tentatively, taking a lock of Ashalea's hair between her fingers. "I'm sorry, child, for not being there when you needed me. I did what I thought was right, what I thought was necessary to ensure your survival. That is all I've ever tried to do."

Ashalea swallowed the lump in her throat, risking a glance into her mother's hazel eyes. They shone with regret and sorrow. But there was something else there too, something Ashalea couldn't place. She had her mother's hair, her nose, her lips, but they were not her eyes, and she did not know them. Not yet.

She reached for her mother's hand instead, smooth and silky against her calloused palm. The hand of someone who didn't know hard labour, the grip of a sword or the curves of a bow. Not even the simplicity of feeling dirt beneath one's nails, planting roots into the ground, giving sustenance, giving *life*.

But she pushed those thoughts away. *Tired, so damn tired.* And she was sick of pushing Celiana from her, sick of being angry. What point is there, in holding onto such notions when the one person who truly deserved it would stand before her soon? And should she defeat him, should they all live to see a new world? Well, she was an elf, and a long life spent brooding or harbouring old hates would make for a miserable one.

"I can't ..." She faltered as she tried to find the words. "I can't say the words you wish to hear yet, but I want to. I want to move on, to build a relationship with you. And I ... I want to know you, Mother. To restore this family."

Celiana beamed bright as the moon from which she was blessed, and she inched onto the bed, tentatively curling an arm around her. And it was too soon, and it felt too strange, but Ashalea nestled in, remembering what it was to be held by a mother. To have a parent's love.

They sat there for a time, talking of old tales, dreaming of new dreams, and forgetting the impending battle entirely. Ashalea listened as Celiana told her about The Meadows, the city it once was and perhaps could be once again.

It felt nice to test the waters. But like she was so very apt at doing, Ashalea's thoughts drifted to the present. To her duties. She was not a creature of stillness, preferring to take life in her own hands and mould it to her liking. And there was one thing that just didn't sit right.

"Mother," she said gently, carefully. "Why will you not fight?"

Celiana stiffened, her spine rigid as she sat up. "Why do you insist on pushing me?" she said coldly. "Why can't you just accept my decision as your mother? As your queen?"

Ashalea flinched at the reprimand, shying away from the abrupt change in Celiana. She found no evidence of the soft, gentle lady, who had laughed and told stories only moments ago. Those eyes were hard and filled with fear.

But just as quickly as it arrived, Celiana relaxed, a collected calm washing over her features once again. She sighed, stretching long arms above her head before looking back at Ashalea. "I'm sorry. It's been a long day. Would you like some tea?"

Ashalea nodded hesitantly, and her mother trotted outside with a bowl, no doubt to scoop some snow for boiling. She frowned, unsure what had just occurred, but she was so hopeful to see this small seed blossom, she dismissed the queen's outburst and instead set to work on changing for bed. Daylight would be breaking in a few measly hours, but she would get what rest she could, and be cosy about it too. War might be a miserable affair, but she could still take comfort in pyjamas.

Celiana re-entered just as Ashalea slipped under the scratchy covers of her cot. If this was what the dignitaries got, she hated to think what the soldiers must be dealing with. Suddenly her pyjamas seemed rather silly in the scheme of things.

"Here you go, dear," Celiana said, offering a cup as she sat beside Ashalea.

The contents smelled of peppermint and rose petals, and she inhaled the scent deeply, thinking of Denavar as she did. He hadn't come to bed, which meant he was either still in the war room or overseeing the mages. She sighed. He would be exhausted, though the selfish part of her delighted in having time with her mother.

She blew on her tea before taking a sip, relishing the burn as it sailed down her throat, spreading warmth throughout her bones. She felt sorry for all the guards on duty. The nights were only going to get colder and longer as winter settled over the world.

"Tea makes everything better, doesn't it?" Celiana said, drawing her from her thoughts.

Ashalea grinned. "I'll drink to that."

They clinked cups, and Ashalea gulped down the rest of the brew, feeling satisfied from the herbals. The peppermint would ease the stress, maybe even help her sleep. It was a small act, to share tea with another, but to her this moment felt gargantuan. To have moved forward, even just a tiptoe, even just a step, with her mother.

Her emerald eyes found Celiana's, and she smiled, truly smiled. "I'm glad we could do this. I'm happy to have shared this time with you."

Celiana smiled but it didn't reach her eyes, and there was that strange glint again. The hardness, the fear. Her fingers twitched, her hands, even with the warmth of the cup she cradled possessively, were shaking.

"Mother?" Ashalea pressed, the peppermint doing nothing at all for the sudden clenching in her stomach.

The queen turned, eyes pleading, and she clutched at Ashalea's arms, nails biting like claws and almost breaking the surface of the skin. "I've done something terrible," she said, voice a deadly whisper.

A shiver ran down Ashalea's spine. "Whatever you've done," she said slowly, "I'm sure we can make right."

Her mother looked her in the eyes then, and Ashalea felt true fear at what stared back. The hazel eyes were wide and flat, the usual sparkle lost, making room for a terrifying emptiness. "You don't understand," she insisted. "I'm running out of time. I have to go before ..." Her voice faded as she shook her head. "I have to go."

Ashalea tried to shake her mother off, but her arms felt heavy, her fingers not obeying. Panicking, she grunted with the strain, trying to haul her legs out of bed. All she got was the curl of her toes, and even then, they started to still one by one. "What have you done to me?"

An unnatural stillness claimed her mother. "I poisoned your tea," she said, eerily calm. "I shouldn't have risked trying to persuade you, but I had to try."

Ashalea wanted to scream with frustration, utterly perplexed at Celiana's behaviour. But she knew, deep inside, that whatever happened next, neither of them could come back from this. "Please," she pleaded, "tell me what you've done and maybe we can fix this."

Her mother smiled at her sadly, both knowing it for the lie it truly was. She sighed, leaning forward to stroke Ashalea's hair once more. Then she leaned in, her breath cooling on the tips of Ashalea's hot ears. Celiana's next words were cold and hard as ice.

"I killed the elf."

Ashalea's eyes widened, her skin breaking out in goose flesh despite the sweat working up her spine as she tried and failed to move. There was nothing, no reason for the crime, and Ashalea squirmed with what little power of her body she had left, bile rising in her stomach.

"Why?" was all she could say, and the question went way, way back, warranting a thousand answers. But instead she got three.

"Because I am a coward. Because self-preservation is all I have left. Because *he will win*."

Ashalea's heart dove into her stomach, lost beneath the violence of a sorrowful storm. A single tear trickled down her cheek, and it curled down to her mouth. The salt tasted of rage, and betrayal … and death. The realisation that in doing this violent act for the darkness, Celiana had chosen him.

He who murdered innocents. He who stole mothers and fathers, husbands and wives, friends and lovers. A killer, a thief, a curse.

"He came for me," Celiana whispered. "He knew my heart better than my own—knew I could not fight him." She was sobbing now, as if Ashalea were a priestess, and she were at confession. "He promised he would spare me, that he would rebuild The Meadows, see the city thrive. I was afraid Ashalea. I didn't"—she choked on her words—"I didn't have a choice."

Ashalea's eyes blazed. "So you murdered a Guardian, your own kin! What of Razgeir?"

Celiana trembled, the cup in her hands escaping her grip, crashing to the floor and shattering, just as final as the breaking of Ashalea's heart. "I tried, but he was too fast. I missed my mark and I—I failed. He was wounded. He won't last more than a few days."

"No," Ashalea croaked. She thought of Razakh, of his last chance to see his father. She had to tell him, had to get out of here. But her body would not budge, almost fully paralysed now, little more than a minute left before it took her entirely.

"Come with me." Her mother pawed at Ashalea, scrunching

the silk of her shirt. "Come with me. Join us, my daughter. He won't harm you if you come willingly. He might even spare your friends. I have the tonic in my pocket. I can heal you right now."

But Ashalea barely heard the words, barely registered the small vial Celiana pulled from her tunic. All she could see was the blood beneath Celiana's nails, the stains upon her milky white palms. They had been washed, but they would never be clean again.

"I would rather die by his sword than go anywhere with you," Ashalea whispered. "I would rather you take one of those shards on the floor and stick it in my neck than look upon your face for one more second." She mustered all her strength, twisted her tongue in her mouth before spitting on the queen's face. *Her* face.

Shocked, Celiana sat frozen, as if that final act undid her entirely. She peeled the spit from her pale cheek, slowly pocketing the vial. "Shame," her mother said with a sigh. "I had hoped tonight would go differently, but it was worth a shot. I really am sorry, you know. For everything I've done, and everything I'm yet to do. He needs to know your plans, girl. And I have everything I need, thanks to tonight's meeting." Her eyes were cold as she glanced at Ashalea. "The poison will wear off with the aid of a healer, but by then I'll be long gone. Don't bother coming after me."

Ashalea felt the paralysis creeping up her neck, and it was all she could do to snarl at the female before her—the wretched, cowardly creature. Her mother by blood, but not by heart. As she poured every ounce of hate into her stare, Celiana gave her one last kiss on the cheek and turned to leave.

"I will ... kill you ... for this," Ashalea seethed.

Celiana turned, smiling sadly, and her answering whisper was chilling, resigned.

"I know."

A Mournful Lament

DENAVAR

E FOUND HER AT DAYBREAK, sprawled across the bed, hair in silver whisps around her face, curled up in a foetal position. Nothing unusual to note. Ashalea was queen of their bed, and a royal hog at that. She was much less dignified in her sleep, which he found rather amusing, a fact, of course, he kept entirely to himself.

But as he slipped off his boots, shucked off his tunic, and bit back a yelp from the icy cold, he stepped on something sharp, its smooth edge slicing the bottom of his foot.

"Son of a—" He studied the culprit, a clay shard, once the proud piece of an unassuming cup, judging by the handle not two feet away. But Ashalea was hardly one to leave such a mess, and he glanced at the cot with narrowed eyes only to find emerald ones burning a hole in him.

"Ashalea," he muttered. "What …" He trailed off as he really looked into her eyes. They were burning with hate, with anger, with rage. And as he sat back, a tendril of fear spiking through his belly, he saw the preternatural stillness with which she lay—impossibly still, even for an elf.

Shoving down his alarm, he raised his palms over her stomach, white light glowing as he assessed her body, searching for injuries or sickness. It was a different kind of Magicka now that he was a wizard. With Wezlan's power coursing through him it was as though he became the Magicka itself—the energies an extension of his soul, his being.

His Magicka dove into her veins, identifying anomalies in her bloodstream, and what he found sent white-hot rage of a different kind through his body. Someone had paralysed her, had managed to sneak past guards—hells, a whole camp full of soldiers.

The darkness? No, even he had his limits. Even in ethereal form, he would have needed to know her location, the ins and outs of the camp. And there was no possible way he still latched on to her; the piece of him that had festered in the inner workings of her mind had long since burned away. She had made sure of that in the otherworld.

But he would have no answers until Ashalea was healed, and so he worked. Hands hovering, they rhythmically moved from her ankles, the toes wiggling in freedom as he moved up, up, up until finally she gasped, breath hitching until it turned into ragged sobs, tears tracking down her skin.

He stroked a palm against her cheek, his Magicka finding no physical injuries. But he asked all the same, knowing it wouldn't help, knowing the real pain would be inside. "Are you hurt?"

She merely buried her face into the hollow of his neck, and

he held her, one hand cradled against her head, rocking her gently into a calming rhythm. He could be patient. For her, he would wait.

He fisted his free hand, and no words were required for the Magicka within to bend to his will. Heat steamed off his skin, and small holes sizzled the sheet down to the very metal of the cot. A beast unleashed itself in that moment, roaring his anger at anyone who dared hurt Ashalea. To see her devastation, the wreckage of another being's doing. And as her shaking frame stilled, as she quieted, he gritted out between clenched teeth, "Who?"

She looked up at him with wide eyes, and there. There was that burn. That fire he knew so well. She would need it, and she would wield it in days to come. "It was her," she breathed.

His brows pinched together as his suspicions were confirmed. It was obvious. Painfully, unbearably obvious. His parents had sent word that she'd been absent from The Meadows for a few days, but he'd been so caught up in the council meetings and running Renlock, he hadn't given it a second thought. And this ... this was the price.

Ashalea watched him carefully as he worked through this, but when he finally said a name, she nodded just once.

"Celiana." It was ash on his tongue, poison to his lips. And if Ashalea didn't end her, if her own treachery didn't sign her death warrant, he would kill her. And he wouldn't do it quick.

"Ashalea, Denavar!" Shara came charging into their tent, skidding to a halt at the sight of his Magicka melting into the bedframe, at Ashalea's face streaked with tears for someone unworthy of her salt.

He glanced at Shara's face; tired, drawn, uncharacteristically solemn. And he knew, the worst of their troubles wasn't over. He ran a hand through his hair, bracing himself, holding Ashalea tighter, as if that could shield her from unfortunate news.

"What is it?" he asked, exhaustion lacing the words.

"It's Razgeir," Shara said softly. "He's ... he's dead."

He sucked a breath through his teeth, forcing himself into stillness, to be strong for the elf in his arms. She stiffened, a strangled cry tearing from her mouth. Denavar risked a glance, but she merely stared, her mind somewhere else, her body having no tears left to give. Something told him she already knew ... that this was all part of some greater plan.

Shara stumbled to the bed, and she took a hand each, the three of them sitting in silence, the frosty air creeping in through the open flaps, numbing their hardened hearts, dulling the pain. There would be no waiting anymore. Their time was up.

Their time was up ...

And in the distance, somewhere in the camp, a Diodonian howled—a broken, discordant sound.

Lamenting a father, a leader, a friend.

A Terrible Tale

TOFIN

THE HOWLS BEGAN AT DAWN, the sky a miserable shade of grey. Even the sun had little shine left to give, confirming the dark was indeed headed their way. He didn't understand it, couldn't comprehend how one being threatened to erase them all from the land, but for his father, for his people and for hope, he would stand against this evil.

The camp was a riot of motion as soldiers of all races ran the lines, their commanding officers barking orders. The clang of hammers sounded amid the mournful tones of the Diodonians: an eerie song of sorrow, a marching band for the dead.

He had not slept, spending the night poring over blueprints, working alongside his brothers to see Jyorden's ranged weapons come to fruition. They made a good team, their individual minds like the inner workings of a mechanism, each cog necessary to keep the unit whirring into motion.

And despite the crusty grains making his eyes sticky, despite the weariness in his bones, Tofin was glad they had pushed on. With some help from the mages—from all parties—these weapons could be completed within days.

He sighed, huddling into his furs, glancing at his companions. Tofin didn't know a lick about his new allies; they were not his friends; he did not owe them anything. But as he watched them—all four, huddled together in comfort and solidarity—he was reminded of his brothers. Of the loyalty they shared, the fierce protectiveness, that unbreakable bond.

And, odd as it was, he felt somehow attached to these people. Two elves, a human, and a Diodonian. Now what where the chances of that? They sat around a luminous fireball, the snowing crystals that descended from the heavens fizzling into nothing upon impact.

His frown deepened. They were all snowflakes, and one by one they would melt before the darkness. If they gave up ... if they surrendered. But he glanced at their faces, warriors all. Their eyes blazed with anger, fury, pain.

He didn't need to know their story to understand that all had lost something—or someone—to the darkness. The scars ran deep enough, reflected in the windows of their eyes and caged beneath their chests. And though his hands twitched with the need to act, though his toes wiggled with an urgency to move, he felt he should be here, with his new companions. Felt he should try.

It wasn't much, but he leaned forward, elbows to his knees, and looked the Diodonian in the eyes. "We'll avenge him," he said gruffly. "We'll avenge them all."

Razakh stared at him then, with eyes that seemed to hold the secrets of the world and the knowledge of all others. But there was a sadness too, even if there were no pupils to discern, even if Tofin didn't understand the depths of those orbs.

Tofin bit back a yelp, stifling his shock at the voice echoing in his head. Something he thought he'd never get used to.

"It was his time. I am thankful his life was long, his post an honourable one. Our ancestors will bless his journey beyond our world." Razakh's reply was simple, blunt. But Tofin could hear the bitterness behind them, sense the sorrow. As if the words carried down that taut line held every ounce of emotion the Diodonian was feeling.

Tofin smiled grimly. "It is hard to lose the ones we love," he said, thinking of his mother.

Razakh hummed, an odd vibration that sounded from deep within his chest. *"Tell me about her. Tell me anything to take my mind off this."*

The others looked at him curiously. Not a private conversation then. He grumbled, rummaging in his pocket for a flask. He'd surely need some liquid courage if he was going to share this story.

The flask was carved from the bones of a great beast many seas from here. A gift from his mother, after his first successful hunt. It was perhaps his fondest memory of her, and his saddest, for it was also the beginning of the last.

He took a swig, the honeyed mead a perfect blend of smooth and sharp, its bite taking the edge off the cold. The assassin held her hand out expectantly and he grunted, tossing it to her. She marvelled at the smooth edges before taking a large gulp and holding it out to Razakh.

He sniffed uncertainly, and she let a few drops trickle on his tongue, to which the beast sneezed, his fangs flashing as his pink tongue lashed against the air in protest. "I didn't think so," Shara said smugly, but it lacked the bite he had expected.

Tofin sighed, rubbing his hands together to ward off the chill. It was not so much the cold bothering him, but the memory. And he didn't know why he offered this piece of himself now. Why he allowed the memory to claw itself to the surface, to reveal his biggest regret and his deepest shame. But perhaps it was needed. Perhaps a burden shared is a load lessened after all.

Once he might have offloaded all kinds of colourful curses to them, told them to mind their business, told the elves particularly to shove it where the sun doesn't shine. But as he looked to the sky, shrouded in a roiling, malicious cloud, he realised they all sat under the same brewing storm. And they would all wither under its gaze as the eye blinked in fury.

Now was as good a time as any to share, for he might not have the chance again.

"Her name was Ereasha, and she was the greatest shieldmaiden of our time. Respected for her fighting prowess but loved by the people too. Tales of her exploits spread by bird wing across the oceans, and once my father heard of her, he knew there could be no greater match. No greater dwarf to be his wife."

The flask made its way into Denavar and Ashalea's hands, and the latter drank deep, nose puckering in protest at the taste. But a flush of colour began blooming on her face, and even Tofin was grateful to see her health returning. He tightened his fists, knuckles cracking violently. To be poisoned by a friend—by family—to be betrayed like that, he could think of no fouler deed.

And Celiana? She was a snake of the deadliest variety. Finally shedding her skin to reveal herself as a creature of chaos. A frightened, cornered beast, and those, Tofin had learned, were always the first to bite.

He shook his head, not wanting the Diodonian to read his

thoughts, nor the elf, for that matter. Ashalea leaned forward, flask in hand, and Tofin took it from her with a nod. Her face was all hollows and dark shadows; a ghost of the girl he'd met on the slopes of Kingsgareth Mountain.

He hadn't realised their destinies were connected then; not as she summoned the very storm itself, frying those creatures upon the mountainside. Not even when the Magicka—that strange, otherworldly sensation—lit his blood on fire, as though invisible cords tied their souls together.

Her eyes had been brimstone then. He remembered those emerald jewels burning on the battlefield, and even after, when he'd met her in the armoury, they had been lit with purpose ... even if he had thought her a little mad.

But now they were empty. Glass on the verge of shattering, steel smelted in a forge of despair. It irked him, to see the strength had waned, to see the fight go out. So, tenuous though times might be, confusing as being a Guardian was, he would help her—would help all of them, if only to unite against a shared evil.

Tofin took a sip, letting the liquid coat his tongue, allowing it to embolden his words. And he realised, this story was as much for him as it was the Guardians. A distraction for them, an unleashing for himself. For he had kept his mother's memory at arm's length, buried deep down and stoppered away. It hurt too much, thinking about her. The person who understood him most, as much a confidant and friend as a parental figure.

"My mother was my father's greatest challenge ... he would say his mightiest conquest," Tofin barked a gruff laugh. "He courted her for a long time before she gave in to his advances, and an alliance was forged with her people across the sea. She came to live at Kingsgareth, and they were happy. In love, which is a lucky thing indeed, for royals are often without the pleasure of such happy marriages.

"But she was not an idle dwarf and certainly not common. Her love was born of the sea, of endless oceans and limitless skies. But water and stone do not pair so well, always fighting each other, and so she would tire of our great dwarven halls and often sail on ships beyond your wildest imaginings."

Shara snorted, interrupting his musings, and he raised a bushy brow. "I'm sorry," she said with a smirk, "but aren't dwarves supposed to like living underground?"

"Aren't assassins supposed to be good at being quiet?" Tofin replied with a huff.

She threw her hands up, chuckling. "Understood. Carry on, Your Highness."

He scowled, clearing his throat loudly, easing himself back into the tale. "On my twelfth name day, she arranged a surprise voyage just for me. We were to sail to her homelands to the east, many moons away. A chance to meet my kin from the Green Gales. A village that nestled not beneath a mountain—but on it, curling up the mountainside to a peak so high it was like—"

"Living on clouds," Ashalea breathed.

Tofin nodded, noting the wonder in her eyes, the slight relaxing of her shoulders. "Aye, from a wee bairn it had been my dream, to go see it. To walk among the oceans of the sky. Unfortunately, my sea legs weren't as sturdy," he said with a grunt. "I'll not step foot on another ship for the rest of my life if I can help it."

Denavar's brows pinched together, lips curling. "I think we all share your sentiments. Our last voyage is not one we want to remember."

Tofin sensed a story there, but he didn't press, seeing the

discomfort on Shara's face, the paling of Ashalea's. He took a deep breath of his own, steeling himself for the crux of his story.

"I never saw the city in the sky," he said sombrely. "Our ship went down in a storm, lost to creatures that have no name, depths not commonly chartered. The beast I saw that day ..." He looked to his flask, thumbing the ridges of bone. "Well, it unleashed its rage, and it plundered our ship of its cargo. Every male, female, and child. But for one. And my mother, she"—he swallowed the lump in his throat, taking a swig to soften the blow—"she went down with the ship. But not before she drove her blade into that monster's heart. They were swept to the bottom of the sea as equals, locked in each other's embrace."

He rolled his shoulders, blinking hard, refusing to allow passage to the tears desperate to be loose. Razakh ambled over, placing his head on Tofin's knee, and the simple act of shared sorrow unhinged something deep in the dwarf. He put a tentative hand on the Diodonian's head; warm, sturdy, solid, even as he felt sick and wobbly.

"She was a warrior to the last," Razakh said. *"She died honourably, fighting for kin, and she may have passed, but her ship sails on. When the storms threaten to break oceans, when thunderclaps sound, that is your mother, roaring her victory, conquering the seas."*

Tofin's heart squeezed, a pang of unfamiliar emotion firing through him. He had hardened his heart long ago, but these people, these Guardians ... perhaps they were a boon for him after all.

Ashalea cocked her head, studying him, and Tofin despised the pity in her eyes. But beneath that sheen of sorrow he saw something deeper. Understanding. From one survivor to another.

"How?" she asked, and he didn't need to clarify what she meant.

How indeed. He was at a loss as to why he didn't drown that day. Why he, of all those unfortunate souls, was the only one to escape the monsters and survive the storm ... But he had been chosen. Whether from a stroke of luck or by some divine being, he would never know, but would be eternally thankful.

He suppressed a shiver as he remembered the moment. Thighs burning, lungs about to burst, chest weighing him down, down, down until he thought he would breathe his last, disappearing beneath those waves. But then ...

"Wings," he said, eyes glassy as he recalled the image. It wasn't hard, for it was forever branded into his brain. "Great wings of glossy brown, a beak sharp as daggers, its lower half that of a giant cat. It swept through skies, riding the currents amid the eye, seeking its prey. Only, it found me. Rescued me, clamping talons as big as my head upon my limbs."

To Tofin's surprise, Denavar barked out a laugh, true wonder plastered on his face. "A griffin?" he guessed, shaking his head. "But they have not been seen for an age."

Tofin grinned. "In Everosia perhaps. But beyond our borders they flourish, living harmoniously with my kin amid the peaks of Green Gales; a shared claiming of the skies. From the stories Mother told me, the dwarves had many roosts built for them—eagries, they were called."

Ashalea leaned forward, chin planted on her fists, and Tofin could see that clever mind at work as her eyes narrowed in thought. "These griffins," she said slowly, "you said they live in tandem with the dwarves across the seas?"

"Aye," Tofin agreed. "It has always been thus."

Her eyes darted to his, a new flame burning within. "And do they fight for the dwarves—with the dwarves?"

Tofin hesitated, racking his brain in effort to remember his histories. But he had never been an academic, never been one for studying for the mere enjoyment of learning. "Well, I was never one for the books but—"

"The griffins fought alongside the dwarves in the Battle of Beliath during The Claiming hundreds of years ago," Denavar interrupted. "A war between humans and dwarves within which cities on both sides were conquered, and the world was reshaped."

Tofin scowled. Apparently, the elf knew more about dwarven histories than he did. He sent a withering glare at Denavar. "And how do you know about our history?"

"*Books*," Denavar purred, sending him a smirk that set Tofin's teeth on edge.

"Did the dwarves and the griffins win?" Ashalea interjected. "They fought together, held their own?"

Tofin puffed his chest out proudly. "Dwarves are the only known civilisation to share such a bond with the beasts. Together, they would have slaughtered the humans." He looked to Shara. "No offense."

Shara shrugged. "Survival of the fittest. Makes no difference to me."

"I don't care about the past," Ashalea said quietly, jerking her chin at Tofin. "I am more concerned with the future."

It clicked, suddenly, what she was pushing for. What she was asking him to do. He rose slowly, his emotions roiling inside. For he knew, deep down, that they would need all the help they could get. That every soldier, every able body on the battlefield could sway their favour of winning.

It ate at him, what he had to ask. The lives he would put at risk, and a small part of him protested, begging there to be another way, clawing at his morals. But this was war, and he was a wolf.

It was time to call in the pack.

He scarfed down his breakfast in a matter of mouthfuls. Cold porridge and fruit. Certainly not a breakfast of champions, but under the circumstances he wasn't very hungry for anything. The porridge lodged in his throat on the way down, the fruit churned in his gut, but it was dread that pooled in his core, cold as it spread throughout his limbs.

He didn't want to do this, didn't want to ask for help. Especially not theirs. Tofin's mind scrabbled for ideas, for alternatives, but there were no other options and deep down, he knew it. But the thought of seeing them fall, of blood and bone and feathers, it sliced deep.

The tea scalded his tongue as he sipped, but the burn was barely noticeable. His blood was already fire and ice, a savage war of emotion that unfurled within. After that griffin had saved him all those years ago, the ties between Kingsgareth and Green Gales had further cemented into a longstanding friendship.

His father and the rulers of the Gales had lamented their loss for a long, long time, but somehow, the death of Tofin's mother had brought them closer together, sealing the family ties between the two cities. If Kingsgareth called for help, they would surely answer, and the deaths that would follow would then be his responsibility.

Tofin shook his head. Was he saved all those years ago only to call on these bonds? Was the life of one worth the many? He had always wondered if the griffin that had saved him somehow knew—somehow understood—who he was and who he belonged to.

He had succumbed to blacking out, after being plucked in its talons. He'd stayed out cold until one morning he awoke in his very own bed in Kingsgareth Mountain, his father's tearful face looking down at him, his brothers' relief evident in the sagging of their shoulders.

The griffin had brought him to the very doorstep of the city, his father had later said. Perched there and waited until someone noticed and called for help. And even still it had stayed there until the king himself came charging out those doors.

Tofin reached into his pocket, pulling a large feather from its depths. The shaft was still sharp, the vane soft as velvet and shining like gold. It was the only thing he had to remember that griffin. It had been tucked into his pants pocket that day, as if in reminder, as if to say the griffin would see him again.

Tofin grimaced. Perhaps he would. Someday soon he might see that glorious beast. And his heart might leap for joy if it were any other circumstance. If it were only for him to bow down and give his gratitude.

He just hoped this time he didn't need saving.

A Message in Blood

YAVAAR

E NEEDED A DRINK. The itch un-scratchable. The need insatiable. Nothing but alcohol would quench his thirst now, but Yavaar had sworn to give that up. It was a vice—sickeningly sweet, blissfully impairing, but dangerous. Too dangerous to allow in such harrowing times. Still, what he wouldn't give for a blasted drink.

Yavaar shivered, hands shaking, skin feeling clammy and feverish as his body protested the withdrawals. His sleep had been fitful of late, plagued by a brain that would not quiet, a body that would not settle. He welcomed the frosty bite of the morning chill, reminding him that he was alive, that he could do this. His heart was strong, unbothered by the extra load insulating his body, regulating his temperature. His blood pumped and he was thankful for every second of it.

The news had spread like wildfire throughout the camp. Dead. The last Guardian was dead, murdered by Celiana of all people. Yavaar clenched his teeth, rubbing his gloved hands together to ward off thoughts of the vile acts committed by that she-elf.

He had felt sorry for her initially. Her joy, her loves, her ambitions had all burned to ashes long ago and, much like him, her city had burned with it. For Celiana, her son had been the bringer of destruction. For Yavaar, it had been his father.

He scoffed at the role reversal. And it might have taken him a while to free himself of his bindings, to stand up, take charge of his life and start being the ruler his people needed—that *he* needed to be—but hers was a cage of her own making. And now she had burrowed even deeper, turned the lock and thrown away the key.

Now she was a murderer. A thief killing her way to submission, stealing a loved one from a son and hope from others. It was too late for her. Celiana, queen of the Moonglade Meadows, was lost to Everosia. To her daughter, most of all.

He frowned, wondering how Ashalea was processing it all. He didn't know the elf, had not yet figured out the workings of her mind, but Denavar had come to be a close ally. Someone whose company Yavaar actually enjoyed, not just tolerated.

The same could not be said for certain other members of the alliance. A prickly and stubborn Tiderion. Shifting in the saddle, Yavaar sucked in a breath, relishing the sting of another blustery winter's day. The snow had come surprisingly swift this year, greedily eating up the land, stripping trees and flowers of their plunder. It, too, was a thief in the night.

Winter was a hard time for his people—the cold brought death to the impoverished, the crops withered with frost, livestock grew sick, and disease similarly spread through the city. Work halted for fishermen, the trading boats became sparse, and time slowed as it worked on the weak.

Usually Yavaar rather enjoyed the colder months, despite the problems it often brought. The days were sometimes tedious when he was cooped up in chambers receiving requests he could not grant, but there were moments, quiet moments where he could slip away. Sneaking out with his horse, becoming someone else, however momentarily. It was a game he liked to play—to pretend to be a commoner, a traveller, whatever struck his fancy. Those days seemed long ago now.

Today he had elected to patrol with some of his best scouts, needing an escape from the cacophony of the camp. The Diodonians had still been howling when he left, quieter than when the news first broke but mournful, haunting. A shiver crept down his spine as he recalled the sounds. His first thoughts had been for his own people. At the risk he was taking—that they all were—in leaving his city without its king. The men left behind would die for their monarch, for their country, if the walls were again breached. But it tugged at him, a small sliver of shame, that he left the city vulnerable.

He studied the white blanket before him, the spindly trees clawing at the sky, and he supposed he could do no better hiding in his keep, a crowned jewel glistening above a blackened city. He might not be a seasoned soldier, might be untested in battle, but charts and maps spoke a language he knew well. Tactics were something he could understand, and so he would work until his very marrow shrivelled and snapped, until he was victorious or dead in a ditch. It mattered little. There was no point dwelling on what could be, only what is.

Yavaar spurred his horse on, wanting to slough off the heavy thoughts, determined to beat back the angry buzz of need. Of an addiction that still clutched at him and ripped into his doubts. Licking his lips, he rode, horse crashing through the snow, his soldiers flanking him.

It was stupid, he knew, to lead the party himself. Kings did not patrol, generals did not stoop to such tasks, but he needed the distraction. The *release*. His blood pumped through his veins with adrenaline, burning away his other need until it hissed, writhing, backing into a dark corner.

And the men. He knew they appreciated his presence; knew they were spurred by action. They also knew he was not a fighter, not really, but he would not have them snigger behind his back, would not tolerate their talk of a weak ruler reliant upon doddering fools and drink to lead. And so, leading this party, exchanging banter with these soldiers, the morale boost, the camaraderie, would do a world of good.

He was charging ahead, feeling the flush of freedom bloom across his face when the captain, Amerie, her name was, held up a hand, calling for a halt.

"Slow, there now," he eased his beast to a stop. A skittish mare—not his usual, magnificent mount, but a hearty horse all the same. This morning he had just wanted to get out of that camp, and so he had taken the first horse he found. He cocked a head at Amerie, and her brown eyes darted to his, sharp, focused.

"Tracks," she said, jerking her chin at the ground. Yavaar ignored the lack of propriety, neither needing nor caring for etiquette in such a place. He studied the sheet of snow, noting odd shapes imprinted there. Not horse hooves or shoes but something ... other.

Judging by the deep indents, they were fresh. "Whatever made these passed by recently," he growled.

Amerie nodded, her gaze elsewhere, searching the fields. "Draw," she said tightly, and the soldiers obeyed instantaneously, the murmur of swords unsheathing as they nudged their horses into a circle around him, guarding him.

Yavaar glanced at the captain, her face taut, her lips pursed. She was a pretty woman, if a little plain, but it was her eyes that captured his attention. Soft like a doe's, the kind that truly sparkled when one smiled. But they were alert, too. Intelligent. And beneath all those lovely things, it was fear he saw now.

And with a start, he realised it was not for herself. Not for the soldiers around her. But for him. She looked at him nervously, as if reading his mind, and dread uncoiled in his stomach. "Captain," he started, but she hissed, an almost guttural sound that had his back stiffening, his lips clamping in response.

He followed her line of sight, eyes locking on what she spied. Dark shapes, little more than black blots against the white, and he briefly wondered if travellers might be approaching, merchants perhaps.

But there was no cart, no horse, no means of supplies, and no sane Everosian would be out in this weather without shelter or cause. His gaze narrowed in on the movements. Disjointed, unsteady, and with a sickening feeling he realised these were no humans, or indeed elves or dwarves.

Ice climbed his spine like hoarfrost on a window, and the hairs on his neck stood to attention as if someone had breathed cold air upon his nape. Amerie looked at him, those beautiful eyes now stern, hard. A soldier's eyes.

"Ride," she breathed. "Ride swiftly to camp."

Yavaar didn't need telling twice. With a hard twist on the reins he sliced them through the air, his mare whinnying in protest. They launched, soldiers flanking either side, the horses' nostrils flaring as they were pushed into a gallop.

Their hooves thundered into the earth, snow lashing into the air as they struck. Gritting his teeth, Yavaar risked a glance behind him, dread unspooling as he saw their pursuers taking chase. Uulakh, if the tails snaking behind them were any indication. They crawled through the snow, alarmingly fast despite the uneven terrain.

"Don't look back," Amerie gasped as she rode alongside him. "Ride, Your Highness."

Yavaar had never felt so afraid, the adrenaline of earlier shifting into a new kind of urgent. Survival mode kicked in, blood pumping so fast he thought his heart might hammer out of his chest. He was so focused on escaping that he wasn't prepared for his horse, that damnable skittish thing, slamming to a stop and forcing him to fly from his saddle.

Any other day he might have cursed, might have felt the fool, but there was no time for embarrassment now. He hurtled through the air, arms up and cradling his face as he curled into a ball and rolled, his bones groaning.

The snow cushioned his fall, even as the wind whooshed from his sternum, and he grimaced in pain. His eyes darted up, searching the playing field.

Uulakh circled from every direction, advancing on their prey, closing off his only chance of escape. For a split second, terror filled him, his first thoughts being that his scouting party had abandoned him. But there they were, swords raised and ready, and the afterthought was worse. Knowing that he had doomed them instead with his recklessness, his clumsy hold over his horse.

Amerie offered an arm, surprisingly strong as she hauled him to his feet. Her eyes betrayed no sign of fear anymore, just duty—a warrior readying for battle. She offered him a grim smile, and they stood together, back-to-back as the Uulakh advanced.

He drew his sword, positioning his feet in a defensive stance as he eyed off their foe. So many—too many—yellow eyes glared back at him, alight with hunger, bodies shivering with bloodthirst.

Bile rose in his stomach, his heart thudding so loud he wondered if his comrades could hear it, wondered how long it would continue to beat until it was ripped from his chest. For Uulakh ate anything, those vile, detestable creatures. They would rip his throat out before tearing into his stomach, prying his ribs open, feasting on his flesh. The thought sent a violent shiver down his spine.

The reptilian beasts were advancing fast now, mere steps away from falling upon them. Amerie glanced at the king, solemn, something like sadness deep within the chocolate depths.

"I would have liked to see the new world," she said to him, little more than a whisper, and Yavaar's heart sank into his stomach. The wind howled in answer, as if it despaired for their fate, for what would happen next. But her eyes burned then, and she grabbed his hand firmly. "Make the darkness pay," she said.

A reptile lunged, thinking her distracted, but the captain's sword was a flash of steel as she arced it down, removing the Uulakh's head from its body with a mighty roar. The soldiers echoed the battle cry, swords whining as they met their marks.

Blood splattered Yavaar's face, tar-like liquid finding its way into his mouth, and he spat out the contents with disgust. His arm moved before he had time to think, slashing wildly at the Uulakh before him. It leered, tongue lashing the air as it tasted his fear, darting backwards to avoid the blow.

Soldiers cried out around him, one falling beneath the

onslaught of three reptiles, eyes wide, mouth gaping as he went down. The man disappeared beneath a tangle of limbs and tails, blood misting through the air as they savaged his body. He did not rise again.

The scouts closed the gap, hacking away at their attackers with vicious determination. Theirs was neither a dance nor a song of swords, but wild, reckless determination. Grunts and hisses filled the air, and Yavaar joined the chorus when an Uulakh leaped, its teeth sinking into his bicep, tongue snaking over the wound even as he pulled his arm back and thrust his sword into the creature's skull with all his strength.

Its eyes widened, expression locked in place as it sagged, a dead weight against his body. Yavaar panted, hot, sticky blood drenching his hand as it trickled down his arm. The Uulakh was still clamped to his body, jaw locked on even in death. He roared as he pried its teeth from his flesh, a spurt of scarlet erupting as jagged holes revealed themselves.

Amerie was at his side instantly, shoving him behind her as he staggered, almost dropping his sword from the blinding pain. Stars threatened his vision and nausea roiled in his belly, the blood loss draining the strength from his veins.

"Protect the king," she roared, and the soldiers regrouped, only a handful left of the near twenty men and women that had set out at dawn. They were everywhere, the Uulakh, as if the very earth had spat them from its depths.

Where are they coming from? There was little time to wonder as another soldier's legs were whipped out from beneath her by a scaled tail, an Uulakh launching at her chest, tearing into her with fang and claw. The woman shuddered, body convulsing as her brain tried to process the pain, rushing to identify the trauma. Blood bubbled in her mouth, a sickening choking filling the air.

Yavaar could only stare in horror, his hand slick with blood where it clamped against his arm, trying vainly to stem the flow. His bicep was numb, and it vaguely registered that perhaps his attacker had ruptured some vital nerve, a tendon needed to move his damn limb and help this woman.

But it was too late, her innards were pulled from her body, like a pink flag waving defeat as they piled, steaming, onto the snow. A last breath huffed from her mouth, eyes wide and unseeing as they stared accusingly at Yavaar, her face somehow even more disturbing from where she lay on her back, her final sight that of an upside-down king. One that had failed her in every regard today.

With a groan he stumbled to his feet, knees nearly buckling as he blinked away the pain, fighting against the dizziness. He stumbled towards the remaining soldiers, but the reptiles were upon them, and one-by-one they went down. He shifted his sword to his left hand, holding it quivering in front of him. It was just Amerie and him now, mere moments away from leaving this world.

Another reptile approached, and Yavaar stood his ground, ducking beneath its swipe to slice a fine line along its belly. It toppled to the snow, the stench of death permeating the air. But another took its place, then another, and Yavaar knew his luck could only last so long.

Claws found their way to his chest and he yelped as searing pain branded him, skin shredding like paint peeling off a wall, and he thudded to his knees, sword clunking to the earth. Breath rasped from his chest as he lifted heavy eyes, Amerie a whirlwind before him as she screamed her fury, guarding him.

And then her scream was a different kind, laced with pain, dripping with fear, so discordant it sent his spine tingling. She sank to her knees beside him, and the picture Yavaar saw ... he would never forget it.

Her eyes were black pools, cold and lifeless, dead as the bodies that littered the snow around them. Amerie's screaming stopped abruptly—not the action, but the sound. Her mouth lay open in eerie silence as her features contorted in pain.

The Uulakh fell back, retreating into a broad circle, preternaturally still as they stood and watched. Yavaar's mind screamed at him to run, but he was rooted to the ground, eyes locked onto Amerie's. When she spoke, fear like he'd never known fired through him.

"King of Maynsegate," Amerie said, but the voice was cold, empty, and unwholly her own. "Lord of the humans," it continued, mocking him, a cruel sneer distorting the woman's usually gentle face.

Yavaar suppressed his shiver, ignoring the cold and the dark swirling in her, threatening to engulf him too. And he knew, before asking, who was speaking—who writhed, uninvited in his captain's body. "Crinos," he mouthed. The name was poison on his tongue, and he spat his sentiments on the ground.

A grating laugh sounded from Amerie, and with a flash she grabbed his hands, squeezing so hard the flesh screamed beneath her touch, the fine bones of his hands crunching, cracking. Agony ruptured through him, and he bit back a sob as he bowed over, unable to move. "If you're going to kill me, Crinos, get it over with," he spat, eyes blazing with fury. "You will learn nothing from me."

The entity within Amerie only laughed. So cruel, so twisted coming from her lips. "I don't want to kill you, Yavaar. I want you to deliver a message to those fools you align with. When we're done, you are to crawl back to camp and tell them everything that happened here today."

Yavaar blinked, despair sinking like a rock in his chest. But he schooled his features, not wanting to give the darkness a lick of information, to confirm or deny anything. The darkness chuckled, and Yavaar cursed himself. He was slow, sluggish from blood loss, crippled with pain, just as the darkness wanted him. A victim to his games, unable to play the part of politics.

"Three days," Crinos whispered through Amerie. "Three days until I bathe in your blood, until the sun shall wither beneath my darkness, and the world shall tremble before me." Amerie's grip tightened on his hands again and he yelped, tears sliding down his cheeks at the sheer agony rippling through him. But he would not give in, would not falter now.

He raised his chin higher, determined not to bow before the darkness, even as his body wished to bend under the trauma, his mind wishing to retreat to black, if only to give his body reprieve. Through Amerie, Crinos grinned as if he knew all this, exploiting that pain even further.

Amerie—the darkness—leaned in, little more than a whisper escaping those lips, and the words were frost upon Yavaar's cheek as he said, "Thousands. Hundreds of thousands will march; beasts you couldn't even conjure in a nightmare. They are coming for you and yours, and they won't stop until the snow is stained red. Everything you know, everything you love, shall perish."

Cold sluiced through Yavaar, as icy as the snow upon which he kneeled. They weren't ready, weren't prepared or equipped to defeat the darkness. An army of that number ... it was unheard of. Impossible.

Yavaar closed his eyes. He couldn't bring himself to answer, had no words left to give. Hate filled his heart, and he let that rage warm his belly and crash through the pain, erasing it momentarily as his anger writhed and seethed, howling to be unleashed.

When that monstrous grip relented, releasing his hands to collapse uselessly at his sides, he opened his eyes. The breath lodged in his throat as he gazed upon Amerie, her hands raising a sword pointed directly at her heart. It wobbled within her grasp, and her eyes guttered from black to brown, as if she fought the darkness with everything she had.

Fear gripped Yavaar again, all the anger melting. He said in a quiet, yet firm voice, "Amerie. I'm here. I'm right here beside you. You must fight him with everything you have. Fight. Just keep fighting."

He repeated the mantra quietly until her breath turned into ragged gasps, and the sword wavered as she pushed against that invisible current, tears tracking down her face as she struggled. Yavaar sat there, still as stone, knowing that if he intercepted, if he tried to free her, the darkness would double his efforts just to spite him.

It was all a game, and Amerie—she was just a pawn to play, a nobody in the darkness's eyes. Not a monarch, not a lord or lady, not someone the darkness would think twice about. Her death wasn't necessary, wasn't integral to the message he wanted to send.

But he would kill her anyway ... because he liked it.

Because he revelled in pain, sated himself on despair. Her death would be forgotten in a moment. But not for Yavaar, not for her parents, her family and friends. Yavaar didn't even know if she was married, if she had children, if there was anyone at all that she'd be leaving behind. Somehow that made it worse.

"Yavaar," she said sharply, and his eyes darted up, landing on hers. "I—"

The sword slid home, so swift, so sudden that it pierced her chest instantly, angled just so to sneak through the ribcage and decimate the heart. Her eyes bulged, and before her head sagged forward, before the light left the eyes now fading back to brown, before her final breath sighed from her lungs, she whispered, "Make him pay."

A single tear slid down his cheeks. The darkness had been watching, always watching, and had planned to ambush these scouts. It was just a happy turn of fate for Crinos that Yavaar had joined them today. Deep down, he knew he couldn't have done anything to stop the carnage, and even if his horse hadn't balked at the horde, that they'd all have died regardless.

But he couldn't stop the thoughts creeping in, settling over his shoulders like a shroud. The lives lost today were on him. If he had done something differently, if he had only tried harder, perhaps he could have saved them. His soldiers—loyal to the last.

A dark shape strolled into view; the figure blurry from Yavaar's dizziness. Black boots crunched in the blood and snow before him, a wicked sword hanging from one hand. The figure crouched before Amerie, blocking her from view, and Yavaar wanted to scream, wanted to roar, but his strength was gone, his body unresponsive.

A sob wrenched from his throat, and he didn't care about the Uulakh skittering away or the shadow figure. He didn't care about the pain racking his body, feeling that he deserved every second of it. He couldn't even clasp his mangled, useless hands together in prayer for the fallen.

And it was all his fault.

All his fault.

34

The Broken King

SHARA

SHARA WIPED A HAND OVER HER SWEATY BROW, the skin clammy and heated despite the frigid air and the strappings binding her knuckles. She threw her opponent a grin as she planted her feet either side of him, victorious ... and perhaps a little cocky.

She had been sparring all morning, needing an outlet for her rage; anything to block out the vision of Ashalea's crestfallen face and the painful silence of Razakh. Pain. That's what it all came back to, really. It stalked them everywhere they walked. Shara was used to it, honed by it, but right now she'd take a beating with a smile, go hungry without a second thought, if only to stop that pain from haunting her friends.

She snorted. Once she would have berated herself, punished herself for being weak, but she was no longer that girl, hiding in shadows, killing on command. She had shed that skin, emerged as something new. And she was stronger for it. Stronger because of *them*. Her friends. Her family.

Unfortunately, that meant shared sorrows, deeper hurts, and it would only get worse from here. She sniffed, offering a hand to the man beneath her, ignoring his wandering gaze over her body. For even simmering from his loss, he remained appreciative of all her talents.

Flicking her hair back, she pulled him up, smiling sweetly as he winced tenderly. She had not gone easy on him. Another bruised body for her to pummel into. Some wicked part of her delighted in that. Her training had been paying off; she had kept at it every morning while in the Moonglade Meadows, and any spare minute since.

Her muscles ached as she rolled her shoulders, cracking her neck, but it was the good kind of pain—one that she understood. She felt strong, her body healthy, and the hollowness that plagued her inside was filling with purpose—with a slow burn of determination.

"If you continue barrelling through our warriors, we'll have none left for battle," Flynn said as he approached, a smirk on his face as he clapped a hand on her victim's back. The man only grumbled, stalking away in defeat. Onyxonites were poor losers, which Shara knew all too well.

"Just sharpening the swords is all," she replied, a feral grin on her face.

Whatever Flynn saw did not convince him. "You need to stop," he warned, "or else you'll burn yourself out. You can't punch your way through this, Shara."

She huffed a sigh, running a hand through the sweaty ends of her locks. "I know," she whispered back. "But it helps me to try. To be doing something."

He put a warm hand on her shoulder, giving it a light squeeze. She didn't flinch, instead feeling comforted by the touch. She blew out a breath in relief, realising their conversation back at Renlock really had been a turning point for their relationship. Before that, she had pushed him away, seeing not the twin, the blood of her own bones, but a monster, a carver of flesh. But that person was no more, had not been for some time. And the man that looked at her smiled sadly, as if he knew where she had disappeared to just now.

The smile she returned was genuine, full of wonder that she had come so far, grown so much. Instead, she shifted and put her arms around him, squeezing with genuine affection. He leaned in, his answering squeeze saying everything words didn't need to. And it was enough, for now. A small comfort perhaps, but it meant more to Shara than he'd ever know.

Shouts broke them apart, a clamour of movement as soldiers ran past them. She looked up sharply, scanning the fields for intruders. Shara had placed herself purposely at the camp perimeter, ready to jump into the fray should any more surprises come for her people.

But it was not monsters she saw, nor the darkness on his black cloud, but a single horse, making its way slowly towards her. A man was draped upon it, too far away for her to glean who it was and no banners to identify.

With a few more steps of the horse he slid off and crumpled to the snow. Just as well that a thick blanket spread below, lessening the impact. Shara narrowed her eyes, scanning for threats, for signs of an ambush or a trap. But the man was alone.

Sprinting towards a horse being led by an Onyxonite woman, she vaulted onto its back and snapped the reins, urging it towards the fallen stranger. She heard hooves at her back, and she turned to see Flynn on her tail, a shadow on her heels.

Their horses trotted to a stop and she slid down the mare's side, unleashing a cry as she identified the man. Not a stranger at all, but the damn king of the merchant city himself. What was he doing outside the camp without an armed retainer?

"Is he alive?" Flynn breathed as he plopped down beside her.

She hastened to Yavaar, turning him gently on his side, and the sight of his mangled body, the smell that wafted from him made her cringe. Dried blood drenched his attire, and his tunic was shredded, jagged wounds scraping down his chest. Claw-marks, she guessed by the uneven rends—and how deep they ran.

Shara couldn't stop the hands clutching at her chest involuntarily. She had received similar wounds at Kingsgareth, and the pain had been unbearable. But this? His skin was in ribbons. His large, bronzed hands were themselves like claws, bent and broken, appearing utterly boneless by the way they sagged.

With the amount of blood he'd lost, by all rights, Yavaar should be dead. Placing a finger beneath his nose, she felt the faintest breath caress her touch; cold as steel yet fragile, limited. Her gaze cut to Flynn. "We need to get him to a healer *now*."

"To the mages then?"

She frowned as she unwound the strappings at her knuckles, carefully blotting them over the chest wounds. Not exactly hygienic, but it was all she could do. His dark skin was now as chalk, practically bloodless. "Tell the mages to meet us in the Onyxonite tent. And find Denavar," she barked.

Flynn was already moving, ordering his mount to kneel as he ripped the clothes from his back to bind Yavaar to the horse. Near dead as he was, they could not risk him falling again. Flynn hissed as the makeshift rope came up too short, and before he could rip his breeches off Shara whispered, "Let me."

She shucked her shirt over her head, stifling a yelp at the burning cold that bit her skin. She had no coat or furs, training as she had been, so she jammed her fingers into her armpits, thankful for the material binding her breasts.

Flynn was already hauling Yavaar to the horse, and she arranged the king awkwardly over the mare before climbing in the saddle and racing towards the camp. "Hurry," she commanded Flynn over a shoulder, and his horse was soon galloping off the field, angling towards the mages for help.

The king's head lolled against his chest as her own horse raced, and she breathed a sigh of relief as the rope kept him firmly bound to the mare. "Hold on," she said to the king, aiming for the largest tent amongst her brethren, every second that ticked by leading him closer to death's door.

"Just hold on."

Three Days

ASHALEA

ASHALEA STOOD BESIDE DENAVAR, brows furrowed, a sheen of sweat glistening on both of their temples as they worked. White light glowed from their palms, cleansing, washing over the ghastly wounds of the king.

How long they had been at it—minutes, hours—she didn't know, but her strength was beginning to wane, and her patience too. Humans clamoured at the tent's entrance, trying to sneak a glimpse at Yavaar over the heads of the Onyxonites guarding the tent, baying and making a fuss. Finally, with the last thread of tolerance snapping, she turned her head and snarled—actually snarled—at them like a feral beast.

They backed away quickly at that.

She noticed the small smirk curling at Denavar's lips, but he said nothing, too focused on healing the king's hands. The chest and arm, gruesome as they were, proved easy enough for Ashalea to cleanse, first removing all evidence of infection and rot, before beginning the arduous task of knitting flesh back together and restoring the structure of his skin.

The hands were another matter. The bones, as they had suspected, were utterly shattered, as if someone had taken a mallet to them and smashed them to oblivion. Had he not been brought straight to a healer the nerves might have been damaged beyond repair.

As it were, Ashalea and Denavar had thought it best they attend to the healing themselves to ensure it was done correctly. They had also hoped to prevent gossip spreading, but there was no chance of that happening.

Yavaar was out cold thanks to a sleeping potion one of the mages had concocted. The pain would have been unbearable otherwise. Ashalea studied his face; high cheekbones, a sharp jaw covered in umber stubble, a straight nose, and his skin ... Beneath the splatters of dried blood it was a bronze canvas, near perfect in its unblemished smoothness.

A handsome politician if she'd ever seen one, for warriors—even elves—were marked by time spent on roads and in battle. Scars, sunburn, freckles, at the very least. It had been reckless, utterly foolish of him to leave the camp regardless of his retinue. And she knew, those scouts would be no more, likely scattered in pieces and left for the wolves.

She set her jaw at the thought, stomach revolting at what Shara had found in the king's saddlebags. If she closed her eyes, she saw it still: a mocking tribute, a warning written in blood. For in that bag was the captain's head, still dripping, mouth still open in a silent plea.

Oh yes, the darkness had been thorough in his message. The king would report his findings when he awoke, but his token had been clear enough. Death was coming. And that bastard brother of hers was so cocky, so eager for the fight that he would come fully announced.

Ashalea knew there would be no tricks, no meaning to his madness except one. He wanted them afraid, he wanted them all to stew in their fear and misery until he could drink it down in a gilded goblet with the blood of his enemies on his lips.

She knew Crinos. She knew that he was proud, that every move he made was meant to hurt, and he wouldn't miss a moment of it. So he would storm the fields in a frontal assault, letting his power wash over them all. But ego, Ashalea had learned, could very easily backfire. Master Erik had taught her that. And so she would use that lesson when the time came.

If Crinos wants to rely on numbers and sheer savagery? Fine. She would utilise that—work with every advantage of the land, the might of each individual race, and she would harness every trick in the damn trade to win.

A light weight on her shoulder pulled her from her musings and Ashalea startled, only to find Denavar's eyes assessing her own. "I'm finished," he said softly, and she almost sagged in relief.

She nodded, eyes once again landing on the king and the now steady rise and fall of his chest. "We need to wake him—find out what happened today. I'll rally the Guardians."

Ashalea closed her eyes, withdrawing to the quiet of her mind, narrowing her focus to tug on that tender thread of Magicka connecting them. She still had much to learn, but telepathy was becoming slightly easier these days. Finding the thread was easy. Holding on, blocking out the background noise—that was the hard part.

Crackling power blared in her head, and she caressed the intricate complexities of Razakh's mind. Being in his brain was like walking through space. Every nerve was alive with activity, the neurons firing so fast they looked like shooting stars, and she marvelled in awe. Diodonian minds were a fascination she suspected the world would never understand. And it was best that way.

She knocked on the door politely, a gentle stroke against his conscience, and he answered, his own thoughts ringing with the clarity of a bell. *"You're finished?"*

"Denavar is waking the king now," she replied, her own words a discordant thrum, like the wrong note struck on an instrument.

His amusement tinkled down the line, as if he were all too aware of her efforts. *"I'll inform the others."*

Ashalea retreated, careening back to reality with a sharp inhale. Her head rang with the after-effects and she sighed, holding a palm to her temple. She closed her eyes, emptying her mind for a few minutes, letting the low drone in her head ease to nothing.

When her lids at last flickered open, Denavar smiled as he ran his hands over the king's body a final time, removing the dregs of the sleeping drug from his system. "It will become easier the more you practice."

"I should hope so," she grumbled. "It might come in handy should we need to update the others during the battle."

Denavar plopped down onto a chair with a sigh. "Only Razakh will be able to respond."

"Not entirely true," Razakh said as he padded through the tent, an anxious Shara and a grumpy-looking Tofin on his heels. Razakh shifted his giant head towards Shara. *"There is the Diodonian ceremony … the linking of minds."*

Shara eyeballed him incredulously. "I thought you rejected that proposal," she said, a slight hint of accusation in her tone.

Razakh hummed in amusement. "*I did nothing of the sort, silly girl. You humans, so sensitive,*" he purred.

She rolled her eyes, but her face brightened. "Do you really mean it?"

"*Indeed. I–*"

"Later," Tofin grumbled. "The king wakes."

All eyes swivelled to Yavaar, whose lids opened slowly, his brows furrowing before giving way to alarm, eyes filling with terror.

"Easy," Ashalea crooned, at his side in an instant. His heart sprinted with fear, and she took his hand tentatively. "You're safe now, back at the camp."

Yavaar sat up, wincing as he pressed his free hand to his head, but he lowered it in wonder, turning it over to see bones where they should be, the flesh of his skin whole again. "You ... you healed me?" His brown eyes glistened with gratitude and ... regret, Ashalea realised.

He snatched his other hand back, flexing it against his chest. Anger flushed across his cheeks and chest, but he schooled his features into neutrality—something he had no doubt been well trained to do. A king could not be ruled by emotions, else his judgement would be skewed, his decisions based off the heart instead of the head.

She supposed she would consider that when the time came for her to rule. For she would most certainly become queen of The Meadows now, she realised with a start. Would sit upon that moonlit throne, now that her mother had—

No, she could not think of that snake now. She did not have the energy to replay those moments in her head. Denavar was at her back in an instant, his warm presence a gentle reminder that he was there. Protecting her from any threats ... and herself.

She threw him a small, grateful smile before turning back to the king. "Yavaar, I can only imagine what you experienced today, but we need to know what happened," she said softly.

His eyes flashed as they narrowed on her, but the hardness dimmed, as if he realised who he was speaking to. The sister of a monster. The victim of his games.

"They ambushed us on the southern plains. We didn't see them coming, didn't hear a thing," he whispered. "They were upon us like wild dogs, ripping, shedding skin and limb."

"Monsters, then?" Tofin asked, his arms crossed over his chest. But even the dwarf was pale, the snarling wolf on his head almost appearing coy in the dim light.

Yavaar nodded, eyes glazed as he recalled the morning's events. "Uulakh, all of them. They gave chase to our horses. My mare shied from the creatures and I—I fell."

Shara eased her way to the other side of the cot, plonking herself gracefully beside the king, but not touching. Not unless he needed. Her presence seemed to help, as if the sight of a human amongst strange faces somehow grounded him. Shara nodded for him to continue.

"The soldiers went down one by one as they fought. They protected me to the last. I took down a few myself but with my arm I ..." He clutched at the phantom wound, as if it pained him still.

Ashalea nodded at Denavar, who filled a glass with water from a pitcher on the adjacent table. Yavaar drank greedily from the cup before licking his lips. "The ranking officer of that scouting party was the last to go down. He took her, before she died. Wormed his way into her mind, controlling her, mocking me."

Anger bloomed once more across his face, lips pulling into a disgusted sneer. "He made her kill herself, after using her body like a puppet. Made her drive the sword right into her heart. I'll never forget it, her face. I'll never forget it ..."

"*Do you remember anything else?*" Razakh asked gently.

Yavaar's eyes narrowed. "There was a figure. A shadow that came after the Uulakh had left. I blacked out before I could see his face."

Ashalea glanced sidelong at her companions. It was a small mercy he had not seen what happened next to the captain, likely blacking out too soon, but it was enough. Ashalea was no stranger to horror, knowing too well what death can do to the soul. What nightmares would follow him for many days to come.

She refrained from reaching out a comforting arm or barking at him for an update, letting him compartmentalise his emotions, giving him time to work through it. Yavaar shook his head, breaking free of his lapse, and when he stared back at her—at all of them—it was with fury.

"Three days."

Ashalea blanched, and Denavar's eyes flicked up in surprise. No one spoke, no one moved an inch as they drew in a collected breath, the air in the very room sharpening, unbearably frigid as those two words sank in.

Tofin broke the strangled silence with a string of vulgar words. Ashalea was inclined to share the sentiments, but she settled with, "Shit."

To everyone's surprise, Yavaar laughed; a bitter, broken thing, snapping them from their shock. "He gloated about it. 'Hundreds of thousands' he said, among other things."

"Gods," Tofin breathed. "But that's—"

"Impossible? Suicidal? How the hells are we supposed to compete with that?" Shara snapped, fingers twitching in her lap.

Denavar angled his head. "What does it matter? Hundreds, thousands? He can blot out the sun for all I care. We fight, as is our duty, and we die with honour, as is our right."

Shara snorted. "Oh, sure, it all sounds so noble now, until your mangled corpse is left to be ripped apart by monsters."

Denavar's head whipped to her, a snarl on his face. "And what else should we do? Cower in our beds? I wouldn't give him the satisfaction. If I die, my body will return to the earth."

"There won't be an earth left to harness your Magicka, elf," Tofin growled. "Every male and female, every animal of land, sea, and sky, will suffocate beneath a blanket of dark. Take away the sun and all shall wither. Let monsters roam ..."

Something Tofin said struck a chord in Ashalea. She chewed over the words, ignoring the sudden eruption of tempers in the room, a squabbling between all members filling the tent. But her mind was elsewhere, cogs turning, eyes shifting as she weighed the scenarios in her head. The land, sea, and sky ... That was it. She saw it now—a beacon in a void of hopelessness. An answer to their prayers. She rose with the fluid grace of an elf, an otherworldly calm filling her soul.

"I know what to do."

The others didn't hear, yelling over the top of each other, rage and despair and pure panic bouncing around the room. This, Ashalea realised, was the result of fear. What the darkness hoped to incite from his 'message'. And that just wouldn't do.

"Gods damn it, shut up!" she yelled. The others stared at her, snapping their mouths shut as she smoothed down her tunic calmly before repeating, "I know what to do."

They stared at her, disbelieving, and Razakh tilted his head, a predatory gleam in his eyes. *"What's the plan?"*

She grinned, conjuring a fireball to her hand, letting that beacon of hope be seen by all Guardians. "I'm going to find our salvation. I'm going to find the help that will win the war."

Shara scoffed. "And who might this person be?"

"Person?" she replied, a wicked smile on her face. "Oh, no, my dearest assassin, I'm not looking for some*one*, I'm looking for some*thing*."

Part of the Charm

SHARA

S HE WAS OUT OF HER MIND. Running off at the eleventh hour? Foolish. And she certainly had no qualms saying so. "You're going to abandon us just as the darkness stomps on our doorstep? Is this some kind of sick joke?"

Ashalea only looked at her stubbornly, and Shara knew what that expression meant. Her mind was made up, and nothing—no one—would change it. Not even Denavar, who hadn't said a word.

Ashalea lifted her chin, the portrait of regal grace. Her skin was pale, cheeks hollowed, lacking that usual luminosity and health. Her hair was coiled in a silver coronet above her head, wisps curling around her face from exertion, but her eyes blazed with emerald fire. Purpose. Her exhaustion gave her a wildness that made her appear even more fierce.

"I do not ask your permission," she said sharply. And then a little softer, "If I don't, we shall surely fail."

"*Trust,*" Razakh said. "*We must trust one another if we are to fight as a unit. Ashalea would not leave unless she believed it worth the cost.*"

Shara sighed. She knew that. Damn it all, she knew it well. And it wasn't that she didn't trust Ashalea; no, that couldn't be further from the truth, but it didn't make it any easier. Razakh was right. They were stronger together, *all* of them.

"Will you at least tell us your plan?" Tofin asked with a huff.

Ashalea winked as she crossed her arms, a stupid smirk on her face. "Where I'm going ... what I plan to do ... it's something I need to do by myself. But if I do this, if my plan works, you'll be nose-deep in ale the night of my return."

Tofin grumbled. "I'd better bloody be bathing in it."

"If you don't get your skinny ass back in time to save my perfectly endowed one, I'll kill you myself," Shara growled, glaring at the elf.

Ashalea grinned, sagging in relief. "I'll be back, and we will go to the Grove together, just as we had planned ... right after we kick some monster butt."

Shara fluffed her hair. "Good."

They looked at each other then, a mutual understanding. There would be no long farewells, Shara knew. This wasn't a goodbye, just a see-you-later. She only hoped that later would be sooner, and that whatever Ashalea had planned would be enough.

Please, Gods, Shara thought, sending a silent prayer to whatever entities still watched, still cared. *Let it be enough.*

<hr />

The dwarven-made catapults were coming together nicely. Shara had no idea how they worked but seeing as she wouldn't be

manning them, she hardly cared about logistics. "What does this one do?" she asked Tofin, a stack of assorted wiring, ropes, and small cogs in her hands.

To her, it looked like a jumble of wood, bindings and metals, but she'd learned Tofin had much more devious notions in mind than the average catapult. "It's a long-range siege weapon. Built for launching projectiles at far-off enemies."

Shara tapped a foot impatiently. "I don't mean in its base form; I mean what do *you* plan for it to do?"

Tofin threw her a lazy grin. "Rather than crush our enemies with rocks and the like, I want to harness Magickal energy, maybe even combine both elements."

Shara nodded appreciatively. "Fireballs raining from the sky."

Tofin patted his weapon lovingly. "Hopefully we'll make it rain more than that. It needs testing, but with the mages, these babies should be razing enemy lines in no time."

"Good. We'll need all the help we can get." Her mind drifted to Ashalea, having disappeared hours ago. The elf had refused to say where she was going and had rejected her offer of company, saying the Onyxonites and the Guardians would need her.

Shara's face soured. As if the Guardians—everyone in the camp—didn't need Ashalea. As if she'd shrugged her self-worth off like she was dirt beneath their boots. With a scowl, Shara threw herself back into work, hauling materials back and forth in the clearing. For once, she didn't mind taking orders, letting the dwarves usher her around for whatever they needed.

She had been a human mule for the better part of the afternoon. It was better to quiet her mind, to have something to do, something for her hands to grasp. She had always been a doer, never one to sit around and plan. Leave that to the soft-hands—those politicians, ambassadors and the like—who'd never worked a day of hard labour in their lives.

They would all be crammed into the royal pavilions now and, if so much wasn't at stake, she might have placed bets on who barked the loudest, who puffed their chest the most or donned the most garish attire. Theirs was a game she was happy not to play.

Razakh was with the Diodonians again, and she'd politely declined joining him. They were still vocally deep in mourning, and Razakh's voice in her head was enough to deal with, let alone others of his Klan. She still planned to corner him about the Diodonian ritual and connecting their minds, but for now she would let him be with his tribe. Mourn the loss of yet another loved one.

Denavar was off with the mages, preparing them for the tasks ahead. Everyone had a duty; everyone was knee deep in work.

"You're worried for your friends," Tofin interrupted her musings, and she looked at him in surprise.

"And you're not?"

He ran a hand over that snarling wolf, shocking black against his pale skin. "Aye. But fear only clouds one's judgement. We dwarves take stock in fate. What will be, will be, and all that."

Shara raised a brow. "You believe in destiny?"

Tofin glanced at her with steel-grey eyes. "More now than ever. Although mostly, as a general, I just hope not to get my head chopped off in battle."

He grinned again, and Shara chuckled, noting the way his eyes crinkled when he laughed. It transformed his grumpy exterior, lighting up his features. She wondered just how often he'd smiled over the years or whether he, too, was guilty of pushing everyone away.

Shara raised a brow. "Keeping our heads, both physically and

mentally, would be ideal."

Tofin punched her lightly in the shoulder. "Shouldn't be any trouble for an assassin, eh?"

"Careful, dwarf, you'll put an arm out if you stretch it much farther above your head," she teased.

He scowled, but it was half-hearted, the metal of his eyes melting just a little. "Lass, there are beasts far worse than you waiting for us. And you'll see," he said with a small smile, "my axe arm goes the distance. Much better than those trinkets you carry at your hip."

Amused, she fingered the slots at her belt—the deadly six-fingered stars in their usual pride of place. "These? They have proved their worth more times than I can count." She patted them fondly.

Tofin snorted, noting her affection for the inanimate objects. "You're a scary woman, you know that?"

She smiled sweetly, tossing her hair behind her shoulders. "Aye. It's all part of the charm."

He shook his head and began tinkering with the catapult again. It was nice, this companiable silence, the ease of being around the dwarf. Surprising, but nice. Not so long ago this exchange would have gone very differently. Or not at all. Gone was that closed off girl, scared of opening up to others, of attachment. She had feared emotion—things that kept her tethered.

To love was to risk being hurt in ways beyond the slice of a sword. But as she looked around at the dwarves, at the other races—all of them working together and setting aside their differences—what it was to really be a part of this world became clear. To live with her whole heart, to want more than to exist and serve. She was free, and she wanted to see the wonders of the world, to explore, to laugh and love and live—really live.

Tofin followed her gaze, and he whistled. "It's amazing. How people can come together in a time of crisis. I can't recall the last time all races allied for a fight."

Shara nodded, thoughts drifting to Telilah; that woman full of love and laughter—joyful and free and so full of life. It sparked something inside her—a slap in the face to open her damn eyes. She realised she didn't just want to live, she wanted to live with her, do all these things with *her*.

She turned to Tofin, a broad smile on her face. "That's the thing, isn't it? The one thing above all else that brings us together."

Tofin's brows raised in confusion. "Aye? And what's that?"

She thought of brown eyes, long curly hair, a smile that lit up the room. And her heart pulled with longing. "Someone to fight *for*."

⬥ • ⬥

"I want to perform the ceremony with you. I've given it some thought and, well, it makes sense. And if I had to be linked with anyone, I'd–I'd like it to be you."

Shara smirked at Razakh's stumbling. He seemed nervous, which was so unlike her furry friend that she couldn't help but take advantage of it. "Oh, you want to be pen-pals now? You've deemed me worthy of you?"

"I–that's not at all what my hesitation was about."

Shara picked at her nails as she leaned against the cot in her tent. "It's fine," she sniffed. "I understand. You're only offering now to save my pride."

Razakh blinked. *"I didn't realise ... I only wanted you to be sure. The connection that's formed can be invasive, as I said. It goes beyond verbal communication, extending so far as to share emotions—fear, rage, joy, even ... even pleasure.*"

Now it was Shara's turn to be on the back foot. Her face reddened as she realised his implications. At what he might see glimpses of if she ever ... "Oh," she muttered.

"*Indeed,*" Razakh said, his tone now dripping with amusement. "*Some things are better left behind closed doors,*" he huffed. "*But be that as it may, I would be honoured to form this bond. But be warned, once formed it cannot be undone. Not until one of us passes from this life.*"

Shara snorted. "That might be sooner than we'd like. And I understand the gravity of this. I know, to the Diodonians, this is a gift that should be treasured and respected. And I will until Crinos takes my soul."

Razakh growled. "*I would not allow him to take you—any of us. We're family, and we cannot be undone.*"

His words settled in her heart, bolstering her determination, and she raised her chin defiantly. "Right then. Let's get this show on the road."

━━◆•●•◆━━

Shara hadn't known what to expect from the bonding ceremony, but it was over almost as soon as it began. Surrounded by Diodonians, Razakh and Shara sat within a circle of flames, an elder Diodonian standing opposite to conduct the ritual.

He towered over them, his once silver eyes now milky with age, the lines of his muzzle wrinkled, the gloss of his red coat peppered with scars. Evidence of battles and sun-drenched days within the deserts.

Fireballs flickered and glowed from the spines and tails of the beasts surrounding them, their eyes glinting eerily in the dark. It was silent, which only served to make Shara more uncomfortable as the eyes of hundreds settled on her face and back.

Razakh offered her a droopy smile, somehow sensing her unease before the connection had even been formed. She laughed at his goofy expression, feeling her bones relax as she ignored their audience and breathed deeply.

"Bend your foreheads so they're touching," demanded the elder.

Shara suppressed a giggle as Razakh lowered his shaggy head, the golden fur soft and slightly ticklish as it met her skin. She closed her eyes, his warmth calming her, his presence comforting.

"Bridge the gap between your minds. Let your consciences be clear, your minds empty of all but this bond," the elder said. His voice seemed to echo in her brain, powerful and vibrant.

Shara inhaled and exhaled, forcing noisy thoughts aside and focusing on the beast before her. On her friend. The thought of being bound to anyone would have once terrified her. But now, it felt right. This was a safety measure—a means of protecting a fellow Guardian, the ability to always communicate regardless of distance.

Razakh nuzzled her temple ever so gently, and she felt these thoughts drift away until there was nothing but silence. A blanket settled over her mind, and she felt herself falling into a sea of consciousness.

The elder said something, but it sounded far away, and she floated as if in a dream. When she opened her eyes, she was in a sea of stars. No, not stars ... thoughts. Nerves sparked as these thoughts drifted, flowing around her—through her.

And she realised with a start whose thoughts they were. She was in Razakh's mind—so deep within the recesses that her own body felt detached, limbless. Shara gaped in awe at the colours flashing around her—beautiful, ethereal.

A sense of calm washed over her, an awareness that she welcomed with open arms. This place was not a cage or a void to be forgotten in. It was a hive to explore. A sanctuary. And she gave her consciousness to it freely.

A low drone seemed to hum within the space, and she felt a tingle of power flood her being, drenching her in its essence.

"Wake," a soft voice said.

Again. "Wake."

"Wake!"

She hurtled back to reality, to her body and her own mind until she was gasping, her forehead still pressed to Razakh's.

And there was something there that hadn't been before. A bridge. A connection.

Razakh opened his eyes and grinned in his usual clumsy way. "*Hello heathen.*"

Shara grinned as his words echoed in her mind. "*Hello right back.*"

37

A Most Formidable Creature

DENAVAR

"HUNDREDS OF THOUSANDS," Nirandia whispered in the stillness. Her words frosted in the air, and a deep cold settled in Denavar's body despite the warmth of the many crackling fires suspended throughout the room.

The rulers of all races had dined together along with the Guardians and, for once, there was no bickering, no small talk. The evening attire was also decidedly plain; the etiquettes of royals all but forgotten with everyone feeling too tired to rise to the occasion.

Good, Denavar thought. Shedding such cloaks meant they could converse on steady ground, just one person—or Diodonian—to the next. Equals.

The dinner itself had been a morose affair, the tension so thick, the worry so apparent, that more food got pushed around the plates than eaten. Except for Shara, Razakh, and Linar, of course. The wine, on the other hand, was passed around freely, drank greedily by all except the Diodonians.

"I bet your history books don't recount wars of this size," Shara grumbled to Denavar after the meal.

"If there are some, I've yet to find them," he huffed, poring over stacks of tomes at the table. He'd been perusing military tactics and historical anecdotes of wars waged long ago. In none had he found stories of battles with beings from other worlds, and he'd had to wonder what they'd done in this age to deserve the wrath that awaited them.

Razakh's tail twitched—the only sign of his irritation. "*The knowledge of dead men will not help you now. The threat that looms is beyond anything Everosia has ever faced. You cannot fight like you normally would, clashing swords and shield. These creatures know one thing: hunger. They are primal, driven by their predatory instincts.*"

"So what do you propose we do?" Yavaar said from beside Denavar, his face weary and drawn.

Razakh cocked his head. "*The darkness thinks us weak. Beneath him. And in doing so he underestimates our abilities, expects us to scatter before his horde. But what if we shuffle the cards, change the game.*"

"Become the hunters," Yavaar breathed. "Not the prey."

Razakh's low growl was a confirmation. "*And what does one do when they go hunting?*"

Denavar grinned. "Lay the bait, set a trap ..."

"And wait for it to spring," Shara finished.

⸺ ◆•●•◆ ⸺

Denavar slumped at the table, utterly exhausted from the day's events. After healing the king and seeing Ashalea off, he had spent the remainder of the day with the mages. First to train, then to talk strategy. It had been a long time since he had trained purely with Magicka. Melee, cardio, strength exercises, were all something he practised often—his aching body could attest to that—but his Magicka training had been ignored.

Today, he worked with each quadrant from Renlock to test not only himself, but the abilities of his flock. Most were passable with elementals—the more aggressive Magicka of the five—but all mages would be utilised to full effect when the fighting began.

The healers, of course, would not be risked in battle, and would wait behind the lines for wounded soldiers. Dimensional users would hang back for the most part, wielding their Magicka to assist archers and long-range fighters. But the psychics would flit between parties and, if Denavar's ideas worked, would wreak havoc on the enemy.

Psychics were not only adept at telepathy, but they could also manipulate the minds of others to blanket their visions—causing hallucinations, heightening their fears, even make them turn against their allies if the mind was frightened enough.

If played right, they would be devastating, but his plan was not without risk. Psychics would be assigned a bodyguard of sorts, to protect the mage whilst their Magicka was busy wreaking havoc on others. A handy skill that unfortunately left the user vulnerable while they worked.

He sighed. The mages were formidable as a unit, but they were not ready. They weren't during the battle of Renlock, and they certainly weren't ready now. But he had learned war made warriors of everyone; they would fight until their last breath. As would he. It was all any of them could do.

He leaned back in his chair, enjoying companionable silence

with the Guardians and Nirandia, who had joined them for a nightcap back in their tent.

She laid a gentle hand on his arm, and her smile was sad as she studied him. "To be a ruler means to make hard decisions," she said. "I've had many years to live with some of mine."

He angled his head, studying the lady of the woods. Her long blonde hair glistened in the firelight; her lovely face lined with concern. "I did not ask to be a ruler, to hold lives in my hand."

"And yet here we are," she said with a wave of her own. "Those who hold power bear the weight of its consequence. It's how you use it that matters. Will you bow to power, or will it bow to you?"

Tofin grumbled from across the table, "You elves, always so fond of your riddles."

Nirandia raised an immaculate brow. "When you live as long as I do, young one, you can wield words as weapons. Of course, some miss their mark through no fault of our own."

Tofin's cheeks turned scarlet, darkening even further when Shara burst out laughing, clapping a hand to his back. "Oh, she likes to play," the assassin grinned.

Nirandia shifted gracefully in her chair. "An educated female is a most formidable creature." Denavar shared a smirk with the lady, even as she shot a bemused smile to the dwarf. "How do you think I've put up with you-know-who for so long?"

Shara snorted from her perch in the tent corner, snuggled up beneath an exorbitant number of furs. She twirled a wine goblet idly in her hand. "I'm sure he doesn't agree with that sentiment."

Nirandia grinned wolfishly. "On the contrary, he's been on the receiving end of my bite. Two hundred years and he's not made that mistake since."

Shara choked on her wine. "Two hundred—you should be a

crone! How old are you?"

Nirandia's spine stiffened, Denavar blinked, and silence blanketed the room, several jaws dropping at the sheer audacity, the nerve. Even Razakh's silver eyes were wide.

Shara fumbled over her words. "My lady, I'm so sorry, I—"

Nirandia's body shook as she leaned over, her face hidden by a sheet of gold, and Denavar held his breath. It took all his willpower not to cackle at the look of utter dismay on Shara's face—and the slight hint of fear, too.

And then laughter. Melodious, joyful, howling laughter erupted from Nirandia. Her answering gesture was so vulgar coming from the usually graceful queen that his own laughter came roaring out of him. So ridiculous, so contagious, they were all howling within moments. Razakh's rumbling pleasure was so decidedly human it only made him laugh even more.

It was a strange thing, to feel joy in what could be their final days ... but fitting too. Denavar only wished Ashalea was by his side, and his thoughts drifted to her as the party drank well into the night.

He prayed she was safe, that she would return to him soon. And when she did, he prayed she was not alone.

38

The Ultimate Price

ASHALEA

SHE STOOD UPON A FROZEN LAKE, its pale blue sheet glittering like a sapphire in the light of the setting sun. The waterfall that hid the entrance to Windarion—the elven city of the Aquafarian Province—was blocked from the elements, sealed from the harsh winter that had been so quick to snare the land this season. She wondered if it was the darkness's doing, that the cold settled so fast, but it was little matter.

It was a small mercy that the elves on the other side were offered this scant protection. No match for the darkness, should he choose to portal there, of course, but not so easy for a horde of monsters to attack.

And there were other things. Beings that kept this land safe. Her eyes roamed the lake, almost expecting to see movement from the creatures beneath its surface. Many would have succumbed to the cold, settling in for the long sleep, but she knew there were others unbothered by the frigid temperatures.

But there was only one she wished to see from the deep blue. Only one who could help her now.

Closing her eyes, she inhaled deeply, shutting off her connection to the world—the sounds and lights all winking out one by one as she focused on her power. The Magicka roiled in her chest, flitting through her nerves. Almost eager, as if it knew what her task entailed.

Hands curling into fists, she dug her nails deep into her palms, and when even that pain had dulled into nothingness, she scrambled through the sea of consciousness until she found one mind that thrummed above all else. Utterly alien, unbelievably powerful, and yet its song was so familiar. A rhythm calling to her, beckoning.

She clamped down on that line, and when the crackle became a crescendo in her mind, the song roaring in an ancient language she could not fathom, she commanded its attention.

"I call to thee," she summoned, both a gentle stroke and a humble bow.

The connection severed, and she came hurtling back to reality, emerald eyes blinking as the glare off the ice and snow burned her vision. She sucked a breath through her teeth, pulling her cloak tight around her shoulders, trying not to shiver as the sun's warmth began its descent behind the cliffs before her.

She held her breath, waiting, hoping, as still as the world around her; so quiet not even the chirp of birds broke the silence. She shut her eyes, and when she opened them, an ethereal glow sprang forth from the lake.

Purples and whites shimmered beneath the surface, flashing one after the other. A great rumbling sounded deep below; a churning so forceful she feared the lake might explode from its wrath.

She backed away a few steps, retreating to the edge of the lake when the ice erupted. Blocks cascaded with a boom as the water cracked and quaked, and a monstrous being twirled into the sky. Circling in a blur of blue and white and pearlescent scales, the beast unfurled its wings, water glistening in a rainbow spray.

Ashalea gaped in awe at the sheer size of this ancient creature, mesmerised by its otherworldly beauty, the impossibility that something so magnificent still graced these lands.

The dragon glided into the sky, stretching out the membranes of its wings, diving and swirling in the air with a grace birds could only dream of. And then it plummeted, spearing for her, flapping its wings so hard before it landed, she had to alter her stance, putting all her weight into her toes so she didn't fly away like a leaf stripped from a branch.

When it landed, the earth shuddered, and it craned its long neck, peering at her with yellow eyes that burned. Its wings rippled, the curved spikes upon the tips deadly, the blue stripe that ran the length of its spine coursing like a river down its back.

"So the war arrives at last, young one."

She bowed gracefully, dipping her head low before gazing into the fiery depths. "Yes," she said simply, for the dragon would know—would have seen her arrival, surely.

His chest vibrated, humming, as if he knew her very mind too. *"And you call for aid, that you might defeat the darkness with my help."*

Ashalea lifted her chin, staring him boldly in the eyes. "You told me once that should I call, you would answer. I have come to claim that offer."

The dragon perused her thoughtfully, and she had to will

herself not to shake, not to tear her eyes away or show any sign of fear. Not at the dragon himself, but for fear of rejection. There could be no such outcome, not if they were to stand a chance of winning this war.

His tail snaked around her form, and still she did not bend, did not quaver. His chest rumbled again, and she realised he was chuckling.

"You came to me but a girl, yet before me I see a queen. One who would rule justly, who would see a better world come to fruition. I know what you would ask of me, and it is a mighty price indeed."

"Then you know none other than a queen could pay such a price."

The dragon's tail tightened around her bones, not to hurt, but to remind her of her place. That she might be a queen, but he was close to godliness in his strength, his purity.

She continued, a smirk growing on her face, a fire of her own burning in her eyes. "I offer you a bargain. A life for a life. Help me save my people, help us win this war, and in doing so, I can close the portal for good. I will relinquish all ties between the dragons and the elves. None shall call on you again; all debts, all allegiance owed, shall be wiped clean. And you—you will be able to join your brothers and sisters in peace, knowing a free world awaits us all."

The dragon leaned so close she felt as though she might be swallowed in the depths of those yellow slits, marked unworthy. It cocked its head, ruminating over her words. Then, as if satisfied, he leaned back on his haunches. *"So you know the cost of closing the portal then? The ultimate price only one can pay."*

Her mind screamed at her to walk away, to run from the future, to curl into a ball and hide, but she would do no such thing. Nor could she run from her destiny for, like it or not, it had always held her in the palm of its hand. She had refused to believe it once, but her eyes were open, and her future was clear. Her life was a coil, and slowly it had unspooled, nearing the end of the line.

And she knew, what that end would be. She had slowly realised it, ever since the great tree in Woodrandia had called to her, ever since the dragon had prophesied the words, ever since Wezlan had died.

And she hated it. She despised that her life had never truly felt her own, that it had always been tethered to this end. And she might have been broken, might have fallen apart once before, but somehow knowing what was to come made her feel stronger. She could not change the outcome, but she could damned well alter the course.

She lifted her chin, inhaled deeply, exhaling until there was nothing but her, the dragon, and steel purpose. "I am the key that breaks the lock."

It was enough. For her, for the dragon, for Everosia. The dragon looked at her, a glimmer of sadness blinking at the knowledge he shared, but there was pride, too. "*Come,*" he said, and they stood side-by-side as the dragon conjured a portal to a distant world.

Together, they stepped through its folds ...

When We're Free

SHARA

THE DRUMS SOUNDED A FEW HOURS BEFORE DAWN, shrieks and howls and discordant screams rending the night air. The darkness's army was close, and those in the camp listened quietly, an eerie stillness having settled over the Everosian army like a shroud. Soldiers walked the rows like wraiths, backs bent, faces pale, eyes haunted as they listened to the sounds of death.

Elves, dwarves, humans, Diodonians, all huddled around suspended orbs of fire, whispering in low conversation. Some said nothing at all, merely seeking solace amongst allies—amongst friends.

Whatever differences they all held seemed forgotten, inconsequential, as they joined together. Even the Onyxonites shared fires with the others, somehow unsatisfied with the bawdy rituals that usually took place before war.

Her people did not enter battle with emotion in their hearts, but instead gave it all to the nights before. Eves spent feasting and drinking and finding pleasure in one another. Indeed, the Onyxonite camp might have been utterly ignorant to the oncoming army, refusing to be silent and instead welcoming music and the sensual song of the bodies that danced.

Curious onlookers of all races had sidled over to the camp, some joining in the feast, some submitting to the dance. Others still found willing partners to take into darkened corners, or to bunker down for the night in a tangle of flesh.

War made wonderers of everyone.

Shara crept down the aisles, little more than a shadow all in black. She did not care for conversation now, did not wish for goodbyes or heartfelt stories. She had few to share. Most of her tales weren't inspirational or joyous ... her childhood had indeed been anything but kind.

The Guardians had gathered for supper, a quiet affair between friends. All but one, and the empty space which should have been filled by Ashalea had glared at her for the duration of the meal. Cheese and breads and cold meats that formed a lump in her stomach. She missed her friend. The Guardians were incomplete without her, and it felt wrong that she was gone.

But Shara knew, despite the lingering anger she felt at Ashalea's sudden need for heroics, her friend's actions would either save them or doom them. She just hoped it was the former, and that she achieved whatever she had planned before it was too late.

Sighing, Shara studied the folk around her; those that instilled hope, still able to conjure a smile and a joke to break the mood; those that retreated into the dark of their own minds; friends hugging friends; lovers embracing each other with a passionate kiss or a gentle hand upon a thigh.

It seemed everyone had found someone to spend their final moments with. Once she might have taken someone to bed, to release the tension and enjoy simple pleasure from another, but there was only one her heart yearned for.

Only one who could satisfy her beyond the needs of the body. And she was far from here, safe within the halls of Renlock. She sighed, her steps dragging, her heart heavy. She ached for Telilah—to hear her laugh, to see the dimples in her cheeks, to feel the curve of her body and the kiss of her lips.

She might never see her again, and while every inch of her body longed to hold that woman, she was glad that Telilah would be safe, and her innocence would not bear the sins of tomorrow.

Lost to the warring of her heart and mind, she found herself back at her tent, and with a defeated sigh, she entered its confines hoping to find solace in sleep. She had just tossed her cloak when an odd smell regaled her. Jasmine and sandalwood.

"Did you miss me?" a silky voice crooned, and Shara's heart leaped with joy as a woman stepped from the shadows, hidden beneath a cloak of midnight blue. She might have cursed herself for being sloppy, but she didn't care. She could not think of anything as Telilah removed the hood from her face, brown, curly locks cascading down to her waist, lips curling into a smirk.

"You're here," Shara breathed. "You came." But then, as if suddenly realising what that meant she stiffened, hissing, "What are you doing here?"

Telilah laughed. "Did you really think I'd let you march into war without saying goodbye?"

"You reckless, foolish woman," Shara seethed. "Do you realise the darkness's army will be upon us in a few hours?"

Telilah did not falter, her lips set into a stubborn line. And as she approached, Shara ached at the nearness, the urgency with which she wanted to pull her into her arms. But it was a mistake, for her to come. A risk Shara had not been willing to take.

The minstrel stopped a foot away from Shara, raising a hand to stroke her cheek. Her skin was velvet, the touch warm and inviting, and Shara wilted just a little, allowing herself to nuzzle into that touch.

"I have arranged a mage to take me back before the sun rises," Telilah whispered, her hands trailing down Shara's chin to the hollow of her throat and around the nape of her neck. "I will be safe, back at the Academy, out of harm's way."

The featherlight touch of Telilah's nails had Shara almost shivering. "You have to promise," Shara breathed. "Swear that you'll return, or I'll toss you over a shoulder and haul you back myself."

Telilah smirked before she curled around Shara's back, fisting a handful of hair as her lips placed soft kisses on Shara's neck, up her jawline, nibbling her ear. "I promise," she echoed, and Shara's toes curled.

Her breath grew short and heavy as Telilah wrapped both arms around her. A hand trailed down the front of her shirt to cup her breast, teasing the nipple with her finger, eliciting a sharp gasp from Shara.

Overcome with need, Shara swivelled, her mouth crashing to Telilah's with urgency. Their tongues collided, twisting passionately. She pulled Telilah to the cot, fingers working at the lace and buttons until the skirts fell, the tunic was chucked off and Telilah stood there, bare and breathtaking.

Shara halted. She too was now naked. They stared at each other for a time, content to just take each other in, to lay bare not just their bodies but something deeper.

"You're so beautiful," Shara breathed, and Telilah's flush was the pink of dawn, of carnations in spring and pure happiness.

She felt suddenly too exposed, as if her nakedness brought to light all the bad beneath her bones, unravelling the stitches of her past, unveiling the worst of her. It felt different now, being with Telilah. It *was* different, for the weight of her feelings bubbled in her chest, threatening to explode, and the fear in her heart was not of love itself, but not to be loved in return.

Her eyes shuttered, and she stood there near shivering, until a soft hand tilted her chin firmly up. "Do not hide yourself from me," Telilah said gently. "For I would have the chance to know all of you from today until always if you'd have me. I would fight those monsters out there just for a smile from your lips and a laugh that is weightless of the worries you now carry."

Shara's eyes burned, those words a balm to her heart, lifting part of that weight from her shoulders, unlocking a door inside her that kept hold of the monsters within. But they did not claw and writhe as the gate swung wide; instead they left in peace, content, and understanding that she could be more than her past. That she deserved a future.

Silent tears tracked down her face, and she released a breath. "Telilah ..."

But the girl placed a gentle kiss to her lips. "Tell me with the new dawn," she said, leading Shara towards the cot once more. "Tell me when we're free."

"*Razakh*," she thought, "*whatever you're doing right now, I advise you close the blinds for a while.*"

The answering hum she received down their connection only laughed in amusement.

40

Death on Swift Wings

Razakh

BLACKNESS SWALLOWED THE WHITE BEFORE HIM, feeding upon fear and soon to feast upon the flesh of the living. Razakh scanned the endless lines of monsters across the fields; a writhing pit of despair come to claim them all.

The allied army waited in position, not moving a muscle, hardly daring to breathe in the stillness. Where the Everosians were poised, the monsters pulled at an unseen leash, desperate to taste their enemy.

Razakh glanced at his chieftain. Proud, strong, a beacon for his Klan. Somehow the scar on his muzzle made him seem all the more fitting for the role; a badge of honour to wear into battle.

It made his heart swell to stand among his tribe, to fight alongside them in a battle much like the stories his father used to tell him. Only this wasn't like those tales. This would be a bloodbath of epic proportions. And he had no desire to die today. No plans for martyrdom or heroism.

He scanned the lines, admiring the many flames of the Diodonians that, when kindled together, blazed bright as the sun. Dotted throughout, the white wolves of Kingsgareth Mountain dug their paws into the ground, fangs snarling, their alpha poised and magnificent. Razakh dipped his head when her eyes met his, and she blinked slowly; a confirmation that the wolves would fight to the last.

At the very front stood the dwarves, Kano and his sons standing proud at the head of their people. They were a formidable force with weapons of the finest steel and shields emblazoned with an emblem of the proud wolves at their back—warriors eager to prove their mettle ... or die trying.

Flanking the Diodonians were the Onyxonites, garbed all in black armour, their faces streaked in black too. Vicious, coldly calculating, he expected they might be the most fearsome of all. Together, these three units would charge. The armies depended on them to break through the swell of creatures, but many would die almost instantly.

Such was the price of war.

A horn blared from the darkness's ranks, and all fell still, tension pulsing through the soldiers like a shockwave. Razakh bared his fangs as Crinos rose from the army, and growls from all races echoed down the lines as the darkness floated on a cloud of his own making. Wispy tendrils branched into the air, choking out the light.

He flickered as he rose. Half elf, half something *other*. As he glared down at their army with eyes red as rubies, he sneered, throwing his arms wide as he gestured at their forces. "I bring death on swift wings, and this is what you muster?" He laughed, a cruel, bitter thing, his voice enhanced by Magicka. "I'm disappointed Nirandia, Tiderion, that you would provide mere morsels for the feasting."

Razakh glanced back at the elves, glittering in finery; Nirandia resplendent in full armour of burnt copper; Tiderion in his usual aquamarine. Most of their soldiers were mounted knights shining in their respective colours, their faces stoic and graceful even before the yawning jaws of death.

Nirandia glared at the darkness from her horse. "Our numbers might not match yours, Crinos, but every elf is worth ten of your monsters. Death on swift wings you say?" She smirked. "Then we shall strip you of your feathers and watch you fall to ruin."

The darkness's eyes glittered dangerously, malice leaking from the red pools. "I'd like to see you try." He floated higher on his cloud, safe above the armies, settling in for the show.

Horns sounded from both sides, and Razakh searched their army for his friends. Tofin nodded from the dwarven front, his face stern, a deadly axe glinting in his hands. Razakh's keen eyes shifted, honing on Denavar upon the rise behind him, garbed in full armour of steel blue, a silver cape clasped over his shoulders, fastened by a crescent moon. He stood before the mages, a beacon of hope, the only wizard of Everosia.

Denavar caught his eye, and his voice echoed in Razakh's mind, "*Strike true, my friend. Break them apart like a storming sea.*"

Razakh bared his teeth in a promise. "*My Diodonians shall drown them in waves of red.*"

Denavar nodded, and the connection broke. Which left Shara; he couldn't see her amid the Onyxonites, but he sensed her presence, her emotions—the bond between them now a solid link that tethered them together. She was calm, detached, and Razakh was relieved to know that the brutal training of her childhood would pay off now.

She was a warrior, and she would not make space for fear, not bow before panic or anger in this moment. All the same, he sensed the sliver of anxiety pooling within her gut, and he knew it was because of the darkness, floating high above, watching with eager eyes. He knew the darkness terrified her like no other could, the trauma of what she went through at his hands still raw.

Razakh glanced above, and the darkness caught his stare. He snarled, hackles rising, flame bursting to life upon his back. Crinos only sneered back, bearing a mouth of sharp daggers as he looked on in his phantom form.

A final horn sounded, and Razakh whipped his head before him. It was time. "*Let them bleed,*" he told Shara, and he imagined her smirking as her anticipation sparked down the line.

"*With pleasure,*" she replied coolly.

The dwarves broke first, sprinting towards the darkness's army, their roars of battle echoing down the line, their axes, broadswords, spears, all raised high. And then the Diodonians were on their tails, snow crumbling beneath their paws as they pounded across the earth.

The monsters were closing, their shrieks and growls drowning out the world. Feathered, winged, and scaled beasts surged towards them in a sea of black. They crashed in a sickening thud of metal on metal and bone on bone, and the forward lines of the monsters were a wall that did not crumble.

Dwarves lunged, their steel flashing in the scant sunlight breaking through the clouds; a roiling, foggy black leaching from the darkness as his evil stretched greedy fingers throughout the air. It was dark—so dark that it might have been midnight, the sun spluttering

like stars blinking out. But the flames off the Diodonians' backs dotted throughout the army like fireflies, providing much needed light to fight by.

Razakh's muscles bunched as he gave chase and, as one, the Diodonians roared in deafening glory; so mighty that even the monsters seemed to blink and shrink just a little. At the signal, the dwarves collapsed in a wave down the front lines, crouching to their knees and raising their shields in one collective platform of reds and golds and silver.

The Diodonians and wolves pounced, and in one leap they pushed off those shields and dove into the fray beyond. Razakh fell upon an Uulakh, and his fangs sank into its scaled skin, tearing its throat from its body. Blood splattered in an arc of black mist, jugulars and limbs scattering over the fields.

Monsters fell in droves, their skulls and spines either crushed by the Diodonians or their vital organs being removed. The dwarves roared their first victory as the Everosians broke the front lines of the darkness's army, and the army at their backs howled in a collective cry.

Razakh fought with a fury he'd never known. There was no time to think, just the animal inside taking over, claws out and fangs bared as he leaped and slashed and sank teeth into the monsters time and again. The field was little more than a blur as he moved, and he wholly surrendered to his predatory instincts.

The alpha joined his side, and they were fire and ice once more, burning together. The wolves decimated monsters one after the other with their veins of ice, splintering through bodies and snow alike.

Arrows rained down from above, archers at the army's back finding their marks in creatures unable to move within the army's centre. Those that fell were trampled in a stampede of writhing bodies, the shrieks of the dead and dying piercing the sky.

Blood pooled beneath Razakh's paws as the savagery of both armies bathed the earth. Dwarves and Onyxonites screamed as winged beasts took them to the skies and released, sending their bodies careening to the earth, their cries abruptly ending as they slammed to the ground.

Razakh was mid-lunge when the catapults begun. Wood groaned before the contraptions sent great balls of rippling blue and crackling oranges whooshing through the air. The contained Magicka exploded in blazing trails that fried the monsters, the stench of charred skin joining the coppery tang of blood.

He heard shouts to his right, a tendril of fear rippling down the bond he shared with Shara, and whipping his head in alarm, he coiled his muscles to bound towards his friend ...

Only to see a spear flying right at his face.

41

The Might of Mages

DENAVAR

"ELEMENTALS, RELEASE," he barked at the mages behind him, their faces pale and stricken with fear as they watched the slaughter before them. It was carnage. Blood and ash smothered the atmosphere, the metallic taste of blood coating his tongue as he looked on.

The dwarves and Diodonians had done well to breach the lines, but the monsters fought with a savagery even he could not have imagined. A buzzing wave of black, breaking again and again like waves upon a shore, crashing upon the Everosians with unrelenting force.

Steel could only go so far; it was time to test the mages' strength.

He gathered his power, igniting every spark in his body, pulling from nature; every electrical current, every pulse of static, every charged ion in the atmosphere. Tunnelling deep, he hauled, building the strength within.

He'd been drawing on his energy for days, meditating in quiet moments, fully resting his body for this battle. And he wouldn't drain himself dry on this one move, but it wouldn't tickle either. The darkened sky roiled to a deeper black, the clouds seeming to shiver with anticipation, flashes of blue and white cracking above.

"Volley!" he roared, and the mages unleashed their respective powers, lighting up the sky in a brilliant flash, like meteors of cataclysmic proportions. And, as they streaked through the churning canopy of black, he fired.

Thunder rolled across the battlefield and bolts snaked down to the earth, explosive upon impact and charring all in their proximity. He made sure to hit deep within the stretching lines of the darkness's army, far from the Everosian allies.

And the damage ... each flare took out hundreds of creatures, their screams choked to stillness, their bodies reduced to ash. Snow continued to fall—no longer white and crisp, but horrible, blackened flakes of ruination.

Lightning struck right above the darkness and, with a sharp breath, Denavar could only watch as Crinos simply shifted out of existence. His shivering body disappeared, only to reappear seconds later in his elven form just long enough for a sneer to spread across his cruel features. The hatred in his eyes—the mockery—only enraged Denavar further. He wanted to gouge out those orbs, rip that smile from his face.

But not now. Not yet.

The mages' Magicka descended in unison, and the black void became alight with a galaxy of stars, each one flaring bright before it winked out—the bodies with it. In one hit Denavar and the mages had decimated thousands.

He dared to hope, brows furrowed as he scanned the darkness's army, but his heart sank as the creatures regrouped, closing those expansive gaps to reform as one unit. They'd barely made a dent, barely scratched the surface of that unearthly army.

He gritted his teeth, smoothing his sweat-slicked hair back from his face. He swivelled to look upon his soldiers, each one terrified, but all willing to sacrifice themselves for the cause. For a future.

They all looked to him, their leader, their wizard. Pride swelled within his chest that they deemed him worthy, that he was the helm to their armour, the shepherd of their flock. He nodded at those he recognised, forced a grim smile for the rest, and then he turned back to the fray to look death in the face.

"Again."

The Greatest Peace

ASHALEA

I F IT WEREN'T FOR THE DRAGON'S HOT BREATH huffing upon her back, she might have pinched herself to wake up. For the world before her defied reality—so beautiful in its natural state she could only gape in awe.

Meadows teeming with wildflowers graced the ground beneath her feet, stretching in undulating waves of colours her elven mind could barely grasp—had never known. Pools of pristine lakes glistened all around, water trickling into their depths from cliffs that hung high above, suspended in the air as if held by a string.

It was impossible. She swivelled, dodging past the dragon behind her to look upon the drop. They were suspended on land within the sky, as were the many rocky outcroppings that dotted the air around her, waterfalls with seemingly no source erupting from their edges.

Rainbows arced in triumph all around, the delightful result of a world bespelled with a Magicka so ancient, so unique that Ashalea could only cackle with glee at its wonder.

She turned to the dragon, noting the pride burning in his eyes. "How?" she breathed, fumbling for the words. "How does this place exist?"

The dragon scanned the environment, snaking his long neck out to bask in the warm, pleasant glow of the sun. "*It's a haven for our kind—other wildlife too. Birds and bees and other creatures that live harmoniously ... a natural life cycle for all here.*"

Ashalea frowned. "But surely, you'd have to feed, right? How can you co-exist in peace?"

The dragon huffed in amusement. "*Dragons can survive off flora, but it is true we find most nourishment—and satisfaction—from hunting prey. We still feed on flesh, but we do not take more than we need. The natural cycle of our world means all species are non-threatened. Something that cannot be said for life lived in Everosia.*"

She snorted. "Don't I know it." She hadn't stopped thinking about it since she'd left; the nagging urge to return home was worsened by the dragon's revelation that time worked differently in this realm. Faster. She shuddered at the thought; every second would be minutes, perhaps even hours, back home. She'd need to be in and out as fast as possible.

Ashalea strode through the meadows, breathing deeply. The air was so clean, so crisp compared to that of Everosia. Florals filled her nose, the air warm and inviting. Her fingers brushed the petals and stems of the various flowers scattered around her, thriving in this environment.

"*It is beautiful, no?*"

She turned to face the dragon, nodding slowly. "It's the most stunning place I've ever seen. So peaceful—I feel as though I could lose myself forever in this bliss."

The dragon hummed, his white and blue tail fluttering behind him. *"This place is ancient, a Magicka even I couldn't begin to understand thrums at its core. The beating heart of our world. While the properties of this land do not change, it is said to reveal to oneself what one most desires."*

"That can't be true," Ashalea said softly. The dragon cocked his head, and she took a breath. "I wish for peace, to experience life and all its pleasures, to love with my whole heart, but I couldn't do those things here. Or anywhere for that matter," she added bitterly.

The dragon brought his face beside hers and she felt its amusement rippling. *"But I didn't say your desires would be made real here, young one. This world is many things, but it does not alter your future, nor does it make your wishes a reality. You must fight for those yourself."* His tongue lashed out from his mouth, as if tasting the air. *"Then again, why fight at all? Why not stay here and live? To find inner peace is to look at one's flaws, one's regrets and pains and sorrows, and to not shy from the reflection. Is that not the greatest peace one might hope to find?"*

She considered it, if only for a heartbeat. What might be if she could forget fighting, the war, the bloodshed and vengeance, and simply just be? To choose something without being dictated to. To live somewhere even destiny might struggle to reach.

For one shining moment it seemed too good to be true, too wonderful. But ... "I can't," she breathed. "I am not a coward; I will not hide from my fate and leave my friends to suffer. And I—I could never find happiness. Not without Denavar or my family. To live without love is to live half an existence. So I will fight. I will die. And I will do so gladly to keep them all safe. So that they may *live*."

The dragon regarded her carefully, and she knew, somehow, that it had all been a test. She had been offered an eternity of peace—one not given lightly. Tears welled in her eyes at what she was leaving behind—not just here, but back home. She nodded slowly, breath shuddering out of her chest. This was what she was made for. This was her destiny.

"So what say you?" she asked the magnificent being before her. "Will you fight alongside me? Will you answer my call?"

The dragon arched his wings, the great membranes shuddering as they opened fully, and Ashalea marvelled at the sunlight glowing through the tissue, veins creeping through the skin in a tapestry of life.

He roared, and his call was received with answering bellows that echoed, blasting through her bones and waking something deep within. Her knees buckled, collapsing under the weight of what she asked and of what answered.

Wings—hundreds of wings flapping, sounding like thunderclaps. And then she saw them; breathtaking, utterly beautiful and wholly terrifying. Tears streamed down her face, and she wept openly—half afraid, half joyous.

She looked at the dragon, vision blurred as she blinked away the salt. "I was wrong," she said as she gazed back at the horizon. "*This* is the most beautiful thing I've ever seen."

The Work is Never Finished

SHARA

SHE HAD NEVER SEEN SO MUCH DEATH, never felt so much pain. When she closed her eyes, all she saw was the dying, all she heard were the screams of the wounded tearing open the night. It had been a long day. Long and yet fleeting; time she could not turn back, lives she could not save.

It was a blessing that a storm had snapped, sending a slurry of ice whipping through the armies, blinding both Everosians and monsters alike. It seemed to have been the only deterrent for the monsters' bloodthirst, and well timed at that.

The Everosians had fought well, but many had fallen. As they would tomorrow, the day after—however long the allied armies could last. Too many militias had given their last breath today. Honourable deaths but wasted all the same.

Tofin had fought like a dwarven God, his axe blazing like

hellfire on the battlefield. Denavar, too, had struck hard and fast with his Magicka. Indeed, Shara had been gobsmacked to see such power, such control.

But Razakh was the first of the Guardians to take a hard hit. Shara had felt the connection falter when it happened—felt his conscience sever from her own mind. She'd never moved faster. Swinging her blades like a tornado of wrath, she had slashed her way through the masses, screaming his name only to find the Diodonians and wolves had formed a protective shell around him. The alpha's maw was bloody and snarling as she had stood her ground guarding him.

Razakh had risen—dizzy, confused, bleeding from half an ear— and she'd sighed in relief, scolding him for being so careless. To that he'd offered her that clumsy Diodonian grin. His hearing had not been impacted, thankfully, but he'd bear that loss forever ... however long that would prove to be.

Thank the Gods it had only been his ear. She suspected if he'd moved half a second slower, he might have lost much more than that. It was not something she cared to dwell on.

Shara stalked towards the basin within her tent, her movement sluggish, her body protesting at every twist, every lift of a muscle.

A ghost looked back at her from the mirror. Her warpaint had sweated off hours ago, replaced by dirt and blood and bodily fluids of the most vital kind. Swallowing back her revulsion, she tipped a pitcher of water over her head, scrubbing her face until it was raw, scraping aggressive fingers through her limp hair.

She felt something caught in the strands, stubbornly refusing to brush out. A sob choked out of her as she ripped and ripped and still it would not give; the trivial thing suddenly feeling like the most arduous task after the day's events.

Finally, she snatched up her blade and sawed the chunk off with her teeth bared. Pulling it back, she felt the bile rise again, and she threw the lump into a dish with revulsion. Soft, pink, and squishy, and it had been in—Gods, it had been in—

Her stomach revolted and she barely made it over the basin when vomit erupted from her throat—acidic, searing, and peppered with dirt. Slumping down against her cot, she cupped her palms to her cheeks, seeing only the faces of the deceased, hearing only the strangled moans of the dying.

She sat there and sobbed for minutes, maybe hours. And for the first time in her life, Shara prayed to anyone and everyone that would listen.

But the Gods didn't answer. They never did.

No one spoke. No one made a sound except for the scraping of cutlery against bowls. Shara fiddled with her own spoon, drawing idle circles within her soup, forcing herself to swallow the slop despite the angry churning of her stomach.

The broth was cold. She barely noticed.

She was sitting in the mess tent beside Tofin and Jyorden, watching common soldiers as they came and went, everyone too busy to remain idle for long. She glanced up at the faces around her. All drawn, all haggard. Even the elves looked like mere mortals—the usually smooth lines of their faces now pinched, the bright skin a dull, tired grey.

A cool, calloused hand settled on her arm and she looked up, startled to see Tiderion's grave face peering down at her. But there was no anger in his eyes, no hardness. "You fought well today," he said softly.

Her amber eyes darted up, assessing, searching for any mockery or jab. But his face was perhaps the sincerest—the most human— she'd ever seen it. "Thank you," she croaked, and he offered her a goblet of water from the table. She drank deep, grateful for the cleansing effect of the liquid.

Tiderion collapsed into the chair beside her, still garbed in full armour. It had barely a scratch, still relatively untouched by the events of war, but she knew tomorrow would be a different story.

"The knights will lead the front tomorrow," he said, noticing the path of her eyes. "We must change our tactics if we're to have any chance. Militia will not be enough to break the front lines tomorrow."

"The darkness knows that," Shara replied. "He'll be expecting something new."

Seated beside her, Tofin stroked a meaty hand over his chin, looking haggard, his stern face exceptionally sour. "Arrows will need restocking; I suggest we appoint a rotation to restock during the night."

Tiderion nodded. "I have my fastest fletchers on it. But we'll need more arrowheads."

"Aye," Tofin grumbled. "It shall be done."

"And blades need sharpening, armour cleaning," Shara added.

Tofin glared at her. "Soldiers can clean their own damn armour." He sighed, shoulders sagging. "Jyorden?"

His brother only grinned, somehow still managing a smile after today. "Heading there now. And you may want to steer clear of Sven and Father. Someone messed up the allocation of food stocks and they're raging like bulls back in our quarters."

Shara raised a brow. "Don't get between a dwarf and their

food. Noted."

Tiderion frowned, his shocking blue eyes glazing. "Enjoy it while you can. Tonight's might be the last we have."

The Abyss

TOFIN

OFIN STEPPED INTO THE PORTAL ON SILENT FEET, one hand tightly clasped around the leather grip of his axe, the other curled up and through the bindings of his round shield. He adjusted the weight, shifting his body so he could move quickly in a crouch.

The night was dark, still about an hour away from dawn, and he was thankful for the cloud cover making it near impossible for the moonlight to shine through. He supposed he had the darkness to thank for that too—the roiling black of yesterday still lingered above, casting ominous shadows over the land.

Now those shadows only served to benefit them. He rolled his muscles as he crept along the snowy ground, precariously icy after the cold night. After cracking the plush layer of snow yesterday, the slush would pose new problems for the fight today. Ice was tricky on a good day. Fighting on it was another matter.

Low hoots mimicking owls echoed as the last soldiers slipped through before the portals zipped closed, and the group moved as a unit. Dwarves, Onyxonites, and Diodonians advanced in a casual phalanx; mages, too, not closing the gaps until they were close enough to do some damage.

They had fought well together yesterday, the collision of skills—and weaponry used—proving an effective onslaught against monsters that were less tactical and more savage, their ranks scattered and unplanned. The Diodonians had done the most damage on the frontlines, their size and ferocity combined with their agility proving them a worthy ally. And then there were the flames that burst like golden banners upon their backs, fireballs blazing upon the tips of their tails; nothing else made the monsters warier.

But today would be different. They were not waiting to line up for slaughter. They were bringing the fight to the darkness, changing the game. The mages would make sure of that. Tofin breathed deep in his nose, ignoring the burn of the cold, his veins thrumming with anticipation, the thrill of battle igniting his senses.

He squinted in the dark, wishing he possessed the keen eyesight of the elves or Diodonians, not wanting to miss anything of importance. The darkness's camp lay dead ahead, and the sounds he could just make out threatened to undo him. Beneath the expected shrieks and grunts and hissing were the undeniable sounds of screams and moaning.

His stomach dropped as he realised who they belonged to. Everosians—humans, dwarves, even the odd roar that sounded suspiciously like a Diodonian. No one standing on the field today had been taken prisoner, the monsters were too vicious for that. Which meant ...

"The wounded," Denavar said softly beside him, his face grave. "They took those we were not fast enough to collect. To feed on, to torture."

Disgust fizzled as pure rage boiled in Tofin's blood. "I expected they would feast on the dead but—" he shook his head.

Denavar shot him a sad smile. "They don't feel anything, Tofin. Don't presume to understand them. They are monsters, nothing more."

"Oh, aye. But they are not long for this world."

A glimmer of icy fire glowed in Denavar's eyes. "No. They aren't."

Tofin looked to the camp once more, studying the creatures as they scuttled around. Uulakh guarded the perimeter, patrolling at intervals where the lights of the camp strained to reach. Curling horns of bone nestled in several towers encircling the army, and Tofin growled in frustration.

"Beasts they may be, but that's not all the darkness has up his sleeve," Tofin said, jerking his chin to the watch towers.

Denavar scowled. "Bandits and outcasts no doubt. Expecting to reap the rewards on a war-torn country." He swore under his breath. "I should have expected he'd utilise them for such things. The camp is primitive, but if even one of those Uulakh spot us coming, our plan will fail."

"I can help with that," a voice said, and Tofin whipped his head around to see Shara had crept up beside him.

"How did you … never mind." He shook his head in annoyance, cursing himself for not hearing her approach.

She only grinned insufferably. "Are you forgetting I'm an assassin? Not to mention my brothers and sisters fighting alongside you. I'll take care of it."

Before anyone could object, she dashed into the night, her black armour not so much as clinking as she prowled across the snow. To Tofin's astonishment, another figure darted from the Onyxonite ranks—tall and lithe, and suspiciously akin to Shara.

"Flynn," Denavar explained. "I expect this is little more than a game for them."

Tofin's cheeks heated. "A game?" He all but threw his hands up. "You want to risk a war on a game?"

The elf smirked, and Tofin wanted to punch that smug smile off his face. "Relax, General, she'll get the job done. If anyone can, it's Shara."

Tofin rolled his muscles. "Elves," he muttered, and Denavar patted him on the back.

They waited in silence, Tofin's eye twitching, muscles bunched as they crouched behind a slight rise in the snowfield. When he couldn't stand it anymore, he growled, "Blast you all. If my plan goes to the shitter, so help me I'll wring her neck like a rag in—"

"If you fools argue any louder, you'll rouse the whole damned camp," Shara said as she popped back into view, a victorious smirk on her lips. "It's already done."

Tofin gaped like a fish out of water, and to his surprise the towers were empty, their occupants no doubt slumped, dead on the tower floors.

"Gentlemen," Flynn said, the slightest hint of urgency in his tone. "If you're finished with your tantrum, I suggest we move. Now."

Tofin huffed, but he glanced at the others. "Don't die," he commanded, and he received crooked grins from all three.

Denavar signalled for the unit to move, and the silent soldiers at their backs rose in unison. It was time. The whine of swords unsheathing clamoured, and the chink of armour accompanied their steps as they bolted past the shoddy gates and into the camp.

Before the first few creatures could blink, they crashed upon them, blood spurting as throats were slit and heads rolled. Tofin swung his axe with abandon, breathing deep as he propelled his strength into the sweeps, hacking at the beasts without pause.

The sounds of monsters waking began to echo throughout the camp, and Tofin knew any second the horns would blast, and the beasts would find their bearings. Mages set fire to tents; those inside burning alive, their screams rending the air, and everywhere blood rained.

It wouldn't be long before ... there, the darkness rose out of the writhing bodies, up into the air, his wispy tendrils of black now roiling viciously as he hissed in anger. He stretched out his arms, and Tofin winced as he waited for the ungodly power to smite him but—

A horn blasted. Long and solemn and somehow melodic, drowning out the screeching of war. The elves. The cavalry was coming. Tofin heard horses whinnying in the distance, the earth rumbling as thousands of hooves descended upon the other side of the camp, too far for Tofin to see past the angry buzz of black bodies before him.

They had the darkness's attention, and Tofin breathed a sigh of relief as he continued barraging the monsters. His axe was slick with black blood, the ground so slushy he almost slipped as he swivelled to avoid a swipe of claws that would have seen his guts spill to the ground.

He roared, sending his axe plummeting down, cracking the Uulakh's head in two. It lodged into bone and Tofin grunted as he tugged at the handle, trying to jimmy the axe as if he were merely chopping wood for a fire.

Searing pain sliced through his back, and he howled, staggering forward, palms burning as he slid along the ground. He twisted, edging along the ice as an Uulakh approached, fangs already dripping scarlet, claws glinting with malice.

It lunged, and with a bellow he raised his shield, almost passing out at the blinding pain racking through his back and up his arm. The reptile snapped at him, seeking purchase behind the steel.

The next second was a blur. Gold flashed before his eyes as the Uulakh was struck down, throat ripped by the jaws of a mighty Diodonian. Tofin gaped as the beast turned, staring into his eyes, dipping its head in acknowledgement.

Right before it was swarmed with more Uulakh—these ones carrying spears that jabbed over and over into the Diodonian's side. "No," Tofin choked, shock clutching his body as he could only watch the blood gushing over the earth, the gold now overrun with red.

It had saved him. Died for him. Tofin felt a darkness rise within that overtook all senses. A desperation he'd not felt since that day long ago, standing on a ship beside his mother before the tides swallowed her whole. He thought he'd join her then, but the abyss had not claimed him.

It would not claim him still.

And if the Gods were determined he should live, he would show them what true mettle was. He would be the sea and the storm and the ringing of thunder. He wasn't that helpless little boy anymore, not that cursed child. He had outgrown that mould, re-shaped it.

And he was not afraid.

45

An Unlikely Sacrifice

YAVAAR

BODIES FELL BENEATH HIM. Slithering things that would never hiss and spit again. Horses crushed the skulls of these beasts, swords swept across arteries, severing limbs. And for every enemy that fell, several more replaced it.

His men were dying, dropping like stones in a lake, collapsing like cards in a makeshift castle. The pawns fell first, then the cavalry, the knights. He knew how the game went—had played it as a child. Stacking those cards one on top of the other, seeing how high he could build his towers before a breath or a touch could blow it all away.

And nestled at the top would always be the king. Always the last to fall. It had only been a game then, a way to pass the time while the real king had scorned him, pushed him away, locked him in rooms where he could not be so bothersome.

Now, it was just a matter of time before the cards gave way to chaos. His soldiers fell in droves, serpents lashing out at the horses, mares collapsing, breaking bones—theirs and their riders'. The bats continued to pluck them from the air, tossing them into the winds to fall like porcelain dolls before they shattered on the ground.

Some didn't even make it that far, the beasts holding them ripping them apart. He watched them now, even as he charged, and revulsion rippled through him.

"Fire," he screamed, pointing at the sky, and archers pulled bowstrings in perfect harmony, an arc of white-feathered arrows soaring through the sky. The beasts went down, and the men within their grasp.

Yavaar searched the skies. The darkness had disappeared, choosing to vanish right after the cavalry had charged. It was a temporary relief, and their strike couldn't have been timed better. For his arm had been outstretched, claws pointed towards his friends as they led the attack on the eastern front, ready to unleash his fury upon them. Thankfully, the cavalry's advance had been the distraction the allied warband needed.

Fear coursed through his veins as he considered where the darkness had gone. Why he had chosen not to strike. All that power … why did he not use it? Yavaar's stomach curdled. Perhaps he had fouler notions in mind, preferring to watch as his minions did the work for him. Or perhaps he was waiting for someone else to arrive. A silver-haired elf. A sibling.

He ducked as a bat soared towards him, narrowly missing his shoulders and instead feeling the truth of his sword as it plunged into the creature's chest. Its blood splattered over his chest, ringing on steel like rain on a tin roof.

Yavaar swung viciously, nimbly, feeling alive now more than

ever if only because he was so close to death. One tended to appreciate their limbs, their lungs, everything that made them human in moments such as these.

Tiderion reined in his horse beside Yavaar, Nirandia at his side. Tiderion was made for battle: rippling muscles, a grace that seemingly defied natural gravity. The way he moved was nothing short of a blur, the dance of his sword like painting a canvas with patient, careful strokes.

His armour shimmered as brightly as the lady beside him. A Goddess in elven form, her blonde hair braided for war, her autumnal armour a beacon of hope to all around them. Her lips were still painted red; a daring slash as her lips curved into a grim smile.

A marsh creature stumbled up beside her mount, long arms outstretched, slime dripping as it reached—

She swung her double-headed spear without blinking—without even looking—thrusting its deadly end into the creature's heart. It was dead before it hit the ground. She cocked a head at Yavaar, eyes glittering with amusement as he clamped his gaping mouth shut.

"I suggest you fall back, Majesty," she yelled, fighting to be heard over the uproar of battle. "You are too important to Maynesgate, we cannot risk you on the front. Your people need a leader to return to them."

"Certainly not one of your politicians," Tiderion grunted as he swung with a long, curved blade, its elegant arch and gilded hilt glittering as the early morning sun hit its keen edges. "And you have"—he sucked in a breath as he lopped off a monster's head—"no heir to speak of."

Yavaar's heart sank. They were right, of course. He was not trained for battle and leaving this world in the greedy hands of politicians was not an option. But the war was his fight too. Only he could not bear to be the cause of more deaths, more soldiers protecting him. Not after Amerie and the scouts. Shoulders slumping, he nodded, beginning to turn his mount towards the camp. Nirandia and Tiderion had already broken off, returning to their respective units; both elves fighting side-by-side in a rainbow of brilliance, their sleek weapons curling in sync, the steel singing in symphony.

A boom shuddered the earth—ice cracking, snow dripping—and Yavaar latched onto the horn of his saddle as his black stallion skittered nervously beneath him. All around, the world seemed to still; the skies emptying of Magicka and arrows; the flashes of blues and whites and reds coming to a halt. Even the creatures fell deathly still as all looked towards the source.

The ground vibrated as a portal opened ... not perpendicular, but instead quaking the earth itself, causing the soil to crack and yawn open in jagged holes, swallowing up soldiers and monsters alike as the land split and their screams were lost. Yavaar watched in horror as shapes began to crawl out of that portal, and his skin tingled—a shiver spider-walking down his spine.

Creatures with disjointed arms and legs scrabbled for purchase as they climbed out of the hole, their rotten skin peeling away from their bones like vegetable scraps. Yavaar looked on in horror at their bodies; grotesque moulds of body parts that appeared to be inside-out, the pink flesh oozing rot and infection.

And then he saw their faces.

Humans. Once, at least. Now the eyes that looked out from twisted faces were dead, soulless, the skin of their mouths pulled back into leering grins or snarls. Worst of all were the deadly blades that sprang out of limbs, embedded into their skin. These things did not wield weapons, they were one.

Experiments, Yavaar realised with a sickening jolt. These were the experiments Shara had mentioned. Murderers, rapists, sadists, reborn into wretched creatures bent on death and destruction.

They moved faster than he could blink, leaving blood in their wake. Limbs and organs and heads peppered the ground. "Good Gods," Yavaar breathed as they sped towards him, slashing anything that got in their way. Hundreds, scores, all spat out of that pit. Senseless things devoid of emotion, only serving to make them more dangerous.

Yavaar's eyes rose, landing on the darkness as he resumed his place above. Crinos laughed, the cold, empty sound echoing down upon them, eyes feverish, drinking in the spectacle from the best seat in Everosia. High above, safe on his cloud of pluming black.

His eyes flitted to Yavaar's, lifeless as cool metal, shining bright with amusement. Somehow it was more terrifying than his phantom form, to see how insane he was, how bloodthirsty. Tendrils of his wisps reached down until they were all around Yavaar—inside him, seeking to choke their way down his throat.

He had never known hate, never understood it so much as in that moment. Not even for his horrible, abusive, greedy father. Not for the politicians that tried to strip the weak of their dignity, their lives. And he burned with it, refusing to bow before the darkness again, not even as the black found its way to his eyes and the world grew blurry and dim.

Shouts sounded in his ears, and the invasive presence that was the darkness withdrew. His vision cleared only to show a horde of the experiments mere metres away. Panic overtook his senses, body freezing like a deer sensing a predator. With a cry he managed to lift an arm above his face, waiting for the impact.

A double-bladed spear swished before him, and Nirandia was there, her long hair whipping as she swerved and curled and vaulted through the air. Then Tiderion was beside her again, the elves fighting in tandem, their blades whistling in unison.

Screams rang out as those disgusting creatures ravaged the elven unit, their ranks dwindling little by little, the faces of those fair and noble warriors tainted in death, their mouths wide.

They were all headed this way. Every mutated creature that crawled out of that hole was careening towards them. Towards ... the realisation cleaved through him. Three integral leaders of the allied armies were bundled neatly together. Right where the darkness wanted them.

"Get out of here," he yelled at the elves, his voice little more than a rasp. "The darkness wants us together; he's using them to—"

Tiderion turned toward him, and it was that split second, that momentary lapse of concentration that did it. A blade slammed through his throat, Tiderion's blue eyes widening, a hand rising to the ruined flesh.

The roar of battle could not stop the sounds from reaching Yavaar's ears as the male's ragged breaths filled with blood until little more than gurgles sounded. The sword withdrew, blood spurted, the light in his eyes flickered momentarily, and then it was gone.

Nirandia never stopped, her weapon swinging, her face stricken with fury and pain. She snarled as the experiments began to overwhelm her, as she was so overcome with monsters her beautiful face showed the first sign of fear. It reminded Yavaar so much of Amerie that he snapped himself of his stupor and charged, barrelling his horse towards the elven lady.

He slashed, reaping, again and again, ignoring the slashes to his arms, the cuts to his face, the blade that punched clean through his calf. It wasn't until his horse was taken down that he rolled to the ground, using the momentum to strike the belly of the creature again and again, until at last the stalwart thing fell. It looked into his eyes before it died. They were still a golden brown, a haunting memory of what—who it once was.

He fought beside Nirandia, breaths wheezing, leg trembling with pain, about to cave any second. As he looked into her hazel eyes, he noticed there was a small ring of gold he'd never noticed before. Never would have seen if not for being so close. And he focused on that tiny detail of beauty, the last thing he would ever see before he died.

A sword pummelled through the break in her armour—right beneath her underarm—and she thudded to her knees, gasping. Her weapon clattered uselessly to the ground. She reached a hand to Yavaar, and he clasped her palm; still warm, still strong even now.

She smiled, a soft and beautiful thing, and he nodded, ready to accept his fate when screams tore the air. Not those of the monsters or soldiers below, but mighty winged beasts, and when he raised his eyes like all the others, he blinked, fearing himself delusional with blood loss.

But there could be no hiding the beat of their wings, the shrill demand to their call, the mighty tails that streamed through the air. Griffins. And riding them were dwarves, bellowing their war cries, twirling axes and swords and all manner of weapons.

Yavaar smiled so wide his cracked lips dribbled blood as the mighty beasts plummeted towards them, drawn by the fastest and strongest of all monsters. Their talons shredded the monsters one after the other, cruelly curved beaks ripping.

And the hunters became the hunted.

Names on a List

DENAVAR

HE BODIES THAT LITTERED THE FIELD WERE COUNTLESS. Denavar sighed as he took in the blood-soaked snow. Winter was indeed harsh this year. The fallen were already crusted with a thick plume of white, their bodies frosting in the evening air. There were so many—too many to count—but Denavar knew the toll would number in the high thousands.

They would be lucky to last another day. If not for the griffins and their riders, they'd likely be dead already. Denavar ran a hand through his sweat-slicked hair, still drenched with blood from the day. He was beyond exhausted, but he couldn't stop yet. The living still needed his attention, and the dying couldn't wait.

His palms glowed as he swept them over his patient; one of many waiting for care. So many that the cots set up in the healers' tents were now spilling into soldier's quarters. Like him, the mages hadn't stopped to breathe since the darkness pulled his army back, many of them stretching their strength to portal travel to Renlock for medical supplies, blankets and food.

The healers gave everything they had, the tent a beacon for anyone in need of assistance. Denavar watched them while he worked, their faces pinched in concentration, brows furrowed and faces pale as they gave all of themselves to the wounded. Some worked in silence, while others chatted to their patients, distracting them from the pain or the things that haunted their thoughts. Denavar understood, for they occupied his mind too.

The darkness's experiments had been relentless. Vicious, untiring, fast as an elf and strong as a dwarf. It was unnerving, not to mention the barbaric mutation of their bodies. Twisted, horrible mockeries of humans.

They had obliterated much of the ground soldiers, with Yavaar's army suffering the most losses. But fortunately, they weren't as effective against aerial units. Something Denavar sent a prayer of thanks to all the Gods for.

Still, his heart ached. Today had been devastating for too many reasons, and he would mourn many who had fallen. Friends from Windarion and Woodrandia, mages he had taught at Renlock Academy. And then there were losses that would hurt not only the many hearts that would mourn them, but the chain of command.

Linar, the Diodonian chieftain; Jeelu and Neefu, Flynn's second and third in command; several of Nirandia's high-ranking officers; most of Yavaar's generals, captains, and so on; the list too long to name. And then the last.

Tiderion.

Denavar winced just thinking his name. The male he'd come to dislike so strongly. Now he just felt guilty, sick with the thought that he'd not tried harder to overcome their differences, to not look past his temperament and instead see his brilliance. For he was that. Strategic, clever, fierce in battle.

He had died protecting Yavaar and Nirandia. There could be no nobler death than that. Unfortunately, Yavaar knew that too. The man had been a shivering wreck after the battle, and Denavar feared even if he were fit enough to fight tomorrow, his mind would not allow it, too broken to piece back together. If Yavaar lived another day, Denavar did not want to risk what might come out of it, for it certainly would not be a king.

He sighed, feeling the last of his energy leaving his bloodstream, his bones growing more exhausted, more brittle by the second.

"Save some of that for yourself," Shara said, sidling up beside him, jerking her chin at his palms.

He could barely move his head, his neck spasming from having it locked into looking down for hours on end. "These soldiers need my help."

Gently, she pulled his hands back before lifting his chin so his stare would meet her eyes. "And you need rest," she said. "If you give any more, you'll be of no help tomorrow and I'll have to go rescue your ass." Shara's keen eyes scanned the room, and she snapped her fingers, much to the glares of the mages. "Hey, can we get some help over here? Wizard needing assistance."

At the mention of wizard they practically ran over each other to assist him. Denavar rolled his eyes. "Really? You're pulling that card?"

"Of course, Divine one. Your health is our greatest concern," she said with an exaggerated bow.

"Hardly," he scoffed, but when he opened his mouth to shoo the mages, he was delivered a withering stare. He shut his mouth instead.

The Magicka felt good as it surged through his veins. A little strange, coming from so many mages, their Magicka all leaving a uniquely subtle trace in his body, but he wasn't complaining. Feeling lighter, the aches and pains of his muscles and the numerous gashes and scrapes littering his body beginning to smooth over.

Shara raised a brow, still perfectly shaped even if she was a splattered, stinking mess. "Better?"

He sighed, relenting. "Better."

Her answering smirk almost made him laugh. Almost. "I'm assuming you didn't come for my welfare alone?"

Shara frowned, amusement quickly fading. "You've been summoned. A funeral ceremony will commence in an hour or two. As the mages who fell are—were —your charges, you're ... needed."

Denavar's brows shot up. "Here? Now? We don't have time for such things. At this rate, we'll likely all be dead tomorrow."

"I know," she muttered, and her resignation stopped him cold. She looked into his eyes, her own amber orbs gleaming. "Even with the assistance of the griffins, his numbers are too many. We would need something drastic to win the war tomorrow. And I have an idea but ..."

She shifted uncertainly, which made Denavar's back stiffen. "Oh, don't play coy now. What has that devious mind of yours concocted?"

Shara smiled grimly. "I want to pull our armies back."

Denavar blinked. "I'm sorry, you want us to retreat? Are you out of your Gods damned mind?"

Shara stared at him. "I believe I said something similar to Ashalea, and we all let her go play saviour, didn't we?"

Denavar fumed. "Don't go there. Don't you dare use that as a weapon against me."

"I'm not angry at Ashalea." Her nostrils flared, and Denavar raised a brow. "Well, I am a little seeing as she's late to the party, but that's beside the point. I'm asking you to trust me. Let me do something to help."

He looked into her eyes, assessing her intentions, but beneath the sadness and the tiredness from today, there beamed a pinprick of hope. He shook his head, a quiet, absurd laugh bubbling from within.

"Shara ..."

"Yes?"

"When have you ever asked to get what you want?"

47

Keepers, Awaken

SHARA

"THIS IS SO STUPID. AN UTTERLY IDIOTIC IDEA."

"*Need I remind you that said idea was entirely yours,*" Razakh purred. "*And I happen to think it has merit.*"

She stood before the wall of trees, hands on her hips as she gazed at the canopies of unending green. "The Grove," she whispered to her friend. "To think our paths have led us around this damned place the entire time. Yet here we are at last and I find myself not wanting to go in."

Razakh rubbed against her leg. "*Scared of some big, bad trees?*"

"No," she said indignantly. *Yes.* "Not at all." *Absolutely terrified.*

"*I can sense your fear down the connection, oh mighty Onyxonite. Maybe your bark is worse than your bite.*"

She looked blandly at the tree closest to her as his amusement trickled through her senses. "Oh my Gods. Did you? Was that a

JOKE, Razakh? Did you just make a funny?"

He thrust his muzzle in the air, looking like a snobby housecat pleased with having left its master a surprise on the new carpet.

Shara burst out laughing. "We're going to talk about this later, because if I don't die tomorrow your horrible material will surely kill me. But first ..."

"*The Keepers,*" Razakh said. His tail fluttered cautiously behind him, flames licking up his back, embers spitting into the dark.

"Would you put that out?" she hissed. "It's practically inviting the darkness to come play hide and seek here."

He growled but snuffed the flames of his mane. "*No more than your screeching might raise the dead.*"

Rolling her eyes, she took a step towards the treeline. It wasn't that the forest itself was ominous—in fact it was quite ordinary, despite the canopies fat with growth, spilling with green leaves in the middle of winter.

She would have expected nothing less, being a place of Magickal energy. It was the centre of Everosia, the beating heart of everything within their world. And at the forest's core was the portal, the gateway to other realms and the potential harbinger of doom, should the darkness gain possession of it.

This forest reeked of Old Magicka that she could not begin to understand, nor did she want to. It was best to leave such things to their natural state—undisturbed and peaceful. Which meant not earning the ire of the Keepers.

Shara cleared her throat, looking nervously at Razakh, who only nodded his encouragement.

"Keepers of old, protectors of this sacred place, please hear me. We are the next Guardians of the Grove, those bound by duty to keep hidden that which is dear."

Razakh hummed, and she realised he was laughing at her grandiose speech. She reddened, sending him a glare. The trees remained quiet, still, not a leaf moving out of place. Breathing deep, she raised her arms. "I beseech you, please, help us. Defend our armies, help us win the war before the darkness can overthrow all the good in this world."

At the mention of Crinos the trees seemed to whisper, their boughs shaking—in anger, Shara realised. Their canopies shuddered violently, leaves whipping out towards her and Razakh, and she ducked her head with a yelp, arms lifting to protect her face from an onslaught of debris.

Razakh leaped before her, shielding her frame with his bulk, standing tall despite the forest's wrath. *"I don't think we're welcome,"* he whispered.

"I'm not giving up that easily," she bit back. She opened her mouth to spit out more eloquent speech but ... damn. To hell with that. Pushing out from behind Razakh she planted her feet in the ground, strong as the roots of the trees before her.

"For God's sake stop your tantrum and listen," she bellowed. Razakh roared beside her, flames blaring to life, and the trees quietened just a little. "We are going to die tomorrow if you don't help, and should we fall, your beloved forest will be next. *You* will be next. You have to understand," she implored them, her tone growing desperate. "We don't just want to protect the portal; we want to close it."

The trees fell wholly still, and the sudden silence was more unnerving than the whirlwind they had just tossed towards her. She stilled, muscles tensed, Razakh's shoulders bunched as they waited.

A single root tore from the ground, and it twisted in the air, curling towards her. Shara did not move, didn't flinch as it hovered before her, as if curious. A sudden surge of Magicka flitted through her, warm and inviting, and it filled her with gratitude.

The root lifted to her face, stroking her cheek before playfully flicking Razakh's tail, and Shara knew they were not alone in this fight.

For the first time, her prayers had been answered.

48

Homage to the Fallen

RAZEKH

HE HAD FORGOTTEN THE PAIN OF LOSS. Forgotten the sharp stab of sorrow that pierces the heart and takes root in the mind. The beginnings of depression and despair. He had never been absent of it—not after his mother had been taken from him at such a young age—but that was an old hurt. Familiar. A scar imprinted on his soul.

Now he had lost both parents, and his closest friend. His chieftain. He deserved a burial within the Diodon Mountains, back home in the desert Linar had loved so much, amid the sweeping red sands of their ancestors.

Razakh couldn't give him that, not with the threat of disease that festered within corpses. Instead the races would burn their dead—cremating the bodies, freeing the souls trapped within.

Perhaps the ceremony could do some good, morbid as it may

be. The elves believed their energies returned to the earth, a show of faith to thank the Gods who granted them such gifts of immortality, beauty and grace. Shara had told him once of a seer who had set the wheels of fate in motion. Harrietti, her name was.

She had died for the cause, and with her death came life. Shara had thought the woman to be gifted from the Gods themselves, and her service had been rewarded with an oasis that would bear her name should it stand beyond the war.

Razakh liked to think Linar's death—Tiderion's and all the others, too—might one day do the same. He had searched the battlefield for his friend, to bring the frozen shell of his body back to the camp. He had tried not to look at the faces of the dead staring back at him, shoving the guilt deep down, ignoring their silent pleas to save them, to return them to their families.

But it could not be. Too many bodies littered the fields, too many twisted remains of all races. He wondered, even with the return of all the elven souls, if this place would always be marked by death. If the fissures in the earth would remain thus forever, or whether the earth could heal its wounds, restore growth once again.

He supposed it didn't matter. All that mattered was they win.

The lords and ladies of the allied races all gathered before the pyres of their respected fallen, sending prayers to the Gods and Goddesses of their faith, imparting a final farewell to their friends and comrades.

Razakh did not step before Linar's body. His friend never cared much for small talk or wasted words. If he were still alive, Linar would know how much Razakh respected him, cared for him. His Klan would instead celebrate the lives of their fallen in their own way, should they ever have the chance.

They would honour the dead in their own land.

"It's time," Shara said down the connection, and he startled from his musings, looking up to see the rulers approach the pyres, each with a torch in hand. Or, in Denavar's case, a fireball.

His friend looked exhausted; dark shadows under his eyes, sagging shoulders, and grey skin that spoke to the energy he'd spent on healing others. He gave so much of himself, asking nothing in return except the loyalty of his people, the strength to fight for a better world.

Denavar would say that was the highest price one could ask, but Razakh did not agree. They were all here for the same reason. To fight so their families and friends might live. And if it came to it, they would die for that cause. Honourably, willingly, knowing they had given their loved ones a fighting chance—or at the very least time to flee the shores of a broken land before chains could ensnare them.

Razakh caught his friend's eyes and nodded as he approached Linar's pyre. He bore no torch, no Magicka except the fire upon his back, and he realised what a gift it was to have such a thing, to have Magicka engrained into his genetic makeup.

Not many creatures still lived in Everosia that could say the same. Those old, forgotten things were long gone from this world. Hunted to extinction. The very same thing the darkness lusted for, only all were at risk now. Every living, breathing, growing thing in Everosia would suffer his wrath should they fail.

Razakh's hackles raised. *No.* His flames raged along his back, crackling his anger, rippling with blue heat, echoing his protest and defiance. He raised his tail, igniting the kindling of the pyre.

And as he stepped down, he felt Shara's leg brush his side, Denavar's hand on his back, Tofin's presence beside him. Paying homage to the dead.

Standing strong for the living.

Colossal Power

Tofin

"**B**LASTED BATS," Tofin roared, ducking the outstretched claws of the creature as it descended upon him. A griffin's piercing cry rang in his ears right before its talons shredded into the bat's wings, a hooked beak tearing its throat out.

A single gilded feather escaped the griffin's golden chest, and Tofin swallowed his emotions as it drifted down into his open palm. He almost choked at the familiar tickle against his calloused hand, reminding him of his saviour from so long ago.

That griffin had known, somehow, that their peoples were linked beyond more than blood. That Tofin held a greater purpose. Whether it knew he would one day request this call to arms, or that he would one day become a Guardian of the Grove, he didn't know.

And yet ... he still couldn't believe it. The dwarves across the seas, his mother's people—*his kin*—had answered his call, choosing to fight in a war that wasn't their own. The thought gave him renewed vigour as he swung his axe again and again, forcing his enemies back with a thrust of his shield and a stroke of his weapon.

His brothers fought beside him, the wolf pack flanking them, forming a wedge as they advanced into the thick of the battle. And his father! His father took to the skies upon a gigantic, glorious griffin, his war cries stoking the hearts of his soldiers, spurring them on. Kano had trained with the aerial legions of their kin, having fought in battles of his own upon a griffin's back. All for his mother, to win her heart, to prove himself a true warrior worthy of the Gods.

He searched the skies hopefully for the griffin of long ago, but that beast was nowhere to be found, and disappointment surged through his gut. But it was enough, to hold the memory of that creature instead.

Pride struck true to Tofin's heart as he watched his father fight above, tackling the winged creatures that blotted out the sun—what little of it managed to creep through the darkness's black shroud.

The dark seemed to be growing, shadows roiling angrily today, and Tofin feared Crinos might tear a hole in the sky, his rage at the griffins' arrival announced in every sneer, every narrowed glare of those red eyes.

It wasn't just the griffins that had provoked his anger, but a change of scenery too. For their armies had shifted the battlefield, and today they had pushed the darkness's army back. Not by sheer numbers, but a constant barrage of Magicka that hailed upon the creatures. It had taken hours to achieve, but they skirted the ring of the forest now, so close to the Grove that the darkness might be tempted to push through.

But he couldn't, not yet. Not when the Keepers barred the way.

Those ancient beings, sentient and yet not, peaceful but utterly vicious when they had to be. And it seemed Shara's little visit last night had certainly awakened them now.

Vines lashed out, impaling bodies from underground, wrapping thorny leaves around throats and sending creatures careening into their comrades. Thorns blocked the entrance to the Grove, and not even Magicka could harm them as a wayward fireball barrelled into the barrier, fizzling out, appearing to be absorbed into the fortress of thorns.

Tofin snarled as the darkness's eyes met his own, and Tofin's determination flashed like lightning as he peered into that being—no longer an elf, not quite a monster, but something else entirely. Insanity glimmered in Crinos's eyes, but he would not back down.

He banged his axe upon his shield, slow and steady, the steel ringing loud, and one by one his people joined him, his brothers at his side; one of fire, one of ice, and he, the thunder to ignite them.

The dwarves bellowed and stomped, marching forward. The song of war was a summons to the allied armies; elves, humans, Diodonians—all joining their ranks, bolstering the lines and closing the gaps.

The monsters wavered uncertainly, the united front causing them to retreat and re-gather. Tofin kept his eyes locked on the darkness, daring him to make a move, to risk the drawing of blood. For powerful as he was, the darkness was not immortal—not immune to the kiss of a sword or the burn of fire.

And Tofin would see to it that he bled before the end.

The darkness took the bait. Slowly, ever so slowly, he descended on his dark cloud, halting just above the heads of all soldiers. He looked into Tofin's eyes and smiled with closed lips, and Tofin knew in his heart he had made a mistake, goading Crinos. Felt it in his bones as that empty, crooked smirk widened. He raised one arm towards the elves—

Black erupted from his fingers, spearing like an arrow through the armies, obliterating all in their path as it consumed every ounce of flesh and blood, an explosion of black and red as bodies disintegrated. Thousands—both elves and creatures—dead in seconds, their existence wiped from the face of the earth.

When the power stopped, the air seemed to choke itself before rippling out in a shockwave, throwing Tofin on his ass and knocking the wind from his chest. He wheezed, trembling as he sat up, and his eyes widened in horror.

A tidal wave of red loomed before him, and his stomach clenched as he realised it was blood. The darkness clicked his fingers and it fell, cascading over the army, drowning them in the lifeblood of their friends. Tofin choked as it slipped down his throat, his stomach rebelling as it came back up and he vomited all over himself.

"You think you know what death is?" The darkness's wicked voice sounded above. "You think your armies can defeat me?"

Tofin met his eyes once more, and this time they were utterly black. Pools so dark no light could reach them, and he shuddered, body still wracked with shock.

The darkness laughed as he caught Tofin's stare, and the words felt directed at him, when he said, "I'm just getting started."

He lifted his arm once more, and Tofin prayed. Prayed with everything he had that something might save them.

50

Gone

Denavar

HE THUDDED TO HIS KNEES as anguish flooded his bones, mouth wide, hands raised to his head as he looked on in shock and denial. Seconds. It had taken only seconds for the darkness to decimate scores of warriors.

Denavar's eyes burned, but the tears would not come. His insides were hollow, his body stripped of hope, his strength waning.

He had been fighting among them earlier. His people. His kin. Woodland elves and warriors from the Aquafarian waters of the north. All gone in a moment. Wiped away from the face of the earth.

And Nirandia ... he choked on the bitter taste of ash on the wind, raising his dirt-streaked face to the sky.

Gone.

51

Half a Heart

SHARA

IT HAPPENED SO FAST. One moment she was fighting amid the mages, protecting the psychics as they forged fake realities, inflicting the minds of the monsters as they fought. The next, black spewed forth from the darkness, and she could only stare in shock as his hand changed direction, arm lowering, fingers pointed right at the heart of the Onyxonites.

Towards her brother.

She sprinted, sliding under a sweeping blade, boots skiing over the ice as she ducked her head back and let momentum push her forward. Her two swords snaked out as she righted herself, disembowelling a marsh creature, twirling in the air as she slashed at the chest of an Uulakh and the neck of a bat.

Everywhere she looked, wings, claws, fangs leered before her. She cut them all away, her skin burning feverishly, breath coming in ragged gasps as she forced her legs to move, pinwheeling as fast as she could towards him.

"Flynn," she screamed, voice drowned out beneath shrieking and guttural groans. She could see glimpses of him now—swords arcing, boots dancing, his form perfect as he moved with precision and grace.

His face was smooth even in battle, the calm before a storm, his instincts and training forcing fear and recklessness aside, the predator within taking over as he battled. His brown hair was plastered back, sweat glistening on olive cheeks, chocolate brown eyes focused on his enemies.

She willed him to look at her, willed her twin to hear her words, and to her surprise, he did, eyes shooting to hers as he killed the monster pressing in. "You're in danger, Flynn, get out of there," she shouted, but he cocked a head, raised a finger to his ear, indicating he couldn't hear her.

But he must have sensed her fear, seen the panic etched into her face, for he began moving towards her, slowly, too slowly, as more enemies pressed in. She growled in frustration, shoving at the slimy marsh creatures as they closed towards her. They blocked her view, and she snarled as she slashed with all her strength, sending those closest to her toppling.

Sprinting again, she slipped on the ice, one knee crashing down with a thud, and she ignored the bite of pain, seeing a glimpse of the back of his head, then his arms, then his blade raised high.

She glanced at the darkness, his arm lowering, his eyes filled with madness, lips curling into a smile as he saw her sprinting. Lower, still lower until his hand unfolded, a finger stretched out. A sob wrenched from her lips as she looked back to Flynn.

His gaze snapped to her, and she shouted, "RUN."

If he hadn't heard her, he must have read her lips, for he noted her arm pointing towards the darkness. He saw Crinos's hand pointing back, and when he turned back to Shara, he smiled softly, gentle acceptance filling the light of his eyes, and he mouthed the words, "I love you."

Her eyes widened and she reached out a hand as all-consuming black raged over him, decimating the soldiers and her brother until nothing but ash floated on the winds, and a scorch seared the ground where he'd stood.

A strangled cry escaped her throat.

Blood cascaded down before the blast had her tumbling head over heels to crumble into a heap upon the ground. Shara looked at the sky, drenched in the blood of her brother, her kin, and she screamed. The battle seemed to fall away as she stared at the spot her brother had just been, the sounds of her grief echoing in the sudden silence. She couldn't believe—didn't want to believe—that Flynn could disappear in one violent instant. Her visceral wails faded into hoarse sobs, tears streaming down her cheeks, leaving tracks in the blood coating her skin ... his blood.

She heard the darkness's laugh rumbling over the armies; cruel, full of delight at her pain, and the destruction wrought not only to the Everosians, but his own witless creatures.

It filled her with blinding rage, consuming her so greedily she might burn herself alive. She rose to her feet, one boot in front of the other, plucking her fallen swords from the ground.

And turning, she bellowed her war cry and tore over the fields towards the darkness, unable to see anything other than her target, unable to fill the empty hole in her chest where her twin had resided. He would never fill that space again, she would never hear his laugh, never see that smile. Never, never, never.

With tears still streaming down her face, she lifted both swords, readying to lunge into the sky when something else stole her attention, fettering the need for revenge.

A rift cleaved through the black of the darkness's making, striking through the fog leagues above the battlefield, filling the plains with light. Shara glanced at the darkness, whose stillness indicated this was not of his making. And, as the world rumbled around them, the rift grew larger, strange clouds pouring from the opening.

No, she realised, heart leaping with hope. Not clouds. She spied gigantic wings, long necks and scales glinting in the newfound sun. Upon their backs were riders, bedecked in full armour of creamy, shining steel. Elves, the many hues of their white, golden, and black skin seeming to shine like pearls in the sunlight, their hair glittering in braids, their weapons wicked and curved.

And at the front of the unit, on perhaps the biggest dragon, was an elf who shined brighter than all. Garbed in moonstone steel known only to The Meadows, she shimmered like the sun, all the colours of the rainbow reflecting off that armour. An emerald-crusted scimitar was raised in one hand, her hair rippling silver behind her, braided for war, the crown of her head bound by a silver circlet.

Shara wept, knees caving before her.

Ashalea had done it. The queen of The Meadows had come.

52

Fury Burns

ASHALEA

FIRE SCORCHED THE EARTH, blazing in trails so smouldering, so blinding, her eyes watered from the heat rising. The dragon she rode soared, the arrowhead to the spears at their back. Dragons of all colours, born of all elements, riding the current behind her.

"Shields," she screamed to the soldiers below, amplifying her voice to carry over the field. "Raise Magicka shields, protect yourselves from the blasts."

Rippling waves seemed to gel together as, one by one, the mages erected transparent shields of Magicka, combining their strengths to push them farther, encapsulating those without the power to protect themselves. An extra precaution in case the dragons' breath blazed too far from the monsters, burning allies in their wake.

The ground quaked beneath the wrath of brown and green

dragons, their powers those of dirt and rock and seed, snatching at monsters from underground, pulling them down or burying them beneath waves of dirt. Their gigantic tails like spiked clubs as they whipped into hordes, sending them flying, little more than a nudge from the primal beasts.

Ashalea stared in awe as they turned the tides of war, the power of fire and ice dragons combining into deadly spirals of freezing flames; the scales of the red dragons gleaming in the reflection; the seemingly smooth surfaces of the white ice dragons shining, their eyes bluer than the brightest sky.

And then there was him. The one she rode. The last of the water dragons. She had thought him magnificent before, but in battle he was beyond glorious. Graceful, strong, and fast—so agile for such a large creature. Water spurted from his mouth, drenching the monsters, scattering them and crushing bones beneath its strength—raging rivers and currents unstoppable.

It was chaos. They weaved between the dragon's kin, swerved beneath the wings of ... griffins, Ashalea realised with a surge of wonder. Tofin must have sent word after all, and thankfully so, for as Ashalea's eyes roved the armies, her heart sank once more.

Too few—there were too few soldiers left, their numbers dwindling before the crawling mass of the darkness's minions. Her heart dropped. Those left standing were drenched in red. Far more than an average battle should allow for. Horror coursed through her veins, and she cursed herself for being so late. For not being here when they needed her. But they had not given up. Fighting with tooth and nail to live, to *exist* in this world.

She would not give up either. Ashalea crouched upon the dragon's back, nails clawing on to the scales of his neck, a slight hollow providing the perfect grappling point. She searched, hoping, praying to find her friends.

"*Here*," a voice said in her mind—soft and sad, yet demanding, urgent.

"Denavar," she breathed. Ashalea knew where to look, she needed only follow the flares of Magicka peppering the battlefield. Flashes of reds and brilliant blues arced across the sky, but she saw the balls of lightning that crackled, growing until they exploded in vast mushrooms of electricity, far stronger and brighter than all others.

And beside him, another warrior drenched in red, in blood. Ashalea's breath caught in her throat. Not her blood. No, Shara moved too gracefully, to freely. A Diodonian fought at her side, protecting her with everything he had, snarling and vicious, and something about the way Razakh shielded her told Ashalea something had changed.

The connection maybe, or perhaps it went deeper than that. Someone had fallen, someone Shara cared about. Ashalea had no time to consider as a dwarf charged into sight, bellowing, axe swinging ferociously as he circled his flock, fighting for them.

They were caved in, encircled by hordes of monsters, all seeming to gather around one central point of the map. All gathered around Crinos.

Ashalea bared her teeth, rage filling her bloodstream as she embraced the fury burning in her veins. "Get closer to the darkness," she informed the dragon, and he swerved, gliding towards that being in the centre of it all, one wing dipping as he plummeted.

Her hair whipped behind her and, rising slowly, she stood upon the back of the great beast and jumped. Weightless, she fell, using momentum to curl her body inwards and flip before landing on the ground with a thump, right in front of her friends.

She turned to the others, a triumphant smirk on her face. "Did you miss me?"

Tofin barked a laugh as his axe cleaved a marsh monster in two. "Girl, I'll get on my knees and kiss the toes of your boots myself after this."

She grinned. "Don't thank me yet. We still have work to do."

Shara stalked towards her, eyes ghostly, face pale. "You're late," she said.

"Some might say fashionably so," Ashalea retorted with a wink.

"You do look quite the part with that new armour. Very flashy, *great* craftsmanship." But her friend's smile was weak, her usual witty bravado gone.

Ashalea prowled to the assassin, leaned her temple against her friend's. "You with me?"

Shara's lower lip trembled, her knees buckled, yet Ashalea held her shoulders fast. "Hey, Onyxonite, don't go breaking on me. I need those wits sharp, your aim true. We're not finished yet, you hear? We cry, we rage, we give in when we're dead. So, you with me?"

Shara closed her eyes, breathing deep, and when she opened them again the amber glowed with purpose. She nodded once, seeming to find herself again.

"Good," Ashalea breathed in relief. Denavar smiled at her as she released her friend, and she frowned at the slight limp, the wounds marring his body, the pain that lined his own eyes. "You're hurt," she said.

"We all are," he replied, and she didn't need him to clarify to know he meant bone deep, in their hearts and souls as well as their bodies. She let her palm glide over his thigh, analysing the bones, finding a fractured shard causing the limp. Light flashed, and she sent her purity searing over that wound, mending the bone, re-stitching the skin.

She felt strong, full of hope and determination, and her Magicka healed him in an instant, his relief huffing out in a long breath, shoulders straightening again. The superficial wounds she left, reserving all her strength for the final task at hand.

Denavar took her chin in his hand, and the world faded to nothing as they stared at each other. She committed his face to her memory—every scrape, every line, the stubborn determination in that cut-glass jaw, the tempest of his eyes. And, beneath it, the love he held for her. Never faltering, always binding them together.

Fire blazed around them, earth upturned, water flooded, and through it all there was only him. Embers floated by as they simply held each other and, finally, she kissed him. Deeply, passionately, giving all of herself to this moment, neither one wanting to voice what would come next. Whether this might be the last time they held each other.

"Isn't this a touching sight?" a voice crooned, and Ashalea immediately dropped her stance to the defensive, sword raised in one hand, a ball of lightning crackling in the other.

"Crinos," she spat, and he had the nerve to smile at her. Almost fondly. Some sick, twisted drop of affection. Perhaps it warred with the disdain he held for her. She didn't care, didn't give it more than a second's thought as he approached.

The cloud of black disappeared, and he dropped to the ground before them, reverting to his elven form. His was in full armour, though his shadows seemed to writhe across the steel, a living tapestry of darkness.

"I was surprised to find you missing from the fight," he said idly, lazily, as he picked at a nail. "Disappointed, actually, that you wouldn't see them all fall."

Her hands curled into fists, nails biting into her skin as she watched him. He noted the movement, smirking as he stood before her. The Guardians flocked to her back, muscles tense, spines rigid as they crouched, ready to lunge at any moment. The darkness noted that too, and a slight flicker of irritation pinched his lips.

Ashalea clucked her tongue. "A real shame. The view is so lovely from a dragon's back."

Crinos's eyes narrowed. "It won't stop me. Your winged wyrms will fall like all the others. Like those left to die while you were gone, sister. Do you know how many you doomed while you were off being the hero?" He breathed deep. "It gave me such pleasure to see it. Especially my little doll's brother. If only you could have seen her face when I burned him from existence. Her screams ruptured the earth. So utterly delicious."

Ashalea's heart sank to her stomach as she looked at her friend. A single tear trickled down Shara's cheek, even as the assassin fought against Denavar and Tofin, their arms holding her back.

"Should I play with you again, my dear? I'm sure there are many blades yet waiting to taste your pretty flesh. Pity that your twin shan't be the one to do the job for me."

"My blade shall be the kiss of your lifetime," Shara spat vehemently. "It lingers just a little before leaving you breathless."

Crinos merely laughed, his eyes flashing with delight at her rage.

Ashalea turned back to her brother, emerald eyes blazing. "You bastard," she breathed. "You will pay for Flynn's death, and all the others. I swear it."

He raised a brow and the steel grey of his eyes glinted with challenge. "Such threats, one can only wonder when you'll follow through. Or if you'll get the chance." His gaze travelled past Ashalea and the others; past the soldiers clashing and the monsters biting; past griffins that fell in feathered heaps from the skies; or the dragons with arrows protruding from their chests. His gaze swept over all those things to land on the forest, somewhere deep within.

"No." She lunged, sword raised high, thrusting to his heart right as his body blinked from existence, his chuckle vibrating through her, twisting her insides with disgust. She turned to the others, eyes wide, fear coursing through her. "The Grove," she whispered. "He's trying to open the portal to the other worlds."

"Not if I can help it," Denavar said, and he opened his own doorway of crackling blue, the window reflecting the entrance to the forest. It was now a firestorm of burning trees and split logs. The vines that had thrashed and churned with anger before now stood silent, still.

Ashalea's hand flitted to her mouth, sorrow cracking through her heart. "My Gods, the Keepers they're—they're all—"

"We can't think about that now. Go," Denavar commanded, and they stormed through one by one.

The window had shown but a fraction of the devastation, and as Ashalea stepped through the portal, she saw a path cleaving through the forest, deep into the growth until finally the burning trail stopped. "He must not have been able to enter via portal or from the air," she stated.

"Why didn't he take advantage of the battle? Come to the Grove when we were distracted?" Tofin said.

Ashalea's blood burned, her fingers curling into fists. "Because Crinos does nothing without an audience. Because he delights in pain—*our pain*. He wanted to break us, wanted to take those we loved before he kills us one by one and watch the pain consume us all. He will kill me last as punishment."

Razakh stepped beside her, assessing the destruction. The eerie stillness, the emptiness of the too quiet forest. *"The Magicka within this place hangs by a thread. The wards guarding the perimeter are gone."*

She sensed his anger, the sorrow at the devastation of something so ancient, so precious to the world. She felt it in her own heart, but she shoved it down. *Use the anger,* she told herself. *Use the pain against him.*

"We'll never get to him in time," Tofin said gruffly. "Not by walking."

Denavar sighed in exasperation. "I can't portal somewhere I haven't been. We'd have to do it in short distances as far as the eye can see, which isn't much in the middle of a forest."

"I have a better idea," a voice called from behind them, and Ashalea turned, her blood turning to ice at who she saw before her. Celiana. Her mother looked gaunt, skin sickly and pallid, hair limp. She looked like the life had been drained from her, and given her latest company, Ashalea wouldn't be surprised if that were true.

It took every effort not to lunge, to wrap her hands around that neck, but Ashalea watched her calmly, her words poisonous. "Give me one reason why I shouldn't drive my sword through your chest," she spat.

Her mother flinched, but she straightened her spine, thrust her chin high. "Because I'm your way in. This forest was my home once, I know it well. I can portal us to the Gate of the Grove ... and to your brother."

Ashalea searched the elf's gaze, looking for signs of deception. But they didn't have time, and the eyes that looked back at her were resigned, hopeless. The she-elf before her was a broken, empty creature. Whatever her brother had done, it had taken the old

Celiana, chewed her up and spat out something else. She could not hurt anyone now.

Ashalea nodded at last, and her mother bowed her head, drawing her remaining strength to conjure a portal. She stepped aside, one arm gesturing the way through, but Ashalea was having none of that.

"You first," she jerked her chin, and Celiana flinched at the venom in her words, the hostility rippling from the Guardians, Tofin's menacing axe raised in warning should she try anything foolish. But she stepped through and out of view as she retreated from the portal's side.

Ashalea breathed deep. And she stepped through the doorway.

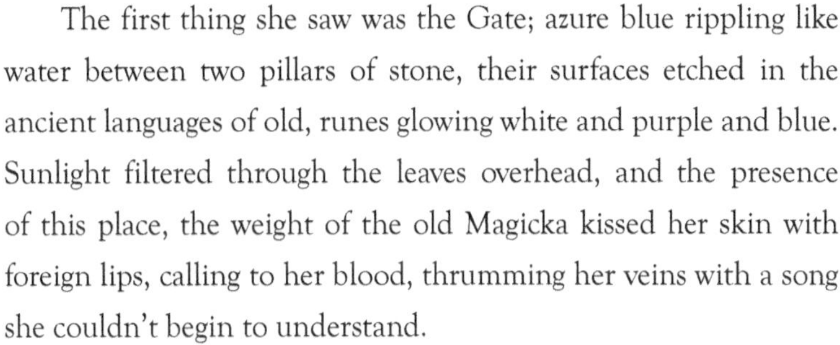

The first thing she saw was the Gate; azure blue rippling like water between two pillars of stone, their surfaces etched in the ancient languages of old, runes glowing white and purple and blue. Sunlight filtered through the leaves overhead, and the presence of this place, the weight of the old Magicka kissed her skin with foreign lips, calling to her blood, thrumming her veins with a song she couldn't begin to understand.

It was pure serenity, unattainable bliss, and she knew that living beings were not meant for this place. For greed lived in the hearts of all men and women, males and females of the different races. And to have such power, to harness the energies and be a master of worlds, could only end in madness.

Which, if the darkness succeeded, would come to pass—and soon. She forced her gaze from the gateway ahead, emerald eyes landing on the darkness ... and her mother.

A curved blade pressed to Celiana's slender throat, the serrated edge glinting in the sunlight, as was the drop of blood trickling down her neck.

Ashalea took a step—

"Careful, Ashalea, wouldn't want to hurt mother dearest by any sudden movements. My hand might slip." He pressed the blade deeper on that last word, let Celiana know the sting of steel, and she gasped, hazel eyes wide.

"She did your bidding, killed for you, and you'd still cast her aside?" Tofin asked in disbelief.

Crinos smirked at the dwarf. "Ah, the last Guardian, a prince of dwarves, no less. My, my, what a party we have. A princess, a prince, the daughter and son of two chieftains, and the last wizard of Everosia. How does it feel, Denavar, to hold such power in your hands? Can you feel him lingering—Wezlan's essence now flowing through your veins?"

"Don't say his name. Don't ever say his name in my presence again," Ashalea snarled.

Her brother's eyes sparkled with malice. "He was pitiful in his last moments. A snivelling, old fool. To throw such power away ... what a waste. And on you and your pet dog," he said coolly, glancing at Denavar.

Power crackled up Denavar's arms as he fisted his hands, and Ashalea sucked in a breath as the ocean blue of his eyes flashed with white warning. "Loyalty and love," Denavar said slowly, "is one of life's greatest gifts. One that—once shared—can be a dangerous weapon."

Crinos scoffed. "Loyalty. You place such high stock in it. But I've known what it gets you. Have felt the repercussions of it all my life. To have parents that would hold you back from your calling, that would punish you for being different, let others abuse you for being special. All the while those who are meant to care and protect you, demanding your silence, expecting you to stay quiet about it, to fade away until you are but a shadow of your former self.

"Loyalty," Crinos spat, his voice bitter, "is giving yourself wholly to your lessons, to your teachers. It's caring for someone so much they were like a father. And yet, when the time came to advance, they denied me once again, bid me hide amongst the sheep like a useless acolyte."

Ashalea's breath whooshed from her lungs. Wezlan. He was talking about Wezlan—the man who had taught him, shielded him, encouraged him to grow. But the seed had been tainted from abuse, blackened from a broken childhood. And once it sought to flourish, the darkness was the result. And she understood—even pitied him a little, for all that had been done to him.

He was not a monster of his own making. Life had not been kind—had not looked gently upon his gifts. People feared what they didn't understand, mistrusted it, abused it. She had learned that from the seer, Harrietti—that kind old woman who had known pain and sorrow and loneliness all her life.

But it was a choice, to let the pain fester into rage, to see only darkness and shut out the light. Crinos had made his choice, as she must now make hers.

"I'm sorry," she said softly, and the forest fell so silent she swore everyone held their breath upon hearing those words. "I'm sorry for the hurts others have bestowed upon you, for the misery, for the loneliness. I wish you might have held out a little longer. Waited for me, so I might have shed some light, might have been a friend, might have loved a brother. And it's not too late, Crinos, for you to do something good. Let us close the portal, let us end this before more blood is spilled."

He looked at her, gaze darting between Ashalea and her friends. His eyes were desperate, longing, as if he had been waiting for a sliver of kindness, for an escape from his own making. Her heart leaped, silently begging for him to find that kernel of goodness and let it flourish.

The silver steel of his eyes softened momentarily as he searched her, the likeness of her face, bearing so many similarities to his own. But that light, that glimmer, it faded; the ember dying until it was consumed by hatred and distrust. His eyes shifted to red, the black wisps of his phantom form began to curl and writhe at his feet, and Ashalea knew her brother was truly dead.

"Love," he murmured, teeth morphing into fangs, face misting into shadows, into the monster. "Love ... is a good way to get one killed."

His blade moved faster than Ashalea could blink, the wispy tendrils blocking her vision as he shifted, disappearing and reforming besides the Gate, and when Ashalea could see again she gasped, her hope shattering into a thousand pieces, rage filling the hollows of her heart.

Celiana fell to her knees, one hand raised to the slash of her throat, blood bubbling as she tried to breathe, tried to speak. Her other arm lifted, and Ashalea lunged, catching her mother before she could crumble to the ground.

Beyond, darkness rose in a shield of black, blocking the Guardians from the portal while Crinos worked his Magicka, no doubt attempting to wrest control of the gateway, to bend the Grove's will to his own.

Her friends screamed and yelled, banging on the shield, wisps of black curling around their waists and throwing them across the glade. She ignored all of it, focused only on the dying elf before her.

Blood spattered the grass, pooling on Ashalea's moonstone armour, and her mother stared at her, hands shaking, body spasming. She opened her mouth, nothing but sickening chokes, blood and wheezing spilling forth.

Celiana tried again. "I'm ... I'm—"

Tears filled Ashalea's eyes. This female had wronged her in so many ways, had failed her in every regard as a mother but one. And she didn't know if she meant it, wasn't sure if she realised the gravity of her words, but she said, "I forgive you."

Her mother's eyes welled, and in them Ashalea saw the regret and sorrow and pain, but beneath it all ... love. Celiana leaned her head back, taking one final breath, and as the air rushed from her body and her lungs gave out, peace filled her eyes before they glazed for eternity.

Ashalea bit back a sob as she laid her mother's head gently to the grass, crossing her hands over her chest. She must have known what her actions would do—what the darkness would do to her after helping them. And she had done it anyway. It was perhaps the greatest courage she had ever shown.

Ashalea rose slowly, steeling her resolve. The black wall writhed just ahead, shadows of monsters snapping and howling and slithering in the darkening light, her friends still trying to slash their way through.

"You cannot win, Crinos," Denavar yelled, his face stricken with anger, muscles bulging in his neck. "You drained too much power on the battlefield and we both know power comes at a price." The darkness did not answer, and Denavar seethed, hurling fireballs, lightning bolts and great tidal waves of water. Nothing worked. No blade would break upon that shield, not even Magicka.

Except one. The only kind the darkness could not wield; a gift the Gods had seen fit to withhold from him. It was all for this—this moment, this fight to end all fights.

"Pull back," she said with quiet calm, and Shara, Razakh, Tofin—they glanced at her, not one questioning her motives, instead bowing their heads, perhaps knowing that this task was meant for her and her alone. The deliverer of vengeance, the bringer of retribution, the fury that burned brightest ... the searing heart of their flames. They gathered at her back, silent yet steady.

Denavar kept his attacks up, his movements desperate, his power so bright it was blinding as all the elements raged against those walls. But she took one step. And another until her hand was on his shoulder, and he sagged beneath her touch, head bent, eyes watery with frustration and pain. She took his face in her hands, forcing him to look at her until his rage subsided, until his logic returned. "Let me do this," she said gently.

He nodded and shifted to her side, a warm and solid presence. Not touching, but close enough to tell her he was there, that he'd always be there. No matter what.

She smiled at him, and it was free, light, feeling totally in control of her emotions and her body. Ashalea winked, and his lips twitched slightly. It was all she needed, to know he was in control again. She glanced back at the others with a smirk. "Might want to close your eyes."

Shara grinned fiercely, latching a hand to Razakh's fur, and much to Tofin's surprise, grabbing his palm in her own: a united front.

Ashalea raised her arms, palms flat, fingers curling, and she burrowed down into the depths of her soul, into that place reserved for this wild, wondrous thing. Ashalea dove into the wellspring before shooting back to the surface. She unleashed white blinding light, spilling over the Grove, blasting into the black whirlwind.

It churned, surging, forging a hole through the darkness's shield, eating up the black greedily, lapping at the shadows. The shadows hissed, snapping back, slithering around her bright light, threatening to devour it whole.

She could sense her brother's hate in the power; his anger, his sorrow, but she would not be broken again. She would not bow or lose herself to the dark. Her light burned even brighter—not hot as the sun, but cool and calming as the moon. And the night? It belonged to that celestial keeper, ever present, never faltering.

The moonlight broke the wall, the shadows peeling away and flaking into ash. Crinos stood beyond, dark power of his own crashing into the Gate, the azure waters beginning to wriggle with black, a steady poison filling the surface. His form flickered violently between elf and monster, as if the Magicka took too much of his strength, his concentration to hold onto. And she knew Denavar was right. He had drained too much, and all Magicka had a price.

Ashalea drew her sword—the blade of kings and queens, the weapon of her people. It had killed her foster parents at the hands of Crinos, had tasted her own skin, the scar still white upon her belly.

But, wielded by the right person, in the right hands, it would deliver justice and peace. She gazed at the sword, at the white hilt carved with the cycle of the moons embedded into the crest. The steel a rainbow of starlight as it glittered, deadly sharp, the blade itself engraved with runes of ancient elvish.

She raised it to her cheek with both hands and roared. Her friends' battle cries sounded behind her and, together, they charged. The darkness was ready; with one hand he sent an arc of black racing towards them, only to be batted aside by Ashalea, her light flicking it away.

Razakh reached him first, pouncing upon the darkness, knocking the elf from his perch before the portal, his spell broken by the contact. Razakh lunged, teeth snapping at Crinos's face, but with strength unknown even to an elf, her brother tore the Diodonian from him, claws digging into Razakh's skin, something crunching beneath his touch.

The Diodonian yelped as he was hurled across the clearing, thudding to the ground in a tangle of limbs. Crinos grunted, his Magicka seeming to sputter as he reverted to his elven form. He drew his sword, the cruel curve of that serrated blade still wet with their mother's blood.

He grinned as her eyes travelled to the red, and she thrusted, his body angling out of reach, his own blade singing as it swept down to her head. She side-stepped, twisting gracefully before whirling her blade behind her.

Denavar barraged him with an onslaught of lightning balls, the darkness either swerving out of the way or batting them aside with black Magicka. Tofin took his chance, axe swinging as it descended upon the darkness's side, missing his skin by an inch, taking only a swathe of the sash fastened at Crinos's side.

Her brother lunged back, slashing a cruel cut down Tofin's back and kicking him away. The dwarf howled, stumbling, Shara positioning herself in front of him. She fought viciously, her blades swinging in unison, a blurry dance of movement and grace, her strikes fast as a snake, deadly and dripping with her rage.

But the darkness was fast—too fast for a human, blocking every hit, slamming her own defence with a strength that set Shara's teeth to rattling, arms wobbling as her muscles quaked against the elf.

Her body dripped with numerous cuts, enough small slices that her skin was a weaving thread of pain.

Ashalea whirled at Shara's back, switching places with her friend, giving her a breather. They battled—for seconds or minutes, she didn't know. Theirs was a storm, a dance, their skill with a blade equally matched, their steps perfect. Not one foot was out of line as they parried back and forth, ducking and jumping and twisting around one another.

"I could do this all day," the darkness sneered, but his words came out ragged, his chest heaving as he moved. "Unfortunately, duty calls," he said, waving a hand at the Gate.

It was pulsing, black growing within its surface, the gateway seeming to spit and crackle, as if angered by the intrusion, growing more unstable by the minute. Fear clanged through her, but she would not give her brother the satisfaction of seeing it.

Ashalea smiled at him, eyeing him off as a predator does its prey. "Is that sweat I see, Crinos? How very mortal of you."

His growing rage was enough. She struck, a single swipe across his cheek, a slash of blood upon his pale, creamy face. He rose a hand to the cut in shock, as if surprised he could be harmed at all. The blood was red ... normal.

Ashalea smirked. "See? He bleeds. Just like any other living creature. And what bleeds will die," she snarled.

It was the push they all needed. The sign to keep pressing their attack. But it wasn't enough. She glanced at her friends. Razakh. Shara. Tofin. Denavar. The only way to win was as a unit. As one.

She smiled at them all, letting a crackle of energy curl over her arms, the white light twisting through her veins as she raised one arm towards the darkness. "Together?"

"Together," they panted.

Her brother was already moving when she glanced back at him, his face ravaged with rage, teeth bared, hate sparking in his eyes. White light burst from her fingertips, surging deep into the darkness's chest. He howled; agony written in the lines of his face. He took one step, then another, and was shocked into place by Denavar's mighty lightning bolt that cracked from the sky and thundered into the earth, scorching the ground around them.

Wisps of black ruptured from the darkness, snaking around their ankles and slithering up their bodies. Crinos roared in pain, his arms twitching as he tried to move. His body shivered as he fought against their power, still threatening to break free from the might of their Magicka.

Shara and Tofin struggled against the shadows, taking one slow, agonising step, their bodies almost overcome by darkness. Razakh burned through as much as he could, his tail searing the dark as he whipped it, slicing the cords binding them all.

The black reached into Ashalea's mouth, choking her, suffocating her lungs, but still she did not let go, her power surging forth. She was nearing her limits now, but they could not stop until he was gone.

Shara roared, breaking free from the black and, in one swift motion, she lunged for the darkness, spider-walking up his torso to curl her legs around his neck, pulling his throat back as she *squeezed*. Tofin broke free next, grabbing Crinos with arms of corded muscle, holding him firmly in place while the darkness writhed. But elven strength, though extraordinary, was matched by that of the dwarves—and a proud, stubborn one at that.

Denavar sent short bursts of power into the darkness, enough to shock him, to numb his system just enough for Ashalea to take her chance, letting go of her power just long enough to strike.

The darkness regained some movement, flinging Shara off, blasting Tofin with black power, and sending his blade careening into Denavar's shoulder, his cry of pain ringing through the clearing.

Crinos raised his arm—

And Ashalea plunged her sword into his chest, driving it through his heart and right up to the hilt, bone cracking as she twisted the blade and leaned in close. His silver eyes widened, his body shook with tremors, and he stumbled into her, arm clutching at her shoulder.

She shifted her weight, allowing his arm to curl around her neck, and she held him close. The only embrace she'd share with her brother ... the last. His breath came in ragged pants, blood beginning to fill his lungs.

"I would have liked to have known you," he said into her ear as he wheezed. "Would have liked to have—to have known a sister. Perhaps you are right. We might have been ... might have been friends."

She leaned back to look in his eyes, surprised to see the silver orbs glistening, just as surprised to feel her own wet with remorse. "I would have loved you, brother—would have loved you as family."

"Love," he chuckled in between choking, "is a good way to get one killed."

"No, Crinos," she said softly, stepping back into the circle of her friends, her family, their hands warm and strong as they clasped her shoulders, and Denavar's calloused hand slid into her own. "To love is to truly *live*."

He stumbled, falling to his knees as he looked upon them all, shaking his head in bewilderment. His eyes landed on Ashalea once more, and he smiled, and for once it was genuine, full of something she couldn't determine. But his smile grew wider as his eyes glazed.

"Then live well ... sister."

Crinos slumped to the ground. Ashalea breathed deep, a tear tracking down her face. So much death and destruction. So much sorrow.

But they weren't done with it yet.

53

Let Me Go

DENAVAR

"THE PORTAL IS IMPLODING," he yelled, the angry rumble of the Gateway beginning to crack fissures in the earth. He knew that this ancient Magicka, this old and sacred thing, was angry. Furious at the corruption leaking from its heart.

"*We have to close it,*" Razakh roared. He was burning the darkness's body with his fire, having hoped it would appease the Grove, but the very world seemed threatened of being ripped apart.

Wind whipped through the clearing, lashing them all, and plant matter and various debris hurtled towards the portal, sucked through its tainted waters. Denavar looked to Ashalea, mouth set in a hard line, eyes squinting against the force.

His shoulder barked in protest, blood dripping down his arm and chest, and he knew his friends ached from the wounds they too had received during the fight. But they had to push, had to keep going until they stopped the explosion that was surely looming.

Ashalea stood silently, boots planted in the grass as she watched her brother's body burning; Razakh concentrating wholly on removing the last of his body, the black still seeping from it. She looked up, sensing his stare—the question within it—and she nodded.

She was okay, bearing nothing but bruises on her soul from today. Killing the darkness, she knew it would leave a mark on her, perhaps haunt her for many years, but they had all known there was no other outcome. Just as they had known the world relied on them to end it. To close the portal once and for all.

He gestured to the others. "Gather before the gateway. Clasp hands."

They did so, Ashalea on his left, Shara at hers, and Razakh and Tofin on his right; the latter laying a hand upon the Diodonian's back. Instantly, Magicka rippled through his body, sparking from his veins through those of his friends.

"Holy shit," Shara gasped. "Is this ... Magicka? Because I could get used to this."

She was grinning wildly, the adrenaline and kickback of the Magicka coursing through her, igniting her body as it was with all of them. Though Denavar could only guess at the elation one without the ability to wield Magicka daily would feel right now.

"*The bond,*" Razakh answered. "*It's the thread that binds us—the Guardians.*"

"And how we'll close the portal. Pull on that power, grasp it in your mind's eye and imagine tightening your grip, wielding it in your palm," he yelled over the wind.

The power crackled between them, growing stronger and stronger, hurdling faster as it moved between their bodies.

"Steady," Ashalea demanded. "Don't let go yet."

Shara shivered beneath Denavar's grip, her hand shaking with the force. Even Ashalea quivered, the strength building to a crescendo until there was nothing but that power, nothing but the Magicka blocking out everything around them.

He clenched his teeth, closing his eyes as the light grew, flaring brighter, brighter, brighter …

"Denavar." His eyes snapped open, and he whipped his head to Ashalea. "I love you. So much. I will always love you, even in the beyond, even in death."

He shook his head, confused, fear clawing at his heart, filling his stomach with dread. "I don't understand," he said. "I love you too."

She smiled. Beautiful, utterly breathtaking as the light reflected in her eyes and atop her head; so bright that it looked like a crown upon her silver hair. She kissed him, long and tender, lips so soft yet so urgent as her mouth crashed to his and her tongue curled.

Her hand squeezed, so warm and right in his own. And then she whispered, "You must let me go, Denavar."

Panic filled his being, his Magicka wobbling under the weight of that threat tying them all together. He opened his mouth to speak, to tell her not to do anything reckless, anything foolish. That it would all be okay, and they would finish this together.

But she suddenly roared, "Let go," and the Magicka crashed out of them and into that portal; so bright he thought he might be blinded; so powerful the ground rumbled beneath his feet. A boom sounded, he felt himself being ripped apart from his friends, and then he was hurled onto his back, head slamming into the ground with the force of a tornado.

The world fell utterly still, and he eased upwards, spine

groaning, head smarting as he pressed a hand to his skull, now wet with blood. Blinking back stars, his eyes focused as he searched the glade.

The portal was nowhere to be seen, nothing but a pile of broken rocks where the shimmering surface of the Gate had been. Elation soared through him. They'd done it. They'd really done it.

He scoured the glade, seeing Shara, Razakh and Tofin grumbling as they rose unsteadily to their feet. He remembered then. That panic—that hopelessness—and he felt it scrabble over his heart as he looked for her.

Denavar lurched to his feet, stumbling around, yelling her name again and again. The others soon realised what he was doing, their own voices echoing through the forest. Denavar bent over, his fists pulling at his hair, a frustrated scream wracking from his chest.

He'd known when she'd said those words. He'd felt it deep down the moment she had said 'I love you.' And he bowed his head in despair, tears crashing down his face as he fell to his knees.

"Let me go," he mumbled, repeating her words. He wept, already missing the touch of her skin, the lips upon his, the warmth of her body. He felt Shara plummet beside him, no doubt coming to the same conclusion as he. She buried her cheek into his neck, her face wet with tears, and then Razakh curled up between them, even Tofin coming to put a tentative, awkward arm around his shoulders.

They sat in silence for an age, the only sound to break the stillness was that of Denavar and Shara's tears soaking the earth.

'Let go' she had said.

And he had.

54

Free

ASHALEA

SHE WAS FLOATING THROUGH A CLOUD OF BLACK. Amid a sea of stars she drifted through the endless ocean, wondering if she were dead or alive, if this was the bridge between worlds or the very end of all things.

Her hair curled over her shoulders as gravity pulled, sucking her away from the window beyond. She saw his face, and those of her friends. One last glimpse, one last chance to lock that picture into memory, to give it permanence in her heart and mind's eye.

Their own eyes had been closed, squeezed shut as the last of the Magicka flashed and the portal began to pull itself apart, shredding and shredding until it tore itself asunder, and their faces snapped out of sight.

She felt the snip of scissors as the connection was clipped, her tether to the Guardians vanishing as she left that duty behind, sealing that Magicka away for eternity, closing the Gate of the Grove to all others.

Something that should have been done long ago, as many things might have come to pass differently, should other actions have been taken. Should a little boy not have been treated as an outcast, bullied for his strength, stripped of his dignity.

But all things were easy to reflect on when one was not long for the world. In truth, she thought she'd be dead already. Wasn't that the deal she'd struck with the dragon? A life for a life. A death for the freedom of many.

Perhaps she was dead, lost to this quiet space. And if death was this calming, this peaceful, she would welcome it with open arms. She wondered, as she twisted through the dark, if the dragons were home already—how many had fallen on the battlefield, if the war was still going or if they'd smote the monsters to ruin.

She suspected the latter. One dragon was terrible enough to behold, let alone those that blotted out the skies. And without the darkness to lead them, the monsters would have likely broken rank. Ashalea sighed, imagining her own water dragon at peace with his kin. He wasn't hers, of course—wasn't anyone's now, nor owing allegiance to anything. Finally. No more tethers to Everosia, no more elves to protect.

She sighed, letting her arms flutter before her, feeling weightless, free. Closing her eyes, she felt like she might sleep, but a tug to her body had her eyes snapping open, and the drifting path began to roll with alarming speed, hurling her into a tunnel of flashing colours, sending her spiralling down.

Ashalea was plonked into a vast meadow; flowers of every colour imaginable dotting the green, impossible waterfalls tipping from the sky. Dragons swept past on swift wings and bees buzzed on nearby petals.

Life flourished all around her. Peaceful. Joyous.

"*Hello, young one,*" a voice boomed behind her.

She stood, lips curling into a broad, beaming smile. "You lied," she said. "You broke your side of the bargain."

The water dragon huffed in amusement. "*I did nothing of the sort. You said a life for a life, but you didn't say whose. The darkness is dead. The war is done. Whilst you were in the Grove, the Everosians fought fiercely, and the dragons fulfilled their oath to you. Your armies can rest safely now.*"

Ashalea gaped at the dragon incredulously. "But the portal, my friends—"

The dragon reached its long neck toward her, one yellow eye blinking. "*The Gate needed to be sealed from both sides: a necessary sacrifice on your behalf. Your friends are safe, and monsters of other dimensions shall never walk your land again.*"

"If the Gate is truly closed then how did you get back?" Ashalea asked. "Did all the dragons make it?"

His golden eyes flashed as he regarded her. "*Some will never feel the kiss of the wind upon their wings again, but it was a sacrifice gladly made. A choice they did not shy from. As for our return ...*" The dragon blinked one eye lazily, and Ashalea realised it was winking. "*We had measures in place to ensure our return. A failsafe portal to send us home if we didn't make it before the Gate closed. Magicka will always be at our disposal, but we will not return to Everosia, this I promise you.*"

Ashalea shook her head incredulously, still coming to terms with it all. The war was over. It was *done*. She wanted to whoop and holler her victory, and yet sadness crept into her veins, dulling the joy of such knowledge. "So many died," she said softly. "So many lives lost."

"*War isn't cheap ... and what bleeds will die. Those soldiers might be lost, but how many were saved today? How many souls will live long, free lives because of that sacrifice? You saved them all, Princess.*"

Her heart soared with happiness to know they were all safe. That they had won. "I did what anyone would do, if they had the power."

The dragon hummed. "*Not all would be so willing to sacrifice themselves for a cause. It won't be forgotten by your people.*"

She stared into his one, sun-filled eye, so bright it made her eyes water. "Will I ..." she bit her lip. "Will I be able to go home?"

The dragon pulled back, studying her. "*That depends. Do you have the power?*"

No. Not even close. Moonlight powers and her Magicka skills aside, she knew she could not traverse worlds—would never be strong enough to portal to Everosia. "I don't," she said softly. "But perhaps you could send me back?"

The dragon dipped his head. "*I am sorry, little one, if I gave you false hope. Our connection with that land is lost. We can never travel to that world again.*"

Ashalea released a shuddering breath. She straightened her spine, breathed in the fresh air, let peace fill her heart.

She could live—longingly perhaps, but happily—knowing her friends were alive, that they had a chance at a future. They were free, their lives now their own. And together they would build a better world, a united Everosia.

And Denavar ... Ashalea's heart squeezed, tears threatening to well. She shoved the thoughts away, refusing to dwell on that. Not yet. For now, she would learn to love herself, forgive herself, and accept her actions. The blood on her own hands, whether deserved or not.

The dragon must have sensed her turmoil, for he swept his long tail aside and flattened a wing to the ground. "*Care for a ride?*"

She would. Oh, hells, she would. Ashalea nodded, scrambling lightly up his side to settle into the hollow of his neck, barely grabbing on before he lunged into the sky, great wings taking them to greater heights, the world even more stunning, even more impossibly beautiful from above.

She felt the wind pull at her hair, somehow warm despite the altitude, fresh and floral and smooth. She flung her arms out and laughed, truly laughed at the weightlessness, the simplicity of such a thing.

And for the first time in a long time ...

She felt free.

55

Heart of my Heart

DENAVAR

DENAVAR PORED OVER COUNTLESS MAPS AND SCROLLS, dusty tomes written by old scholars, shrivelled parchments about Magicka and portals and traversing different realms. His study was a sprawling mess of book towers and mugs, the half-drank contents beginning to take on a life of their own.

He scrubbed a hand over his eyes and down his cheeks, his jawline now covered in a healthy dose of stubble. Shara said it made him appear 'worldly', whatever that meant, but he kept it simply because he didn't care.

He didn't have time for appearances, sleeping for only a few hours at a time as he worked himself to the bone. He ate well enough; spring had certainly bounced back with a happy flourish this year, and with it the crops and animals that had shied from winter—and quite possibly the darkness's presence.

It had been months since the war—since he'd seen *her*. And he had spent every waking minute since Ashalea's disappearance rebuilding The Meadows, organising treaties with the other races, rebuilding the various cities dotting the country and, of course, searching for her.

He didn't believe that she was dead—couldn't even think it without feeling like he might implode. His heart still beat too strongly for her, and though he could not feel her presence in this world, he believed with his whole heart she was waiting in another. Denavar prayed every night—to the moon beyond this window, to the Gods that sailed the stars—hoping she was okay. That she was safe. The alternative was unthinkable, unbearable, and so he worked … and worked … and worked.

The Guardians had stayed with him, attending to the restoration of this once great city and acting as ambassadors for their respective races. But he supposed they weren't Guardians anymore. They were free; free to live their lives and be whatever—whoever—they wanted.

Yet the world was not finished with them, not to mention their own peoples, and it had been tough.

Razakh and Shara especially spent much of their time flitting between their homes, stepping in for the fallen chieftains. Shara had been affected the most by her loved one's loss. The death of a twin was something he would never know, couldn't begin to comprehend.

She still laughed and smiled, still joked and tossed her hair in that aggravating, eye-rolling way. But there were times when the assassin drifted, present and yet not, her eyes falling dark, her memories haunting her.

It would perhaps be that way for all of them. And time was the only thing that could heal those hurts now. Time that he didn't have.

He was close to a breakthrough, feeling in his bones that he was a hairsbreadth away from finding the piece of the puzzle. He was today reading a book titled *Talismans and True Meanings*, scouring the pages for more information on bespelled items and those which bore energies—objects containing memories or worldly significance, in which many were said to be effectively tethered to said location in the world.

And if he was right, the Moonglade Meadows would surely be such a place. The Magicka here was ancient, the reign of rulers a long one, dating back thousands of years to the first forefathers and mothers of his kin, and those of the royals.

Denavar wracked his brain, absentmindedly spinning his letter opener on the table as he thought of Ashalea's possessions. His mind landed on the Onyxonite talisman, wondering if she had still been wearing it that day. But even so, he doubted the spell bound in that item would be enough—certainly not something that connected her to The Meadows.

He leaned forward, gazing at the sky beyond. A harvest moon, big, bright and yellow, a good omen for the land, a beacon for his people. He gazed beyond the violet curtains fluttering in the gentle breeze, over the fields dotted with wildflowers, past the construction and stone piles, the rolling hills and gentle creeks.

Laughter filled the air, and music. Two things he had not heard in this place for too long. And his soul rejoiced to hear it, his heart longed to join them, but not yet. Not without *her.*

The letter opener slipped beneath his fingers, and he winced as the knife clattered, the small blade leaving a bead of ruby red on the pad of his thumb. He studied the fine edge of the blade, its silver gleaming with his blood, and it hit him then. The obvious solution:

an item of such symbolism, such importance to the Moonglade monarchs that he cursed his stupidity.

"My Gods," he whispered, and he leaped from his seat with such ferocity it groaned in protest. He snatched the blade and a map of constellations, and he paused, looking out the window once more, at the moon and the starlit sky beyond.

"I'm coming, my love. I'm coming." And he could have sworn one of the stars shimmered fiercely in answer.

Denavar sat cross-legged in a circle of glyphs he'd painted in the clearing, eyes squeezed shut in concentration as he dove deep into his Magicka, into his core where the strongest of his power slumbered. He would need every drop, and if that were still not enough, well, he'd called for backup too.

They were in the Grove once again—Shara, Razakh, Tofin and himself—and if it brought back bad memories, no one had complained. All were eager to help, to bring her back to them. Shara's eyes had filled with tears when he told her his plan, and even she had been speechless, shakily nodding her approval before they had all immediately jumped in a portal.

Razakh crouched opposite Denavar, Shara and Tofin on either side, and they all formed a connection—clasping hands or gripping fur. Denavar didn't know if they still held any power, whether the Grove might help them tonight, but he had to try. They all did.

The Magicka washed over him, calm and cleansing, and it was refreshing to use his power for something good, instead of feeling that urgent adrenaline to destroy, to unleash fire and lightning upon enemies.

Some small part of Denavar wondered if perhaps Wezlan had known it would come to this; that one day the Guardians might find themselves short a she-elf with silver hair, a laugh like sunshine and a smile bright as a moonbeam.

Without Wezlan's power now coursing through his veins, he knew he would never have considered such a feat. But now ...

He breathed deep, feeling himself reach the centre of his power, bringing it surging to the surface—the waves crashing again and again, still calm, still steady. Opening his eyes, he unsheathed that tiny blade, slicing his palm before letting the blood drip onto a glyph, then to the items placed in the centre of them all.

A crown of The Meadows, blessed under the eyes of the Gods, imbued with glowing ancient Magicka, and a dagger of the same starlit steel as Ashalea's sword, its hilt carved with pearlescent moonstone. It was to the dagger's sister that Denavar would call—to the sword of kings and queens that had disappeared with Ashalea on that final day of war.

Items of symbolism, strength, purity, honour. The others followed suit, Shara gently drawing blood from Razakh before they sprinkled their drops upon the collection.

They clasped hands once more, and Denavar looked them each in the eye. "This is it," he said, veins singing with nerves, stomach fluttering, equal parts excitement and fear.

"I'm with ya, laddie," Tofin grinned, and Shara squeezed his hand tightly, the touch saying more than words could.

"*Let's bring her home*," Razakh said, and Denavar nodded, overwhelmed by gratitude. But he swept everything aside, leaving room for only two things; the spell that would link them to the sword, and the image of Ashalea, burning brightly into his mind.

He exhaled ...

And the power flooded between them, the world seeming to slow. The cool caress of that power stroking their cheeks, sighing in their ears, gentle waters lapping over the glyphs. They flashed brighter one by one as Denavar squeezed his eyes shut and searched.

For they weren't just any runes etched into the Grove, but stars—a map of constellations, and one of them hosted Ashalea.

The worlds flashed before his eyes, so dizzyingly fast he thought his head might break upon the force of this power, his mind only able to take in so much information at once. Razakh's own conscience stroked a gentle claw against his mind, and Denavar opened to him, allowing the Diodonian—that strange and beautiful mind of the telepath—to share the burden.

Together, they searched the stars, sailing, wading through the seas, and he felt the drain of such power, the cord growing taut enough that it would snap if he pulled too much further. So he took from Shara's obsidian strength, drawing her energy; that kernel of Guardianship within her stretching until he heard her gasp and he retreated.

His power lapped greedily from Tofin until that same small gem of Grove-given grace—that connection of Guardianship—shrivelled until he was utterly spent. But he didn't let go, they all gritted their teeth, their breaths coming in ragged gasps until even Razakh had nothing left to give.

Denavar soared through the black and white canvas, a shooting star burning bright, a beacon for Ashalea. His body shook, he felt blood pool in his nose, dripping down his ears. He heard the shouts of his friends, but still he did not let go. And, vaguely, he realised he was never going to, even if he might die, he would never *let her go*.

Something shimmered at the end of the line. Something bright and warm and familiar, and he pushed, his pulse thinning, his heart slowing. Pushed until, finally, bright light flashed, and he was shoved backwards in a gust of wind.

And before him was a portal. Bright and crackling. Full of goodness. Full of *hope*.

He looked up, eyes squinting, tears running down his face, mouth slack from disbelief and pure wonder. On the other side, in a world so vibrant, so full of life, was a face crowned by silver hair, emerald eyes full of joy and ... peace.

But it was the smile that filled him with pure happiness. A smile so free and so happy, it almost broke him to see such joy in her, such delight.

She stepped through the portal, and tears fell down his face as he kneeled before her in awe.

His friend. His love. His queen.

Returned at last.

Epilogue

"You know, since I returned you've been fussing over me like a mother hen," Ashalea said with a click of her tongue.

Shara smirked. "My baby's all grown up and leaving the coop," she teased, twisting a lock of Ashalea's hair into place and pinning it. She leaned back, assessing her work and nodding with satisfaction, but her face fell. "It's just ... when you left us, I—I wondered if it was forever. If you'd come back to us. When three months had passed and still no word, no sign?" She shook her head. "I was out of my mind."

"We all were," Razakh said from his perch on the bed. *"Babysitting this one was worse than dealing with Diodonian cubs,"* he huffed. *"At least their fire doesn't come in for a while. Shara's temper is more dangerous than those dragons."*

Shara hissed at him, but before she could utter any rude retorts Telilah barged over to re-do some of the pins in Ashalea's hair. "They were fine," Shara said, rolling her eyes.

Telilah snorted. "For an assassin maybe, but we're working with a queen here, and we must have perfection," she clucked.

"And *I'm* the mother hen?" Shara said, swiping up a flute of bubbling wine and sculling the contents with a smack of her lips.

Telilah turned from her work to plant a tender kiss to Shara's mouth, the latter melting like butter; a soft, dreamy smile on her face once they broke apart.

Ashalea grinned to herself. The two had been inseparable since she'd returned, and it made her heart swell with joy to see Shara truly happy, her walls slowly coming down as Telilah gently chipped away at them.

They were a good match. Telilah's easy, caring nature seemed to settle Shara's fiery temperament, all the while stoking the passion and zest for life in Telilah. Ashalea truly believed they could conquer kingdoms if they set their minds to it, but for now rebuilding this one was the first step.

Telilah handed her a mirror. "Here, dear," she said gently, "take a look."

Ashalea took a deep breath before gazing at her reflection, and what stared back ... she gasped. Golden, dewy skin that gleamed, the slightest rosy rouge on her cheeks and lips, lids glittering with a pearly sheen and glitter like stardust, lashes curled. It was subtly stunning, and even she had to admit she looked nice.

More than nice. Her silver hair had been curled, the soft waves dropping to her waist, the top half pinned and plaited in complex braids, tiny roses sprinkled within the locks.

Shara grinned crookedly as she snatched Ashalea's hand,

dragging her to the floor-length mirror in the bedroom chamber. Her hand flew to her mouth. If she thought her hair and makeup were nice, this ... this was something else.

The gown shimmered like pearls, subtle embroidery woven into the fabric glittering like stars, the sweetheart neckline plunging. Every slight swish set her sparkling; the bodice tight before gently flowing out. The sheer panels at the side of her dress showed her curves off—and she did have them, Ashalea realised with a start.

Curves. Her body had filled out again since being back in the Moonglade Meadows, her shape one others might desire or envy. But she didn't care about all that. This was for her. Feeling good, feeling healthy again—it was for her.

"One more touch," Telilah chirped happily. Her long brown hair bounced as she pulled something gingerly from the gilded white dresser. A silver crown shaped in roses and vines; feminine, stunning. At its heart was a moonstone gem, glittering brightly, its colour changing shade depending on where the light hit.

Telilah set it upon her head with the utmost care, and Ashalea almost burst into tears as she looked at herself—at the reminder of what the crown meant, and who had once worn it.

Shara walked up to her side, leaning her raven-haired head on Ashalea's shoulder. "Today is about the future," she said. "About you. Don't spend one minute of it in the past or let it stain today. We're here for your happiness, and that's all that matters."

Ashalea took Shara's hands in her own. "Thank you. For everything."

She didn't have to say what that entailed. Shara beamed, winking in reply. Razakh hummed, jumping off the bed to pad towards them.

Ashalea laughed. "Don't you look dapper."

Indeed, he wore a silver bowtie around his neck, looking prouder than a peacock as he sat beside them. Shara and Telilah were resplendent too; the former in a gown of sapphire, the silky fabric complementing Shara's darker skin and amber eyes; the latter in dusky rose, highlighting Telilah's heart-shaped face and certainly her curves.

Ashalea breathed in deep. "Let's go get 'em."

She walked down the path that looked like a river of stars under the night sky. Vines and roses crawled around cream pillars, and flowers of all varieties scattered the ground beneath her feet.

Tiny balls of Magicka floated like candles in the air, and a looming willow spread open arms in invitation before her, a small lake sparkling beyond. She saw friends in the crowd—Razakh, Tofin, Yavaar, Kano, her first female friend, Erania of Woodrandia, even Ringarr Bonodo, the seafaring captain she'd met in Windarion. So many faces smiling back at her, and so many she wished were here to do so again.

But all of that faded to grey when she saw Denavar. He was magnificent in a tunic of navy blue, a silver cape clasped at his back, his brown hair swept ruggedly, his face clean-shaven, revealing that strong jaw. His blue eyes gleamed with desire and admiration.

And he smiled, white teeth sparkling, those lips curved a little to the left in a crooked grin—her favourite smile of all.

She walked towards him under the weight of everyone's eyes, and yet she felt none of it. She felt fully free as she stepped towards her future, her light. As she stopped before him, she spared a glance to the canvas above, sending a prayer to those she knew were watching over her. Most of all, she thought of one man, his sparkling grey eyes, his razor-sharp wit, his sage advice and warm hugs.

Wezlan couldn't be here today, but he'd always be with her in the space that mattered most. As they all would, the Guardians at her back. Their destinies had linked them, but what they had went beyond blood or fate or friendship.

What they had was a family, and it would last the ages.

She glanced at Denavar, felt the warmth of his palm slipping into hers, fingers curling, love blooming through his touch. His eyes sparkled, and peppermint graced her as he leaned in close.

"Together?" he whispered with a wink.

She smiled, squeezing his hand, and Ashalea thought perhaps that might be her favourite word. She grinned.

"Always."

The End

Acknowledgements

First, to my readers. You've stuck by me for three books, and I will always be grateful for your support, love, and loyalty. This trilogy is the first of many to come, and I hope to continue many conversations about this world and the characters. I'll always have a place in my heart for this crew, who have taught me so much from conception to completion!

To my editor, Aidan. Your advice is always a delight to receive, less so for the pickiness than the delightful comments that make this job easier! Thank you!

My cover artists, Erica, and Niru. You are both beyond talented and I'm still in awe at the beautiful art you have produced. Thank you for bringing my visions to life and adding your own flair of creativity to these projects.

To Emily and Julia. Your talents are, yet again, whimsical and delightful to see. I love your work and I'm so happy to have had the pleasure of working with you.

Special thanks to my beta readers! Your feedback and real-time reactions make my heart warm and fuzzy ... and the shock-horror moments make my blackened author heart do a little jig haha!

Thank you to the many wonderful businesses who have taken a chance on these books—produced merch, shown support, extended the love, drawn fan-art and so much more. Special mentions to Ariel at No Shelf Control, Sandra Winther, Read & Relax, Off the Book Pages and Sarah's Self Checkout.

Last, but certainly not least, to my family. My husband, Jason, whose support and love made these books possible. I am so thankful, and I love you so much. My dogs, whose demands for pats during writing and editing were ceaseless (but welcomed). To my family interstate and overseas who never stop supporting me. To the inventor of tea ... I downed many pots during this process. That will never change.

So, from the bottom of my heart, thank you all so much. Much love, and hopefully see you soon for the next adventure!

About the Author

Chloe Hodge was born in Adelaide, South Australia, to New Zealand parents and a Hungarian heritage. In 2017 she completed a Bachelor of Journalism and Professional Writing at the University of South Australia, then proceeded to work for the ABC as a radio producer and news reporter. Thereafter, she worked as a journalist for a technical grape and wine magazine before founding small editing business, Chloe's Chapters, and starting a career as a YA Fantasy author. Her trilogy, Guardians of the Grove, is available on all major online retailers, as well as her home website, chloehodge.com

When she's not writing or editing fantasy novels, she is ... not able to be found. Most likely curled up with a book somewhere, playing video games, or adventuring with her dogs.

www.ingramcontent.com/pod-product-compliance
Lightning Source LLC
Chambersburg PA
CBHW020540120726
47903CB00001B/54